KU-032-721

Her Last Assassin

Victoria Lamb

CORGI BOOKS

TRANSWORLD PUBLISHERS
61–63 Uxbridge Road, London W5 5SA
A Random House Group Company
www.transworldbooks.co.uk

HER LAST ASSASSIN
A CORGI BOOK: 9780552165297

First published in Great Britain
in 2014 by Bantam Press
an imprint of Transworld Publishers
Corgi edition published 2014

A CIP catalogue record for this book
is available from the British Library.

Addresses for Random House Group Ltd companies outside the UK
can be found at: www.randomhouse.co.uk
The Random House Group Ltd Reg. No. 954009

The Random House Group Limited supports the Forest Stewardship
Council® (FSC®), the leading international forest-certification
organisation. Our books carrying the FSC label are printed on
FSC®-certified paper. FSC is the only forest-certification scheme supported
by the leading environmental organisations, including Greenpeace.
Our paper procurement policy can be found at
www.randomhouse.co.uk/environment

Typeset in 10.5/13pt Sabon by Falcon Oast Graphic Art Ltd.

Printed and bound in Great Britain by Clays Ltd, St Ives plc

2 4 6 8 10 9 7 5 3 1

MIX
Paper from
responsible sources
FSC® C016897

For Steve Haynes, my Goodluck

'Cropp'd are the flower-de-luces in your arms . . .'

William Shakespeare, *Henry VI, Part 1, I, i*

'My tongue will tell the anger of my heart
Or else my heart, concealing it, will break.'

William Shakespeare, *The Taming of the Shrew,
IV, iii*

Prologue

Nieuwpoort, Low Countries, July 1588

IT HAD BEEN ENTIRELY TOO LONG, GOODLUCK THOUGHT, since he had watched the white cliffs of Dover fade in the distance, and committed himself to this dangerous venture: a new name, a new language, a new mission. All courtesy of Sir Francis Walsingham, the Queen's ever-resourceful spymaster.

'A few weeks,' Walsingham had insisted, passing him a bag of coins with his secret orders. 'That is all you will need to uncover their plans. If the Spanish move against us, they will likely come from the Low Countries first. It is the point nearest England which is friendly to Spain. Do not fail us this time, Goodluck. Do not fail Her Majesty.'

Yet the weeks had stretched into months, and until today Goodluck had been no nearer the evidence he had been sent to discover: the timing of the Spanish invasion, a threat that had loomed over England now for several years but which no one could accurately predict.

It was summer now, and he was homesick for England. Goodluck poured another bucketload of kitchen slops, cold and greasy, out of the window into the sunlit yard below. The low-lying fields beyond the manor house and the makeshift garrison were still flooded, though the built-up paths between them had dried out in the sun, thick with yellow-tipped wild flowers that might have reminded him of English meadows if it had not been for their sickly sweet smell. He was glad not to be looking out to sea, for the sight of the Dutch harbour crammed with high-masted warships, hundreds more of them bobbing at anchor beyond the harbour wall, their bright pennants flapping in the breeze, made him itch to be back in London, making his report to Walsingham.

It would not be long before the Spanish fleet and their allies sailed against England. Goodluck did not wish to be an English spy stranded in an enemy country when that happened.

He turned back and dropped the wooden bucket next to a heap of cabbages. 'Boy!' he roared at the lad whose task it was to keep the spit turning. 'That meat is burning again!'

The lad muttered some excuse, but turned the spit a few times in a desultory fashion, his gaze resting sullenly on Goodluck as he began to wipe down the knives.

Goodluck could hardly blame the boy for his lethargy; the whole garrison at Nieuwpoort lay under a malaise, eager to fight but held constantly on the leash as they waited for the order from Spain. An order which never came.

A red-faced porter ran back into the room with an empty platter. He wiped his brow on the inside of his sleeve. 'The Spanish lord is calling for more wine. Sir William says his noble guest is thirsty. Too much salt on the beef tonight.'

Goodluck shrugged, and spat on the earth floor. He laid the Dutch accent on thick, his voice rumbling through the narrow stone room. 'Don't blame me, Jeggers prepared the beef.'

'Where is Jeggers?'

'Gone for a piss.'

'Well, when he gets back—'

'What am I, your errand boy? I'm a cook. So let me cook.' With a furious bellow, he turned back to the lad drowsing again on the warm hearth stones, the pink-fleshed porker hissing and singeing in the heat of the flames. 'Up, up! The meat, boy!'

Goodluck waited until the porter had gone in search of the cellarman, then decided it was time to end this masquerade – and not a moment too soon as far as he was concerned. He had to make his report to Walsingham before the fleet sailed and it became redundant. He knew Sir William Stanley had received orders today from Spain.

Surely this was the message they had been waiting for?

Goodluck dragged the leather apron from about his neck and threw it on to the grease-covered floor. He was bare-chested underneath, for the heat of the kitchen made it impossible to work any other way. First dipping his head in a bucket of cold water, Goodluck shrugged into a clean shirt and jacket, his face still dripping. Then he took out his leather purse from the knife chest, clipped it to his belt and went to the door.

'When Jeggers gets back,' he told the boy, 'tell him he's to finish up with the pork. I'm off to see the play.'

Pausing, he took a small coin from his purse, then threw it to the boy. 'Here, get some salve for that,' he said, not unkindly, and nodded to the burn reddening the back of the lad's hand.

The boy looked surprised but pocketed the coin in silence, no doubt fearing a beating if he spoke out of turn. He was not to know that Goodluck, bad-tempered Dutch cook from the outlying provinces, was in fact an English spy.

Treading heavily down the short flight of stairs into the courtyard, the Englishman waited there a moment, checking that he had not been seen. The summer evening was still hot, the sky darkly flushed to the west with a hint of rain to come, though the day's heat was lessening as dusk fell. Small black flies crowded about his head, perhaps attracted by the smell of grease, and he shook them away with an irritated flick of his hand.

As he had suspected, everyone was still enjoying that evening's entertainment in the hall. Travelling players on their last night in the Low Countries – a troupe of shuffling men he had seen arriving earlier, their carts loaded with theatrical chests and scenery – had come here to perform an English play for the soldiers. Something to keep the exiled Catholics happy as they waited for the signal to sail against their own people.

Keeping his head down, Goodluck trod softly through the narrow grassy maze of lanes about the ancient manor until he reached the back of the hall and began to skirt its high windows. He caught a burst of raucous singing from within, then enthusiastic whistles and applause. A song and a jig to start them off. He recalled the days of play scripts and costumes, and the crude banter of the players' tiring-room. Not that any of his old friends would recognize him tonight, for his famous beard had been shaved off to play the Dutch cook.

For the briefest of moments, he allowed himself to feel again how homesick he was. It had been too long since he was back in his old house at Cheapside, frequenting the playhouse or dicing with friends in the poky taverns beneath the city walls.

He did not know how Lucy Morgan had fared without him, or whether she was still allowing herself to be courted by that married good-for-nothing Shakespeare. He himself had proved useless as her guardian, seemingly never on hand when she needed him most. His ward had fallen pregnant by Shakespeare, saved her reputation by marrying a man repugnant to her, then been attacked by Master Twist, Goodluck's enemy. It was a miracle she had come through such troubles unscathed. Well, perhaps not unscathed. Though she might not see things that way, losing her child had been a blessing, given how hard her life would have been if the boy had survived.

At the edge of the hall, Goodluck stopped dead, squeezing flat against the wall. He had seen a sentry passing the entrance door ahead. Well, he did not need to go that way, but up. Glancing about once more, hoping the falling dusk would mask his climbing, he found one rough foothold in the wall, then groped above until he found a stone jutting out. Thus anchored, he hauled himself up the wall, grunting under his breath with the effort.

He had been this way before, up the wall and across the tiled roof to listen to Stanley's deliberations under cover of darkness, and tonight there should be no trouble repeating the manoeuvre. Stanley's noble guest had come with a substantial entourage, many of whom would no doubt come milling out of the hall as soon as tonight's play was done, though for now they were safely inside. All the same, to try this climb before sunset was dangerous.

He could not let the chance go by though, dangerous or not. It had been weeks since any messenger had come from the court, and he had heard Stanley discussing this visit two days before, claiming it would 'settle matters once and for all'.

What could that mean but a new plan of invasion?

To hear confirmation of such a move against England, after months of wasted nights listening to empty talk, must be worth a man's life. Even if it was his own.

Reaching the roof above the commander's quarters, he slid forward on his belly, keeping as flat as possible against

13

the still-warm tiles. From here he could be seen by anyone crossing the dyke to the rear of the old house, now head-quarters to Stanley's army. But with everyone inside, except for the guards in the inner courtyard and at the entrances, there should be no one to see him.

Goodluck came to the broken tile and lifted it until he could see down into the room below. There was Stanley's curly head, and there the darker hair of his Spanish guest, both men standing together by the commander's broad-topped table.

Putting his eye to the crack, Goodluck's heart quickened. A map had been spread across the table, weighted down at its four corners to prevent it curling up, a map that he did not recognize as any he had seen Sir William Stanley consult before. It must belong to the Spanish lord who had arrived from court, whose name he did not know, but for whom he had dutifully cooked a fine venison pie in wine gravy before turning to the cruder culinary tastes of his entourage, the bare remains of which could still be seen on the sideboard.

'Here,' the Spaniard declared in his own tongue, stabbing at the map with a long dark finger, 'this is where your men will join ours, and together we will sail for England. It will be a great victory over the Protestant rabble and their whore queen.'

'Indeed,' Stanley agreed in heavy, well-accented Spanish, and his voice held no irony. 'And when we take London, it will be my pleasure to see Queen Elizabeth forced to kneel before her new masters, then to order her harlot's body whipped through the streets. She will cry out for mercy, I have no doubt, as so many Catholics have cried since she came to the English throne. But she will receive none from me.'

The Spaniard laughed, stroking his pointed beard. 'You have no loyalty to your Queen, señor? I hope you will show more to Spain.'

Stanley came into view below, a tall, gaunt fellow with a shock of dark hair tinged with silver, his thin cheeks flushed either with the heat or with his own natural belligerence.

Goodluck studied him curiously. Here was a man who rarely slept, a leader of fierce conviction and renowned courage, and yet he was a traitor. Stanley's resentment towards England had reputedly been fuelled by some perceived slight during his long service in Ireland. If so, he had covered his tracks well since then. Indeed, he had served his country brilliantly during the initial conflict with Spain. Goodluck recalled hearing after the battle at Zutphen, where Sir Philip Sidney had received his fatal wound, that the Earl of Leicester himself had praised Stanley's bravery in dispatches, claiming he was 'worth his weight in pearl'. And yet it was also said that he hated Protestants beyond reason, and Queen Elizabeth above the rest.

'I will show Spain the loyalty she deserves, sir. Your king at least has supported me this past year. My family's estates in England are all now forfeit to the crown. What loyalty has this Queen shown me?'

'Forgive me, Señor Stanley, I did not mean to question your allegiance.' Adroitly, the guest turned the subject. 'My officers were pleased to hear there would be a play tonight. It is a long journey from Spain, and a little wine and entertainment are most welcome. Your own troupe?'

'Travellers.' Stanley offered the Spaniard a dish of sweetmeats. 'They sail for France tonight. No, do not look alarmed. Even if they speak of your presence, it may work to our advantage. I do not want any interference from the French, and I'm sure news of a great fleet here will keep our Froggy neighbours quiet.'

Someone knocked at the door and both men fell silent.

Stanley threw his cloak across the map and called, 'Come in,' in English.

Out of sight the door creaked open and someone came in. Goodluck recognized the sweaty porter's voice. 'More wine, sir, my lord. Forgive the delay, I could not find the cellarman.'

'Set it there on the sideboard, light the candles, then leave us. But remain within call. I will need you to escort our guest to bed when we are finished here.'

Once the two men were alone again in the book-lined study flickering with candlelight, Stanley pulled the cloak off the map. 'You have me doubting my own men, my lord, with your stories of treachery.'

'Let us hope I am wrong.'

Stanley poured them both a glass of wine. 'You will find my men loyal. I can vouch for every one of them.'

'In my experience, the ones deemed most loyal are those most likely to betray their masters. And we know someone within your camp is passing back information to that great whoremonger Walsingham.'

Goodluck lay very still at this. Who could have betrayed him? It had to be someone in England, perhaps one of Walsingham's own men. His disguise as a Dutch cook was too good for anyone here to have penetrated it.

'I will investigate your accusations, trust me. And if I do find a traitor within our midst, I will open him with my own sword.'

'I am glad to see the rumours of your bloodthirsty nature have not been exaggerated. You make a good friend for Spain.'

'*Gracias, señor.*'

Sipping his wine, Stanley wandered back to study the map, which even upside down Goodluck could see showed the coast of the Low Countries and France. The southern coast of England had been marked with several large black crosses.

Proposed invasion points?

'The south is very well for His Majesty's magnificent Armada,' he murmured, pointing to the southern coast, 'but coming from the east, we must concentrate on attaining the mouth of the Thames.'

The Spaniard sounded impressed. 'You intend to put London to the sword yourself, then?'

'*De verdad.*' Stanley was poring over the map, his body between the table and Goodluck's view. 'To take London will be the hardest and yet most vital point of our campaign. When they see their own countrymen sailing up the Thames, doughty soldiers led by exiled Englishmen, the men of London will soon surrender. I can hardly wait to witness our day of triumph.'

'Your wait is almost over,' the Spaniard told him softly. 'The fleet is under way. It will reach the English coast in a few weeks.'

'My men will be ready.' Stanley sounded like an excited schoolboy at the prospect of attacking his own country. 'And the signal to embark?'

'The arrival of our fleet. Post lookouts along the shore, señor. As soon as the admiral's ship is sighted, give your people the signal to embark. Your men must remain ready at all times, both day and night, for I cannot say for sure when the fleet will arrive.'

'But it will be soon?'

'Patience, señor. Your day will come.'

Goodluck studied the map keenly, committing to memory every enemy position he could make out. It had taken months, but at last he had some useful news for his master. The Spanish Armada was already at sea and would soon be joined by other forces sailing from the Low Countries. No doubt they would meet in the straits

17

between France and England, or at the mouth of the Thames.

This was the news he must carry home. And at once.

On the next tide, if possible.

The Spanish lord spoke again. 'But what of your other plan? His Majesty asked me to enquire after the letter he sent to support a domestic plot against the Queen. In case our invasion force is not able to reach the Queen before she flees for safety, is your man in position?'

'I am gratified His Majesty takes such interest in my humble plans. Yes, a letter has been sent by courier, with a small incentive. The courier is a most trusted spy. He works for Spain under the guise of being a true Englishman.' He hesitated. 'I needed someone skilled in diplomacy, for there have been problems with our assassin. Though nothing that cannot be resolved with a little persuasion.'

'I trust you will not disappoint His Majesty again?'

Stanley seemed on edge. 'We were close at Kenilworth, I know. You do not need to remind me of our failure there.'

Watching from above, Goodluck cursed silently. Was this man the unknown plotter behind the assassination attempt at Kenilworth Castle, which he and his ward, Lucy, had helped thwart?

This betrayal was too vile. Stanley had been a knight of the realm, lauded for his brilliant service in Ireland. Yet as soon as Leicester had left the Low Countries, he had surrendered his garrison and troops at Deventer to the Spanish without hesitation. Now he was plotting his queen's death. And not for the first time, it seemed.

Stanley poured himself more wine and drank heavily, then wiped his mouth carelessly on his sleeve. 'It was not my fault we did not succeed. I was busy in Ireland that year, and could not make sure of her death myself. We came closer to success with young Babington's plot. But some at court who might have supported us turned cold after Babington's execution, and the illegal beheading of the Scots Queen, God rest her martyred soul. It seems the English Catholics wish to bring England back to the Church of Rome, but not at the risk of their own necks.'

Would these Catholics never give up their attempts on her life? Goodluck felt sick, and wished he could kill the man. But there was more to learn here, and further traitors to uncover. He must be patient.

'So the appointed assassin is one of us?' The Spaniard sounded sceptical. 'Not another hired mercenary like the female you used at Kenilworth? No, do not give me his name. Names are dangerous. Just assure me that your man will kill England's most infamous whore with his own hands, and draw your country back into the Roman fold.'

'Amen to that,' Stanley muttered, also drinking a toast. 'It is well past time this queen was stripped of her fine jewels and made to burn naked, which is how she would die if I had my way.'

Even the Spaniard sounded uncomfortable at this extreme display of vindictiveness. 'You forget yourself, señor. Once the country is ours, it will be up to His Majesty to decide her fate, not the English. He will be your master then. Let us not forget, heretic or not, Queen Elizabeth is still of royal blood.'

'Only if King Henry was her true father,' Stanley spat out, 'and few Catholics believe that. Her mother Anne Boleyn was a proven whore and died on the scaffold for her adultery, leaving her bastard child rightfully disinherited. Why, Elizabeth could be any man's child.'

'I had forgotten her mother was a whore. His Holiness the Pope has declared as much himself.'

'That a common bastard has ruled unchallenged for so many years is a travesty of English justice.' Stanley paused.

'I will accept His Majesty King Philip's ruling on her fate, of course. But I cannot hide that I shall be *overjoyed* to tread her bones into the dirt where they belong.'

'Hey, you!'

A shout from the yard below made Goodluck lift his head in alarm, realizing that he had been spotted. He slithered to the edge of the roof and looked down at the drop, wondering how to lie his way out of this one.

'What do you think you're doing? Come down!'

The man spoke English, but with a strong Irish accent. It was dusk and he could not make out the figure clearly, but guessed by his pike that he was a soldier. No doubt one of Stanley's men from the garrison sent to guard the back gate on to the marshy fields.

Acting dumb, Goodluck nodded. He jumped down, but kicked the man hard in the head as he dropped.

The luckless soldier staggered backwards, his pike clattering to the ground. At once Goodluck was on him, dragging the dagger from his belt and pressing the blade against his throat, between the helmet chinstrap and his jacket collar.

'Another word and you're dead,' he promised the soldier in English.

The man struggled.

'Don't be a fool,' Goodluck said warningly into his ear. He had no wish to kill the man. 'Keep quiet, and we'll both live to see another day. Now, what is it to be?'

But the man *was* a fool. He stared at Goodluck through the gloom as though trying to judge how serious he was. Then, seeing one of his compatriots patrolling in the darkness a few hundred feet away, he struggled hard to escape and opened his mouth to yell for help.

The cry was choked off in a gush of blood as Goodluck thrust home the dagger in his throat. The man twisted against him for a few horrific moments, arms flailing, his face contorted with pain. Then he sagged back, a dead weight.

As quietly as he could, Goodluck let the man's lifeless body drop to the ground. He dragged the knife free from his throat – he might need it later – then turned and sped silently to the now unguarded entrance to the yard.

Keeping flat against the wall, he reached the gate without being spotted again, glad of the shadowy cover of darkness, though he could hear the other soldier's footsteps a short way behind him in the yard.

He felt sick at what he had been forced to do, though this was not the first man he had killed in the Queen's service. But he had certainly been one of the youngest, and his stomach rebelled at such a duty.

Goodluck stopped to listen to the sounds of revelry from the hall. It gave him a moment to think. He bent to wipe the knife and his sticky hands on the grass verge outside the gate. The play must have finished long since. Yet the men inside the hall were still dancing and singing. Straightening, he could still smell blood and knew some of it had stained his jacket as he wrestled with the dying soldier.

'Silas, are you there, man?' Someone had come wandering out of the hall. He sounded drunk. 'I heard a shout just then. What is it?'

There was a startled exclamation in the dusk as the man stumbled over the body of his fallen comrade.

He raised his voice, shouting to his friends inside the hall. 'St Patrick, there's a foul murderer among us! Come out here, in God's name, all of you! Silas is dead!'

Goodluck did not wait to hear more. His brief comedy as Dutch cook to the Stanley household was done. It was time for Master Goodluck, English spy, to take his place.

He ran, heading for the narrow marsh-flanked path which he knew would lead him through quiet backways to the town of Nieuwpoort, and the ship-filled harbour beyond it.

Before he even reached Nieuwpoort, he saw his salvation. The departing players, still hooded like monks and shuffling, were following their carts on foot as they rumbled back to the harbour. Stanley had said this was their last stop before sailing for France, that he had given them permission to leave port after their performance. If Goodluck could somehow insinuate himself into their number, or perhaps squeeze aboard a covered cart, he could reach France, and from there buy his passage home.

He kept his distance, not wishing to be seen. Back at the garrison he could see torches flaring in the gathering dusk, and heard shouts echoing across the low fields.

Occasionally one of the players slowed his pace and looked round, his face hidden under his cowl, and Goodluck had to crouch suddenly in the tall grasses, keeping out of sight until they moved on again.

They had played in English tonight, for the sake of the exiled soldiers under Stanley's command, but could be any nationality – French, Italian, perhaps even Spanish. Italians and Spaniards would promptly hand him over to the authorities if they discovered a stowaway. But if they were French, he might have a chance . . .

There would be a moon tonight. They might even sail on this evening's tide if it was bright enough.

Down on the docks, Goodluck waited in the shadow of a wagon being loaded with ale barrels from one of the merchant ships. Luckily, nobody seemed inclined to pay any attention to the stout man who knelt to adjust first one uncomfortable shoe, then another, and who later bought an apple from a passing tradesman on his way home for the night. Goodluck stood munching on the apple in the dark mouth of an alley, waiting patiently for the players' carts to move.

Out to sea, he watched the assembled warships bob slowly up and down, chafing at their anchors.

He had almost given up hope when the carter came back at last, and with the help of the other players unloaded the long wooden theatrical chests. These were hoisted on their shoulders and carried aboard a small sailing ship, its narrow mast insignificant beside the vast forest of masts all around it, their warships' pennants slapping gently in the sea breeze. While the cargo was brought aboard and the players stood arguing the fee with the captain, the crew began their preparations to cast off, loosening the ropes and giving Goodluck hope they would indeed be sailing with tonight's tide.

He wondered why the players were in such a hurry to quit the country, but then reflected that a night's lodging might have cost them any fee from their performance at the garrison. No doubt they were keen to move on to the next town instead, perhaps in France, which was only a short voyage along the coast for a quick, light vessel like this.

Finally the crew disappeared below, leaving the deck empty but for one man huddled in a cloak, smoking a pipe as he gazed out across the harbour.

As silently as he could, Goodluck climbed down one of the ropes that hung along the harbour wall, cursing his weight under his breath. He landed on the deck with a thud that set the small ship swaying, and had to duck out of sight as the man with the pipe turned to stare.

There was a coil of ropes to one side of the open deck, and some old sails lying across them. Pulling one of the damp sailcloths over him, Goodluck flattened himself as best he could to the deck behind the ropes. It would do for the hours of darkness, at least. But before day dawned he would have to find a better hiding place.

Preferably one which did not reek of fish.

After another agonizing wait, he heard the sailors calling out to each other in Dutch, and felt the deck sway beneath him at last in a horribly familiar way. Never a good sailor, he gritted his teeth and lay waiting for the ship to clear the choppier waters where the warships were moored. He thought fleetingly of the soldier he had killed back at the garrison, wondering if he'd had a wife or any children to miss him. His belly churned, and the sickness worsened. After that, he thought instead of the message he would bear to Walsingham, then counted slowly backwards from a thousand to pass the time.

Through gaps, Goodluck could see strips of torchlight on the deck, and occasionally a man passing by. Finally daring to raise the sailcloth a little higher, he caught a glimpse of the moon rising over the water, gleaming silver on rolling black waves, and the harbour of Nieuwpoort becoming smaller in the distance.

He was safe.

At that moment, the sailcloth was twitched away from him and he met instead the flash of a dagger blade in his face.

'On your knees, Master Stowaway,' a man ordered him coolly, 'and keep your hands where I can see them! I hope you were not bound for sunny France. For you will find the English air a trifle sharp, even at this time of year, and may receive a sterner welcome than you were expecting.'

It was one of the players from the garrison, still cloaked but with his hood thrown back. Goodluck stared up at him, raising his hands slowly away from the dagger in his own belt, and almost choked in his amazement.

Even in the moonlight he knew that lean, sardonic face.

'Kit Marlowe!'

Part One

Part One

One

Tilbury, England, August 1588

PENNANTS FLAPPED DOWN THE MISTY WHITE AVENUE OF tents, their bright devices revealed, then hidden again, with each gust of wind. Elizabeth drew rein, hearing the shout of 'The Queen!' go up along the ranks. Robert, Earl of Leicester, glanced back at her: reassuring, almost close enough to touch, her bridle in his gloved fist.

Queen Elizabeth blinked at her favourite, and the mist blurred, then disappeared. Her head jerked. 'On, on.'

The soldiers needed to see her in sturdy health and upright, despite the weight of the silver cuirass Leicester had caused to be made especially for her. She had come to ask these men to die for her and for England. How could she demand such a sacrifice when she could barely sit on her horse, or inspect their ranks without tears?

Man after man looked up at her as she passed, good trusting faces smeared with dirt, sunburned under the brims of their helmets, and she could not look them in the eye.

By her own decree, albeit hurried through by certain of her advisors, her royal cousin Mary, Queen of Scots, had laid her head on the block. Now little over a twelvemonth later, Spain was at war with England, openly and without pretence, a war she had worked for so many years to avert. All her plans of conciliation lay in tatters, for the enemy's ships were already at sea, had been sighted off the coasts of Cornwall and Devon, might even now be in the narrow straits between England and France. If a Spanish invasion force were to come sailing up the river Thames, as Walsingham and Leicester believed they might, many of these stout-hearted Englishmen would perish at their hands.

A dais had been erected on a sandy mound, furnished with a high-backed chair and shaded from the August sun by a white-canopied roof flapping sulkily in the wind. Elizabeth dismounted and stepped up on to the dais, disdaining her favourite's outstretched hand. She refused to sit but stood instead, gazing out across the motley army Leicester had managed to assemble at Tilbury, some men in livery, some in leather jerkins, others stripped down for the heat, nut-brown and little better than common workmen as they dug out the embankments.

At Leicester's signal, a trumpet sounded, calling the nearest men to attention. Weary soldiers leaned on their spades and mattocks in the trenches, staring expectantly at the dais; others scrambled up the sandy banks, as though eager to hear what she had come to say. Those nearest the dais dropped to their knees with due reverence, baring their heads in her presence despite the strong sun.

A flag whipped lightly overhead. She glanced at Robert, suddenly unsure, then saw that he was looking away at something in the distance. The wind scudding on the river perhaps, or the vast makeshift barrier he had built out there across the Thames, a ramshackle dam of flotsam and other debris lashed together to prevent the Spanish fleet from sailing any nearer to London.

Turning to the assembled soldiers, she found her voice.

'My loving people,' she began, raising her voice to be heard above the cries of the gulls overhead, 'as you can see by my armour, I have come here today resolved to live and die among you all. To lay down for my kingdom, in the midst and heat of battle, my honour and my blood, even in this dust of Tilbury's shores.'

A murmur ran through the crowd at this striking declaration, and she drew breath, seeing the gazes of those nearest her fix on her face, eager for more.

'I know I have the body of a weak and feeble woman, but I have the heart and stomach of a king. And of a king of England too! And I think foul scorn that Parma, or Philip of Spain, nor any prince of Europe, should dare to invade the borders of my realm.' She paused, aware of Robert's keen glance; he had not heard this speech before she delivered it. 'Rather than allow dishonour to be brought upon you by my sex, I myself will take up arms. I will be your general, judge, and rewarder of your virtues in the field.'

One of the men in the fresh-dug trenches, his face hidden behind the raised pikes of the guards who had accompanied her to Tilbury, cried out, 'Aye, there have been few enough rewards!'

She shook her head, seeing Robert's hasty movement, and held out a hand towards the unseen speaker. 'Yes, I know you deserve rewards for your great love of England. And I assure you, in the word of a prince, those rewards shall be duly paid. In the meantime, my lieutenant general shall be here in my stead. Obey and follow him, for never did any prince command a more noble or worthy subject than the Earl of Leicester.'

Elizabeth heard some dissent from further afield, and raised both hands, concerned not to let it grow into outright mutiny. These men were not trained soldiers but farmers, common yeomen, field labourers handed a mattock or a pike and told to stand their ground if the Spanish should land. Only a few squads of mercenaries were there to swell their ranks and show them how to fight for their country.

There was sweat on her forehead, but her speech was nearly at an end. If she could not persuade them to do their queen loyal service, despite a lack of armaments and food, despite poor boots and having nowhere to sleep but under the stars, then England would be at an end.

'I do not doubt that by your obedience to my general, and your valour in the field of battle, we shall win a famous victory over the Spanish and all those enemies of my God, my kingdom, and my people,' she finished, crossing herself with a loud 'Amen.'

Leicester cheered and tossed up his cap, whereupon all his officers threw theirs into the hot blue sky, also cheering.

Men knelt on all sides as she walked among them in the dazzling August sunshine, their helmets off, some bowing their heads in awe, others hoarsely crying, 'God save Her Majesty!'

Afterwards, she could not recall making her way back down the ranks amid the roaring cheers of the men, nor being led to Leicester's tent in order to take lunch with him. But she remembered one bright-eyed man who reached out and dared to touch her armoured side in passing, with a bold cry of 'God save the Queen!'

As though afraid it was an attack by some Catholic fanatic, Leicester knocked the soldier aside like a fly, then called loudly for him to be restrained.

Elizabeth stayed his hand, frowning. 'Let him be, Robert. The man meant no harm.'

Indeed, seeing the blind faith in the soldier's face as he scrambled to his knees, staring after her, she thought he was like the man in the crowd who touched Jesus' cloak in the belief that this contact alone would cure him. Except she was no saviour, Elizabeth thought wryly, offering up a silent prayer against hubris.

Inside the cool shade of Robert's suite of tents, set a little aside from the filth and squalor of the digging works, she was relieved to find a table and cushioned chairs set out for her in a civilized fashion, and several of her ladies waiting to attend her. Helena Snakenborg and Lucy Morgan were among those who had accompanied her from court, with fresh-faced young Bess Throckmorton behind them, still in training to be one of her maids of honour.

'Ah, dear Helena,' Elizabeth muttered, stripping off her gloves and holding out her hand to the Swedish-born noblewoman who had served her for so many years, 'my fan, if you would. And a cup of ale before my thirst overcomes me. I am like to melt in this infernal heat.'

While Robert and his men waited outside, she allowed the women to tidy her face and hair and remove the shining silver cuirass, for her back was now aching from its weight. With so many stout guards about these tents, she doubted it would be required to shield her anyway, its polished silver more a matter of show than protection. Robert had encouraged her to wear armour to address the troops, and she had readily agreed, for she knew the mere sight of their queen in armour would imbue in these common soldiers a stronger sense of loyalty than half a dozen speeches ever could, however stirring.

Lucy Morgan dabbed at her hot forehead with a cool cloth. 'Better, Your Majesty?' she murmured.

'I thank you, yes,' Elizabeth agreed, and favoured her African lady-in-waiting with a smile. 'I heard you had been ill. I am glad to see you back on your feet. A summer chill?'

'Yes, Your Majesty. I am quite recovered, thank you.'

31

Lucy poured a fresh cup of ale from the flagon on the table, and handed it to her with a low curtsey, quiet and respectful as ever in her presence.

She could not fault the woman in manners, Elizabeth thought, for all she had shown other faults in the past. Faults that irked her still. Yet whatever whispers she might occasionally have heard of Lucy's lack of chastity, there had never been any proof to bring her to book. And she was Robert's little pet; there could be no doubt of his favouritism where Lucy Morgan was concerned. Indeed, she had only been permitted to return to court after her last disgrace at Robert's express request. Accused of being unchaste, banished from court, married without permission after some indiscretion, according to Sir Francis Walsingham – another of her senior courtiers who took an oddly keen interest in Mistress Morgan's activities – and now widowed, and back in Elizabeth's service. Well, a widow was respectable enough. Helena was a widow too, and had never looked at another man since her beloved husband died. But there was something unsettling about Lucy Morgan, something not quite respectable . . . Elizabeth could not put her finger on what it was about the woman that made her uncomfortable at times. Was it the colour of her skin? Black as the devil, some of the crueller girls whispered behind her back, though Lucy Morgan had shown herself to be a good and diligent servant since returning to court.

Having unlaced the silver cuirass, Helena handed the heavy breastplate to Lucy, then hurried to the tent entrance at some unseen signal. She returned with a smile. 'His lordship the Earl of Leicester is outside, Your Majesty, and would have luncheon served. Will you admit him?'

'Of course,' she agreed impatiently, and settled herself at the table. Lucy knelt to straighten the folds of her silver and white gown, which had become entangled, then stepped back out of the way, hands meekly by her side.

Yes, Lucy was a strange and unsettling creature, and not quite the same as Elizabeth's other women. Yet it could not be denied that she had served both queen and country well since entering service at court. Sometimes it was best not to question a servant's character when their loyalty had proved useful to the throne.

But Robert! She smiled up at him, and saw the answering smile in his eyes. 'How was it?'

Her favourite knelt and kissed her hand as though for the first time, his upward glance one of admiration. 'You were magnificent. My men saw a great prince today, Your Majesty, at the height of her powers.'

'*Your* men?'

Robert gave a little chuckle. 'Forgive me, I forget sometimes who I'm speaking to.' He rose, then nodded to the men in the doorway to enter. 'Are you hungry? I have arranged for us to take a light meal. I must admit to being famished, will you permit me to sit and eat with you?' Without waiting for her nod, her general drew out the chair opposite and threw himself into it, all legs, his lazy smile for her alone as he dragged off his dusty gloves. 'I was up before dawn, preparing this place for your arrival, with no time to take a bite except the merest crust.' He smiled at the steaming dishes being laid out for her inspection, then nodded to the taster. 'I take the precaution of having all my food tasted now, do you mind? Since we are so openly at war, one cannot be too careful. I know you have your own man, under Sir Francis's command, but while you are away from court . . .'

She waited until the dishes had been pronounced safe, then nodded Helena to set aside a small selection to cool on a trencher. She disliked eating her food too hot these days, for her teeth were easily inflamed by an excess of heat or cold. While she waited, her glance secretly devoured her general. War became Robert Dudley, where peace had left him bored and forever embroiled in pointless arguments at court. His face was more bronzed from the sun, it was true, but she did not find that unhandsome. Indeed, the deepening colour of his skin set off his dark eyes, that sombre gaze which had earned him the soubriquet of 'Gypsy' as a youth.

So now they sat together, Queen and Gypsy, monarch and general, while outside the tent their men dug and swore and sweated in the sun for her sake, and that of England.

'Robert,' she ventured quietly while her women were busy with their own meal, 'if Parma should come down the Thames . . .' She hesitated, almost not wishing to ask the question, though she knew he at least would not lie to her, where her other councillors had been at pains to conceal the truth at every turn. 'That barrier you have erected across the river . . . It will hold his fleet back, will it? And then these men here . . .'

'Will in all likelihood be slaughtered where they stand,' he muttered, and stabbed his knife into a chicken quarter. 'We have done what we can. The river approach to London has been blocked, though how long our barrier will last, I could not say. One good storm might break it apart, and you have seen for yourself how the wind has risen today. We have locked up all the Catholics we can find to prevent a rising from within the country. But Parma's men will be trained, they will possess strong, modern weapons – not spades and cudgels like the bulk of the rabble out there!'

'But their hearts are stout.'

'Aye, stout enough to die in your defence.' He drained his ale, then wiped his mouth. 'Swear truth, it makes me rage to see them so poorly clothed and equipped. Not a coward among them. But they need weapons, and hot food in their bellies . . .' He stared gloomily at the meal before Elizabeth. 'Some of the men arrived here footsore and starving. *Starving!* Sent here by their lords to swell our numbers but with no provisions and little attempt at furnishing them with proper weaponry. It was all I could do to have bread and ale brought in daily for so many thousands, let alone meat. And as for steel . . .'

Elizabeth sat and watched him in silence for a moment. Robert looked across at her, resentment in his eyes. She said, 'You blame me for having delayed so long. You think I should have accepted months ago that war was inevitable.'

'You have always done as you see fit, and you are the Queen,' he managed stiffly.

'Yes, I am.'

A smile tugged at the corners of his mouth at her gentle emphasis. 'Though in this case, Your Majesty, an earlier decision might at least have improved our munitions, if not our chances of defeating Parma and Spain if they choose to invade.'

'Which you believe they will.'

He nodded sombrely. 'I fear so, yes. And this is the likeliest point they will choose for an invasion. Tilbury is where we will resist them, Your Majesty. Or die in the attempt.'

She picked in a desultory fashion at a dish of wildfowl. It smelt good, but her nerves had been so delicate since leaving court, she was not sure she could keep any food down. She saw Robert watching her though, a frown in his eyes, and made an effort to eat a tiny sliver of meat. He had already chided her for refusing to come down to dinner last night in the small manor house in which she was staying, but in truth she could not have faced either the meal or the company. All she seemed able to think of these days was the threat of invasion, and what it would mean to surrender herself to King Philip in the event of his victory. That, and her own weakness as a prince in failing to avert this war with Spain.

'God willing, it will not come to that. Our own fleet may yet drive them back.'

Robert met her gaze. 'Your Majesty, we both know they outgun us. The descriptions of their ships . . . like floating fortresses. We are like David sent against an entire fleet of Goliaths, with nothing but a rough catapult in our hands. No, our chances of routing their great Armada at sea are barely worth spitting on, though I grant we may do some small damage there. But most of their ships will get through, and then—'

He glanced sharply at the entrance to the tent, for there was some commotion there that could be heard even above the shouts and clamour of the busy camp.

A dark-suited servant came to the doorway and bowed to the earl. His face was concerned. 'My lord . . .'

'Yes, Furley, what is it?'

'A messenger, my lord. He swears it's urgent.'

Robert stood, knocking his cup over with a clatter and seeming not even to notice it rolling away under the table. 'Then do not delay but tell him to approach at once, man.' He turned to Elizabeth, frowning. 'Forgive me for disturbing your meal, but—'

She pushed away her trencher and shook her head, suddenly aware of a sick fluttering in her belly. What urgent news could this be? Had the fleet been spotted on the Thames?

'No, we are at war. Let him come in.'

A man stumbled in, travel-stained, his hose besmirched with mud. He saw the Queen and dropped to his knees, yet delivered his message to Leicester, as general of the army. 'My lord, the Spanish fleet . . .' he began breathlessly, then dissolved into a paroxysm of coughing. 'The Spanish . . . fleet . . .'

Elizabeth clicked her fingers and Lucy hurried to her side. 'A cup of ale for the messenger.'

'Yes, Your Majesty.'

The man drank gratefully, then began to relay his message again, this time more slowly. 'The Spanish fleet has been put to rout.'

'*What?*'

He turned to the earl, nodding. 'The message I was set to bear, my lord, is that Lord Howard's fleet engaged the enemy a week since and the Spanish Armada was broken up. Some ships were wrecked in bad weather, others burned, and those that remained . . . Well, some say they have been chased away up the east coast and will not come back.'

'Where was this engagement?'

'Gravelines, my lord.'

Robert's face lit up with rare laughter. 'So Howard's done it! I would never have believed it could be done, but by God, I owe the man an apology.'

The messenger did not seem to share his joy, however. Still on his knees before them, he looked from the earl to the Queen, his face apologetic. 'Forgive me, my lord, Your Majesty, but . . . there is more.'

She waited, suddenly tense. 'Speak, man. What else? This is no time for squeamishness.'

'No, Your Majesty.' He swallowed, then said, 'There is a rumour that more ships are already on their way from Spain to join those which wait in the Low Countries. And that a great force of thirty thousand men and horses waits only for the signal to sail for England and invade.'

Leicester's smile had vanished. 'Rumour?'

'That is all I know, my lord. But a detailed report follows me. It was being written even as I left the coast to bring this message. The Earl of Cumberland—'

37

Rising from her chair, Elizabeth dismissed him with an impatient gesture. 'Enough! Go now and take food, rest yourself a while, then come back and speak with his lordship here about your return message. You have done well and will be rewarded.'

The man bowed and left the tent.

She looked at Robert. 'A force of twenty or thirty thousand men? How are so many to be resisted?'

He shook his head, speaking as though in a daze. 'I do not know. But it will be done, Your Majesty. It *must* be done. More soldiers must be found to fortify our coast against the Spanish and their allies. There are still nobles at court who have not sent men as requested, but kept them back to guard their own lands. I shall write tonight to demand they be sent. Every man must be spared, and quickly. Yes, even the men from the fields, the grandfathers and the young boys too. If they can dig and hoe, they can hold a pike.'

Fool that she was. She had delayed so long, and now look. Yes, Howard had triumphed, it would seem, and put the mighty Spanish fleet to rout. But to what avail, if more followed, and in greater number than before? This war had been disaster heaped on disaster from the first, and never any help to be had, except what God might yet send out of His great mercy.

That it should come to this. Scratching about for a handful of straw-chewing villagers to stand at arms and guard England's shores . . .

Her own head could be on a pike by this time next month, paraded about the streets by some crowd of cock-a-hoop Spaniards with gold earrings and oily beards, her vanquished people grovelling beneath the boot of the invader.

'Oh Robert, what have I done?'

She sank down on the floor, her legs no longer able to

support her. Helena and Lucy came to her at once, horrified, trying to lift her back to her feet, but she thrust them away.

'I do not need your help. Leave us!' Still they hesitated, glancing uncertainly at the Earl of Leicester, who had stood motionless throughout. 'Get out, I say!'

When the women had gone, Robert knelt before her, the sword by his side scraping along the sandy floor. The tent roof rippled above him, the intimate space so warm and close, she could scarcely breathe. She remembered another summer's day in a tented hunting pavilion, long afternoon shadows on the tent walls, and Robert's voice outside, asking when the Queen would rise. Many years ago now, she thought, yet she could still remember how Lettice had risen in her place and gone outside to speak with him, their heads close together, two shadows entwined on the wall of the tent.

He is still mine, she told herself fiercely. Still my creature.

'Your Majesty,' he murmured, taking her hand and raising it to his lips. 'None of this is your doing. Dismiss that thought from your mind. King Philip has been planning this since the day your sister died and lost him the English throne. He has kept his followers in your service for many years, men like Sir William Stanley, who we know now to be traitors. You cannot prevent a man like that from betraying his queen and country if he is intent on doing so.'

'I had the chance to move against them first.'

'Let us dwell instead on what must be done now. You are not well, I shall call your ladies back.'

'No, not yet. A moment longer.' She saw the concern in his dark eyes and loved him for it. 'Robert,' she said, and watched how his gaze narrowed on her face. 'I am well enough. But this heat . . .'

He stood and fetched ale from the table. 'Here.' He put the cup to her lips and she drank obediently, like a child again, looking up at him with wide eyes. The tent swayed in a gust of wind. Outside someone was shouting. The Spanish, come already? A wave of panic seized her, but when she looked, he was calm, paying it no heed.

She shuddered, coming back to herself slowly, and held out the cup. 'Take it, take it. Help me up, Robert. I would not have them see me like this.'

The earl supported her to her knees, and thence carefully to her feet. His arm was tight about her waist, still narrow as a girl's. She wondered if his wife had grown stout in middle age. The thought amused her, but only for a second. Death was too close to them all these days.

She looked into his face and smiled. 'Thank you, old friend.'

Robert hesitated, then bent his head to kiss her. His lips brushed hers in a dry mimicry of what they used to have. But she felt his affection and accepted it in place of burning passion. The only burning passion she had time for now was the desire to rid her seas of their enemies.

'But now you must return to the safety of the court,' he told her, his eyes serious. 'It is too dangerous, Your Majesty. If Parma should essay the Thames, as so many have told us he must, there will be no protection for you here. We have the beacons in place, you will be kept informed of any invasion.'

'As you wish.' She stroked his cheek, and smiled when he turned his head, tenderly kissing her palm. 'Whatever danger threatens, I know you will do your best for me and for England. What would I do without you, my Robin?'

Two

Finsbury Fields, London, August 1588

LYING ON HER BACK, LUCY STARED UP INTO THE SUMMER SKY, watching idly as one tiny cloud scudded past overhead. It was difficult to connect that vast blue expanse with her life here below, the noisy city they had left behind for the afternoon, the ebb and flow of the Thames, so thick with ships that a man could almost walk from bank to bank without getting his feet wet, and everywhere a frenzy of joy that the Armada had been smashed and the Spanish foe defeated. Yet somehow the sky and the earth must be connected, for God had intervened and brought England triumph just when things seemed most hopeless. Now it was as if every bell in every church tower in London were ringing, the streets awash with men dancing drunkenly with their tankards raised to the cry of 'Gloriana!', their wives clapping their hands to the beat of the pipe and tabor. And somewhere along the east coast, the tattered remnants of the Spanish fleet were listing home empty-handed or wrecked upon the rocks.

She should not be here.

Pleading a sick headache, Lucy had slipped away from

her duties at court yesterday. And this was her reward for lying: to be with Will for the day, his shoulder warm against hers, his eyes closed as he slept, curled up like a cat in the hot sunshine. She loved how he felt by her side, his wiry body beginning to fill out now that his pay had increased enough for him to eat a decent meal now and then, that brooding hungry look gone from his face. He had even let his hair grow a little longer, the dark strands brushing his shoulders, his beard trimmed to a point and neatly oiled like the other young men's.

It was less plain to onlookers now that she was the older of the two, and she was sure Will preferred it that way. Burning with curiosity, she wondered again how old his wife was and whether her looks were dark or fair, for he had flatly refused to speak of her.

Perhaps it was best not to dwell on his marriage. For while they were together like this, Lucy could almost forget that Will was not hers, that she had merely borrowed him from another woman.

To be in love was surely the cruellest fate, she thought, and closed her eyes against the light.

It had been Cathy's suggestion that she find an excuse to leave court for a few days. 'Go, dearest Lucy, do what is in your heart,' her maid had insisted, dragging her away from the high window where she had been leaning, bored and listless, watching the crowds gathering in the streets below.

Cathy had been her friend for years, one of the prettiest and most popular court dancers until she left court to get married. With her husband dead in the war, and never able to dance again after an accident which had snapped her ankle, Cathy now served as her maid.

'The Queen won't miss you, not with all these madcap celebrations. The only time you're ever happy is when you're at the theatre with that good-for-nothing

Shakespeare. So go, wipe off that lovelorn face and enjoy yourself for a few days.'

'But what if the Queen should send for me?'

Cathy had smiled, helping her into a simple gown of coarse linen, a gown that would allow her to pass unremarked through the crowds in the city. 'Then I shall tell her ladies that Mistress Morgan is sick with a headache and will attend Her Majesty as soon as she can rise from her bed. And indeed you will be sick if you do not go, for I know that look.' Her smile had made Lucy squirm, aware that she had betrayed herself. 'You are pining for your player.'

Shakespeare stirred beside her, disturbing her thoughts. Drowsily his hand groped for hers in the grass and squeezed. 'Lucy? Still here?'

'Where would I go?'

He turned towards her, nuzzling into her bare throat. 'You might have slipped away like a faery in the greensward. I was asleep.'

'You snore.'

'Forgive me, dearest, sweetest Luce.'

Lucy smiled, and let him kiss her. His lips made no demand, yet desire kindled in her like a too eager flame, scorching her starved body. She felt blind in the bright sunshine, her face turned up towards the sun. Their fingers intertwined, then she felt him roll away and sigh, loosing her hand.

'If only I could lie here for ever by your side,' Will muttered, staring up at the blue sky just as Lucy had done. 'But I am called to work. I must tour with the other players. And I must stop a sennight in Stratford at least, to see my family . . .' His voice tailed away. 'I must do my duty by them.'

'And I must return to court before I am missed.'

'You risk yourself for me. And what can I ever give you in return but a kiss and a farewell?'

She smiled drily, sitting up and beginning to pick grass from her loose, uncombed hair. 'You are not on stage now, Will. Come down out of the clouds and speak plainly.'

Will sat up beside her, his dark eyes watchful. She knew there was a restless intelligence behind them, but neither understood it nor wished to share it. Sometimes she felt his brain must burst with all the wild, teeming ideas it held, and that was not a comfortable thought. It ate away at her to know he belonged to another woman, to lie with him in this secret disgrace and dishonour, to *steal him* from his wife. Yet her passion for him could not be contained. It was as wild and dangerous as his brain.

'And yet there are no clouds today,' he murmured, indicating the wide blue sky above London with one of his stage gestures. 'So I am already plain.'

She glanced up and her mouth twitched. 'What's that, then?'

His keen gaze followed the line of her pointing finger. 'I fear that is no cloud, mistress, but your sultry displeasure. Come, let me blow it away,' he told her, and seized Lucy by the waist, pushing her down again into the grass.

She laughed, trying to push him away. His mouth found hers, and then she was lost, her body prickling and hot, twisting beneath him in the most telling of silences.

'Blow or kiss?' she managed huskily, her lips freed as his mouth sought her throat. Her laughter died when his mouth moved lower, tracing the swell of her breasts cupped high in the coarse linen gown, untrammelled by the ruff she would have worn at court. For she was in disguise today, a mere woman of the streets, out with her lover to celebrate the fall of the Spanish Armada. 'Master Shakespeare!'

'Mistress Morgan?'

Lucy groaned as he tugged a nipple from her gown. 'Someone will see!'

44

'There are none up here at Spitalfields but apprentices and their girls, or young men practising their swordplay. Now hush, and let me practise mine.' He suckled hard on her nipple and she closed her eyes against the dazzling sunshine, her face hot. 'My sweet black Luce, your body is a dream of pleasure. May I never wake up from it.'

The cries of the young men from across the field shattered the illusion that they were alone. Lucy dragged her bodice up to conceal her breasts, then sat up, not looking at him. 'I should go back.'

'To court?'

'Not yet.' With shaking hands, she attempted to tidy her hair, repinning her cap across its unruly curls. They had slept at Goodluck's empty house the night before, and she felt guilty at having left the place that morning without cleaning it. 'I must spend a few hours at my guardian's house before I return to my duties. I do not know when I will be free to leave court again, and there is food left out that will attract vermin.'

Will looked at her, his face unreadable. 'Still no word from the man himself?'

'He is often away for long months without word. I have known years to pass . . .' Lucy moved his hand, which was creeping stealthily along her ankle. 'Will, we must go!'

'What is it? I thought we had put the past away. Now you seem troubled again.'

'What decent woman would not be troubled in my place?' she muttered, but shook her head when he would have kissed her. 'Forgive me, I accepted your terms, and knew what was offered me. Now I find those same terms chafing at my heart. Love, but no marriage. Always to love in secret, sharing you with another woman. It is hard.'

'You share me with no one,' he told her shortly. 'I have told you how it is between me and Anne. I have not lain with her since she told me of her love for another man.

But she is still my wife, and mother to my three children.'

'I know,' she agreed.

'I cannot simply put my wife away, as though I were the King of England and cared nothing for how people might talk. I am a man and she is the woman I married.' He stood and held out his hand. 'Come, let us go before the afternoon turns sour. It is a long way back to Moorgate.'

She allowed him to pull her to her feet, shaking out her full skirts, checking them for grass stains. The grass was flattened in a rough circle where they had lain together, two bodies on the greensward. Yet even as she watched, the long blades of grass began to spring up again, like an army of slender green soldiers springing to attention. Soon there would be no sign that they had ever been there.

For a moment she watched the heavy white arms of the windmill turning in the distance as the breeze increased, a creaking sound floating across the fields.

Will stooped and picked something up, a white ribbon, one of the lacings from her gown. 'Mistress Undone,' he murmured, and handed it over with a wry smile.

She tried not to laugh but could not help it. 'You are a fool, Master Shakespeare.'

'And if I am, what does that make you?' he asked drily. 'A fool's fool, which is to say nothing at all. The shadow of a shadow.'

She shivered and looked up. The sun had gone behind a cloud for a moment, the wide blue skies above suddenly dotted with white. He took her ungloved hand and kissed it, then together they began to wander down Finsbury Fields towards the city wall. The clouds moved on, casting sun and shadow alternately across the long grasses. A group of men in green were practising their archery where the ground levelled out, watched by women waiting for their laundry to bleach in the sunshine. The bushes round about were strewn with the white outstretched arms

46

of shirts, like dozens of penitents begging for mercy.

Bells had been ringing all day in the great churches of London, a strange discordance that jangled on the air. Even from that distance she could see crowds thronging the river banks as small sculls and barges continued to sail back into the port from where they had been blocking the Thames against the feared Spanish invasion. Some of the poorer boats had been hung with brightly coloured rags, in the absence of standards and flags, and men were standing along the decks of the barges, waving at those on the banks.

Near the river, a fire had been carelessly started not far from the gate to London Bridge, its smoke drifting thickly above the city. She hoped it would be put out soon, for the path of a fire could run swiftly among so many timbered houses, especially after a dry summer like this one.

'What is she like?' she asked shyly, not wishing to anger him with her questions but unable to contain her curiosity any longer.

He had been whistling a tune under his breath as he too studied the rising smoke. It was one of the soldiers' marching songs that were heard everywhere in the city now, the words crude but memorable.

'What is who like?'

'Your wife.'

He stopped whistling. There was a long silence. Behind them she heard the thud of an arrow finding its target. She looked at him, seeing the taut lines about his mouth, and wished she had not spoken.

His gaze searched the horizon as though hunting for the answer. 'I cannot . . .' A moment of hesitation. 'Forgive me.'

It was not the first time she had asked about his wife, the woman he had left behind in Stratford. He had given no answer before either. Lucy felt her temper rise but clamped her lips tight on her reply, swearing to herself this would be her last time of asking. He was a keeper of secrets, this man she had taken as her lover, a player like her guardian. Though he did not possess Goodluck's iron core, a straightness of nature that somehow enabled her guardian to speak the truth even when he lied. Not that Will was crooked. But he was cunning; he knew how to stretch a silence out, and tender it as his answer.

If only Will Shakespeare had been honest and true from the start, she would never have become his lover. But now that she was in, there was no climbing out. Not without leaving her heart behind.

But what of her soul?

Will stopped walking and turned to face her. He had dropped her hand when she asked about his wife, but gripped it again now, that restless intensity back in his face. 'Listen, when I am in London, I am sworn to you. There is no other woman for me. But what you see here, this man, this player, this is not all I am. We are all bound by our choices, whether made in error or with full knowledge. When I was too young to judge it a fault, I got a good woman with child and was forced to marry her. I was in love, yes, but it was a boy's love, and a marriage made blindly. Now I am a man, a father, and I must stand by those choices. But this,' he brought her hand to his lips and kissed it, his eyes closed, 'is also my choice. Forgive me for what I cannot change, though it must hurt your heart to do so, and trust me when I tell you, you are truer and dearer to me as my mistress than if you were my wife.'

'I do trust you, Will,' she whispered. But it still hurts, she thought in anguish, leaving the words unsaid.

What would it avail her to speak of the pain in her heart, how she wept some mornings on waking early, racked with loathing for what she had become? His kisses were true enough, he loved her as any man loves a woman;

perhaps even as he loved his wife, or better. But it did no good to close her eyes to his consummate skill as a player.

Will Shakespeare could bring the groundlings to silence with a single word. He knew which words would stir and which deceive. She had no such skill, nor any way to tell his truths from his falsehoods. Nor, in her most secret heart, did she wish to know, for fear of what she might discover of his character.

Sometimes she felt like a plaything in his hands, spun this way and that, while he took what he wished from her.

'But?'

Could he read her thoughts? She tugged her hand free, staring at Shakespeare. His dark head. His eyes. His mouth. Then smiled wearily, remembering that she loved him. What else mattered?

'But you are too subtle for me. I must disappoint you.'

Will laughed then, relief in his face. The clouds shifted and the sun poured around them, balmy and golden. 'You? Lucy Morgan? Disappoint me?'

He walked on down the path, turning to look back at her, beckoning her after him with a schoolboy's wink and open hands. He was a magician, she thought, and began to follow, jerked along by the invisible cord between his heart and hers.

'Impossible!'

Will left her outside Goodluck's house, suddenly more sombre now that the time for his departure had come at last. His arm was tight about her waist as they kissed in the cool shade between houses. 'Do you go back to St James's after this?'

'The court has moved to the Palace of Whitehall. The Queen was restless.'

'What woman is ever not?' His kiss found the warmth of her throat, nuzzling there with passionate intent.

'Dearest Lucy, I can hardly bear to leave you. I will not see you nor lie with you again until the autumn. I do not wish to leave London, but—'

Her heart ached with a pain she could hardly bear. She hushed him, laying a finger on his lips. 'I pray you, no more farewells.'

'I love you, Lucy Morgan.' He kissed her once more, then backed slowly away, studying her as though imprinting her face on his memory. His voice was uneven. 'I shall dream of you every night until I return, sweet Luce. Do not forget me. Remember Will Shakespeare in your prayers.'

She could not help but suspect that he would too easily forget her once back with his wife and family in Stratford. Yet how could she complain? That respectable woman had borne his children; she had more right over Will than Lucy would ever have as his mistress, sharing his bed in this shameful, covert fashion whenever she could escape from court. She should finish this affair and swear herself to chastity again. But it was impossible. She loved him so much, never to see him again would feel as though part of herself had been torn away. Even now, just losing him for a mere month or two, she found herself as weak-hearted as a girl in her first flush of love.

Clutching the wall for support, she watched in silence until Will Shakespeare reached the corner, his hand raised in a last salute as he disappeared round it.

So he was gone, and it felt as though her life was over. How would she survive until his return?

Wearily, she turned to unlock the door to Goodluck's house, only then realizing that she was being watched herself.

There was something familiar about the shambling figure leaning against the wall a few doors down. An odd-looking man, his shoulders were hunched, cloak drawn up around his chin and hat pulled down despite the summer's heat.

Instinctively, she backed away, fearing to be attacked. It was not unknown for the neighbours here to spit at her in the street, knowing her to be without any male protector when Goodluck was away. Nor could she entirely blame them, for they all knew she had taken a lover. Indeed, Will was becoming so well known as a player in the city, some even knew his name and profession, and whispered the louder for it. No doubt they saw her as a player's whore, and felt she should not be dwelling on this street among more respectable folk.

'Mistress Morgan!' he croaked, shuffling forward in muddy boots fastened with knotted lengths of string. 'Stay a moment, mistress. I would have speech with you.'

She looked more closely. 'Master . . . Mistress Jensen?'

It was the strange ragged woman who had come to tend her two years ago after she had lost her baby in a fall, dragged downstairs by Goodluck's enemy, Master Twist. Lucy remembered that she had smelt of fish, and looked uncomfortably more like a man than a woman, yet she seemed to have the gift of healing and Lucy had soon learned to trust her gentle hands on her badly bruised hip and spine. But she had not seen Mistress Jensen since she had healed enough to walk again, and Goodluck had said the woman had gone back to her river barge.

'Jensen,' her visitor corrected her gruffly. 'That's how I'm called. May I step in?'

'Surely.' Lucy opened the door and moved aside. 'Can I offer you ale?'

'Thank you, no. I'll not keep you. Only, the thing is,' the barge woman shuffled inside, glancing about cautiously, her hat still pulled down, 'I've your man aboard and need you to take him away.'

'My man?' Lucy did not understand. Then she inhaled,

seeing the woman's sharp gaze and suddenly understanding only too well. 'Master Goodluck?'

'Aye, Goodluck.'

'On your barge?'

'Aye, mistress, that's it.'

Lucy looked out at the street. The sun was beginning to dip, and the shadows were lengthening between the high timbered buildings. It was well over a year since she had last seen her guardian. What trouble was he in that he could not walk back to his house from the river?

She found this woman's masculine garb unsettling, and the odd way she was prowling about the room now in muddy boots, peering into every dark corner. Yet if Goodluck trusted her, Lucy might as well put her faith in his judgement too, for all he had been mistaken in his old friend Master Twist.

She made up her mind. 'Take me to him, Jensen.'

Three

GOODLUCK SPRAWLED AT HIS EASE, FACING KIT MARLOWE across the upturned crate which served as a makeshift table below deck. At anchor, the barge swayed gently on the Thames, a motion he had grown accustomed to over many weeks when this craft had been his home. Here, some years ago now, he had recovered from a near-mortal wound, and learned to hope again that his time on earth was not finished.

The owner of the barge, one Jensen, a brave but shambling woman who lived as a man, had reluctantly agreed to let him and Kit rest and drink here awhile. Now she had vanished.

He did not smell a trap. Jensen was to be trusted, he felt it in his gut. But there was still the question of Kit Marlowe's loyalties. It would be good to know what he had been doing in the Low Countries. And there he was still very much at sea.

'More ale, master?' he asked, gesturing to the young man's tankard. He took care to slur his words, though in truth he had not drunk so much as he had spilt these past few hours. 'There is yet a little if you are still thirsty.'

'No.' Marlowe hiccuped, then held up his hand. 'I have

taken sufficient, I thank you. What I need now is . . . is . . .'

Kit Marlowe stood unsteadily, fumbling at his hose which seemed to have become unfastened.

'A piss?' Goodluck suggested, his eyebrows raised.

They both laughed uproariously, then Kit shook his head, stepping back to wag an accusing finger at him. 'No, good master, for I . . .'

The young man blenched suddenly, and made for the upper deck, his hose almost falling down in his hurry, clambering up the narrow ladder just in time before he was sick over the side.

Goodluck followed the unpleasant sound of retching and found his companion hanging over the side of the barge, his face quite white in the sunshine, spittle on his lips.

'You are unwell?'

'Too much . . . ale.' Marlowe rolled on to his back, staring up at the smoky air. 'And I smell fire.'

Goodluck looked down the river, feigning a loss of balance as he staggered to the side and clung on. 'Ah! Some fool has lit a bonfire by the bridge. To celebrate our famous victory over the Spanish, no doubt. But now it . . . it threatens the houses.'

'Damn the Spanish though. May they rot in hell. Damn their black . . . black hearts!'

'Aye, aye,' he agreed rather too loudly, slamming the side of the barge with his hand so that the vessel rocked uneasily in the water. 'Damn the Spanish and God save the Queen!'

Marlowe wiped his mouth, staring up at him fixedly. 'You serve the Queen. No, do not try to deny it, man. Why else would you have been there, amid the enemy?'

'And you?'

The young man threw his arms wide. 'A poor player,

54

that is all I am. A maker of scenes. I have told you this a thousand times. Yes, I have worked for Sir Francis Walsingham in the past, when I was a student at Cambridge. But do not think me a master spy like yourself, Master Goodluck. Pray excuse me that. I do not have your . . . your nose for trouble.'

Goodluck grunted and turned away, the warm sun behind him as he looked downstream towards the bridge. Coming back to London from the Low Countries in Marlowe's company, he had made up some fanciful story about having fallen on hard times abroad and taken work reluctantly to earn his keep. Not quite believed, he had been forced into a drinking match with the young man, who seemed determined to stop him making his report to Walsingham. Although impatient to leave and be reimbursed for his expenses, he was also curious to see where it would lead, this drunken charade with Kit Marlowe. He had a suspicion the boy was no more drunk than he, though putting on a good act.

Not that it mattered. By the time they had reached the port of London three days ago, hindered in their approach by bad weather, the news he bore had grown old. The Armada had sailed and been assaulted, they had heard on arrival, first by a storm and then by their stout English warships, smaller by far than the vast Spanish ships, but faster in the water and more manoeuvrable. Now those ships that remained intact were limping back to Spain, much to King Philip's shame, and it seemed likely to Goodluck that the exiled Catholics in the Low Countries had not been able to sail in time to bolster their numbers.

'Nay, do not go,' Marlowe had insisted whenever Goodluck stirred and tried to leave, itching to make his report. 'Not yet, not yet. Take another cup of ale, good master. It's not every day I am honoured to drink with one of Her Majesty's greatest spies, and with our war half-won. Let's play another game of thimblerig.'

'I am no master spy,' Goodluck had told him several times, but Marlowe was having none of it. He just kept smiling and tapping the side of his nose as though to indicate some secret knowledge.

'Are you afraid that I will speak of it abroad? I am not one of those loose-lipped fools, for all I am a player. Your profession is safe with me, Master Goodluck. Come, another cup? Let us drink to England, and the Queen's good health!'

After a day of drinking in the riverside taverns with Marlowe and his player friends, Goodluck had staggered away, thinking to sober up before he made his rendezvous with Sir Francis Walsingham.

He had made his way down to the waterside, sick of the stench of ale and smoke, and had found Jensen's barge moored alongside the quay, low tide making it sit several feet below the wall. Hailing the man-woman hunched on deck with her ubiquitous pipe, he had come aboard only to find himself followed by Marlowe, bearing more ale and apparently not yet ready to stop his debauchery.

'A new place to drink?' The young man had slapped Goodluck on the back, nodded to Jensen, then made his way below deck, shouting back, 'Come down here, man, there is a crate for a table and a good light. I was sick of the taverns' prices anyway. Here we can talk more privately, for I know you spies dislike long ears wagging about you, even at your play.'

A night and a day later, Marlowe was only just beginning to show signs of weakening, while Goodluck himself had grown sick with fatigue, no longer able to hold his own with these young drunkards.

They had drunk long into the night, playing cards and thimblerig while Jensen reluctantly fetched more ale and hot pies for them. Then they had dozed uneasily until first light, neither man wishing the other to slip away unnoticed, and started drinking again as the sun came up. But though Marlowe had questioned him hard and relentlessly, under the guise of drunken banter, Goodluck had held his peace. There was only one man to whom he would talk of what he had learned in the Low Countries, and that was Walsingham, the Queen's spymaster.

Now it was late afternoon and the river stank in the heat, the north bank of the Thames shrouded in smoke from the fire near London Bridge. He could hear shouts from those watching out of windows on the bridge, crowded with narrow houses, as the flames were doused with river water, one bucketful after another.

Goodluck looked impatiently at Marlowe, stretched out on the deck and groaning now like one in mortal pain. He had to get away somehow and make his report to Walsingham. But this young man was tenacious, and an expert dissembler. Even his groans sounded realistic. But Goodluck was convinced it was all for show, merely a distraction while the young man studied Goodluck in his turn.

Certainly he was still a spy. There was no other explanation for it. But in whose pocket? Was Kit Marlowe working for the Queen these days, or the Spanish?

If the former, then Goodluck was once more under suspicion, for it was clear that Marlowe was intent on discovering what he knew by whatever means possible. If the latter, it was his duty not to let Marlowe out of his sight, for God alone knew what information he might have gained in Nieuwpoort, or one of the other places under Spanish control he had visited in his guise as a travelling player.

'Master Goodluck!'

Hearing his name called, Goodluck turned in shock to see a tall, dark-skinned lady standing above him on the quayside. She was not dressed as a lady would be, but simply, her sleeveless gown plain-cut and of coarse stuff, more like a peasant woman than one of the Queen's own ladies. And yet that was what she was, her face as well known at court as any wealthy noblewoman's, the one-time protégée of the Earl of Leicester himself, and still one of the Queen's favourite singers. And Goodluck's ward.

'Lucy?'

He stared, momentarily confused by her appearance. It was indeed Lucy Morgan, though how and why he did not know. Then he saw Jensen's heavily cloaked figure behind her, the barge woman's brow threaded with sweat in the sunshine, and understood.

Lucy's hands were on her hips, her full lips pursed in disapproval as she looked down on him. Even in that poor gown she looked regal, he thought, straight-backed yet somehow elegant, a dancer's grace in the way she held herself. And for a thoughtless second, he forgot his mission and was overjoyed to see her again. It had been too long. And as always, Lucy seemed more alive than everyone else, her dark eyes sparking with emotion, her tight-curled hair spilling out from under the neat white cap, a strange humming vibrancy in the very air about her.

Then Goodluck recalled himself. He did not want Lucy to meet Kit Marlowe. It had been one thing to bring her up around the likes of Ned and Sos, and even that foul traitor Twist. But this was different. Those days were gone and life was colder here on the edge, the old ways almost vanished and nothing new in sight.

This was no place for his ward. He wanted Lucy to go home, to remain free of this dangerous, wearying net he had woven about himself.

Then their eyes met and his fatigue fell away.

'What happened to your beard?' she asked directly, staring.

'It's a long story.'

58

He hesitated, thrown off balance by her sudden presence. Two worlds had collided. He struggled for something to say, to distract her, belatedly remembering to sound drunk.

'I can't believe you're here,' he said uneasily. 'Did Jensen hunt you down at the Palace of Whitehall?'

'No, I was at your house in Cheapside.'

'How so?'

'It's a long story,' she repeated his own words back to him, then smiled slowly. 'Catch me!'

He caught Lucy in his arms as she jumped down on to the barge, and smiled when she rested her hands on his shoulders, kissing his cheek in welcome.

Marlowe was staring at Lucy in frank admiration. An introduction could not be avoided without arousing suspicion that he was trying to hide something. Or in this case, someone.

Goodluck did not want these two involved.

'Kit, this is my ward, Lucy Morgan.' He hesitated, thinking back over the implications of what he had just said. Then added, 'Though too old now to be under my charge.'

'It seems you must be under mine today,' she said pointedly. She too had taken a step back, though their hands were still touching. Just the fingertips. 'You stink of ale.'

'Forgive me. I . . .'

He tailed off, seeing how she had looked sideways at Marlowe, an odd expression on her face.

She nodded to the young man. 'Master Marlowe.'

'Mistress Morgan.'

Kit scrambled to his feet, managing a sketchy bow. The pallor of his face was less marked now, and although he swayed where he stood, he too no longer seemed as drunk.

'You already know each other?'

'Indeed we do,' Marlowe said, coolly enough for a man

in his cups. He looked at Lucy with sharp, clever eyes that seemed to see so much and which Goodluck would gladly pluck out if Marlowe did not keep his hands to himself. The rumour went that Kit Marlowe preferred boys to girls, but Goodluck was taking no chances with a fellow spy. Not this time. 'Let me see, the last time we met was at the playhouse. How is Shakespeare? Still smoothing his beard with Master Burbage's oil?'

Lucy glanced at Goodluck. 'I do not know. That is . . . Master Shakespeare was well when I saw him last.'

'Which was when, exactly?' Goodluck growled, releasing her hands.

Her dark gaze fell before his, a sure sign of her guilt. Had she been wanton with Shakespeare again in his absence?

He surprised a desire in himself to kill that arrogant young man who had seduced his ward, left her pregnant, then failed to marry her because he was already married. Was she a simpleton, that she must continue to love a man who had brought her once already to the edge of ruin?

'But an hour ago,' she admitted. 'We walked out to Finsbury Fields together. There was no harm in it.'

'Is his wife dead?' Goodluck demanded.

She looked shocked, then shook her head.

'Then there is harm in it.' He climbed up the ladder on to the quayside, clasping Jensen's hand in farewell. 'Jensen, I must thank you again for your hospitality.'

The barge woman grunted something, then looked sharply at young Marlowe until he too ascended the ladder. 'Farewell then, masters,' she muttered, and climbed down on to her barge with the agility of a cat, dragging the rope away as she did so, so that soon the barge was adrift on the low ebb of the current and heading sluggishly down towards the bridge.

'What an odd creature,' Kit remarked, watching her go.

He slapped Goodluck on the shoulder. 'It's been good drinking with you. Let's do it again some evening, when I shall hope to wheedle more secrets out of you than you were willing to give this time. Now you must forgive me, but I have an appointment to keep with a tankard of ale.'

He bowed again to Lucy, this time with more of a drunken swagger, as though he had only just recalled that he had been drinking all night and day. 'Fare you well, friends.'

Lucy looked at Goodluck once Marlowe had disappeared. There was an accusation in her face which he chose to ignore. 'Where have you been all these months?'

He took her hand and dragged her up the street after him, following Marlowe as covertly as he could with a woman in tow.

'What, did you think I must be dead?' he demanded, unable to contain his frustration any longer. 'No wonder you took up so readily with William Shakespeare again.'

'You think it has been easy for me to meet with him when I know he is married?' Her eyes glittered angrily. 'All London has been in an uproar this summer, with tales of Spaniards landing in the night, setting fire to our houses and slitting our throats. You were not here and had left no word of your whereabouts. You could have been dead for all I knew. There was some comfort in that Shakespeare and I were in love when the whole world was going to hell.'

Marlowe, climbing briskly away from the river with no signs of being drunk, turned as if to check he was not being followed.

Goodluck ducked into a recessed doorway, pulling Lucy after him. The space was dark and cramped. Their eyes met.

'Why are we following Master Marlowe?' she asked in a whisper.

'Because he is a spy and I wish to know who he is working for. And to what purpose.'

Her eyes narrowed, watching him. 'Is that why you were with him on Jensen's barge today?'

'I needed to watch him in a place where I would not be watched myself. And I would trust Jensen with my life.' He smiled, remembering how Jensen had once nursed him back to health after he had nearly died, and his own horror on discovering her sex. 'I am only sorry she got it into her head to come and disturb you. It was not necessary.'

She frowned. 'Where have you been, Goodluck?'

'Nieuwpoort.'

'I thought the Spanish held most of the ports in the Low Countries.'

'They do.'

He peeked out of the doorway. Marlowe had continued climbing and was almost at the top of the hill now. Soon he would be out of sight. It was imperative that he did not lose the boy.

'Come!' he jerked Lucy after him, hurrying up the steep hill with her at his back, both breathless and sweating in the warm afternoon.

When they reached the top, he was relieved to see that Marlowe was still in sight.

The young player had stopped to talk to someone. A bearded man with a dog at his heels. Goodluck did not recognize him, but then he had been out of London for a while. Besides, this man had the air of a foreigner.

Goodluck waited in the shadows until the man moved on, limping along beside Marlowe, no doubt taking him to a place where they could talk more privately.

'Time to move on again,' he whispered to Lucy, and began to follow, watching all the time in case Marlowe entered any of the taverns or private houses. 'Keep close.'

Lucy was still breathing hard after the hill, though the heat was not so intense here, the old timbered houses leaning in close, shutting out the sun. The street was busier too, people crowding past on their way down to the river, perhaps to spend an evening on Bankside. He had heard the drummers and fife players on their way up the river, and men shouting all afternoon about the celebrations to be held across the bridge that evening, out of reach of the city fathers.

He glanced at her, and was surprised to see anger in her eyes.

'I had no idea you were in the Low Countries,' she told him, pausing to catch her breath. 'Even Lord Leicester abandoned the fight there when they were overrun by the Spanish. Most of the English-held forts fell after he sailed for home, the fighting was so fierce.' She squeezed his hand. 'You could have been killed, Goodluck. Do you care nothing for your life?'

'Those forts did not fall to the Spanish,' he corrected her, his gaze still on Marlowe ahead of them. 'They were surrendered without a fight.'

'I don't understand.'

'Treachery,' he explained shortly. 'Not every Englishman has his country's good in his heart.'

'Is that why you went there? Into the enemy's camp? On Walsingham's command, to smoke out a traitor?'

'Where there are traitors, there are plots against Her Majesty. I go wherever Walsingham sends me. He has been a good master all these years. I have no complaint to make against him.'

'So trusting!'

He was angry himself then, the blood beating loudly in his head. But then he noticed Marlowe step aside into a doorway further up the street.

'Wait here,' he ordered her.

Goodluck pushed through a crowd of black-capped students arguing fiercely in the middle of the street, and came to within a few doors of the house Marlowe had entered. There he stopped; the windows on the first floor were unshuttered, due to the heat, and he did not wish to be seen from within. He stood flat against the wall and listened, but could hear nothing over the noise of the crowd.

The door opened and a beggar came out, limping, a wooden crutch under one arm. His face was swarthy, his hair long enough to touch his dirty collar, and when he called out a cheery greeting to a passing acquaintance, Goodluck realized that he was an Irishman.

Hurrying to catch him up, he put a hand on the man's shoulder. 'Friend,' he said with a ready smile, 'I could not help hearing your voice there, for you speak with the self-same accent as my own dear mother, too long departed from this earth, God rest her soul.'

The beggar halted, squinting at him against the setting sun. 'Your mother was Irish?'

'Indeed she was, and I thank you for reminding me of her sweet face. But I see you have not the use of both legs.' He fumbled in his purse for a coin. 'Unless it gives offence, would you accept this small token in memory of my mother?'

The man's eyes lit up. He took the coin, but cautiously, biting on it, then slipping it hurriedly into some pouch concealed under his tattered coat. 'Thank you, sir, thank you. And may your mother's soul rest in peace. From what part of Ireland did she come?'

'From Dublin.'

'Ah, it's a beautiful city. Well, good day to you, sir, good day.' And touching his cap, the beggar began to limp away, supported on his crutch. Goodluck fell into step beside him, which surprised the man, but his easy smile seemed to set him back at his ease. 'Will you take a sup of ale with me, sir?' the Irishman said. 'There's a tavern on the corner will serve me if I sit outside and make no fuss.'

'Alas, I cannot, for I am to meet a man in this street. But so far I have not seen him. Perhaps you would know him? His name is Marlowe.'

The beggar looked at him hard. 'Marlowe? You know Marlowe?'

Goodluck nodded, watching him. There was a moment's silence. He felt himself begin to sweat, thinking he had baited the trap wrongly. Then the man shrugged, wiped a hand across his brow and gestured back down the street. 'The house with the carved elephant above the door. You'll find him within. I go there for alms sometimes, for I served the master of that house before I lost my leg in battle.' He slapped the crutch. 'If I had not been cut down, I would be there still. For I left many good men and friends behind.'

'In Ireland?'

'No, sir, in the Low Countries.'

Goodluck's mind leapt ahead. 'You served under Sir William Stanley?'

'Aye.'

His heart was racing. 'And that is Stanley's house?'

'One of them.' The beggar's eyes narrowed suspiciously on his face. 'What did you say your name was?'

'I didn't,' Goodluck said shortly, then nodded his head. 'Good day to you.'

Returning swiftly to where he had left Lucy, Goodluck took her by the arm and steered her towards the network of tiny lanes and alleys which he knew would take them back to his house, only rather quicker without having to push through the crowds.

'Whose house was that?' she asked once they had traversed several lanes.

Goodluck glanced over his shoulder, but no one was

following them. It felt safe enough to share what he had discovered. 'It belongs to Sir William Stanley, though he is not at home at present. Nor will he be, once Walsingham learns of this house, for his estate should be forfeit to the crown. Indeed, I rather suspect Stanley will be occupied for some time with leading Spanish forces against the English.'

'Sir William Stanley is the traitor you were watching abroad?'

'The very man.' Goodluck frowned, thinking back over what he had seen and heard. 'The question is, why is Marlowe visiting one of Stanley's houses while Stanley himself is far away on the other side of the sea? Marlowe and his men performed before Stanley and the garrison at Nieuwpoort. Did Stanley charge him with some errand once he was back in London?' He shook his head. 'It makes no sense.'

'You think Marlowe is a traitor too?'

'I think he has some questions to answer, certainly. And I must see Walsingham tonight. But first, I shall take you safely home.'

She handed him the key as they approached the house in Cheapside, and he unlocked the door. It was not often these days that he spent much time at home. He looked about the place in dismay while Lucy hung up her cloak and tidied her springing hair under the tight white cap. The fire had been recently lit, but had not warmed the stones. The house felt damp and unwelcoming. It needed to be lived in, not left to stand empty for months at a time.

'When you marry again,' he told her, 'I will give you this house for your own. I will find somewhere else to live. This house needs a family. It needs you, Lucy.'

Lucy was staring. 'When I marry again?'

'Your last marriage was a fraud. Would you have your whole life a lie?' He felt some long-repressed emotion

66

begin to rise inside him and struggled against it, keeping his voice level. 'Let Shakespeare go. Find yourself an honest bachelor instead and marry him. These sad looks do not suit you.'

'You do not understand what is between us or you would not tell me to find another man,' she whispered, standing very still before him. 'I need William Shakespeare. I desire him.'

'You *desire* him?' He took his ward by the shoulders. 'Do you know what the Latin word *desirare* signifies? It means to watch for a star in vain. We look for what we lack, and love comes hand in hand with looking. This man, Shakespeare, this adulterer . . . He is not what you lack.'

'Then what is it I lack?' Lucy lifted her gaze to his. 'Goodluck?'

The look in her eyes almost undid him.

Four

Palace of Whitehall, London, September 1588

'MORE HOT WATER, YOUR MAJESTY?'

Reluctantly, Elizabeth opened her eyes. Helena was standing beside the tub with a pitcher of steaming hot water, ready to reheat her bath. It was surprising to her that not more of her people took baths, for they were a most pleasant way to keep the body clean. She had drifted away in the steamy warmth of her bath, remembering the magnificent celebrations laid on last week by Robert, the young Earl of Essex. She had looked down on his pageant from a high window here at Whitehall, clapping her hands in delight at the scurrilous verses Essex had penned for the event, casting doubt on Parma's manhood in the wake of England's famous victory.

'Your stepson becomes a most excellent courtier,' she had told Leicester, who had been by her side every night of those victorious celebrations. Then added slyly, 'And so handsome. One would almost swear he was your son, not Walter Devereux's.'

She smiled now, recalling Leicester's swift sidelong glance, his lack of a denial. It was well known that he and his wife Lettice had been intimate during her first marriage to the unpleasant Walter, Earl of Essex. And the boy's name was Robert, after all.

Coincidence, or a covert nod to his true parentage?

Either way, she thought the young Robert, Earl of Essex, a most fetching young man, and very like his stepfather in looks, even if his disposition was inclined to be somewhat wild and impetuous. But as some had murmured about the court, in dangerous times like these, warlike temperaments were more in demand than the flowery and poetic natures who seemed to populate her halls.

'Your Majesty?' Helena prompted her kindly.

Elizabeth found she had closed her eyes again. So tired! It had been another long day in council. It seemed winning a war involved almost as much paperwork and discussion as waging it. She had given strict instructions for the soldiers to be paid off and dispersed at once, and all warships retired as soon as the council was sure no further Spanish incursions were anticipated. But this, of course, had excited furious comment from those warmongers who were keen to see troops marching up and down the land for the next twelvemonth, their upkeep and training costs eating into her slender reserves of money.

No, the war was won, and the soldiers must all go home or England would soon be bankrupt. It was as simple as that.

Besides, Lord Leicester had taken himself off to the healing waters at Buxton a few days after victory had been declared, saying he needed to rest. If Robert felt it safe to abandon the troops and their fortifications at Tilbury, then why should she not send his men home?

She nodded to Helena. 'Pour on,' she agreed, pulling her feet back from the steaming water now filling the bath, then murmured, 'and add more rosewater. The scent is so delicate, it reminds me of my younger days.'

Her lady-in-waiting returned with the rosewater, then gently soaped Elizabeth's neck and back with a soft, perfumed cloth.

Elizabeth stared up at the stately portrait of Leicester in armour which hung on her wall, carefully positioned so she could see her favourite from her bed at night. Robert had been handsome in his youth as well, though perhaps more graceful than his stepson, with a certain presence at court that young Essex lacked. Now he was grey-haired and a little stout, his health uncertain, as his last letter had indicated. But whenever their eyes met, she saw the man he had been and was herself a young girl again, her heart fluttering. With Essex, although he was charming and attentive, there was always some reserve on her part, perhaps a fear that he might find her . . . too old.

'I shall order a new portrait of myself, Helena. It shall be very regal, and strike fear into the hearts of our enemies.'

'Is it over, then? This war with Spain?'

'For now.' Elizabeth put that difficult question aside; she did not wish to consider the possibility of further strikes against her country. She inhaled deeply, enjoying the sweet scent of rosewater. 'Tell me, what do you think of young Robert, Earl of Essex?'

Helena hesitated, slowly soaping her shoulders in the rising steam. 'Lord Essex has a goodly face. And they say he is clever, and might make a good statesman when he is older. But he is a little rash and impulsive for my tastes, Your Majesty.'

'Loyal though?'

'I would hope so, Your Majesty. He is always at your knee. You cannot fear disloyalty from that quarter, surely?'

'No, but like so many of these young bucks at court, Essex is full of ambition. And though he is charming, he is, as you say, rather too headstrong. He does not yet possess

Leicester's political skill, nor his restraint in the face of my displeasure.'

Elizabeth lay back in her bath, closing her eyes as she thought of the two men side by side at court, one young and wilful, the other entirely her servant – if she disregarded his unfortunate marriage.

'I wish Robert would take the boy more in hand, teach his namesake how a nobleman should behave to his queen.'

'No doubt he will, Your Majesty, when his lordship returns from his travels next month.'

There was an abrupt knock at the door to the bedchamber. Helena glanced round, surprised.

Elizabeth sat up, a touch exasperated by the interruption, the cooling bathwater slopping over the sides. Was she never to be left alone? But no one would knock this late unless the matter was important. 'Put the screen round, then see who it is.'

Helena did as she was bade, dragging the tall wooden screen around the bathtub. Elizabeth stared through the narrow gaps in the screen but could see nothing of any use, the room too dim with the shutters closed and curtains drawn against the evening light. She stared instead at the mahogany screen, thinking how very fine it was. The three generous sections were decorated with excellent latticework traced in gold and carvings of naked mermaids and dolphins sensuously riding the waves; a coronation gift from some foreign prince, she could not remember which.

After a whispered conference at the door, Helena returned, looking almost fearful as she came round the screen. 'Your Majesty, it is Lord Burghley. He says he must speak with you at once on a matter of grave urgency.'

'What, are the Spanish back and burning Cornwall again?'

'Your Majesty, will you permit me to dry you and call

the other ladies back in so you can be properly robed?' Helena's smile was strained. 'The bathwater will be cold soon anyway.'

While the women came in and dressed her, Elizabeth stood silently, examining her hands. In her youth, the pale beauty of her hands had been famous throughout Europe.

'Such long elegant fingers!' the Spanish ambassador had exclaimed once, watching her play the virginals.

Now her skin was discoloured, her nails brittle. Her women rubbed in cream every morning to smooth out the slackening skin on the backs of her hands and around her wrists, while delicate gloves hid them from visiting dignitaries. But with every year that passed, she saw the signs of her ageing and despaired.

'We will wait with you, Your Majesty,' Lady Mary Herbert assured her, settling a lace nightcap on her head.

'No,' Elizabeth said quickly. Some premonition of horror crept over her and she shuddered, waving her women away. 'There, I am ready. Leave me, all of you. I would speak with his lordship alone.'

Leaning on his cane, Cecil came in and bowed low, his face gaunt, a sombre expression darkening his eyes.

Elizabeth stood to receive him in her furred night robe. She knew it must be bad news, and she could not bear to sit for bad news.

'Your Majesty, you must forgive me for being the bearer of evil tidings, but . . .' Lord Burghley hesitated, not quite able to meet her eyes. 'Perhaps you might prefer to sit, Your Majesty? I fear this news concerns his lordship, the Earl of Leicester.'

'Robert?'

She faltered, taking a step back towards the bed as though to deny him.

What did Cecil mean, *evil tidings*? What could have happened to Robert? An attack on the road north perhaps, some concealed enemy taking him and his entourage unawares? Or a tumble from his horse? He always had ridden too wildly, even now . . .

Elizabeth saw his face. It was the worst news imaginable. She halted, gripping her hands together tightly. She would stay on her feet to hear it.

'Speak on, Cecil. I am neither tired nor in my dotage, I do not need to sit. What is the matter?'

'It is my sad duty to inform you, Your Majesty, that his lordship, the Earl of Leicester, is dead. His body was found by his servants early this morning, at a house near Oxford where he had broken his journey north, having been taken ill on the road.'

She stared, unable to speak.

He continued doggedly, compassion in his eyes, 'Do not fear that it was poison, Your Majesty. I wondered that myself until I read the doctor's report which accompanied the news of his death. It would seem to have been his lordship's old malady, the fever and shaking, that struck him down. I fear his weeks at Tilbury, camped among the fly-ridden marshes there, may have exposed him to further harm on that score. I am very sorry indeed, Your Majesty, for I know that you and he . . . that his lordship . . .'

'Robert,' she managed in a whisper, then laid a finger on her lips as if to silence him. She refused to hear more of this news.

'Should I fetch your ladies, Your Majesty?'

Mute, her body numb with icy shock, she shook her head, and saw Lord Burghley take a cautious step towards her.

'I cannot disguise that I did not always agree with his lordship,' Cecil continued, watching her closely as though he feared she might collapse, 'but no one could doubt Leicester's loyalty to his country. Nor his loyalty to you, Your Majesty. And his handling of our recent defences against the Spanish was masterful and inspiring. His death is a great loss to the court, and indeed to England.'

Empty words. But well intended, she had no doubt. Elizabeth found her voice again in the silence that followed. Miraculously, it did not shake.

'I thank you for bringing me this news. Would you leave me now, my lord?'

She followed Lord Burghley to the door, and as soon as he was safely outside, shut it behind him and turned the key in the lock. There was some urgent knocking from outside, then raised voices. Helena spoke softly through the door, offering comfort, but she closed her ears. It did not matter. None of it mattered any more.

Alone and unobserved at last, Elizabeth tottered towards the high curtained bed, but sank to the floor before she reached it, blind and deaf to everything but the terrible grief racking her body.

'Robert!' she cried in a strange, high-pitched voice, rocking back and forth like a child, her face hidden in her hands. 'Why have you forsaken me? Robin, ah Robin!'

Five

HER FACE VEILED, LUCY HELD THE DIFFICULT POSE AS LONG AS possible after the strains of music had died away, her arms lifted wide in a gesture of triumph, her gaze on the Queen. Her lavish costume of cloth of gold with a vast overarching ruff and wing-like sleeves was meant to signify an angel, while the lords and ladies posed about her were white-robed shepherds, Magi in exotic cloaks and turbans, and cherubim or lesser angels with golden trumpets set to their lips.

'Bravo!' cried the Earl of Essex, who had been kneeling by the Queen's side throughout the performance. Now he came gracefully to his feet, glancing about the assembled court in the Palace of Whitehall, and clapped his hands in a clear signal for applause.

The court stood silent, looking at the Queen expectantly.

Elizabeth sighed, but said nothing.

It was the first time the Earl of Essex had arranged the Queen's traditional Christmastide pageant without his stepfather's assistance. Perhaps it had not met with Her Majesty's approval.

'The tableau is very fine. It reminds me of another

pageant, another Christmastide . . .' the Queen murmured, looking straight at Lucy. Her voice tailed off into silence.

'Your Majesty?'

Helena offered her a jewel-studded goblet and the Queen took it absentmindedly, though she barely sipped at the wine before handing it back.

Queen Elizabeth straightened on her cushioned seat and turned to look at the earl in some consternation, as though suddenly remembering where she was. Behind her elaborate headdress, a rich red backcloth glittered with gold thread, embroidered with a lion rampant. Next to such finery, the Queen's face seemed whiter and more paper-thin than ever.

'You arranged all this yourself, Robert?'

'I did, Your Majesty.'

'You have done well.' Elizabeth set her hands together briskly, and the rest of the court followed, their applause rising to the rafters of the high-ceilinged hall. Her smile seemed to be for his lordship alone. 'I am pleased, my lord.'

Lucy was able to move at last, turning with the other performers to bow before the Queen.

For a moment she had feared the Queen might be returning to that state of despair and apathy that had haunted the court in the aftermath of Leicester's death. For after hearing the news, the Queen had locked herself in her bedchamber for several days, weeping as violently as a woman widowed, and had refused to respond.

Eventually Lord Burghley had ordered the door broken. They had found Queen Elizabeth inside, lying pale on her bed, staring at nothing. For days afterwards she had not spoken, in a trance of despair over her favourite's death. Yet she had rallied at last, taken proper food, and sat stony-faced with her councillors to discuss the funeral arrangements.

The crisis had been over.

Yet even now it seemed to Lucy that Her Majesty sometimes mistook the earl's passionate young stepson for Leicester, for the two Roberts had been very alike. So alike, many believed Leicester to be his natural father, though none would have dared stir Essex to wrath by suggesting this calumny aloud, not least because it would make him a bastard.

The musicians had begun to play again, a light and lively tune that soon had even the Queen tapping her foot.

'Your Majesty!' The Earl of Essex approached the Queen, his hand outstretched, his smile teasing. 'Would you do me the very great honour of partnering me in this dance?'

With a pearl in his ear, Essex looked rakish and even more like Leicester than ever, Lucy thought, watching the Queen return the young man's smile.

Even Elizabeth seemed younger when she was with him, her cheeks suddenly flushed, her eyes sparkling. He lifted her lightly by the waist and whirled her round, smiling into her face.

Slipping into the shadows behind the raised dais, Lucy looked about the Great Hall. As she had suspected, the entire court was watching them too, from behind fans and raised hands, with a curiosity to equal her own.

Was Essex the Queen's new favourite?

He was wild, to be sure, and not always respectful towards Her Majesty. But there could be no doubt of her liking for Robert Devereux. The only question was to what degree Elizabeth liked him. For a marriage could not be ruled out, even at her advanced age. And it was clearly in the earl's head too, his hands familiar on her waist, his smile just the wrong side of intimate.

'Lucy!'

She turned, frowning at the unexpected summons. Her

heart leapt and she struggled not to respond too openly, suddenly glad of the veil.

William Shakespeare was leaning against the wall by the arched east doorway, his arms folded, his smile enigmatic.

In an unhurried fashion, she wandered across the hall, nodding her head to Lord Burghley and several other courtiers on her way, and swept past Shakespeare without a word.

Her Majesty's ladies-in-waiting were expected to maintain strict chastity, never allowing themselves to be alone with a man. If she was seen with Shakespeare . . .

Her heart thudded sickly, but she kept herself steady and upright, listening to the applause from the hall as the dance came to an end.

His face alive with a similar tension, Will followed her along the narrow corridor and into a deserted cold store that overlooked the river. As soon as she had closed the door quietly behind them, he threw back the heavy veil and took her in his arms.

'My sweet Luce,' Will murmured fervently, and kissed her on the mouth. The room was cold and she shivered; he stroked the delicate silken sleeves and back of her gown, pulling her close against his furred jacket. 'Forgive me, I know this meeting could be dangerous for you. But I could not bear for us to be apart a moment longer.'

Lucy looked into that dark, intense gaze and felt her mouth curve most unwillingly into a smile.

Master William Shakespeare.

He was handsome, and still so young. And he was becoming quite renowned for his skill at the playhouse. She had seen his name in the street on playhouse bills, and heard him mentioned at court as a promising new poet.

Lucy's smile faded as his hand cupped her breast in a possessive gesture. A shocked tingle ran through her, and she gasped, biting her lip. Her belly ached for his

78

more intimate touch, not caring for the consequences.

Yet she must care. Her liberty could be at stake.

'Will!' she managed in a strangled voice, placing her hands flat on his chest.

'My love?'

'Not here,' she whispered urgently. His heart was beating too rapidly under her fingertips; she looked into his face and knew they would be in mortal danger if she could not stop this madness. 'We might be discovered.'

His voice was low in her ear. 'Explain to me how I can let you go. You are so beautiful tonight, Lucy. You are the apple, you are temptation itself. I came in search of my mistress, and have found this exotic creature in her place, all gold and glittering.'

Will stroked her cheek, then placed a soft kiss on her lips. She should be cold and chastise the unwary playwright for pursuing her so openly. Her reputation at court was as fragile as a widow as it had been as a maid. She was watched less carefully, it was true, but even the suggestion that she had taken a lover could ruin her.

Yet how to push him away?

At times like this, his warmth charmed her like a summer's day. And the intelligence in his gaze spoke to her of love, and reason, and the agony of this enforced separation.

She recalled another time when William Shakespeare had appeared unexpectedly at court, kissing her in a small, dank room not unlike this one. How young and naive she had been then, and how ready to believe him free of worldly shackles. Even now she knew the truth, that he was a married man with three young children and a home far away in the country, she could not seem to shake this desire.

Lucy laid her forehead against his chest, listening to the erratic heartbeat beneath. 'This love . . .'

'I know, I know,' Will agreed when her voice faltered. He stroked a hand down her back, his warm touch making her shiver with pleasure. 'It is foolish and ill-advised. Yet here we are again.'

'The Queen suffers with grief over Leicester's death. She is in no mood for a deception like this. A widow and a married man meeting secretly.'

'A singer and a player.'

'A lady of the court and . . .'

Again she hesitated, and he whispered in her ear, 'A lewd and undisciplined country bumpkin?'

Lucy smiled then, looking into his face. 'You are hardly that, *Master Shakespeare*,' she told him, emphasizing his name. 'They have begun to talk of you at court these days.'

His eyes widened slightly. 'They do?'

'You are no longer an unknown,' she assured him, and felt a stab of pride at how rapidly he had risen to prominence.

'Lucy,' he murmured, and she raised her arms in a flurry of silken gold, linking them about his neck, surrendering herself to his mouth, even if it was for only the briefest of moments.

His lips nuzzled her throat, then dropped lower to the swell of her breasts above her glittering bodice. Oh, this was dangerous indeed, she thought, her eyes closing on a wave of desire. His kisses were like a physician's honeyed syrup, drugging her into forgetfulness.

'Damn this costume.' He tugged impatiently on her bodice. 'I love your ruff. But this gown is too tight for a lover's embrace. What are you meant to be? A star?'

She shook her head, gurgling with laughter at his expression. 'I am an angel.'

'Where are your wings?'

Lucy stepped back and lifted her arms to either side, so he could see the gossamer-thin material hang down in its many shimmering folds, and he smiled. 'Of course.' His hands reached for her again. 'I must remove your wings, alas, for you are too naughty to be angelic. But there will be pleasure in the act, I assure you. Come, my sweet, let me show you.'

'You should not be here,' she told him, taking the opportunity to retire to a safer distance, 'and you know it.'

His gaze followed her across the room, but his arms dropped. She had the impression he had known what she would say before even reaching for her.

'So you grow tired of me at last, my sweet mistress. I wondered when it would come.'

Lucy shook her head. She hated the bitterness in his voice. If only she could be free to kiss him back, to be his lover, his wife. If he had not been married, they could have been together.

'I could never be tired of you,' she whispered.

'But you have found another lover.'

Her smile hurt. 'Fool.'

'I am love's fool, yes,' he agreed simply. She saw the pain in his eyes and could not bear it. 'And yours too, if only you would have me.'

'You have a wife.'

Will closed his eyes. He covered his face with his hands as though ashamed. For a long moment there was silence in the small room. From the Great Hall came the strains of music. She stood still and thought of them dancing, the lords and ladies of the court, and the Queen with them, pretending to be happy though all the world knew she was still grieving for Lord Leicester.

'Must we go through this argument again?' His voice was muffled. 'I thought it resolved.'

'It can never be resolved while your wife still lives.'

Will's hands dropped from his face. He stared at her, and she feared he was only half in jest when he demanded,

'You do not mean me to do away with Anne, surely?'

Lucy turned to the door and he caught her, his hand almost rough on her arm. She drew a sharp breath, but did not shake him off. His touch was a bittersweet pain that jarred through her. She hugged it to herself like a secret. Never again, never again, never again.

'Speak sense for once, Will. Our affair must end.' She looked down at his hand on her arm, willing him to release her. 'I love you. And I hope you love me. But we can never be together as man and wife, and we should not be together as lovers. Your wife and children deserve more than a few days of your company every summer.'

His face was sombre, brooding. 'I know it. Do you not think I know it?'

'Let me go.'

He released her, but reluctantly, his gaze still locked on hers. 'This was inevitable, I suppose.' His smile was grim. 'I always knew you would refuse me again one day.'

Lucy opened the door and he followed her into the corridor, close on her heels.

'Then why endanger me by coming to court?' she asked him, keeping her voice low, though the courtiers were still dancing in the Great Hall and nobody could hear them. The walls and high painted ceilings of the palace rang with the haunting notes of pipes and hautboys, the compulsive beat of the tabor. 'Why pursue me here?'

'I could not help myself,' he admitted. 'And I still had hope.'

They were nearly at the doorway into the Great Hall. It had grown dark outside the narrow windows and freshly lit torches smoked in their sconces, the air about them suddenly acrid.

'There is no more hope to be had,' she told him flatly, and tried hard to believe it herself. 'Hope is dead.'

But telling her heart not to love him was like telling it

82

not to beat. The death of love could not come to pass just by the willing of it, and they both knew it.

'Are you sure of that, my love?' Will asked softly, and traced the back of his fingers down her cheek.

'No,' she whispered, staring into his eyes.

His smile was crooked. 'I did not think so,' he murmured, then bent his head to kiss her.

She did not resist but leaned into the kiss. Her body burned sweetly against his. They should part. She did not want this to be farewell though. Not yet. Oh please, not yet.

His arm came about her waist. 'I know this tune,' he muttered. 'I have danced it on the boards many times. French, is it not?'

She nodded, enjoying the warmth of his body against hers, the masculine scent she had missed.

'Then let us dance it like the French, my lady. Hand in hand, and face to face.'

She looked up at him then, suddenly breathless, stunned by such a shocking suggestion. 'Dance together? In front of the court?'

He laughed, his eyes appreciative. 'Indeed, that would take some courage on our part. No, I mean we should dance here in the corridor. With none to see us but the shadows.'

Dance in the corridor? Out of sight of the rest of the court?

Lucy smiled and shook her head. 'Madness.'

'But a pleasant madness.' Seemingly undeterred by her refusal, Will took a step back and bowed very formally, then held out his hand to her. 'My lady?'

She hesitated, glancing up and down the empty corridor. What harm could there be in such a jest?

'I thank you, my lord,' she murmured, and curtseyed to the ground with her skirts spread wide, as though accepting an invitation from a great dignitary. 'It would be my honour.'

'Ah, your honour . . .'

He was laughing, mocking her. But she did not chide him for it. Her hand felt snug in his. Will pulled her gently forward, and they began to dance, rising on to tiptoe as they swung about, circling each other like wary animals, their eyes locked, breath catching. In a crowded room, this was an entertaining and complicated dance. Alone together in a narrow space, it was breathtakingly intimate. Dangerous, even.

There was not room for a full turn, except where they stood, and Will miscalculated the time, lifting her slightly too early for the leap.

There was a pause as they waited for the distant musicians to catch up. His hands gripped her waist tightly, a few inches below her glittering bodice. His gaze was sombre, intent on her face. For a few seconds, Lucy hung above him there in her golden gown, looking down with laughter in her face. She wondered why it was she always doubted his intentions when he was not there, yet forgot her doubts as soon as they were together again.

Could this be a trick her heart played on her mind?

Or was William Shakespeare a magician, conjuring her to fall in love with him anew whenever they met? Certainly he knew how to woo her with words.

'My heavenly star,' he whispered, lowering her towards him. Their mouths brushed, then he was kissing her compulsively, still holding her by the waist, her feet not quite touching the stone floor.

Her body hummed with a sensation she recognized. Heat flooded her face, and she clutched at his shoulders, kissing him back, uncaring what he would think of such a response. Will groaned, then abruptly lurched forward, still holding her against him, and she felt the cold stone wall press into her back.

'Lucy,' he muttered, tugging at her bodice to release her breasts. They spilled into his hands, and she moaned, eager for love. 'God, I want you.'

She kissed his throat, touching him wildly, her hands shaking on his body, deaf to everything but the rush of blood in her ears. Her womb ached with need, her desire for him much sharper than it had ever been before. Sharper and less easily put aside by the voice of caution. It was as though the needs of her body now overrode the warnings in her head. The danger was quite forgotten until a sudden noise behind them reminded her where they were.

'Forgive my intrusion,' a man said in a cold, amused voice. 'I did not know this was a bedchamber.'

Will drew back, hurriedly dragging her bodice back up. He swore under his breath as his fingers faltered over his own clothing, his cheeks flushed. 'No,' he told her urgently when Lucy tried to see over his shoulder. 'Say nothing. Lower your head. Do not look at him.'

But it was too late. The man had recognized her.

'Mistress Morgan?'

It was Henry Wriothesley, the Earl of Southampton. She did not know him well, for he was still young and fresh-come to court from university. But it was clear that he knew her.

Her heart thundered violently as she considered how she had been discovered with a man, kissing him so lewdly, letting him touch her, make love to her. What might Wriothesley do with this dangerous information? It was not unknown for ladies of the court to be imprisoned in the Tower of London for lack of chastity. And their admirers with them, sometimes for many years.

She was no longer the Queen's favourite. The Earl of

Southampton could ruin her with a few well-placed words in Her Majesty's hearing.

'Ah, it is indeed Lucy Morgan.' The earl inclined his head so slightly, it was clearly intended as an insult. Then he looked Will over, his eyes narrowed. 'But who is this gentleman? I know him not.'

The music had long since finished in the Great Hall, and they could hear the buzz of conversation instead, the courtiers beginning to disperse for the night. At any moment, some of those within the hall might come pouring out into this narrow corridor and find her in the forbidden company of men.

There was a breathless silence as Lucy stared from Wriothesley to Shakespeare, still unsure what to do. His lordship had not called for the guards, at least. Nor did he seem angry, though she sensed a certain distaste in his tone.

Perhaps they might yet escape censure.

Lucy gathered her wits. 'My l-lord Southampton,' she stammered, dropping to the floor in a respectful curtsey, her head bowed. 'Pray forgive my ill manners. This is Master William Shakespeare.'

Wriothesley's brows rose steeply. 'The player?'

Straightening from his bow, his velvet cap in hand, Will stared at the young nobleman. The flush in his cheeks had begun to recede. 'You have heard of me, my lord?'

The Earl of Southampton nodded, still examining him closely. 'I was at the Rose with some friends but a few days ago—'

He was interrupted. A group of laughing young men in rich attire had tumbled through the doorway, coming to a noisy halt behind him. Wriothesley turned to remonstrate with them, and several hooted loudly, slapping him on the back, mocking him for having left the dancing early. She knew a few of them by sight, others from their flirtations with the Queen's other ladies. Then she saw the nobleman

86

in their midst, the handsome Earl of Essex with a pearl in his ear, and her blood froze in horror.

'I must go,' she muttered to Will, and turned swiftly away, picking up her skirts so she could hurry.

Lord Southampton would be offended by her rude departure. But he was a youth, barely eighteen years of age. Essex had the ear of the Queen, and if he were to report having caught her alone with a player, she would almost certainly lose her place at court.

She was almost at the end of the corridor before Will caught up with her. 'Stop,' he insisted, his hand on her arm. 'For the love of God, Lucy, don't run from me. Not after that. My heart is still in my mouth from kissing you. Where are you going?'

'Back to the Queen's chambers,' she muttered, trying to hide her panic as other courtiers began to fill the corridor. The dancing was at an end, and the court was dispersing, just as she had feared. 'Before I am missed.'

'You kill me with your coldness.'

'Please, Will . . .'

But he would not be budged. His voice grew hoarse. 'I love you, and I came here to tell you that I cannot live without you any longer. Do not dismiss me like a hound to kennel.'

Lucy threw the thick veil over her face, though it did little to disguise who she was. Her head wild with misgivings, she led Will to a darkened alcove, letting the crowd pass them by. At least in this jostling throng they would be less easily noticed.

'You must stop coming to court in pursuit of me. If the young Earl of Southampton tells his friend Essex what he saw tonight, and Lord Essex tells the Queen, our lives might as well be over. I am not a free woman, and you are most certainly not a free man. This is impossible, Will, and you know it.'

'Then leave court tonight and come home with me,' he urged her in a low voice, his hand still tight on her arm. 'You may never be my wife, but you could be my mistress. No, not like before. That was a mistake. I was too young, I did not know how much I was hurting you. I have a little money set aside now, I could look after you properly.'

'Make me your whore, you mean?'

'No!' He was abruptly angry, his gaze flaring, releasing her at once. 'I love you. Don't cheapen this.'

Her heart stuttered under his intense stare, suddenly pounding. The offer was tempting. To be Shakespeare's wife in all but name, to watch him in the playhouse every afternoon, then lie with him every night and not fear discovery . . .

But Lucy was only tempted for a second. She would be giving up everything she had struggled to regain after her disgrace. If she followed him tonight, she would throw away her position at court, and very likely be condemned for disobedience and lewd behaviour. And for what? To become a player's mistress for so long as he wanted her, and after that to become a whore for whichever man would promise to feed and clothe her and keep her off the streets?

No, a thousand times no.

She sought for an answer he would understand. 'The Queen would never permit me to leave court.'

'Then do not ask her permission, simply run away with me.' His anger had dropped away, like a summer rain-storm that passed as swiftly as it came. Now he was pleading with her instead. Her nerves jangled before the look in his eyes. 'I need you, Lucy. You understand me. You satisfy me more than any other woman has ever done. Come with me, I will hide you so they cannot find you. I will keep you safe.'

'Hide a Moorish woman in London?'

Will opened his mouth as though to explain his plan, then shut it again. She felt disappointment as well as relief. He had not thought it out clearly, had he?

'Let us keep things the way they are, Will. I will see you whenever I can, I promise you that. But please do not ask me to leave court. This is where I belong, where my duty lies. If I cannot be your legal wife, then to be the Queen's lady-in-waiting is what I most crave from this life.' She hesitated, studying him through the thick veil. 'I would never ask you to leave the playhouse for my sake, or to seek another trade.'

'That is different,' Will said wretchedly, but she could see that he had understood.

Breathing was suddenly difficult. Her vision blurred. She swayed, one hand supporting herself against the wall of the alcove.

Was this how a broken heart felt?

'I love you,' she managed, 'but I cannot be with you.'

His gaze lingered on hers, his body so close it was hard not to reach for him again. She recalled how it felt to lie naked beneath him, to rock against him in the night, for their hands and lips to touch while he made love to her.

'This is not the end,' he told her steadily, as though it must be the truth if he had felt it, if he had spoken it aloud. 'It cannot be the end. We will see each other again, will we not? At least do not leave without allowing me hope of that.'

'I will come to you next time,' she promised him. 'To the playhouse. Or your lodgings. As soon as I can leave court without my absence being noticed.'

'You swear it?'

She could not help smiling at his insistence. Will Shakespeare might be married, but there was no doubt in her heart that he loved her. 'I swear it.'

Six

'TAKE THEIR THRUSTS AND JIBES AS A COMPLIMENT, MAN. Your fellows attack you because they fear your skill.' With an absent air, James Burbage helped him off with his dented breastplate, the old theatrical manager still half listening to the cries on stage behind them. Takings were up again: the Rose had enjoyed a full house that afternoon. But Burbage still liked to keep a finger in every playhouse pie, from ensuring the tiring-room ran smoothly to bowing out their most honoured patrons after each performance. 'Talking of which, is the *Shrew* finished yet? Summer will be upon us soon and we need fresh plays.'

That was the question Will had been dreading. He hesitated, easing off his helmet while he considered how to answer. His hair had stuck to his forehead in the hot April sunshine. The cramped tiring-room, where the players disrobed backstage and changed between scenes, was stifling. The tiremen were talking quietly together in the corner, sorting out the costumes for the next piece to be played, some of which would need to be altered to fit the new cast.

'It has not been easy,' he told Burbage carefully, 'playing a history by day but writing a comic piece by night. Now I am called "upstart" by my fellow theatricals, as though I keep my quill busy to spite them rather than to feed my family.'

'Your fame grows daily. Let the likes of Robert Green rag at you. He is a lesser star.'

Will grinned, pouring himself a cup of ale. 'Hardly!'

'You do not believe me? Why, we even had his lordship the Earl of Southampton sniffing around backstage yesterday, in the hope of meeting Master William Shakespeare, if you please.'

'The Earl of Southampton?' Will was stunned. He struggled to recall the lavishly dressed, soft-faced youth who had come across him with Lucy at court. The nobleman had mentioned the Rose, yes. But they had barely exchanged more than a few words. 'What in God's name could he want with me?'

'The earl is still half a boy, newly released from the cloistered halls of Cambridge University. You are a man of great moment in the city. What do you think he wants? The same thing the merchants' wives and daughters want when they hang about the theatre door after each performance.' Burbage laughed, seeing his expression. 'No, never fear, I do not mean *that*. He wants your fame to rub off on him, that is all. He will ask to be your patron, Will, to make himself look good before his noble friends. For he will be supporting the most popular writer of the day.'

'Kit is that, surely?'

'You surpass Kit with your poetry He writes a stirring scene for the groundlings, but cannot turn a line as powerfully as you.' Burbage took Will's cup away and drank from it, wiping his mouth on his sleeve afterwards. His hair was almost white these days, it had grown so silvered with age. Yet age had given him an authority he had lacked before, with many of the younger players now looking to Burbage for cues on how to speak and gesture, and how to own a stage just by standing on it. Even Will himself was not immune to his eloquence. 'Depend upon it, this noble youth will wish to fête you and carry you about the court on his shoulders. And if you let him, you will be made.'

Will considered that possibility for a moment. A wealthy and noble patron to support his writing?

This could be the chance he had been hoping for. He loved to tread the boards, to see his work played out upon the fierce power and bustle of the stage. But to write poetry, long poems like those by Ovid and Virgil that he had studied as a boy in Stratford – that would lend his career true distinction.

'I wish I had spoken with him,' he muttered.

'Where were you yesterday? I had Robert stand in for your part, though you were missed by the groundlings. These sudden absences are not like you.' Burbage looked at him closely. 'I trust you were ill. Too ill to send word. Or else working on this new comedy and lost in a reverie, so you did not mark the time?'

Will did not meet his gaze. In truth, he had been with Lucy again all day, walking by the slow-rolling Thames, out beyond the city walls where the woods and fields stretched green and peaceful. He felt more at home there than in the city, reminded of Warwickshire's damp woodlands. He knew he should not have missed the afternoon performance but it was rare for Lucy to find an opportunity to escape her duties at court, the Queen guarded her ladies so jealously these days. To be with her for a few hours had seemed worth the sacrifice of his pay.

James Burbage seemed to guess at his thoughts. 'With lovely Mistress Morgan, were you? You are a young fool. But a fool in love writes better than a fool alone. Only do not make a habit of it. Trust a wily old husband and take my advice on this, my young cockerel.' He clapped Will on the shoulder. 'You spend too much time with Lucy

Morgan. Soon you will have two wives, and no mistress.'

Will frowned. 'Two wives?'

Burbage hesitated before answering, for it had gone quiet on stage. The final love scene, no doubt.

'You take her too seriously, Will.'

'How so?'

Instinctively, Will had also turned his head to listen to the players. He knew the scene well, had watched it often enough in rehearsal, had written and rewritten the lines himself. A man making love to a boy dressed as a girl. Out in the wide O of the Rose, a falsetto trembled above the silence of the groundlings; a man answered softly, wooing a youthful apprentice with the shadow of early hair on his chin and rags for breasts swelling out the bodice of his gown.

'A man should visit his mistress with a light heart, and make her no promises,' Burbage told him in a whisper. 'Else he will come to dread her company as much as his wife's.'

'I have no wife,' Will told him flatly.

He turned, dipping his hands into the freshly filled water bowl, and hurriedly washed the sweat from his face, then dunked his head. With water dripping down the back of his neck, he straightened, running his fingers through his wet hair to smooth it down.

'Anne is a woman who shares my bed a few nights of the year, and claims to be the mother of my children. That is all.'

Burbage threw Will a cloth to dry himself. His face unreadable, the old theatrical watched him from under thick brows. 'I am sorry to hear it, Will. Yet she is still your wife in the eyes of the law.'

'I know that only too well,' Will replied drily, rubbing at his wet hair with the cloth. 'Nor am I likely to forget it.'

Music swelled through the theatre, signalling the end of

the play. A jig was played and some of the players danced, their heavy steps thudding and creaking against wood to the rhythmic clapping of the groundlings. Then they heard an excited hubbub of voices and a sound like distant thunder as the crowd moved as one, heading for the doors out into the yard where the stallholders and the whores awaited their arrival, and thence into the busy street.

'I should go to the gate, check that our noble patrons had all they desired today,' Burbage muttered, tidying away the last of the armour in the properties chest.

Just as Will was reaching for his plain brown doublet and hose, the doors to the tiring-room were flung open. In poured the rest of the players, sweaty-faced, tugging at their too-warm costumes and laughing at some joke. With them came a tide of other folk, more tiring-men to assist the noisy players off with their costumes, a woman bearing a tray of ale and roast nuts, and the irascible stagekeeper with his book and broom, complaining about the untidy state of the theatre.

'How now, Burbage? Did you receive my message?'

Will turned, dressed in nothing but his shirt, surprised to hear such a refined voice in the coarse hubbub and banter of the tiring-room. The owner of the voice was a young man with a weary look on his face, his beard fashionably pointed, his eyes heavy-lidded. By his rich doublet and cloak, the soft kid boots on his feet and the large pearl earring he wore, he proclaimed himself a wealthy man.

It was the Earl of Southampton, the young lord who had discovered him with Lucy at court.

Behind the youth stood an older man, wearing livery and with a stout dagger at his belt. A fine cloak was draped over his arm. Presumably his servant.

The Earl of Southampton looked across at Burbage commandingly.

'This is the very man you seek, my lord,' Burbage told him, and pushed Will forward.

The nobleman turned to survey Will, examining him from head to toe. An unexpected enthusiasm crept into his expression.

'William Shakespeare?'

Will bowed respectfully, still dressed in nothing but his shirt.

'You probably do not recall the occasion, but we met briefly at court once. My name is Henry Wriothesley, Earl of Southampton.'

The young man's eyes, oddly intense, never left Will's as he spoke. He did not mention Lucy, but Will felt her unspoken name weigh heavily in the silence between them.

He hesitated. 'Yes, my lord, I remember.'

'I left word with Master Burbage here that I wished to speak with you. I take great pleasure in attending your plays, Master Shakespeare, and wish to encourage you in your work, for I have some knowledge of the theatre myself.'

Will was surprised. 'You write too?'

The earl shrugged, a look of boyish disdain on his face. 'A few little things, mostly to be performed before my friends at university. Nothing of worth.'

The players around them disrobed in near silence, watching the newcomer and listening with unabashed curiosity, for although the nobility sometimes passed back-stage on their way up to the gallery – to avoid rubbing shoulders with commoners in the narrow corridors – they did not often welcome noblemen to the tiring-room after a performance.

The earl glanced about himself with interest, seeming to enjoy his visit backstage. Burbage had stopped to help one of the apprentices who was struggling with his queenly gown. The rags stuffed in the lad's bodice had made convincing breasts, and now he stripped off to reveal padding about his narrow hips and arse, a curly red wig sitting awry on his close-shaven head.

'So that is how it is done,' Henry Wriothesley murmured, turning to smile at Will. 'We did much the same in the university dramas. I played a woman of loose morals once, and was so convincing, I nearly fooled the Dean when he caught sight of me in the cloisters. He became quite apoplectic and shouted for the porters, thinking a whore had been smuggled into the college.'

Will grinned.

'Tell me, have you ever thought of writing epic poetry?' the earl asked, and perched on a side table while Will hurriedly dressed.

'Yes, my lord.' He fumbled with the fastening of his hose, wishing his clothes were not so humble. 'Many times. But epic poems do not sell well unless—'

'Unless the poet can find himself a noble patron?'

'Just so, my lord.'

Henry Wriothesley nodded. 'Then look no further, William Shakespeare. I shall be your patron, and furnish you with whatever help you require to write a poetic epic.'

His gaze flashed over Will's plain brown doublet, then he snapped his fingers at the servant who had accompanied him.

The man drew a leather purse out of his jacket and threw it across to Will.

Will caught it and stood astonished, weighing the purse in his hand. So Burbage had been right when he thought Southampton was looking for a writer to support. But this was more than he had expected. The purse was heavy, enough to pay his lodgings for a few months. Or to put aside in the hope of buying a share in Burbage's theatrical company one day, and so raising himself from humble player to part-owner.

'That purse shall be my first incentive to you. Only for my sake, make it a love poem that you write,' the earl insisted, standing again. He held a pomander to his nose, for the confined space smelt of men's sweat and spilt ale, and he seemed suddenly impatient to leave. He gestured to his manservant, who approached and swung the cloak about the young man's shoulders. 'For poetry was invented to express love. And let it be written on a classical theme, if you know any.'

'Venus and Adonis?'

Henry Wriothesley glanced back at him from the door, smiling, though clearly surprised by the speed of his response. 'An inspired choice. You know the Latin original?'

Will gave an answering smile. 'Yes, my lord. Ovid is a poet of great subtlety and range, and the comfort of my quieter hours since I was a boy.'

'I am glad to hear you enjoyed an education in the Roman poets.' The Earl of Southampton hesitated, looking back at him, then nodded briskly. 'Send it to me when the thing is done.'

Will bowed very low, unable to believe his luck in having obtained such a lucrative commission. 'You have my grateful thanks for this opportunity to prove myself, my lord.'

A playwright was a poor thing in the eyes of the court, he thought, writing for common groundlings and merchants, and paid only a few shillings for his sweat. But a poet was a creature set apart, and held far higher in courtly estimation than a backstreet theatrical. This poem on Venus and Adonis might not simply swell out his empty pockets, but confirm his reputation at the English court.

And who was at court but Lucy Morgan?

Seven

'BUT YOUR MAJESTY MUST SEE THAT I CANNOT BE EXPECTED
to remain at home,' the Earl of Essex complained, turning
impatiently from his contemplation of the bustling river
below the walls at Hampton Court, 'not when men like
Drake are permitted to sail forth in your honour, seizing
foreign lands for England. It is not right that gentry and
commoners should take to the seas in your service,
ungoverned by the hand of any nobleman. My stepfather
would never have allowed such an outrage, and nor shall
I, now that I have replaced him as your advisor.'

'No one could ever replace dear Robert,' she muttered,
but Leicester's stepson was no longer listening to her.

Elizabeth sighed, fanning herself as she watched him
pace the room. The Earl of Essex was still only a young
man of twenty-three years. Yet he expected to be accorded
the same respect and honours as her more experienced
statesmen, some of them twice his age.

Still, Robbie did make her smile at times. She was
amused by this hothead who looked so much like
Leicester, though incensed by his churlish refusal to bow to
her authority. They were alone in the chamber where she
had been dancing galliards that morning to keep her

spirits up and her body strong. The musicians had been dismissed when Essex arrived in a temper, demanding to know why he was not on the list of men sailing out on English raids against Spain.

'It is too dangerous, Robbie,' she told him softly. 'I could not bear it if they brought your body home, laid out cold and stiff under a flag, as they did with young Pip Sidney.'

'I have ridden into battle before. I fought alongside Sidney in that brave charge at Zutphen.' The Earl of Essex sounded almost scathing, seeming to care nothing for the courtesy due her as his queen. 'And I amply proved myself in the Low Countries, did I not? Or have you forgotten the praise my stepfather lavished on my courage and swordsmanship during those early campaigns against the Spanish? I am no child to be held back from war on a woman's whim!'

'Nor was Pip,' she pointed out drily. 'Sir Philip Sidney was a seasoned campaigner and a stout-hearted soldier. Yet he failed to come home from the Low Countries alive. His loss still grieves my heart sorely.'

'Then let me avenge him!'

'No,' she insisted stubbornly. 'I have lost too many good men to death these past few years, both at home and abroad. I would not lose you too.'

'But this is nonsense! Nonsense!' Essex was angry now. He stripped off his gloves, slapping them sharply across his palm. 'What use is a tethered hound when the horn calls him to hunt? Or a hawk with his wings and talons clipped?'

'You forget yourself, my lord, and your sworn allegiance to this throne.' Her temper rose swiftly to match his. 'I am your queen, and I say you shall not go to Spain, but stay here at court where you belong.'

'I belong nowhere. I am a free English nobleman.'

Heat mounted in her cheeks. 'God's death!' she

exclaimed. 'You are not free to do as you wish. As an English nobleman, you are my subject and you will obey me, sir!'

'I am of royal blood too!' he countered furiously, head held high, then saw her expression.

He fell to one knee before her, all at once chastened, his handsome face gazing up at her. 'Forgive me, Your Majesty. My temper is so strong, even my own mother cannot . . .' He hesitated. 'It was wrong of me to address you so churlishly. But do you not see, madam, how I would lay my life at your feet to uphold your throne? Yet you keep me at court like a boy and do not allow me to prove myself worthy of . . .'

Coldly, she raised her eyebrows and saw his proud gaze fall away. 'Worthy of . . . ?'

'You must know that I . . .' He stammered, suddenly a boy again. 'That you and I . . .'

'Speak.'

'That I hold you very high in my affections, Your Majesty!'

She stared, astonished by such an admission, and then amused, hiding her smile before he was wounded by it, her heart secretly flattered.

Foolish boy! Dear sweet child!

He gazed up at her earnestly, his eyes burning with passion. 'Say you hold me in affection too, Elizabeth. Do not kill me with a refusal or I shall not be answerable for my actions.'

'I have not given you permission to use my name,' she reminded him icily. An instant's easing of the rein and this wild colt would bolt with her again.

'Not yet,' Essex conceded proudly, 'but soon. Your royal favour must come to me in the end, as it came to Leicester.'

'Must it indeed?'

Essex rose from his knee, dusting it down with his glove. She watched him thoughtfully. Leicester would have stayed kneeling until she bade him rise. His handsome stepson did not worship her in the same way; he had the temerity to dream himself her equal. It was a charming arrogance. But a dangerous one too, if left unchecked. She did not have the heart to crush him though, for he was still a boy to her, for all he had accompanied Leicester and Sidney to war.

If she broke this young man's spirit, he would never serve her as well nor as faithfully as Robert had done.

'You think me a lesser man than my stepfather, perhaps, and that is why you test me with these blocks and trials,' Essex continued sharply, as though reading her thoughts. 'But I am a greater man, and shall prove my worth or die in the attempt!'

She suppressed her smile. 'I am glad to hear you wish to surpass Lord Leicester in my service, Robbie. But you must content yourself to do so here at court, and not against our enemy Spain. I do not, and indeed never shall, grant you permission to sail with Sir Francis Drake and his fleet. Is that clearly understood?'

He looked at her broodingly, then sketched a careless bow before retreating to the door. 'Your Majesty.'

She had not given the earl leave to go, but said nothing, merely signalling her ladies to attend her as they gathered in the doorway, their expressions sly and curious. No doubt they had heard something of what Essex had been saying to her, the love he had declared so vehemently. Well, there was no harm in reminding the sillier girls in her service that even a comely young nobleman like Essex could be brought to his knees by her queenly presence.

Elizabeth smiled, wandering to the sunlit windowsill where he had stood, and looking down on the barges bobbing at anchor along the river. No doubt it was hard for him to accept her refusal when so many other young men were preparing for war. But she would not lose Essex as she had lost Leicester, even if it meant making his lordship resent and fear her a little.

No, better the impetuous youth should find some corner of the court to sulk in than remain with her a moment longer in that temper. They would soon be at loggerheads again if Essex could not clear his brow of that dark frown.

Walsingham came to her later, limping heavily, coughing behind his hand. She thought she had never seen the statesman look so old. 'Your Majesty,' he began, and handed her a rolled-up letter, 'more bad news, I am afraid. His Majesty King Henry of France is dead.'

She did not open the letter, laying it aside with a shudder. She had taken her fill of bad news in recent years, and the death of fellow princes was not a matter she wished to pursue in too close detail.

'Sickness?' she demanded, half praying that it had been.

'Murder.'

Her stomach churned with an old fear. 'Poison, then?'

'A monk with a knife. They are saying it was in revenge for the Duke of Guise's death.'

Elizabeth closed her eyes. 'Barbarians.'

'Be easy in your mind, Your Majesty. Thanks to your royal father, England is rather short on fanatical monks, armed or otherwise.'

'Poor Henry.' Her eyes narrowed on Walsingham's face, sensing something more in his stillness. Her spymaster had served her for too many years for her not to be able to read the signs that some plot was afoot. 'What else? This is not your only news, is it?'

His smile was wry. 'Forgive me.'

'I pray you do not spare me, old friend. We know each

other too well for subterfuge. Who has my death in hand tonight?'

'You remember last year I told you of some possible scheme against your life, hatched by one already in your service at court?' She nodded grimly. 'Well, my man has been back to the Low Countries in search of a name. He has not been as successful as I had hoped, for those who plotted against your life have moved deeper into enemy territory where he was not able to approach them without arousing suspicion. I fear he is now too well known to them, so I shall recall him to England and send another of my men in his place. He is younger, and his face is unknown to their spies. Indeed, I have high hopes that he will bring us back a name.'

'But?'

Sir Francis coughed again, more violently this time, reaching for a handkerchief as he turned his head away. She waited impatiently while he recovered, knowing there would be more to say on this matter. 'But there is some suspicion that poison is to be the method used, Your Majesty. Accordingly, I will ensure your cooks and their assistants are all loyal men, and from now on would suggest two tasters instead of one. For safety's sake.'

For safety's sake?

She fixed her spymaster with a cold eye. 'If you recall, you and Cecil promised that once my cousin Mary Stuart was dead, there would be no more of these attempts on my person. Well, Mary is dead these past two years. You even showed me a lock of her hair to prove it. Yet still I must fence myself about with these precautions. I am a queen besieged, sir. What do you say to that?'

'I most humbly apologize, Your Majesty. We did indeed believe that the Scots Queen's death would bring an end to these conspiracies, for then there could be no question of a Catholic queen succeeding you on the throne. But it seems we bargained without the strength of feeling among those Englishmen whose personal loyalties are to Rome and who have chosen to make their beds with the enemy.'

She experienced a profound feeling of distaste. 'These disloyal dogs. Do not call them sons of England, it besmirches the good name of true Englishmen. Send out your man, find me this poisoner. And when we have run the traitor to ground, we will cut his belly open in the street, so all may see the colour of his cowardice.'

Walsingham bowed, taking back the letter she had not opened. Frowning, she noticed a yellowish tinge to his skin, and a slight tremor to his hands.

'Are you unwell?' she asked him suspiciously.

'I find that malady touches me more these days than it used to,' he agreed, then glanced at her, clearly hesitant. 'Perhaps I could once again mention my retirement, Your Majesty? My health grows ever more uncertain—'

'As does my throne,' she pointed out sharply, a little panicked at the thought of losing Walsingham as well as Leicester, interrupting before he could ask for the impossible. 'I cannot spare you yet, old friend. Not with Drake planning these assaults on Spanish-held towns. I shall be glad if they bring back heaps of Spanish gold and treasure for our coffers, but not if all we achieve is to poke Philip with a sharp stick and force him to launch a second Armada to defend his shores.'

'I believe the Spanish fleet is not yet up to strength again, Your Majesty. That may be why the King tries other avenues to shake your hold on the English throne, such as this unknown poisoner of ours.'

'Well then, you see my predicament more clearly than most. One more year of service to my crown, with Spain put to rout once and for all, and you may retire to spend more time with your daughter.'

'I thank you, Your Majesty.'

'But take some rest now,' she advised him kindly, 'then get back to work. I cannot have you unwell, sir. We are still at war. The Privy Council needs your guidance on foreign affairs more than ever now, we cannot spare you to a sickbed.'

As Sir Francis bowed his consent, a good servant, always ready to bend to her will, Elizabeth threw out her jewelled hand for him to kiss. Since Robert's loss, she could not bear to think of herself alone and undefended by the men who had guarded her since she had come to the throne.

'Just as I need young hotheads like the Earl of Essex, to rally his fellow countrymen against invasion should that evil day ever come, so I need men like you, Walsingham, to watch for the secret knife in my back and the poison in my food.' She smiled at him, at her most charming, and saw pleasure lighten his dour face. 'I know you will not fail me.'

Part Two

One

Seething Lane, London, May 1590

RAIN HAD BEEN FALLING IN A STEADY DRIZZLE EVER SINCE HIS entry into English waters, welcoming him back to his homeland.

Goodluck trudged uphill from the stinking wash of the Thames towards the corner of Seething Lane, his leather hat pulled down and collar turned up against the wet. Another mission completed, another damp, unpromising homecoming. His clothes were patched and threadbare, his boots were beginning to let in water and he was bone-weary. It had been nine months since he had slept in his own bed.

Perhaps it was time he thought about securing a new line of work. Yet he knew no other trade. What else could he do but spy for England?

Besides, if he was free to idle about, what would he do all day but watch the barges sail up and down the Thames? Or sit in a tavern corner, slumped over his ale or puffing on a clay pipe, telling stories of his life in return for a pinch of tobacco.

Goodluck waited in the shadows until nightfall, unsure whether he had been followed from the docks, then knocked at the back door to Walsingham's house in Seething Lane. The front of the house had been in darkness for hours. But there was a fire burning in the servants' quarters; he smelt woodsmoke drifting from the chimneys into damp air, and heard the crackle of burning logs from within as he waited.

A boy appeared in response to his knock, peering through the door grille at him, a puzzled expression on his face.

'I am here to see Sir Francis Walsingham,' he told the boy, then gave the password to prove he was a friend.

Without a word, the boy disappeared.

Goodluck stood under the persistent rain, listening to shouts and footsteps within the house, and wondered if his master had left London and was residing at court. Yet the note he had received a month ago via a contact in Flushing had told him to wind up his investigations in the Low Countries, and to present himself at Seething Lane on his arrival back in England.

No doubt Walsingham wished to convey his disappointment at the lack of information gathered over the past nine months abroad, posing as a travelling dentist. It was not a conversation he had been looking forward to, for he was acutely aware of having failed his master on this mission.

'I need the name of this traitor in the Queen's service,' Sir Francis had told him at their last meeting, handing him a pass for the ports and a small purse of silver coins. 'Nothing else, just the name.'

Yet although Goodluck had talked in disguise to many exiled Catholics in the Low Countries, painstakingly following Sir William Stanley's trail from Nieuwpoort, he had been unable to discover the name of the traitor hired to poison the Queen. And now he had been recalled to England, like a cur with its tail between its legs, presumably to account for his lack of success.

A grey-haired woman in apron and cap appeared in place of the boy, holding a candle lantern. She squinted out at him through the grille, then opened the door, gesturing him to step into the smoky hallway. He recognized her from a previous visit to Seething Lane. It was Walsingham's housekeeper, though he did not know her name.

'Mistress,' he said, bowing his head and trying not to drip all over the rushes on the floor. 'Forgive me for troubling you at this late hour, but I need to speak with Sir Francis at once. I saw that the house is in darkness though. Is your master away from home? At court, perhaps?'

The housekeeper stared at him, wide-eyed. 'Sir Francis Walsingham is dead, sir.'

'*Dead?*'

'Aye, sir.' She was frowning. 'Where have you been that you did not know it?'

Goodluck's chest hurt. *Walsingham was dead*. He heard himself speak, and barely knew what he was saying. 'I have been abroad for nine months. Tell me what happened, mistress. Was it poison?'

'No, sir, only that same malady against which he had long fought. Sir Francis was a brave man, but he was very sick towards the end and suffered most dreadfully in his last hours. But the Queen would not release my poor master from his duties until he was so close to death, there was nothing the physician could do but give him poppy for the pain.' There was a note of bitterness in the old woman's voice. 'Sir Francis left many debts unpaid. Even this house may have to be sold to pay them.'

'I am sorry to hear it,' Goodluck muttered, then stood a moment like a man at an unmarked crossroads, suddenly lost for which direction to take. He had not thought any further than his meeting with Walsingham tonight. And now it would never happen. To whom should he convey his information, what little there was of it? And how to recoup his expenses from his long months abroad?

'Forgive me,' he asked the housekeeper, 'but Sir Francis left no message on his deathbed? No final instructions?'

She looked at him as though he were mad. 'No, sir.'

A thought struck him. 'But what of his papers? His letters and books?'

'Some gentlemen of the court came by yesterday and took away several chests of his private papers and other items, sir. I know nothing more.'

'His widow?'

'Lady Walsingham has gone into the country, sir.' The housekeeper hesitated. 'Perhaps you should ask at court if there is some special instruction you seek.'

'Yes,' he agreed blankly, realizing that she wished him to leave. And indeed there was nothing here for him any more. Walsingham had summoned him home for some reason, then abruptly died. Though one could hardly blame a man for dying.

Outside on the lane again, Goodluck stood under the rain and stared up at the house. Walsingham's study had been on the corner that jutted out, looking down on to the stable yard below. Its fine latticework windows were unlit, the master of the house departed from this world. Goodluck himself would never wait for Walsingham there again, nor take payment and secret papers from his master's hand, nor be given instructions for any new mission. And whatever reprimand he had been facing would now never be delivered.

The game was at an end, it would seem.

The house in Cheapside was also in darkness. So Lucy was still at court. He felt a dullness creep over his heart and almost laughed, chiding himself for such frailty. She was in her world, he was in his.

So much the better for Lucy, he thought grimly. He would not wish to inflict this broken world on her youth and beauty, his life narrowing and darkening each day towards oblivion. This was her time to shine. His time was almost done.

Goodluck fished a door key from his purse and let himself into the house, finding it cold and damp. He fumbled for a candle and tinderbox on the shelf where they were always kept, and soon the kitchen was full of trembling light. Lucy had not been home for many months, he suspected, inspecting the dusty pans on the table and prodding the crumbling white ashes in the hearth with his boot.

He carried the candle upstairs and stared down at Lucy's mattress. It lay stripped of its linen now, the chamber musty and cobwebbed, her clothes chest shut and locked, a long-dead mouse lying amid the rushes under the shuttered window. He remembered their last meeting, and told himself it was best if his ward never came home again.

What did he have to offer Lucy now? He was a tired old spy, his master dead and his purse empty. That young villain Shakespeare was better placed to provide for her now, even if he was already married.

At least Lucy seemed happy to be Shakespeare's mistress, since she could not be his wife. When life was so cruel and short, surely happiness must count for more than blind obedience to the rules by which they were forced to live? Of that heresy, he was growing more convinced every day.

Suddenly exhausted, he dragged off his sodden clothes, found an old cloak in which to wrap himself, then lay down on Lucy's bare mattress to sleep.

Just before he snuffed out the candle, he wondered again to whom he should report his meagre findings from the Low Countries. But with no answer forthcoming, sleep soon overtook him, and he dropped away into a dream where he was hanging from a crumbling cliff by one bloodied hand, and his shouts for help could not be heard above the roar of the sea below . . .

Goodluck woke to the sound of knocking at the front door. He stumbled down, still wrapped in his cloak, and found a neighbour on the doorstep, red-faced and stout. 'Master Giles?'

'I heard you come back in the early hours,' Giles admitted, looking him up and down with a doubtful expression, then held out two letters. 'These came for you while you were away, Master Goodluck. This one about six weeks past, this one only a few days ago. Though we do not see you often, I told the messenger I'd hold on to them for you, rather than turn the boy away with his errand undischarged.'

'That was very kind of you, Master Giles.' Goodluck took the letters, trying to curb his impatience to read them until his neighbour had gone. 'I would offer you a bite to eat, but my cupboards are empty. I am not a good house-keeper, I fear.'

Giles laughed. 'Well, you are a busy man. Any fool can tell that, for you are never at home.'

'Has my ward Lucy been here lately?'

His neighbour thought a moment, then shook his head. 'Not since the summer. She still travels with the court though, doesn't she? The Queen and her court were out at Hampton, last I heard. You could send word to her there.'

'Yes, perhaps I shall.'

'And feel free to come to us for your dinner,' Giles added brusquely as they shook hands. 'If you've nothing in the house, be sure my wife will always welcome you to our table.'

Goodluck stared, unsure how to respond. All these years he had kept this house at Cheapside and yet never been in any of his neighbours' homes, though he knew some of them to nod to in the street. 'I thank you. Again, you are very kind, Giles.'

'Well, the offer is there.'

Alone in the chilly kitchen, still shivering in the old cloak, Goodluck made sure the door was secure, then lit another candle and sat down to read his letters.

The older letter was from Kit Marlowe, a note asking briefly if they could meet at the Angel on the Hoop one Friday evening a month past. This he set aside, frowning.

What had Kit wished to discuss? Too late to discover it now. But that could be a useful contact to develop now that Walsingham was gone. Kit was well known as a university man and, it was claimed, had friends at court; he might know how the Queen intended to administer her spy network in the wake of his master's death. For there must be many like him who had been cut adrift, unable to make their reports or meet their expenses on her account.

The more recent letter took him aback. Unrolling it, he glanced absently at the signature, then sat like a block of stone, staring down at it.

Agnes Goodluck.

His brother's wife. What could she want after all these years? He had sent word of his address back home when he first took this place in Cheapside, but had never once heard from his brother. Now a letter. It could mean only one thing.

Dear Faithful
You will doubtless wonder at my writing after so long an
age of silence between us, but your brother Julius is in
dire need of you. He fell from his horse yesterday morn-
ing, jumping the hedge at Fletchers' Brook. He was

carried back to the house at once, but the physician fears his back may be broken. I do not know if you are at home to receive this letter, or even if you are yet living. But if you are, I pray you return home to Oxfordshire at once and lend us your brotherly comfort.

Your sister-in-law, Agnes

Postscriptum: I was saddened to hear of the death of your sister Marian. Though she and Julius were not close, she was still family, and it grieves me that we were not there at her funeral. I hope all was done as Julius would have wished it to be.

Goodluck sat a moment longer, re-reading the letter, then laid it aside. Giles had said this letter had arrived a few days ago. It would have taken a good day or two to reach him from Oxfordshire, even by urgent courier. *The physician fears his back may be broken.*

By now his brother might be dead.

The candle flame flickered, surly and reluctant in the shadowy kitchen. He stared at it blindly. *Julius Goodluck.* His older brother. His only kin now that Marian was gone, the woman who had always looked after young Lucy while he was away.

It grieves me that we were not there at her funeral.

No more was I, he thought grimly. He had been away in France when Marian died of a fever nearly three years before, and not even Lucy had heard of her death until it was too late to pay her respects to the woman who had raised her.

He hurried upstairs to fetch dry clothing, pulled on his best kidskin boots – barely ever worn – and a better cloak than the one he had slept in, then locked up the house again and made his way to the stables beyond Moorgate where he occasionally hired a mount.

It would still take two days at least, but the swiftest way into Oxfordshire was on horseback and Goodluck wished to travel swiftly, though he knew there might be little need for it if his brother's back had indeed been broken. By now, he could be going home to bury his brother, not make his peace with him.

Two

it would still take ... days at least, but the swifter way into Oxfordshire was on horseback and Goodluck, who had ... travel swift ... though he knew there ... it to need for it if his brother's back had indeed been broken. By now he could be gone home to lay his brother to rest, make his peace with God.

Two

THAT SPRING, THE COURT HAD MOVED FROM THE STUFFY corridors of Whitehall to the vast, turreted riverside palace at Richmond. Lucy had always thought the grounds and gardens there beautiful, yet now she found she could not lift her heart even with the sight of delicate white blossom along all the woodland paths that surrounded the palace. The Queen had sunk into a deep and heavy-eyed lethargy since learning of Sir Francis's death, to be roused from this state only by her rage over the wayward Earl of Essex, who had run away from court like a naughty boy fleeing his nursemaid and joined the fleet without royal permission. Elizabeth had sent a volley of furious letters after him, commanding the earl to return to court at once. But news had soon come back from the coast that Essex had already sailed for Spain, commandeering one of the ships under Drake's control and swearing he would not be bound by an old woman's authority.

'Let the Earl of Essex return now,' she had been heard to say to a visiting dignitary, 'and the executioner shall have his head before the week is out. He is a rogue who has dishonoured our throne with his unruliness. As we have authority to rule, so we look to be obeyed.'

The expedition to ransack Spanish towns had been a pitiful disaster. Thousands dead of fever and little treasure to show for their efforts. Yet the Queen had forgiven Essex within days of his return. There had been a violent row – Lucy listened outside with the other ladies-in-waiting as the tempestuous pair shouted at each other in the Privy Chamber – and then silence.

They had not dared to enter the chamber, though Helena had knocked and been told shrilly by the Queen to 'Depart!'

One of the younger girls had made a face. 'I expect he is kissing her, to keep her quiet. Such an old woman too! It's horrible.'

'Hush, child! How dare you speak of the Queen in such a rude and impertinent manner?'

Helena had boxed the girl's ears for her impudence, sending her red-cheeked and howling from the Queen's chambers.

But any rumours that Essex would charm her into a late marriage were laid to rest when it emerged that he had secretly married Walsingham's daughter, Frances.

Lucy knew Frances only a little. The widow of Sir Philip Sidney, she was a tall slender woman with a tragic air, and still young. Young enough, indeed, to be an affront to Queen Elizabeth when she heard of their secret wedding ceremony, performed only a short while before Sir Francis died.

'How dare he?' she had fumed.

The court waited to see what would happen. But it turned out to be nothing. After a brief period of disgrace, with the young couple banished to Essex House, Robert was seen again at court.

Lady Helena had shrugged. 'Essex can do no wrong in her eyes,' she commented to Lucy, watching them dancing together in the Great Hall at Richmond. 'This period of favour won't last though. One day he will cause Her Majesty such offence, she will not be able to forgive him.'

Yet soon it seemed that Essex was once more in the Queen's good graces. She gave him leave to sail to Brittany with a small number of ships, to battle the invading Spanish who had landed there.

'You think me misguided to have forgiven Essex so readily?' the Queen asked Lucy one evening, as they sat watching two of the courtiers play chess in the Privy Chamber. The evening was warm. Elizabeth closed her eyes as Lucy fanned cool air across her face and throat. 'You consider him dangerous, perhaps?'

'Not at all, Your Majesty,' Lucy replied. 'The Earl of Essex loves and reveres you as his queen.'

'And as a woman?'

Lucy hesitated, unwilling to lie, yet equally aware that the truth could see her punished for impertinence. 'That you must ask his lordship yourself. He does not confide such thoughts to me.'

'You know, sometimes when we are alone together, I forget that he is not Robert. I mean, the Earl of Leicester. His dark eyes . . .' The Queen's voice dropped away into silence. She sat a moment, musing and humming a popular tune under her breath while she watched the chess match. 'He is a charming boy.'

'A boy, Your Majesty?' Lucy remarked innocently.

Then she saw the Queen's expression and wished she had not dared make such a comment.

'A man, then,' the Queen agreed sharply. 'I had not thought you took such interest in his lordship.'

'Indeed, I have barely spoken with Lord Essex, Your Majesty,' Lucy hurried to assure her, seeing the flush of jealousy in the Queen's cheeks. 'His lordship thinks only of you and how best to serve you.'

That seemed to mollify the Queen, though she watched

120

her closely from then on, and Lucy more than once felt the intent gaze of one of the Queen's spies.

Lucy would go to bed early those nights and cover her face with her arm, desperate to be alone even among the bustle of the other women readying themselves for bed with whispers and prayers. Her old friend Cathy attended to her disrobing some nights, and would often look on her with concern after these bitter exchanges with the Queen. There was little that went on in the Queen's chambers that was not swiftly known throughout the palace, even in the servants' quarters.

'You can always leave court if you are unhappy,' Cathy whispered in her ear as she was unlacing Lucy's gown, 'and set up home with me in the country. I would be glad to return to Norfolk and see my son again. He will be grown tall as a weed by now!'

'The Queen would never let me go,' Lucy replied despondently. 'Not while my voice is still good enough for her to parade me before visiting ambassadors. I am her dark treasure, her noble singing Ethiop!'

'You must watch yourself most carefully, and remember that others will be watching too,' her friend warned her. 'Never allow yourself to be caught alone with a man, nor smile too much. Give the Queen no cause to have you punished. The court is a dangerous place if you will not play her games, Lucy.'

'I am sick of her games!'

'For goodness' sake, hush, before you get us both whipped!' Cathy kissed her goodnight, then hurried away to attend to other ladies. 'Do not forget what I said. Step carefully, Lucy.'

One night after she had sung for the Queen at a masque, then slipped away with the excuse of a headache, Lucy found her path blocked by a masked courtier. The corridor

121

was narrow and windowless, only one torch set in a wall sconce at the far end, flickering violently in the gusting wind. She curtseyed and flattened herself against the wall to allow the man to pass, guessing by his rich finery that he must be one of the Queen's noblemen. But the courtier did not move.

The man was wearing a black-feathered bird mask, inset with seed pearls. He turned it to one side to survey her through its eye-slits, and she saw his eyes glittering as though he had been drinking.

'Mistress Morgan, what a surprise to find you un-attended here, so far from the revelry. Are you in search of someone, perhaps? Or have you lost your way? The court is behind you.'

Aware that it might appear like a secret assignation if she were discovered alone with this man, Lucy said nothing but took a hurried step backwards, meaning to return to the masque.

'Not so fast,' he muttered, swearing under his breath, and caught at her arm. 'I have not finished with you yet.'

She heard a menace in his slurred voice and frowned, trying to recognize the man behind the mask. Did he mean to do her harm? There was none here to stop him if he did.

'Sir, do I know you?'

Silently, he pulled down his mask, which hung from his neck on a length of black lace. It was Henry Wriothesley, the young Earl of Southampton.

Almost sagging against the wall in relief, Lucy managed a thin smile. 'My lord Southampton. How may I help you?'

'I want your promise.'

'My lord?'

'You have taken a lover,' he stated bluntly, shocking her with his directness. 'One Master William Shakespeare by name, a common player of the city. No, do not waste your breath in denying your guilt. After I saw you together at Greenwich, I set men to follow you both. I know that you have gone into the city in disguise since then, without seeking the Queen's permission to leave court, and that you have lain with Master Shakespeare on several occasions.'

The young earl held up a sheet of paper, on which she could see a list of dates and places. 'What I know of this affair would be enough to see you whipped to prison like the whore you are, and your lover with you.'

She stared at the list in horror. Slowly, she remembered what he had said before. 'What is this promise I must make?'

'That you will never meet with Master Shakespeare again, or this list will reach the Queen. I do not need to tell you at what risk of disgrace you stand, mistress, for you have lived at court too long not to know it. But perhaps you have not considered how your lover will suffer if this tale is wider known. Her Majesty's mercy is rarely shown when it is a question of adultery.'

Her eyes widened on his face.

He smiled icily, seeing her expression. 'I have his guilt confirmed in writing. There is a Mistress Anne Shakespeare at home in his native Warwickshire, and three young children born of their legal union. You know the Queen's views on such matters.'

He tucked the list away inside his cloak, which hung loose over a fine red-velvet doublet.

'Now, mistress, do I have your word on this? Or must I force the question further?'

She shrank against the wall as the young Earl of Southampton trod closer.

'What, nothing to say, my dark mistress?' he asked softly, his smile unpleasant. 'You are not so silent with Master Shakespeare, I'll be bound. But perhaps you need a more physical persuasion.'

Southampton grabbed her by the shoulders, holding her still, then his mouth came down on hers, hard and punishing.

She had been kissed by courtiers before, often in jest or in hope of more, but this was not the kiss of a man who held her in any affection. His hands hurt and insulted her body while she struggled in vain, his strength greater than hers, his kiss a scourge on her lips.

His tongue invaded her mouth and she bit down on it.

'God's blood!' the young man exclaimed, springing back with a furious expression.

He lifted a jewelled hand and swept it across her cheek, knocking her to the stone floor. Lucy hit her head and lay winded and in pain, trying to gather the strength to crawl away. The young man stood above her, breathing hard, a dark silhouette against the flickering torchlight, and for one terrible moment she feared he was not finished with her, that he planned to rape or murder her.

'Take that as a warning, Lucy Morgan,' Henry Wriothesley told her, breathing hard. 'Never forget you are only one step from an African slave, however fine the gowns and jewels you have been permitted to wear in Her Majesty's presence. Such favours are easily stripped from a whore. Next time perhaps you will be more welcoming when one of your betters lowers himself to your body.'

He turned contemptuously on his heel. 'Speak of this,' he threw over his shoulder, 'and news of your misdemeanours will reach the Queen.'

After Southampton had gone, Lucy dragged herself into a sitting position and felt gingerly for her swollen lip and cheek. Her mouth was bleeding where he had struck her.

She forced herself to stand, then made her way slowly back to the large chamber she shared with the other ladies-in-waiting at Richmond. Cathy was not there, so she lit a candle, then dabbed the blood from her face as delicately as she could.

Struggling out of her gown on her own, she lay down on her mattress and hid her face from the other women when they came in later, chattering and laughing after the masque. Her mouth throbbed painfully, feeling twice its usual size, and she feared that her face would be badly bruised in the morning.

She would have to lie to the Queen, pretending that she had slipped on the stairs in the darkness and cut her lip open on the stone.

Why was Henry Wriothesley so furious that she had been sleeping with a common player? The Earl of Southampton felt no love for her himself, that much had been clear from the way he struck her so violently to the ground. Perhaps his nature was warped, so that he took delight in causing women cruelty and pain. She had heard of such men, and knew there to be other courtiers whose tastes ran that way.

One thing was clear; she must not go into London again to see Will. The consequences did not bear thinking about. Nonetheless, she should get secret word to Will about the threat she had received tonight, or he would assume she no longer loved him. Yet if Will came to court himself and confronted the earl, he would risk the disclosure of their adulterous affair.

Perhaps it would be better to let Will assume the worst. He might hate her for it, but at least he would not have to face the Queen's fury.

Three

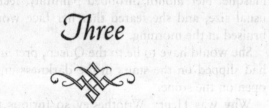

IT WAS A WARM SPRING DAY IN RURAL OXFORDSHIRE.
Goodluck spurred his horse out of the knee-high sweet
meadowgrass and on to a narrow track bordered by old
beech trees in full spread. His brother's farmhouse stood at
the northern end of the hamlet, set back from the Oxford
road at the edge of an old forest. The house had belonged to
Agnes's father, a ramshackle affair when last he had visited it
under cover of darkness. He had been a young man then, his
heart smarting with shame and rage at how their Protestant
family had been treated under Queen Mary's violently
Catholic reign.

But it seemed the farm had grown more prosperous
since Elizabeth had come to the throne. There was a stout
wall protecting the vegetable plot and orchard, the farmhouse had a fresh coat of whitewash and, by the look of it,
new thatch on the roof.

Hens scattered indignantly before him as he rode
through the dusty yard. A slender, fair-haired girl
straightened from feeding them corn, her eyes curious as
she shielded them against the setting sun.

He swung off the hired horse, nodding courteously to
the girl. 'Good evening to you. Is Mistress Goodluck within?'

Slowly, the girl looked him up and down before answering, from his dust-covered boots to his plain cap. She was cautious, he thought, and unwilling to give out information unnecessarily. He liked that, it was an excellent quality in these days of trouble.

'Who's asking?'

He told her drily, 'My name is Goodluck.'

The girl's face drained of colour, and he suddenly realized that she must be his niece, his brother's daughter. If her father lay on the brink of death within, she would hardly find that name amusing.

'Forgive me,' he said more warmly, dragging off his gloves and offering her his hand. She took it, still staring at him wildly. 'I am Master Julius's younger brother. Mistress Goodluck wrote to me in London, asking me to come at once. I am sorry if I startled you.'

'You are Faithful,' she whispered.

He hesitated, then nodded. 'Are you a Goodluck too?' he asked.

'Yes, sir. My name is Eloise.'

'Then I must be your uncle.' He drew breath, asking the question whose answer he had been dreading all the way from London. 'And is your father still living?'

To his relief, Eloise nodded. 'Will you come inside and see him, sir? My mother will not leave his bedside, just in case . . .' Her blue eyes filled with tears. 'The physician says . . .'

'Hush now,' Goodluck murmured. He took off his cap and gave her an ironic bow. 'We Goodlucks are tough, Eloise. It is hard to shake us from this world. If your father has survived this long after his fall, let us hope for the best and not give him up just yet. Now let me tie my horse to this post before he thinks to wander off into the forest, then show me the way to my brother.'

A servant stopped clearing the old rushes in the hall as

127

he entered and stared instead, just as Eloise had done. His young niece, whom he guessed to be about thirteen years of age, led him upstairs to a bedchamber on the first floor. She scratched at the door, then entered, beckoning him after her.

A woman with neatly bound hair sat by the bedside, her back to the door. Although her hair was fair, it showed some streaks of silver, and when her head turned, he recognized the woman his brother had married many years before, and at whose wedding he had danced.

'Faithful!' she cried, jumping up. She took his hands and squeezed them hard, her face lined now, no longer young as he remembered, and grey with strain. 'I am so glad you came. I was afraid . . .'

'I was away in the Low Countries,' Goodluck murmured, answering the unspoken question in her face, 'and did not receive your letter until two days past. Then I came at once.'

His glance moved past her to the man lying still and silent on the bed under a rich red counterpane, his face white as alabaster, his eyes closed. His heart sank at the sight of that strange mask-like stiffness and pallor, for he had seen men look like that before, in the final hours before their death.

'How is my brother?'

'There has been very little change since Julius fell from his horse.' She drew him towards the bed. 'He has been bled, and we try to feed him strong wine and physic to keep him alive, but he can barely swallow. I speak to him and touch his face, and poor little Eloise comes to sing to him, hoping that her father may hear her. But he does not wake.'

Agnes looked at him with desperate eyes. 'Will you try to rouse him, Faithful? I know it has been many years, and harsh words were said at your parting. But you are his brother, and you know him better than any other man alive. Julius may wake for you where he would not wake for us.'

He sat beside his brother and took his hand. Julius's skin was cool and limp. His brother's hair was grey, where once it had been dark, and his face, though smoothed out in sleep, showed signs of age, with deep-set lines about his eyes and mouth. Goodluck wondered if he would soon look the same, for there were but ten years between them, his brother well into his sixth decade. Now it seemed he would not see his sixtieth year. Though to own the truth, as youths they had not thought to live so long, for as Protestants growing up under Queen Mary they had all been marked for a heretic's death.

Julius had escaped that fate by accepting the Catholic faith, only returning to his true beliefs once Queen Elizabeth had ascended the throne. Goodluck himself had travelled abroad, unable to accept the taste of Roman faith in his mouth. There, he had learned to hide in a crowd and to lie as easily as breathing. He had turned to acting soon after, to earn a crust and a roof over his head, and discovered a talent in himself for cunning speeches and dissimulation. A theatrical-turned-spy took him in, one harsh winter when money was scarce, and soon he was running errands that would have seen him hanged if caught.

Julius, of course, had ordered him not to go abroad. 'Your place is here, at our mother's side. To flee is cowardice.'

'If it is cowardice to flee death by burning, then yes, I am a coward.'

'Use your head, Faithful. You need not burn if you will bow the knee to Rome. It means nothing.'

'It means everything!' he had insisted angrily. 'How can you so easily abandon what our father taught us?'

'God knows what is in every man's heart. It is to God you should look, not to our dead father. His refusal to accept Catholicism is what brought him to the stake and took our lands along with his honour. Now our family is ruined. And for what? One man's refusal to go to church along with everyone else in this land.'

Now his brother lay still and pale on his bed, a broken man.

'Julius, it's me, your brother Faithful.'

No response.

He thought for a moment, then said quietly, as though the two of them were alone together, 'Do you remember when we were young, Julius, and I fell from my pony? You made me climb back on, though I clung to its neck sobbing like our sister Marian all the way home, terrified that I would fall again. Now you lie there like a dead man and cannot stir. What, sir, have you forgotten that you are a Goodluck?'

He watched, but his brother did not move, nor did he give any sign of having heard his voice. His daughter Eloise gave a little cry and fled the room. Agnes followed in tears, calling out her daughter's name.

Goodluck said nothing more but bent his head, still holding his brother's hand.

He had thought long on his journey from London, remembering his childhood at the old manor house, how his father had been first accused and then charged with heresy, how Goodluck and his brother had been unable to prevent their father's death. Grown to manhood with such horrors, he had believed himself beyond tears. Now, sitting beside his brother as he lay dying, Goodluck knew himself to be as frail as the day he had watched his father burned to death as a heretic.

He dragged a hand across his eyes. 'I swear, I never thought the day would come when I would weep over *you*, Julius. How you would laugh if you could see this.'

The hand in his jerked slightly.

Goodluck glanced up, surprised, to find his brother looking back at him. '*Julius!*'

His brother's voice was a bare thread of sound. 'What, are you here, Faithful?'

'Let me call Agnes for you.'

His brother frowned. 'Wait!' He gripped Goodluck's hand. 'What happened?'

'You fell from your horse.' Goodluck saw the question in his brother's eyes and could not lie. 'It's bad, Julius. Your back may be broken. You've lain here nigh on a week without waking. Indeed, Agnes feared you might never wake again.'

'My good wife has no faith. Unlike you, Brother.'

Goodluck managed a smile. 'She has been in great distress. Let me call her for you.'

'Not yet.' Julius fixed him with an unwavering stare. 'I was sorry to hear our sister Marian had died. One of her sons sent a letter a few months later, and some small effects she left me in her will. Were you with her at the end?'

'I was in France when Marian died.'

His brother's lips twitched. 'On a mission of the utmost importance to England, no doubt.'

Goodluck saw that he was not accused of neglect. 'Can you doubt it?'

'No, you were always the bravest of us all, dashing off to break your neck in some adventure. But not all men are cut out to be soldiers and adventurers. Some of us prefer the plough to the sword.'

'Truly.'

Julius gripped his hand more tightly. 'Promise me you will look after my wife and daughter when I am gone.'

'You are not gone yet, Brother,' Goodluck said drily.

'Swear to it.'

He nodded. 'I swear it.'

'On the Cross.'

Goodluck hesitated. Then he drew his dagger, placing his hand over the hilt where it formed the shape of a cross.

'I swear on the Holy Cross that I will protect your wife and daughter as best I can in the event of your death. *Amen*.'

'*Amen*,' his brother echoed in a whisper, then looked at him hard. 'So you will stay?'

Goodluck considered that question. Stay at his brother's farm and become part of a family again? He had lived alone too long to enjoy such a prospect.

And yet why not? His old spymaster was dead, and his house in Cheapside dark and cold as the tomb. No one there would miss him. Not even Lucy, who had young Shakespeare to keep her warm.

'It would be my pleasure.'

'Good, you are welcome to share what little we have here.' Julius closed his eyes, clearly exhausted even by that small effort, and seemed to lapse back into sleep.

Goodluck went to the door. 'Agnes!' he called urgently along the corridor. 'Mistress Goodluck, your husband stirs! He is awake!'

Agnes came running at once, her full skirts clutched in her hand, face still blotchy with tears. At the sight of her husband lying on the bed with closed eyes like a dead man, she turned to Goodluck in furious accusation.

'What mischief is this, Faithful? You have called me for nothing. You said my husband was awake!'

'And so I am,' Julius croaked, opening his eyes again. 'It will take more than a fall from a horse to kill me, dearest mutton-head.'

His wife stared, then burst into sudden noisy tears as she realized he was back with them, first embracing him, then hiding her face in her hands.

'Thank the Lord for this deliverance! Oh thank you, sweet Lord Jesus, for answering our prayers!' Agnes prayed, half laughing and half crying, then called for a servant to ride for the physician, her husband having woken from his long sleep.

Eloise stumbled into the chamber amid this noise and chaos, her blue eyes wet with tears, confusion on her face. No doubt she had feared her father lost to her for ever.

Goodluck said nothing but stood aside for the young girl, knowing she must see the miracle for herself.

Eloise stared at the man on the bed, clearly astonished to see his eyes open, then took a hesitant step forward.

'Father?'

Four

ELIZABETH WAS PLAYING AT QUOITS IN THE RIVERSIDE gardens at Richmond when her ladies parted and a red-faced servant came running through them. He dropped to his knees before her, the late summer sun full on his face. 'Your Majesty,' he gasped, sweat on his forehead, too out of breath to continue.

'Speak, what is it?' she demanded impatiently, her knees still bent for the throw, a quoit hoop in her hand. 'Can you not see we are at play here? What is the score, Master Raleigh?'

'You are winning, Your Majesty. By five points.'

'You see, man? I am ahead by a margin of only five points. All depends on this next quoit. Your interruption may mar the game.'

'Forgive me, Your Majesty,' he managed hoarsely, 'but it is the Earl of Essex and many horsemen . . . They are at the gates.'

'Yes?'

Turning her back on him, she threw the quoit with great concentration, as though unconcerned by his news. To her satisfaction, it looped about the post, shuddering on its way to the ground, and the watching courtiers applauded her skill.

'A ringer, a veritable ringer!' Raleigh exclaimed. 'Three points. Bravo, Your Majesty!'

'I am glad his lordship has finally answered our summons and returned from France,' she commented, turning to look at the messenger for the first time. 'His failures have been much in our mind lately. Let the earl approach, but not his camp followers.'

The servant withdrew, bowing.

'You may take my next turn, Helena,' Elizabeth murmured, and stood aside to watch the rest of the game from the shade of a handsome chestnut tree. She refused Raleigh's courteous offer to fetch her a seat. 'I am not yet in my dotage, sir. I am well able to stand and do not need your assistance.'

Sir Walter Raleigh bowed and returned to the game, but she had seen the surprise in his face. She had betrayed her nervousness.

How foolish she was. And over a young man whose headstrong nature had led him to insult and disobey her too many times since he had first come to court in his stepfather's shadow. Yet he reminded her so forcibly of Leicester with his fits and sulks, and his arrogant refusal to do her bidding!

Soon there was a stir at the tall iron gates to the garden. Elizabeth turned and saw a party of young noblemen descending upon the game, pushing aside the guards with pikes who would have prevented their approach.

Essex strode at the front of this unruly pack, undoubtedly their leader, his face shining with determination in the sunlight. His cloak had been thrown back over one shoulder, as though to display the hand which clutched at his sword hilt, his feathered cap set at a bold angle, his expression proudly stubborn.

He came to a halt before her and bowed, flourishing his cap. 'Your Majesty, I have returned from France at your command. Though I am at a loss to understand why I was so prematurely recalled. I have to tell you, madam, that you have done the French King great disservice by thus disenfranchising me as the deliverer of his people. Without our aid, Normandy may be quite overrun by the Spanish. Now that I and my men are no longer on hand, I fear they will be.'

She looked from Essex to his followers, recognizing many noble faces among the crowd, though not one of them could be much above five and twenty years.

Good God, was this a rebellion?

'This is not the first time you have greeted me thus, my lord Essex, with so much discourtesy I fear your brain must have been seized with a fever while abroad. Though that might explain why you managed both little success and great expense in your campaign against the Spanish. Has Rouen fallen yet?'

He hesitated. 'The siege there has not yet begun, Your Majesty.'

'Not yet begun?' She stared, shocked. 'But that was the express purpose with which you journeyed to France. To snatch Rouen back from the Catholics.'

'I left many brave men in Normandy, madam. They will bring stubborn Rouen to its knees.'

'Would that I could do the same to you, my lord. Pray, have you forgotten that I am your queen, to come to me with such show of arms, surrounded by your knights and followers?' She gazed on him haughtily, suppressing her fear. 'Show some respect. Or must I teach it to you with a spell in the Tower?'

She saw Essex flush angrily at such a public reprimand, glancing round at the young noblemen who had accompanied him. 'Do you hear this chilly welcome from our queen, friends? We who have fought the Spanish on behalf of our countrymen, are we to be addressed thus by a woman who has never borne armour?'

'You surly dogs!'

Sir Walter Raleigh appeared behind her in the shade of the chestnut tree, showing his teeth.

'I will make you show your queen respect.'

He half drew his sword, sparking furious shouts from the young men before them, only to sheath it again on Elizabeth's swift command, 'Put up your weapon, sir!'

'Your Majesty,' Raleigh protested, taking up a position at her right hand, 'you must permit me to teach this young puppy some manners.'

'Puppy, is it?' Essex baited him, perhaps taking heart from her refusal to allow Raleigh to act against him. 'Best hope I do not grow into a hound with teeth and claws enough to tear you from this court, Raleigh.'

Elizabeth drew a slow breath, trying to control her temper. No doubt Essex and his followers thought her weak, not seeing how she struggled to keep this broken court together, to knit these different factions into a coherent whole. To be united in a common cause was the only path to peace for England now; if her best men should fall to fighting among themselves while they were still at war with Spain, what hope was there for England's survival?

'At least I am not in thrall to a woman, and must seek to hide my sins from her for fear of punishment,' Essex continued insolently, more flushed than ever.

Raleigh's mouth tightened, but to Elizabeth's surprise he did not respond to this bewildering insult.

'What do you mean by that, my lord?' she demanded, glancing from Raleigh to Essex. 'Is there some secret you share which should be made known to me as your queen?'

'Best ask Mistress Throckmorton there,' Essex said shortly, looking over her shoulder at one of her younger maids of honour. 'For she is as near to this sin as Raleigh.'

Elizabeth turned and stared at Bess Throckmorton, a pretty maid, and one about whom she had heard no scandalous whispers. But Essex seemed to be suggesting that she and Sir Walter Raleigh had been intimate. Since Raleigh was guardian of the Maidens' Chamber, and held a key to that private sanctuary, such a betrayal of Elizabeth's trust would be serious indeed.

Bess Throckmorton flushed scarlet as all eyes turned to her, and exchanged such a speaking glance with Raleigh that their guilt was all but confessed.

Elizabeth longed to box the girl's ears, trembling with fresh anger as this new outrage against her authority was revealed. Her gaze dropped at once to Bess's waist, but if the girl was with child, her sin was cunningly concealed by the drapes and folds of her broad-skirted gown. For now, she would have to give the foolish girl the benefit of the doubt.

'Get you to the Maidens' Chamber, Bess, and there await my summons. I shall speak first with Sir Walter Raleigh, and discover if there is any truth behind this shocking accusation.' She tried to control the temper in her voice, not wishing every busybody at the court to hear. 'Until then, you will not leave your chamber, nor seek to speak with Raleigh.'

'Yes, Your Majesty,' the girl whispered, then turned and fled.

Elizabeth did not dismiss Raleigh, though in truth she would bring down a sharp punishment on him if it was found that he had kissed any of the maids under his charge. If his guilt was proved, he would suffer a stay in the Tower. And young Bess would join him there, if she had indeed lost her virtue to the saucy man. But just now Elizabeth needed Raleigh and his sword, and suspected he would be all the keener to serve her with his life and liberty at risk.

'Now, my lord Essex,' she continued, her voice sounding clear across the gardens, 'will you and your men give up your swords? For you know it is not permitted to come thus weaponed and rebellious before your queen.'

Essex was looking about himself again, clearly determined not to yield to her will. 'I promise you this, I shall give up my sword to no man. No, and no woman either, Your Majesty.' He raised his voice when he saw the palace guards closing in around them, their pikes levelled towards the would-be rebels. 'Friends, who is with me?'

After some hesitation, the Earl of Southampton, a handsome dark-eyed youth who had been ward to Lord Burghley as a child, laid a hand on Essex's shoulder. 'I am, my lord.'

Two beardless youths stepped forward to stand beside them, their hands on their dagger hilts. The rest stood more uncertain, muttering among themselves. Several slipped quietly away, noticed by Essex as he threw his cap aside and cried out, 'By God, you brave fellows, what are you afraid of? For shame, are you not Englishmen?'

'Yes, and therefore we serve the Queen,' one youth replied, and drawing his sword, laid it glinting before Elizabeth on the grass. He knelt awkwardly, and bowed his head. 'I take no further part in this, Your Majesty, but yield to your mercy.'

'And you are forgiven, Master Bacon,' she replied, recognizing the boy, the weaker of two brothers who had often been about the court in recent years.

'Anthony!' Essex exclaimed angrily.

Master Bacon turned and gestured Essex to lay down his sword as well. 'Be sensible to your place, Robert. You have been recalled from France, and must accept the Queen's reprimand. Your campaign is over. Now lay down your sword.'

It seemed that Anthony Bacon's influence over Essex

was strong, for after a moment's hesitation, his face torn between fury and despair, Robert obeyed his friend. He unbuckled his sword belt and threw it down, sword and all, at Elizabeth's feet. Then, again after some urging, he fell to his knees before her, and was joined by the Earl of Southampton and their remaining followers, their heads bowed.

'Your Majesty,' Raleigh began urgently at her elbow, but she hushed him, shaking her head.

Once, yes, she would have imprisoned Essex gladly for this outrage. But with Leicester and Walsingham gone, their country stood in dire need of strong young nobles like Essex and Southampton. Essex in particular seemed to have the rare gift of inspiring followers among his peers and making the commoners love him. She would not yet give up hope of moulding this recalcitrant boy to her will, for the benefit of England's future.

'Rise and follow me,' she told Essex coldly, then swept back towards the safety of the palace, accompanied by an entourage of her guards and her whispering ladies.

Having turned the bustling servants out of her bedchamber, Elizabeth ordered her ladies to wait outside until she was ready for them, then closed the door on the world. The captain of the guards tried to protest, declaring it too dangerous for her to be alone with a man who had just threatened rebellion, but she merely shooed him out as well. The boy was headstrong, but he would do her no real harm. He needed to be trained, that was all.

As though to confirm her thoughts, Essex stood watching her, his arms crossed, a sulky look on his handsome face. She wished he would grow into some good habit of diplomacy soon, for he had none at present, nor good sense, which might have kept him from her displeasure if he had only waged his campaigns a little less wildly in France.

Elizabeth shook her head at him wearily. 'My lord, my lord.' She cast up her eyes to heaven. 'Why must you continue to think of me as your adversary?'

'Are you not?' Essex responded bitterly, not meeting her gaze.

'Tell me this. If I did not love you, both for your own sake and that of your departed stepfather, would you be here now, alone with me in my bedchamber?'

'You play too deep a game for me,' he muttered.

'Oh Robbie.'

She approached him, admiring the handsome turn of his cheek, his dark, shoulder-length hair that curled charmingly like a young boy's. In this dim light, she could almost believe herself a girl again, closeted with Leicester. Surely this boy must indeed be his base son, as so many had whispered on seeing the young earl, conceived on the Countess of Essex in an adulterous liaison. How else could they look so alike?

'I play no game,' she reassured him. 'I am your queen, that is all, and I must have your respect or lose everyone else's. Do you not see that?'

'And am I not deserving of some respect in return?' he demanded, his arms still crossed, his look brooding as he contemplated the portrait of Leicester on the wall. 'I am not merely a courtier. I am a nobleman and a soldier too. I have led your armies into Spain and into France. I served at my stepfather's side in the Low Countries. I have . . .' He hesitated, then blurted out, 'I have skills you have yet to measure.'

She had to smile. 'Skills, my lord?'

'Of diplomacy and scholarly understanding,' he asserted, then looked at her directly, his eyes hungry. 'You have made me your Master of the Horse, Your Majesty, and for that I am grateful. Now admit me to the Privy

Council as you did Leicester, and I shall not disappoint your trust in me.'

Elizabeth stared. 'The Privy Council?'

'Why not?'

The Earl of Essex, to become a member of the Privy Council, the highest council in the land, a body of noblemen and diplomatists whose decisions, ratified by her, governed England? It did not take Elizabeth long to envisage the turmoil he would create if given a place around that revered table, even for a day.

She was horrified. But how to refuse him gently?

'I must admit,' she began carefully, 'that I had no idea your ambitions inclined that way, Robbie. Except that had you asked me to appoint you Archbishop of Canterbury, I could not have been more surprised by this request. Though I am delighted to discover that one so young should take such a keen interest in governance.'

'You have considered others for the position who are not much older.'

She lowered her gaze, a little disturbed by that remark. Had Essex heard that young Robert Cecil, Lord Burghley's son, was being tacitly prepared for a position on the Privy Council? He showed such promise, a true scion of his father, and as blessed with intelligence as he was cursed in looks. Indeed, she hoped to see the younger Cecil installed on the council as soon as it was safe to do so, which would be once Essex had returned to France and could raise no trouble over the appointment.

But Essex seemed unaware of her plans for the promising Cecil. Instead he watched her with eager eyes. 'And your decision?'

'It is a delicate matter, I must think more on this,' she demurred, turning away. 'And consult with the other members of the council.'

His face lit with a sudden fury, the earl seized her by the

arm and spun her to face him. 'Those old men? They hate me, their minds are mired in the mud, they will say no! You are the Queen, this decision is for you to make, and you alone.'

Elizabeth was shocked and taken aback by his violence towards her. Had he no respect indeed? She almost feared he would strike her, such was the anger in his face. She ought to shout for her guards, knowing that one cry from her would bring the door to her bedchamber crashing open, with Essex dragged to the Tower for daring to lay hands on her royal person.

Yet she did not cry out.

The intensity in his face both alarmed and excited her. It had been a long time since any man had held her this way, had shown her such passion.

'Robbie,' she whispered, touching his face.

He inhaled sharply, standing very still beneath her touch. They were so close, she could see warm amber flecks in his dark eyes, his skin rough where the cold winds of northern France had chafed it. Then he gave a small laugh, as though amused. He captured her hand and drew it to his mouth, planting a kiss on her open palm.

'Forgive me if I raised my voice to you, but my ambitions are such, they will not stand to be thwarted. As you love me, Your Majesty,' he said huskily, 'you will appoint me to the Privy Council where I belong.'

Her eyes widened on his face as his words took root in her mind. She felt light-headed, an odd flush in her cheeks as though she were afflicted by fever. 'As . . . I love you?'

Essex dropped her hand and caught her by the shoulders instead. He stared back at her, his gaze compelling. 'What, is this not love between us? Or have I read the signs amiss? We are so different in years, and yet so alike in thought. I see the way you look at me. I have only to enter a room at court and your gaze turns to seek me out.' She gave a small

143

cry of shame, and he smiled grimly. 'Do not fear its power, love strikes where it will and we would be fools to deny it. You watch me as I watch you, Elizabeth, for our hearts know what we secretly desire. Yes, you are a star out of my reach. Out there in your state rooms, you are the Virgin Queen, a goddess of pure gold and ice . . . *untouchable*!'

His hands stroked her shoulders through the fine sleeves of her gown. 'Yet here in your bedchamber, you are but a woman, and I am a man. And a man can love a woman.'

Before she could even gather her confused thoughts, Essex drew her close and kissed her.

His hands gripped her shoulders, refusing to release her, and his mouth took hers with a boldness even Leicester had not possessed. His knee pushed between her skirts, his body hard and youthful, and he seemed oblivious to the possibility that they could be discovered in this embrace. Elizabeth had not experienced such intimacy in years, and although she was afraid, she did not push him away but allowed that old familiar heat to rush in and consume her.

'My love,' he groaned against her mouth, 'my darling Elizabeth. Give me joy of your body. Let me love you.'

She had not thought of Essex as anything but a handsome youth, like so many others at her court. Now though, with his mouth on hers, his hands frankly attempting to open her stiff gold bodice, Elizabeth knew she was in danger of allowing herself to be seduced.

'My lord,' she managed hoarsely, turning her head aside, 'we cannot.'

'My love, we can,' Essex whispered, then took her chin, kissing her more deeply.

Things had gone this far between her and the French duke, Alençon – indeed they had gone further, truth be told – but they had been secretly promised to each other, and such intimacies were acceptable when undertaken in private by a betrothed couple. But if she were to permit the married Earl of Essex to make love to her here, with the door to the royal bedchamber unlocked, her women and guards in the next room, that was an indiscretion that would not be hushed up.

Elizabeth wrenched herself free, strengthening her resolve. She was too old to be got with child and her sin paraded before all the courts of Europe, it was true. But it would be lustful incontinence that drove her to seek pleasure in his arms. The same lust she condemned in her unmarried ladies.

'You must leave, my lord.'

'How can I leave?' he said huskily, following as she hurried towards the door. 'I can be patient, Elizabeth.'

'You will address me as Your Majesty.'

'I see.' His smile was lopsided. 'Now that I have tasted your lips, I am to be dismissed like all the rest.'

'How dare you!'

'I dare because I must.' Essex seized her hand as she attempted to draw her loosened bodice together. 'You want me too, Elizabeth, do not lie to yourself. Another minute and we would have been on that bed together. I know that I am married and you are my queen, but we cannot tell the heart not to love, nor force the body not to feel.'

'Release me!'

His face tightened but Essex let go of her hand, taking a step back. His eyes duelled with hers though, his wayward emotions all too plain to see.

'You came to me for a place on the Privy Council,' she reminded him. Anger made her indiscreet, though she remembered to keep her voice low, fearing they might be overheard. 'Have you abandoned that ambition now, in hope of a place in my heart instead? I must counsel you against such a plan, for it will not be successful.'

He reached for her again.

145

She shook her head. 'I am not yours to hold, nor any man's. Did you not risk my displeasure in marrying Sir Philip Sidney's widow without my consent, in much the same way that you have accused Sir Walter Raleigh of having loved Mistress Throckmorton in secrecy?'

'He *has* seduced her,' he muttered savagely.

'The truth of your accusation is yet to be seen. Indeed, I have heard no word against Mistress Throckmorton's virtue before, though I agree she is a comely girl, and much admired at court for her beauty. Perhaps you admire her too?'

When he did not answer, Elizabeth began to suspect she had hit upon his true reason for accusing the sailor of such a heinous misdemeanour.

'It is widely known, however, that you dislike Raleigh and consider him your enemy. Many say you would be glad to see him at the bottom of the seas he crosses so readily.'

'Do not believe me, then.' He shrugged, sullen as a boy again. 'The truth will out.'

'You claim to have lost your heart to me, my lord, but you had best be content with keeping your head on your shoulders. You shall not get another if you lose *that*.'

'And this is all I gain by my love? Distrust and threats?'

Elizabeth heard the bitterness in his voice, and saw rebellion in his face. Essex would turn against her throne if she could not handle him more delicately. With no elder statesman except Lord Burghley to keep the ambitious young earl in check, she feared a split within the court that could precipitate a civil war.

'I do not distrust you, Robbie. Indeed, I have always favoured you above all the other young men of your generation, for your own sake as much as your step-father's. And I know you wish to serve me and England, but I cannot grant you a place on the Privy Council. Not yet. You have not gained the experience necessary for governance, nor do you possess a cool head for diplomacy. You have boasted instead that you are a soldier, though a scholarly one. Why not see where such talents take you before casting my favour aside in such despair?'

His eyes warred with hers. 'I am to return to France?'

'You were given a duty which is as yet unfulfilled. You will return to France on the next turn of the tide, and see Rouen besieged and the Spanish Catholics who hold it put down like rabid dogs.' Her voice hardened. 'Be assured, Robbie, I shall not receive you at court again until our aim is achieved and Rouen has fallen.'

Sulkily he looked away. 'As you wish.'

'You will not be in France for ever,' she reminded him. 'On your return to England, there is another post which has fallen vacant and might suit your disposition better. It requires a man both subtle and valiant, one who is not afraid to draw sword in my service. A man who can be trusted with this country's greatest secrets.'

His eyes flashed to her face, suddenly intent. 'I am that man, Your Majesty. Name the post.'

'Walsingham's.'

Five

THE STREETS OF COVENTRY WERE QUIET AFTER THE REVELRY in the hall. Will and the rest of the Earl of Pembroke's company had played there all that afternoon, though in truth they could have played out of doors, the autumn weather was still so fine. The summer had been dry; too dry, some said, with food scarce for lack of rain and even the Thames shrunk to a turgid stream in places.

But a dry spell was good for players, for everyone loved to watch a play when the sun shone.

Will walked slowly along the narrow cobbled street, looking out for his father's cart. It was late, and the sun had not yet set in the west, though the walls of the houses and taverns opposite were gently reddening as the hour grew later. He turned a corner and found himself in the shadow of the ancient church, its walls of dusky red sandstone high and imposing, its spire visible from many miles away.

The bells in St Michael's tower rang out to mark the hour – seven o'clock – and from inside one of its side chapels Will could hear chanting in Latin, no doubt the holy fathers at their devotions. He had visited the old church a few times as a child, and still remembered the pageants and plays he had seen enacted in the shady square before the tower, with jugglers and miracle workers, and once several men dressed as a highly credible fire-breathing dragon, which St George had most enthusiastically killed. But then it had been deemed unhealthy for the people of Coventry to see such spectacles, and for a while only Morris dancers had been permitted to perform on feast days.

His father's cart trundled round the corner ahead of him, the old cart set behind a new young horse, a replacement for old Hector who had died the year before.

His younger brother Dick was perched in the back of the cart, his long legs dangling off the open end. 'Will! Over here!'

Will climbed aboard and shook first his brother's hand, then his father's, grinning. 'It's good to see you, sir. Did you arrive in time to watch the play?'

'Only the last part of it,' his father admitted, not meeting his eye, and slapped the reins. 'Get up!'

The cart jerked forward, his father awkwardly turning the horse in the narrow lane to face the way they had come. In the back, his brother sat down again with a thud, holding on to the wooden sides so he would not fall out as the cartwheels lurched violently over the cobblestones.

'I had to buy some new skins to make the journey into Coventry worthwhile,' his father said, his tone uncompromising, 'though business was poor this summer. It's all this fine weather; no one needs new gloves against the cold, and trade is suffering. So you'll forgive us if we didn't have time to sit and watch a play today, but some of us have work to do.'

Will was disappointed but said nothing. There was no point getting angry; this slight was nothing new. His father had never taken much of an interest in his theatrical work, so he would hardly care that the company had been acting one of his son's own plays that afternoon, the Roman tragedy *Titus Andronicus*.

'I cannot stay long, I am afraid, but must rejoin the company in a week's time and travel to Leicester with them on their journey east,' Will told him briefly, not bothering to explain how hard it had been to be excused from work even for a sennight. But he could not resist adding pointedly, 'The Earl of Pembroke is a hard taskmaster; every day is a working day on this tour, and we are already a man short.'

He slung his pack behind him on the floor of the cart, which smelt bad and was piled high with sheepskins ready to be soaked and stripped of the remnants of their wool.

'I am glad you got my letter though, and were able to come and pick me up. How is Anne? And the children?'

'They are well, though Hamnet has been ill again.' His father shrugged. 'A fever, that is all. The boy is prone to these lightning sicknesses that come and go in a few days. I daresay he will grow out of them in time.'

Will nodded, though such news always made him uneasy. Partly it was guilt, for he was hardly ever home in Stratford to see his children grow up. His son would be six years of age now. Would Hamnet even recognize his own father?

Always assuming I *am* his father, he thought grimly.

He thought of the son he had conceived on Lucy, and who had died at birth, brought into the world too soon after her fall down the stairs. It had been a boy, Lucy had told him. She had named the dead baby William, but had him buried with her husband under his name of Parker. So he had one dead son thought to be another man's, and one living who might not be his.

He frowned, wishing he knew why Lucy had not answered his letters of late, nor come to see him since before the summer.

Had he displeased her in some way?

When he returned to London, he would seek Lucy out as soon as Pembroke's Men were commissioned to play at court, and discover how he had wronged her. He could not bear this long absence from her bed, though it was true that his poetry seemed to grow better the longer they were apart.

The three Shakespeares rode the cart in silence, leaving the city walls behind and following the track towards Stratford as the sun dropped lower, staining the land blood red. Now Will could see that his father had not been exaggerating about the dry weather that year; the track was a mess of dried mud-ruts at every crossroads, their cartwheels thumping about drunkenly, the fields on either side bone dry and even the river barely ankle deep at its heart. But where the marshland was still damp, the tiny marsh flies still whined and danced over the skins piled up in the back of the cart. There was no wind, and the evening sky seemed clear for miles, signalling yet more dry weather to come.

It had been a long and tiring day. Will soon fell asleep, lulled by the swaying motion of the cart and the darkening skies. He woke to the rumble of voices, and opened his eyes to find that they had reached Stratford and were passing the Green Man tavern, closing for the night. He shivered and drew his cloak tighter about him. Glancing back, he saw that Dick was asleep, one of the sheepskins pulled up over him to keep out the chill.

'Awake now, are you?' his father said, glancing at Will as he sat up. 'The children will be abed by now, but your mother may still be sitting up for us – and your wife.'

His father hesitated, staring ahead at the track which led to Henley Street. No one was about in the town, and although a few of the houses along the way showed candle-light through their windows, most doors and shutters were closed, the decent folk of Stratford having retired to bed or the fireside once the sun went down.

'Anne's missed you badly this past year,' he said in the end, not looking at Will. 'It's been hard for her, particularly now the twins are older and running about, always underfoot. I know Anne would like a house of her own, and although your mother would miss the children, I think it would do your wife good to be mistress of her own home.'

'I cannot afford to buy a house for her yet,' Will said, frowning.

'Will you ever be able to, on a player's fee?'

'Yes!' Will could not resist showing his father that he was no longer a poor player, but a writer whose work had grown popular in London. 'I am writing plays now, don't you remember? And I have a patron, a wealthy nobleman to whom I dedicate my longer poems.'

His father grunted, seemingly unimpressed. 'And when will you pass on this nobleman's patronage to your wife and children?'

The house was in sight now, smoke curling thinly into the night from the central chimney. So his mother was still up, and most likely Anne too, waiting for him to return. Will thought guiltily of the money he had kept aside for the day when he could buy a share in the company, not sending it home to Anne with the rest of his pay.

But a second epic poem, on the rape of Lucrece, would follow his long poem about Venus and Adonis, and for that the Earl of Southampton had promised him another heavy purse.

'Soon,' he promised, reaching for his pack as the cart rumbled to a halt outside their house.

The house on Henley Street looked smaller and more ramshackle than he had remembered. Since gaining the Earl of Southampton's patronage, he had moved to better lodgings and grown accustomed to visiting much grander houses than this. Even so, he was surprised by how much repair it seemed to need, the thatch scarce and patchy in places, mud splashed up the walls where paint was peeling, one of the upper window shutters hanging loose from its hinge. But to comment would have been a discourtesy to his father.

'Perhaps this winter. It will not be enough to buy us a house yet. But eventually we should be able to buy our own house here in Stratford, as she always dreamed.'

The door opened and Anne stood in the doorway, neat as ever in her housewifely cap and apron, her face half hidden in shadow.

As his brother stirred sleepily in the back, Will jumped down from the cart, not quite sure whether to expect a cold silence or a greeting from his wife.

But Anne held out her hands as cheerfully as though he had only been away a few days, saying softly, 'Welcome home, husband.'

Deep in the night, Will turned away from his wife and covered his face with his arm. A moment later, he felt her hand on his hip, smoothing his heated skin, and had to bite back a curse.

'You are tired,' Anne whispered, 'that is all.'

He closed his eyes. Guilt had overwhelmed him as she undressed, her back turned to him in the candlelight as though hiding her body, no longer as slender and beautiful as when they had wed. He had been away from home too long, and had given his heart and body to another, caring nothing for his wedding vows. How could he make love to her with this guilt gnawing away at him inside?

He had watched her undress, and tried not to compare her body to Lucy's dark magnificence, still strong and firm, a body made for pleasure in a man's bed. The

153

children Anne had borne him had left fine white lines across her body, rounding out her belly and thighs. Yet none of that mattered.

He had taken her in his arms as they lay in bed, intending to kiss away the hurt he had caused her, to show Anne he still desired her as a woman, not merely in duty as a husband should. But as his wife had moaned beneath him, her hips rising wantonly to meet his thrusts, he had suddenly lost his desire and rolled away, too ashamed to face her.

Perhaps it was the thought of Edward, the younger lover she had once taken, that haunted him still.

Anne had sworn never to see his father's apprentice again, and it had been several years now since the lad had left their house and married. Yet he could not help wondering if she had preferred the younger man, suspicious that Edward had possessed skills to arouse her which Will lacked, for in recent years he had found her more, not less, responsive in their marriage bed.

'By tomorrow night, your body will be rested and all shall be well,' she reassured him gently. 'We will take wine and lie together, you'll see. Do not be uneasy in your mind.'

She kissed his shoulder, then turned away and was soon asleep, her breathing deep and steady.

He lay miserably in the darkness, unable to sleep, listening to the Watch as they called the hour in passing. Soon he found himself aroused by memories of Lucy and their last energetic coupling. Her naked beauty came unbidden into his mind and he tried to banish it, but in vain. It had been too many months since Lucy had escaped from court to visit him in secret at his lodgings, or backstage at the theatre, her appetite for love as keen as his, ready to couple with him even in the smallest of spaces. She loved to ride him in bed, her breasts moving freely, her strong thighs astride his hips, working him up and down until he exploded with sharp joy.

Not here, he told himself fiercely, feeling his desire rise. Not in my marriage bed!

But his arousal would not be ignored. An hour or so later, tortured and half out of his mind with longing, he turned and lifted Anne's nightrail, whispering, 'Open for me.'

Sleepily she parted her thighs and let him take his pleasure urgently inside her, her hands stroking down his back. This time when he reached his peak, Will took care not to cry out but stifled his groans in her long fair hair, fearing to speak the wrong name with Anne, as he had once done with Lucy.

Rising early the next morning, Will breakfasted and strolled out into the garden where he could hear his children helping their grandmother in the vegetable patch. The earthen path was dry and cracking, but water had been brought up from the well to moisten the soil where the vegetables still struggled towards harvest.

Susanna, his elder daughter, curtseyed when she saw him, and wiped her dirty hands on her apron as though embarrassed to have been caught at work. Her blue eyes rested on him seriously. Her hair, so dark at birth, had softened to long fair strands, the colour of fresh-laid thatch, and she had her mother's chin, raised proudly as he took her in his arms.

'My sweet Susanna. How about a kiss for your long-lost father?' he asked, kneeling to look at her face to face. 'What, too coy, young Mistress Susanna? I have a remedy for that.'

She giggled when he tickled her, her dignity dropping away. 'Don't, Papa!'

He grinned and turned to the twins, stout Judith digging

155

in the dirt with a wooden trowel, and Hamnet, watching him with cautious eyes from behind a bay tree. The boy was more slender than his sister, his too-large blue smock belted tightly at the waist. His big dark eyes were his own, neither his nor Anne's, a hint of melancholy there which left Will feeling guilty as he called the boy forward.

'How now, young Master Hamnet, are you well?' When the boy just stared, unspeaking, he ruffled his hair and looked at his mother, Mary. 'Does the boy not speak yet?'

'He's shy, that's all,' Will's mother said shortly, and handed the child a woven basket laid with neatly clipped herbs, the blue tips of lavender on top still shining from their recent watering. 'Take that in to your mother, Hamnet. You'll find her in the kitchen.'

The boy trotted inside, the basket too big for him but struggling manfully not to tip it up. Will watched him with troubled eyes. If only he could be sure the child was his. For while he was uncertain, he could not seem to love the boy as he should. Nor his other daughter, Judith, though in truth he could have accepted another man's daughter into his household more readily than a son.

He crouched to embrace Judith, who seemed non-plussed by this kiss from a stranger, perhaps not remembering who he was from his last visit home. 'And you are my younger daughter, and as sturdily built a girl as ever I saw!'

'Aye, Judith has the broad frame of an Arden,' his mother said proudly. When he looked up at her, Mary met his gaze without flinching, adding significantly, 'And her father's stubborn nature.'

Will looked away without replying. He broke off a sprig of rosemary and crushed it between finger and thumb, bringing it to his nose. The sharp, sun-baked fragrance almost overwhelmed him. He held it out to little Judith to sniff, and laughed at her amazed recoil.

'Rosemary,' he murmured, dropping the sprig into the muddied lap of her smock, 'for remembrance.'

It was clear his mother understood the reason behind his reserve where the twins were concerned – no doubt his father had spoken to her when he dismissed his too-familiar apprentice – but Will was not interested in discussing such a delicate matter with any but his wife. The doubt was in his own heart, and none but Anne could ever remove it. So far she had not convinced him that the twins were his. And perhaps she never would.

'I must get these young ones cleaned up, and then walk to the market to buy a few items for tonight's supper,' his mother said gruffly, bending to take Judith's hand. She hesitated, looking back at him. 'Will you come with me? Perhaps you may find a gift for Anne at the market. She has missed you sorely this past year, and might appreciate a little attention.'

He resented his mother's interference, but shrugged. It was true that a gift might lighten Anne's spirits.

'Why not?'

Accompanying his mother to the market, Will found his father already behind his stall. A new apprentice stood by his side, a thick-set lad named Tom who barely spoke while he was there, except to recommend a pair of gloves to a passing farmer and his wife.

Will eyed the boy with some misgiving, but since it soon became apparent that Tom was already enamoured of a local girl, he dismissed the threat from his mind. He could not be forever doubting his wife and seeing potential rivals in every man and boy who entered his father's house. If he was a more honest man, he would admit to being more guilty of the sin of adultery than Anne. But his honesty would not stretch that far. For if he admitted his guilt to Anne, spoke openly to her of his love for another woman, she might take that as an excuse to seek out a new lover herself. And that would break the fragile trust on which their marriage was now built.

'He's a fine boy,' his father remarked drily, seeing his interest in Tom, 'and a good worker, if somewhat shy of strangers. I was glad to get another boy apprenticed after Edward left, for it's been hard work on my own, and it seems your brothers have no interest in following me into the glover's trade.'

'You had better watch the boy, and be careful to give him his due. Some of the apprentices rioted in London this summer, their pay was so low.'

'So we heard. But this is Stratford, Will. The apprentices would get short shrift from our town council if they tried to riot here.'

Will glanced at him curiously. His father had sat on the town council for many years, but debts and a growing reputation as a recusant, one of those who failed to attend Protestant mass every Sunday, had seen him asked to leave.

'Do you miss being a councillor, Father?'

'No more than you miss being a husband,' his father replied sharply, then called out to a passing gentleman and his family, 'Sir? Forgive me, sir, but may I interest you in a new pair of gloves for your daughter? No, the weather is still fine, but autumn will come soon and I can see your daughter's gloves are a little worn.'

Will bowed, and followed his mother, who had begun inspecting the food stalls in search of cheese and fresh meat, a linen-covered basket over her arm. 'So there you are, Mother! I thought I had lost you.'

'Not yet.' She glanced at him, smiling. 'I saw you looking at young Tom. Your father has been more content in his work since gaining a new apprentice. You do not regret missing the chance to become a glover like your father?'

He shook his head. 'The theatre is a better life for me. I am free there, not bound by the rules of a small market town like Stratford. It is good to come home and see my family safe and well, but I would not wish to live here. Not now that I have discovered London.'

'When you are older, perhaps you will change your mind.'

'Perhaps,' he murmured, not wishing to distress his mother by arguing with her, though he could not imagine a time when he would wish to live in the country again.

'Ah,' she exclaimed, laying a hand on his arm as she pointed to a couple ahead of them. 'It is Christopher Dun and his wife. Do you remember Christopher? He was at the grammar school with you. The two of you were good friends as children.'

'I do indeed,' he agreed, and stopped to shake his friend's hand and bow to his wife, Sally, a pretty girl with a rounded belly, who said nothing but looked at Will with a shy smile. 'Mistress, it is good to know you. But I had not heard that you were married, Christopher. I wish to God I had not missed such an occasion.'

'It was but two months ago, and undertaken in haste.' His friend laughed, indicating his wife's belly. 'We were a little forward of the wedding ceremony, I fear. But you would know all about that.'

His mother looked away at that last remark, her face stiff and disapproving. 'I must buy some cheese from Mistress Clovelly before the best is all gone,' she said coldly, and excused herself.

'I have been too frank and offended your mother,' Christopher said ruefully, watching her go. 'Forgive me, Will. That was not my intention. My tongue is too loose.'

'As it ever was,' Will agreed, but shook his head when Christopher offered to go after Mistress Shakespeare and apologize for his coarseness. 'Wives and mothers are easily offended. I would not pay it any mind. But here you are, a married man like myself, and soon to be a father! Are you still hoping to take over your father's farm out on the London road?'

'My father died last winter,' Christopher explained, holding up a hand at Will's hurried apology, 'no, you were not here, how could you know? I run the farm now, with my new bride's help, and hope to borrow enough to buy another property not far from town, out along the river Avon towards Shottery. Then we will have two farms, and two incomes.'

'And will you have four pairs of hands, to take on so much work?'

'In a manner of speaking, yes. My younger brother will run Home Farm for me, so Sally and I can live nearer town.'

'A good idea.' Will was amused but taken aback by Sally's steady stare, wondering why his friend's new bride seemed so fascinated by him. 'I almost envy you this pastoral existence, waking to soft rising mists in the mornings, hearing the cattle lowing at sunset, the Warwickshire fields alive with birds and darting hares—'

'Aye, then stumbling out in a frozen dawn to call the cows in for milking, or waking to find all your chickens have been killed by a fox in the night.' His friend shook his head. 'For a country-born man, Will, you seem to have forgotten the harshness of our lives here.'

'Oh, the city can be harsh too,' Will told him frankly. 'What with the recent rioting, the horror of the plague, and the strange weather we have been suffering this year, it is a wonder so many survive. The days are dry enough now, too dry indeed, but there was a fierce rainstorm a month back over London that nearly drowned us all in our beds. So when the apprentices are not looting shops and murdering innocent citizens, you can see coffins floating open in the Thames where the graveyards have been flooded, or thousands of dead flung into one pit, with only rue and wormwood to stave off the disease for those who must handle the corpses . . .' He caught Christopher's frowning glance at his wife, and hesitated. 'Forgive me, such tales are not for a woman's ears.'

'No, don't stop, Master Shakespeare.' Sally suddenly spoke, her brown eyes wide with fascination. 'I wish to hear of life in the city, however cruel it may be. And the theatre. What is it like, a proper theatre like they have in London? They say thousands can squeeze inside on feast days to hear a play or watch a spectacle. Is that true, Master Shakespeare? I should dearly love to visit London one day and go to the play.' She caught her husband's frown, and bit her lip. 'But I should not rattle on, master. I promised Christopher so faithfully that I would hold my peace if he let me meet you, and now see, I have broken my promise.'

'As soon as I pointed you out to my wife across the square, she nagged me to introduce her to "Master William Shakespeare", for she knows your wife, Anne, and has heard all about your reputation in the theatre,' Christopher said sharply, and pinched her cheek so that she squealed. 'You are not staying long, I hope, Will? For I do not trust my own wife not to sneak off to you in the night, famed London playwright that you are.'

Sally Dun looked up at Will through her lashes and smiled, making her interest only too plain.

Will's gaze dropped inadvertently to her full breasts in the tight country gown, and he felt a stab of desire for his friend's wife that shocked him with its intensity.

Hurriedly he backed away, laughing to cover his lust. 'I fear Anne might have something to say to that,' he told them, pretending to believe it was a jest, though he knew the woman at least to be in earnest. 'Which reminds me, I must find a gift for my wife on one of these stalls. So if you

161

will excuse me . . . .' He bowed to them both. 'I will have left Stratford by Sunday. But perhaps next time I will be in town longer and we can dine together, Christopher. For old times' sake.'

He caught up with his mother at Mistress Clovelly's farm stall, and was almost relieved to listen in to their homely discussion of cheese and butter-making, and look at the new churn the farmer's wife recommended for use at home.

As a happily married youth, leaving for the city that first time, Will had thought to return to Stratford in triumph one day, a well-known playwright with money in his pocket and fine clothes on his back. But never in these dreams of untold success had he thought that a life in the theatre would push his wife into another man's arms, nor bring him so many invitations to love outside his marriage bed.

A better man would be able to resist such offers, Will told himself with scathing self-contempt, but knew it was no use. From being an honest husband, looking only to his wife for comfort, he had gone in a few years of London life to being as lascivious a player as Burbage or Alleyn, men who thought nothing of tupping their mistresses in the tiring-room at the theatre, then going home to their wives for seconds.

It was one thing to keep a secret mistress in London and a wife in Stratford. But to betray Anne here, among her own friends in her home town, would be an insult beyond what any wife should have to bear.

Six

THE YEAR 1592 WAS ON THE TURN INTO AUTUMN; BIRDS could feel it and were gathering in the leaden skies, the leaves beginning to turn yellow when Goodluck finally decided to return to London. For too long he had lived idle in the country, and now was itching to be back in the saddle. He had heard from passing tradesmen that plague had returned to the city over the summer, more virulent than ever, and thousands were dead. Theatres had been closed, and other public entertainments banned. Now though, the air was said to be clearing again and those who had fled the city during the worst of it were beginning to return.

Besides, it had been an age since he had seen Lucy. Foolish though it was, he felt nervous not knowing how she fared at court nor if she still had dealings with that good-for-nothing Shakespeare.

'I wish you well, Julius.' He laid a hand on his older brother's arm. 'I will try to visit you again next summer and see how your recovery is progressing. Fare you well until then.'

He fastened his cloak and made his way outside into the muddy farmyard where his horse stood saddled and waiting amid the noisy geese and chickens. He felt some guilt at leaving them, but this was not the life he wanted, spending his days tending livestock in place of his brother, or walking the boundaries of the farm and brooding on the failures of the past.

After the terrible fall from his horse, his brother's recovery had been slow. Julius was unable to walk even a few steps without a stick, though he could sit up and was carried downstairs to his desk by the servants every morning. His wife and daughter had been forced to take over the arduous business of running the farm, though young Eloise at least seemed to relish the task.

Agnes embraced him. 'We shall miss you, Julius most of all. I am glad you came and healed the breach. Brothers should not quarrel.'

'I only wish I could be in two places at once.' He kissed her on both cheeks, then turned to embrace Eloise. 'But I have stayed far longer here in Oxfordshire than I had planned. I have business in London and cannot tarry longer. Julius seems on the way to health again, but I fear he may never walk without a stick. Will you write if he worsens this winter?'

'With all my heart,' Agnes agreed. 'Though I shall write even if he mends. I fear that once you are back in London, you will quickly forget your family out here in the country.'

He grinned, swinging up on to his horse. 'How could I forget such a beautiful sister-in-law and such a pretty niece?'

Eloise giggled, looking away, and her mother shook her head at him in mock disapproval. 'You are a naughty man, Faithful. But you are good and true to your name, however you may seek to hide it with jests.'

'Farewell,' Goodluck told them, then kicked his horse to a trot out of the farmyard.

He would miss hearing his Christian name every day, though he was glad none in London knew it. Master Goodluck was how he preferred to be known there. But it was time to put aside his fears for his brother's health, and the land they farmed so precariously, and think ahead to what he would do on his return to the city.

It was several years now since he had confided in Sir Francis Walsingham the information that a new plot had been hatched against the Queen's life, and also that young Kit Marlowe might be spying for Sir William Stanley, traitor to the throne and his country. But it was possible that ill health – followed by his final trial, death – had kept Sir Francis from divulging what he knew to the Queen. Either that, or Goodluck's reports had been investigated and found to be fruitless. The man planning the attempt on the Queen might have been caught, for all he knew, and dispatched long ago. Kit might have admitted to playing a double game and been paid to continue, or else defected to the Catholics with everything he knew.

Time to find out how the land lay since Walsingham's death, then. And to see his Lucy again, if she could be persuaded to return from court for a few days. He would dearly love to take her out to his family, let her meet Julius and Agnes, and see how she would get on with young Eloise.

Seven miles down the narrow track to Oxford, he came to a familiar crossroads and paused a while, sitting his horse in silence as it fidgeted.

'Ride on, you fool, and let the past be,' he muttered to himself, but did not obey his own command, his gaze brooding as it followed the narrower track to where it bent away into brambles and hedgerow.

Greenway Manor lay that way.

In all the time he had been staying at his brother's farm, Goodluck had resisted the urge to go home; to revisit the manor house and lands where he had spent his childhood and youth. For Greenway Manor no longer belonged to the Goodlucks. Confiscated at the time of his father's execution, it had been granted by Queen Mary to a family of pious Catholic gentry instead.

Impulsively, before he could change his mind, Goodluck turned the horse's head and made his way down the track. 'Just a quick look at my old home,' he told the uncaring animal as it plodded along, 'and then we'll be back on the road. God willing there'll be no more rain to wet us even if we do not make Oxford before nightfall.'

The track to Greenway was even more narrow than he remembered, barely wide enough to take a cart, the high hedgerows overgrown and even collapsed in places. Twice he had to bend his head to avoid a low-hanging branch, and where there had once been a well-maintained ford at the dip in the valley bottom, the mossed stones were broken and slippery, the stream running across the track with a noisy clatter, picking its own path. His horse splashed through weedy shallows, the water surprisingly high for summer's end, and emerged into marsh-grass and bulrushes on the other bank. There the track climbed another few minutes, then turned sharply to the left, where the gate to Greenway stood open, the path turned to mud by the cattle who still grazed beside it, nothing barring his way to the manor.

He pushed slowly on along the path, remembering each familiar twist and turn, how the way passed by a small green pond where he and his brother had collected frogs and their spawn as boys, then opened out into a leafy woodland ride. This led to the house along an avenue of beech trees planted by his great-grandfather during old Henry Tudor's reign, the Queen's grandfather, their broad trunks mossed with age, leaning mildly above the track.

He could see the house through the trees now, and drew rein, sitting back in the saddle. Whatever angry spirit had driven him here down the track to Greenway, it had vanished, leaving nothing but a bad taste in his mouth. This was no longer his family's place, for all that he had been born and brought up here as a lad. It belonged to somebody else now, and he was nothing but an intruder, trespassing on another man's land.

'Come on, time to go,' he muttered, and dragged on the reins, meaning to turn back towards the Oxford road.

But then he saw a pair of booted feet, dangling from an upper branch in one of the beech trees, and lifted his head to see to whom the feet belonged.

A young boy was sitting in the tree just ahead, staring down at him. He had long curly brown hair that hung over his eyes like a wild pony's mane, and wore a filthy misshapen rag which barely covered his legs and arms. On closer inspection, it appeared to be an old sack, cut open at both ends to make a kind of garment. The boy seemed unafraid at the sight of Goodluck, though he did not look very welcoming either. He piped up, 'What is your name, stranger?'

Goodluck hesitated, looking up at the boy assessingly. He did not wish to land his brother's family in trouble by using their name. 'My name is Faithful,' he replied on a whim, then immediately wished he had chosen another, one of the many false names he kept in his head for just such moments. 'What is yours?'

'I have no name. Nor any parents. I was found in the woods yonder as a baby, wrapped in a blue cloth. So they christened me John Sky.'

'And is that why you spend your days up a tree, Master Sky? To be closer to your namesake?'

'Perhaps.'

The boy swung himself down from the branch, landing

perfectly in front of Goodluck's horse, which whinnied nervously and jabbed at the bit.

The boy shook back his long brown mane of hair and seized hold of the bridle, patting the horse above its noseband. He seemed on easy terms with the animal, and clearly had no fear of it.

'Did you take a wrong turn, Master Faithful? There is no one up at the manor if you were thinking of calling there. I can lead you back to the Oxford road for a penny, if you have one.' He looked dubiously at Goodluck's patched clothes and shoddy boots, still muddied from his brother's farm. 'Are you a farmer?'

'No, by the grace of God.'

'A messenger then, perhaps?' The boy seemed more hopeful of his penny with that possibility. His eyes narrowed. 'I know a shortcut through the forest that will set you on the road to St Giles. Or near it, at least.'

A wind rustled in the trees all around, making a wild sound like the sea. Goodluck looked down at the broad, whitewashed house through waves of shifting beech leaves.

'You say there is no one up at the manor. Where are they, then? Gone to market in Oxford?'

'The house has been empty these past five years.'

'*Empty?*' Goodluck stared down at the boy. 'But how? Why did they leave?' He saw the boy's surprise, and tried to disguise his interest. 'That is, I heard it belonged to a family of Oxford gentry. Do they no longer keep it?'

'The family name is de Bere,' the boy explained, squinting up at Goodluck as the sun came out from behind a cloud. 'They left for the Low Countries just before the Armada came. I served them in the stables or wherever I could earn a crust. Now there are no horses, not even a donkey. I keep the herb gardens free of weeds though, and the chimneys swept clean, just in case they come back some day. But I don't think they will.'

168

Goodluck was frowning as he pieced together the history of Greenway Manor since his family had been evicted from the safety and comfort of its ancient walls.

'Joined the Catholics in exile abroad, did they?' he asked tightly.

It was hard not to let his anger show. His ancestral home had been handed over to these Catholic de Beres, who twenty years on had turned traitor and joined the Spanish when they thought King Philip might be on his way to knock Queen Elizabeth from her throne.

'Aye, master.' The boy's grin was wry. 'A poor choice, I'd say, after our ships swept the Spanish before them and smashed their great sailing castles on the rocks.'

When Goodluck laughed, Sky joined in, then wiped his hand across his face, a mischievous light in his eyes. 'But the place is empty, like I said. Even the housekeeper's not there. She's gone to Banbury for a sennight to visit her sick old mother. I'm left in charge of the chickens and pigs.' He hesitated. 'I seen you looking at the manor a long time before you saw me up in the tree. Do you know the house, master?'

'Yes, I know it.'

'Then will you come up and take a closer look for a shilling? The door's not locked, and there's no one to chide us.'

Goodluck smiled. 'Sure you're not called Providence, boy?'

'I'm sure.' John Sky jerked at his reins, dragging the horse forward. 'Come on then. It's only an old house and it don't bite.' He started cheerfully up the track with Goodluck behind him on his horse; no doubt the boy was keen to earn his fee. 'There's not much to eat but hens' eggs, and the windows are all shuttered against the wind and damp, but you can stop the night for two shillings. I

169

daresay there's chambers enough for ten gentlemen . . . if you don't mind a bit of dust.'

Standing alone in the shuttered and unlit hall at Greenway, waiting for the boy to fetch a lantern, Goodluck felt the hairs rise on the back of his neck. The fading tapestries on the walls were unknown to him, but the flagstone floor, worn smooth close to the door, was the same he had stood on some five and thirty years before, watching them drag his father away to prison. 'Heretic!' they had shouted, searching through his chests of books and papers for the evidence they needed of his guilt. One priest had wagged a finger in his father's face, smug at the thought that he had found another Protestant for the bonfire. 'As a heretic, your title and lands are forfeit to the crown. You'll burn for this, Sir Thomas!'

Goodluck closed his eyes. He turned away from the horrific memory he could not face – his father, tied to a stake in the marketplace, choking as the smoke began to rise – and thought instead of his last argument with Julius, and their subsequent flight from Greenway.

'The authorities will be back soon, to evict us from the house,' Julius had warned him the evening after their father had been executed. 'Our lands will be forfeit.'

Goodluck had come across his brother crouched by the fire that night, burning old letters and documents the priests had not taken. 'It's too dangerous to remain here, so I'm driving over with Agnes to her father's farm tonight,' his brother had told him urgently. 'It's not far, only about seven miles. You and Marian are welcome to come too,' he had added. 'We will make room there for you both until you have decided what to do.'

'I shall not leave. This is my home, my birthright,' Goodluck had replied doggedly.

'Not any more. Greenway belongs to the crown now.'

His brother had straightened, warning him to lower his voice, for Julius suspected that one of the servants had betrayed their father. 'If you will not come with us, then at least join the university at Oxford. I can lend you money if you wish to study, and you will be safer there than here. But do nothing in Oxford to make them suspect you. Wear a rosary and keep a crucifix in your chamber, go to Mass every Sunday like a good Catholic. They will be watching us all.'

'I have no wish to become a scholar. Nor a Catholic. And I will not stand idly by while these thieves take what is rightfully ours.'

His sister Marian had stared in indignation. 'Don't be a fool. They will kill you if you try to stop them. You are a boy of fifteen, barely a man yet.'

'I shall not become a Catholic, Marian. If our father was ready to burn for his beliefs, then so should we be.'

Julius had taken him by the shoulders, shaking him angrily. 'Father is dead. I am the head of the family now, and you are behaving like a child. Do you not see how your wildness endangers Marian and me? If you are taken as a Protestant, then they will come after us next. I will not have my innocent wife suspected of heresy simply because my brother does not know when he is beaten.'

'I am a staunch Protestant, as our mother and father were. I will always keep that faith, even if it means my death.'

'Then you must flee the country.'

'So be it.'

Julius had flung him aside, and Goodluck had hit his head on the stone floor. 'You are a fool, boy!'

'And you are a coward!'

Goodluck opened his eyes, and the dark shifted uneasily. The silent hall seemed to echo with those voices from

171

the past, the tapestries stirring as the door opened.

It was young John Sky, coming back with a lantern.

Goodluck took the lantern and peered up the dark stairs. His small bedchamber had been on the first floor. No doubt it had housed other occupants since, members of this family of recusants struggling to hide their allegiance to Rome in a Protestant country. He wondered if those who held the house now fully understood how and why it had been snatched from its previous owners.

The place was dank and smelt of rot, but it was still his home, just as it had been the night he left it, taking nothing with him but his horse and his father's sword. To his great chagrin, he had been forced to sell both during that first year on his own.

As he lifted the lantern, a large rat darted away into the shadows ahead. He smiled grimly. 'An extra shilling to stay the night, you said?'

'Aye, master.'

'A hard bargain. I hope the roof doesn't leak.'

Five days later, while Goodluck was picking warily at an eel pie in the Mermaid tavern, a heavily cloaked man came to his table.

'Master Goodluck?'

He looked up, frowning. 'Who's asking?'

The man stood over the table. He moved a corner of his cloak to reveal the glint of an unsheathed dagger beneath it. 'You're to come with me, master. And no arguments.'

Goodluck sighed, then pushed away his pie and stood up. It was not the best he had eaten, anyway; he feared the eels were not fresh-caught. 'Where are we going?'

'You'll see. Outside!'

A covered cart was waiting outside the tavern, and he was bundled into it. The reins were lashed, then the cart trundled away, driving a good two hours south of the city into the dark countryside, clouds obscuring the moon's brightness. It came on to rain and Goodluck was glad to be under cover, unlike the unfortunate driver. By the time it stopped, they had arrived.

It was a large private house, with men on patrol out on the roadside and guards on the gate. He climbed out, frowning, and was pushed against the wall by the guards so they could search him for daggers and other hidden weapons.

'Where is this place? Who am I to see?'

'This way,' the man said who had taken him from the Mermaid, and gestured Goodluck to follow him inside.

After several corridors and staircases, he was ushered into a book-lined study where a young man stood behind a desk, examining the papers set before him. He looked up as Goodluck entered, then nodded to the other man to leave them. The door closed, leaving them alone together, and the young man smiled.

'So you are Master Goodluck.'

Goodluck nodded, waiting. He glanced swiftly about the room, but could see nothing to reveal his host's identity.

'From your reputation, which is considerable in certain circles, I had expected your beard to be larger,' the young man commented.

At that, Goodluck fingered his beard ruefully. 'It does seem to be taking longer to grow back after trimming these days.'

'Will you sit?'

'Not until I have your name, sir.'

The young man's eyes narrowed on his face, then he laughed. 'You do not know me?'

'Should I?'

'I am Robert Devereux, Earl of Essex.'

Goodluck bowed low at this illustrious name, mainly to

173

conceal his surprise. 'I am honoured,' he murmured, straightening. 'And what does your lordship want with an old player like myself?'

'You recognize this?' The Earl of Essex threw a document across the table at him. He waited impatiently while Goodluck examined it with deliberate care. 'Well?'

'It would appear to be a list of some sort, my lord,' Goodluck commented, though his heart was beating hard.

His own name was on that list, and he recognized most of the other names too, men true to the late Sir Francis Walsingham and no doubt in the old spymaster's pay at one time or another. Many were dead. Some, like himself, were still alive and probably in possession of information that had never been delivered.

He felt sweat on his palms as he laid it down on the table again. It was a dangerous list to be bandying about, let alone showing to a man who might not be who he said he was.

'But the hand?' the earl persisted. 'You know it?'

Goodluck could see that the time for prevarication was over. He wondered if his life would be over with it. 'It is Walsingham's hand,' he said directly. 'What is this about, my lord?'

'The Queen has appointed me to be her new spymaster,' Essex told him, and drew a large bag of coins out of the chest next to his desk. 'I have tracked down most of the men on that list, but one man had eluded me, a man whom Walsingham trusted implicitly and whose information could be most useful to me as I seek to protect the Queen against her enemies.' Essex smiled. 'That man is you, Master Goodluck. I have had men watching every tavern and port for you for the past six months. Where have you been?'

Goodluck ignored his question and did not look at the bag of coins. 'Forgive me, my lord, but I do not know you

174

and cannot discharge my information to you without some further sign that—'

Essex silently handed him another document, this time a brief note with a bold flourishing signature at the bottom.

Goodluck read the note, then handed it back with a respectful nod. 'So you have the Queen's authority. I am convinced, my lord. But I am not sure how I can help you. The men involved may be dead, their trail cold.'

'I have reason to believe that they are not dead,' Essex told him, sitting down and signalling him to sit too, 'and their trail is still very much hot to the touch.'

Goodluck sat, frowning. 'How can you be sure?'

'You know Master Marlowe?'

'Yes, but I do not trust him. I saw him once entering a house that belongs to Sir William Stanley, who is a well-known traitor to the crown, as I am sure you must be aware. This was on Marlowe's return from the Low Countries, where he may have had dealings with Stanley or one of his agents. I followed him from the port directly to the house, there can be no mistake.'

Essex did not seem to be listening to him. 'A feint. Marlowe is an exceptionally intelligent man. No doubt he considered you suspect as well and sought to throw you off the scent, that is all.'

'An odd way to go about it.'

'I trust Marlowe,' he remarked, but Goodluck could see that the young man was troubled. 'And he has confirmed what you reported to Walsingham in . . .' He riffled through the papers on his desk, knocking several to the floor in his impatience. 'Yes, in the summer the Armada came. You reported a plot engineered by Stanley and paid for by King Philip. A member of the Queen's own household was to carry out the assassination.'

'Indeed. Was the man caught?'

Essex sat back in his chair and looked at him. 'No.'

'You mean he's potentially still in the Queen's household?' Goodluck was shocked. 'Forgive me, I thought that plot must have been foiled years ago.'

'They were difficult times at court. The war was at its height, nobody knew what was going to happen, we expected invasion at any moment.' Essex turned to stare out of the window, toying with his large pearl earring, and Goodluck saw that the earl was not as young as he had originally thought. Either that, or worries had creased his brow prematurely. 'Then Walsingham died, and much of his information died with him. It is only recently that I have begun the task of going through some of his papers and checking that all important information has been acted upon.' He indicated the pile of papers with a sigh. 'An arduous task, I can tell you. First we had to break his personal code, though we had some help with that from his men.'

Goodluck almost smiled. He could imagine that Walsingham would have made it very difficult for anyone to decipher his private notes and correspondence who was not already part of his inner circle.

'So now you have found me, my lord. But I cannot see that I will be of much use to you. I have done nothing for the past two years but live idle in Oxfordshire.'

'On the contrary,' Essex said coolly, and threw across the bag of coins, which landed with a hefty jingle in front of him. 'You are perfect. A man who can blend in anywhere, Walsingham describes you in his notes, with a nose for treachery second to none. And that is precisely what I need.' Essex looked at him assessingly. 'We will need to have you measured. But that can wait.'

'My lord?'

'When you are ready and have set your affairs in order, I will see that you are given a position within the Queen's

176

household, as a steward's assistant. Someone who can come and go without arousing suspicion. You will live at court and discover the name of this traitor who seeks the Queen's life.'

Goodluck shook his head, bemused. 'But all that must be over long ago, my lord. What makes you think—'

'Marlowe recently returned from Spain. He brought back vital information that the traitor is still in position at court, and preparing to strike as soon as the signal has been given.'

'It's simply not credible, my lord.' Goodluck tried to make the earl see the flaws in this apparent plot. 'Marlowe must be mistaken. Either that, or he is feeding you false information. Why would the traitor still be close to the Queen so many years later, but not yet have struck? And what signal could be sent that would not be intercepted by your men?'

Essex raised his eyebrows drily. 'If I knew all that, I would hardly need your services, Master Goodluck.'

Seven

LUCY, SEATED ON THE FLOOR BESIDE THE QUEEN'S THRONE,
had no choice but to stare straight ahead as the players
filed into the Great Hall at Nonsuch Palace. There was an
air of great excitement among the courtiers, for there had
been few plays this past year, the theatres remaining closed
for many months while a terrible plague ravaged the city,
forcing the best companies to tour the provinces. Now
it was November and the weather had turned chilly, so the
only entertainment to be had was indoors. Yet even a
masque or a court play was welcome these days, for the
Queen was grim company.

'Your Majesty,' one of the older players began, his beard
grizzled, his head bent as he knelt briefly before the Queen
and court, 'I present the Earl of Pembroke's Men, who will
play for you a piece by Master William Shakespeare, one
of our company. Our matter tonight is the first contention
between the two famous houses of York and Lancaster, a
popular piece which is otherwise known as the play of
Henry VI, Part the Second. We pray the court lend us their
ears a while, and may our humble entertainments bring
delight to Your Majesty.'

His prologue having been discharged, the man rose,

bowed very low, then disappeared behind the high curtained screens which served to create a tiring-room for players at the palace.

The Queen clapped for silence, and all eyes turned to the stage.

Lucy had seen Will among the players, but not dared to meet his eye. To her right, leaning against the wall among the other noble courtiers, was Henry Wriothesley, the Earl of Southampton.

And he was watching her. Her and Shakespeare.

There would be no escape from his intent gaze for the next few hours while the play unfolded. The Queen had insisted on Lucy's presence in the hall tonight, for she was due to sing during the mid-play interval, and to feign illness now would be to draw unwelcome attention to herself. So she looked woodenly ahead, and dug her nails into her gown, clutching compulsively at the heavy black velvet.

She had not meant to listen to the play, concentrating instead on not giving away her interest in Will. She had not seen him for so many months, it felt like half a lifetime since they had last spoken. Nor had she written to tell him what had passed between her and the Earl of Southampton, fearing the letter might be intercepted. Will must think her love for him had waned, and perhaps that was for the best. Yet even as Lucy schooled her expression to show no partiality for Shakespeare or his work, the action lured her in, the music of his language causing her to forget her troubles and lose herself instead in the terrible past strife between the great houses of York and Lancaster.

When Will acted his part, never once glancing her way but speaking all his lines to his fellow players, she ceased to know him as her lover but saw him as a nobleman fighting in the conflict. When the players bowed and left the stage, a little music from flute and drum signifying that the interval had begun, she had to shake herself awake, as though she had been lost in a dream.

While the music played, a line of servants marched into the hall bearing cups and flagons of sweetly scented mulled wine, and platters of dainty spiced morsels to tempt the Queen's appetite.

'Mistress Morgan, are you ready to sing for the Queen?'

Shocked, Lucy looked up into the sombre face of Lord Burghley. 'Forgive me, my lord. I must have been day-dreaming.'

He held out his hand and she took it, rising to her feet, still dazed by the play's curious power.

'I am to sing one of Master Morley's songs of spring tonight,' she announced. 'Her Majesty the Queen has requested a song to shake away this winter's cold.'

The Great Hall fell silent as she stood before the court, breathing deep and intending to sing unaccompanied by any musician or drummer. Lucy clasped her hands together and looked up at the Queen's faery-like figure, magnificently regal in her bell-shaped gown of gold and silver, a vast angelic ruff stretching several feet up behind her head, the candlelight glittering on its silvered tips.

She felt oddly sick, she realized. Her heart was beating too fast, her belly knotted as though she faced some terrible trial.

She had sung hundreds of times at court. Tonight though, knowing that Will was among the players listening from behind the curtained screen, she was more nervous than ever.

> Now is the month of maying,
> When merry lads are playing, fa la,
> Each with his bonny lass
> Upon the greeny grass. Fa la.

The Spring, clad all in gladness,
Doth laugh at Winter's sadness, fa la,
And to the bagpipe's sound
The nymphs tread out their ground. Fa la.

Fie then! why sit we musing,
Youth's sweet delight refusing? Fa la.
Say, dainty nymphs, and speak.
Shall we play at barley-break? Fa la.

As her last note faded into the silence, Lucy allowed her gaze to slide sideways to the Earl of Southampton. She encountered such a hostile look from his narrowed eyes that she had difficulty not recoiling. Then the young nobleman turned abruptly and walked out of the hall.

Why did Southampton hate her so much? What had she ever done to the earl that he had forbidden her to see Will again?

His dislike was a mystery she could not unravel.

Henry Wriothesley was a dangerous man to have offended, for he was too young to have become politic yet and might at any moment tell the Queen her secret, or force some unhappy argument on her which might lead to her dismissal. She only prayed he would soon forget his enmity towards her. For if he continued in this hatred, her life at court would be difficult indeed.

Lucy knew what her friend Cathy would say. 'Leave court and seek a new life with me in the country. If you feign a serious illness, the Queen will have to let you go, and I would go with you.'

Some days, she was almost tempted by that offer. Yet there was an emptiness inside her that was still unsatisfied, and she feared that life as a country widow was not the answer to such a void.

The steward came out at that moment and struck the

floor three times with his staff of office, a signal for them to resume their seats. Lucy sank on to the floor beside the Queen again. She took advantage of the Earl of Southampton's absence to look for Will among the players as the troupe filed out once more to bow before the Queen.

'Approach us, Master Shakespeare,' Queen Elizabeth declared loudly, summoning him to the dais.

Will removed his cap and came forward, his face intent, and dropped to his knees before her.

'Sir, I find your play much to my taste. Only let there be more music in your next piece, and more comedy, for we have troubles enough in England without dwelling on those of others.'

'It will be as you wish, Your Majesty,' Will replied, bending his head respectfully.

Elizabeth dismissed him with a wave of her hand and Will rose, backing away, cap in hand. As he did so, Lucy saw his glance find her. She met his gaze, and for a few seconds it was as though a light had blinded her, her whole being dazzled by the intensity in his face. His dark eyes spoke to her across the hall, trapping the breath in her chest.

She stared, and could barely hear what the steward was saying as he called the last stragglers to their places.

Will was angry with her. He did not understand why she had not visited him, nor answered his many love letters.

Yet what other course had been open to her? She had acted to save both of them from disgrace.

She longed to slip away from the hall, to escape the brooding accusation in his face, but forced herself not to be foolish. She must sit still and watch the play, or risk dangerous comments. After all, the young earl was not the only one at court to suspect her relationship with

Shakespeare; she had been seen with him in the past by some of the other ladies-in-waiting and their servants, though not for some time. But often enough for them to be curious if she were to leave the hall during this performance of his work.

Southampton sauntered back into the hall just as the first scene began, deliberately taking up a place nearer the Queen, a move which made her feel even more under threat.

Did the earl suspect she was still seeing Shakespeare outside the court? If so, he would be most unjust in his exposure of her past misdeeds, for she had followed his injunction to the letter.

As soon as the play had finished and the Queen had left the hall, a white and golden effigy accompanied stiffly to her bedchamber by servants with torches and her most favoured ladies in procession, Lucy attempted to escape out of the lower door. She heard his cry behind her and knew that Will had seen her leaving.

She must not speak with him, she thought suddenly. Nor risk any kind of physical contact which might be observed by the earl or his spies.

Desperate not to provoke Southampton into exposing their affair, she lifted her skirts and broke into a most undignified run. The low-vaulted cloister outside the hall was cold and unlit, the air chill where the passage was open to the weather.

Unsure which way to take, Lucy hesitated, then turned to the left. There was a small privy garden that way, she remembered, and in this dark she would soon lose him.

But she had bargained without William Shakespeare's tenacity.

Will came upon her in the privy garden, turning her to face him in the frosty darkness. 'Why have you not come to visit me in so long a time, Lucy Morgan?' he demanded, staring at her. 'Nor responded to the letters and poems I sent?'

His throat convulsed when she did not answer. His eyes filled with pain. 'Have you taken another lover? Is that it?' He seized her by the shoulders. 'Speak, do not hide your shame but tell the truth. Are you warming another man's bed these days?'

'No, no!'

'Thank God for that, at least!'

His mouth found hers, kissing her with such hunger she could barely breathe or stand, stumbling backwards until Will was pressing her against the rough stone wall.

'I had meant to ignore you, to say nothing, to let you go. I have hurt my wife enough, it is a sin to keep pursuing you.' His voice was hoarse, his mouth warm on her throat as he held her close. 'In truth, I was happy when I returned to London after the summer, and still you did not come to see me. But when I saw you in the hall tonight . . .'

Will sounded almost wild, his hands clasping her by the waist, their bodies pressed together.

'God help me, Lucy, I have struggled to remain true to Anne, but I cannot let you go. Not without speaking to you at least. Not without kissing you one last time.'

She did not need him to explain. She understood only too well the deep and irresistible connection between them, the tugging of two souls together while the world rebelled against such a forbidden union. And yet even love was not enough. Not to save them.

'We cannot do this,' she told him in a whisper, and put a finger to his lips. It was dark in the small palace garden, but they could still be overheard. 'I should not even be here, it is so dangerous. I did not answer your letters because . . .'

'What is it?'

She was worried by the look on his face. 'Swear you

will not take any dangerous action when I tell you.'

'Lucy, for pity's sake, tell me what has happened. I must return to my company soon before I am missed. Is this about Master Goodluck?' His gaze searched hers intently. 'I know that I have wounded you in the past, and do not deserve your trust as your guardian does, but I still love you deeply and would not for the world have you thinking ill of me. What have I done to incur your displeasure?'

She hesitated, looking over her shoulder. The place was dark and still. It seemed the revellers had all dispersed after the Queen had left, for the palace lay quiet, only the servants moving softly through the corridors, extinguishing the lamps.

'It is not you, nor Master Goodluck, but the Earl of Southampton who keeps us apart.'

Lucy was uncertain whether she should be telling him about the young nobleman's threats. But she could not bear the way Will had looked at her tonight, his cold anger so evident, believing she did not love him any more.

'Lord Southampton came to me and laid our affair before me, saying he knew all and would take the matter to the Queen unless I agreed never to see you nor lie with you again.'

'*What?*'

Lucy saw at once that Will was stunned. His hand had loosened about her waist, and she wriggled free of his grasp, moving away from the stone wall and carefully putting some distance between them. 'That is why I have not answered your letters, Will, nor come to visit you at the theatre, for fear Lord Southampton would learn of it and tell the Queen. You know the penalties for adultery, and worse, for unchaste behaviour by one of her ladies.'

'But how could Lord Southampton know of our love?'

'Perhaps we were not as careful as we should have been.'

'You must be mistaken.'

He was shaking his head. He did not believe her. He did not trust her enough. What could she do but repeat her story? Lucy could think of no other way to make him understand.

'My love, I am not mistaken,' she insisted gently. 'His lordship the Earl of Southampton forbade me to see you again, on pain of discovery to the Queen, and I have only kept away from you out of compliance with his terms.'

She could see confusion in his face now, and a growing disbelief that made her despair. He tried to approach her but she shook her head, holding him at a distance.

He stood rooted then, fists clenched by his sides. 'I tell you, Lucy, this is not possible. I do not doubt that his lordship spoke to you. But you have mistaken his meaning, that is the only explanation.'

When she took another step away from him, Will did not pursue her this time, but watched with cold eyes.

'I spoke with the Earl of Southampton only a few days ago,' he continued. 'He is my patron. He was pleasant and friendly, as he always is. He even asked to hear my new poem. Why would he say one thing to you, and another to me? If our love offends him – and I cannot believe such a thing – then why would his lordship not have approached me about it himself?'

Lucy did not know the answer to that, so said nothing. But she could see that Will did not believe her. Perhaps he feared she was lying to him, blaming her long absence on his patron in order to ruin his chances of advancement. That her lover could be angry with her for telling the truth was hard enough to bear, but that he no longer trusted her, nor believed her story about the young earl, was like a knife thrust deep into her heart, killing her where she stood.

'All I can think is that you must be jealous,' he muttered, staring at her now as though he did not recognize her. 'When I was a humble player and you were a great court lady, our secret love amused you. You could come to my rough bed for the kind of love you would not find at court. But now I am grown to be a man of some consequence, and Queen Elizabeth herself singles me out for praise, you are envious and wish to see me cast down again.'

'No!' she cried, and reached out to him, laying a hand on his chest. 'I love you, Will. Nothing has changed in that respect. How can you think such a terrible thing of me?'

'What else am I to think, Lucy?' Will demanded, and she saw too late that he had grown suddenly furious, his temper whipped up like a summer's storm. 'You tell me what I cannot believe possible, that my lord and patron supports my endeavours with one hand and slaps my courtly mistress with the other. You must be lying, your tale makes little sense otherwise.'

He finished in a rush, 'If you no longer want me, say so and have done with it.'

If only it were that simple, Lucy thought wearily. She longed to have her clever William back, the lover who wooed her with such charm and wit. But there was no talking to him in this mood.

She tried to turn away but he seized her. There was pain in his voice as well as contempt. 'What, sweet Luce, are you afraid to end our love cleanly? I am no villain. I shall not strike you for honesty, only for lies.'

Lucy dragged herself free of his grasp, breathing hard. 'Then you are a great fool, William Shakespeare, if you cannot tell truth from lies when it is your own heart that is involved.'

She let her own temper rise to match his, and did nothing to contain it. Why should she hold back? Shakespeare was more of a deceiver and dissembler than she had ever been, and she would not stand to hear him slight her character so unjustly.

'You want honesty?' she demanded. 'I am glad Lord Southampton has forbidden us to meet, for it saves me from making such a decision myself. Yes, it is over between us. Now go, and do not write to me again, for I shall merely burn your letters unopened. I cannot wish you ill, Master Shakespeare, for that would be to work against my own heart. But I trust that God will go with you, and watch over you, and perhaps one day bring you back to your good senses.'

She stood in silence as Will bowed and left her alone in the small privy garden, his face averted, no doubt still believing her fickle and cruel. When he had gone, she sank down on to the icy grass, not caring that her black velvet gown would be ruined, and covered her face with her hands. But her eyes were dry and her hands did not tremble.

I will not weep, she told herself fiercely. *I will not!*

No, not for a man who could court her for years and still think her capable of such evil. William Shakespeare was not worthy of her tears. Nor should she weep when the fault was not hers, but his alone. And yet her heart was broken and might never be mended again.

'Lucy?'

She looked up, hurriedly rising as she saw the dark shape of a man blocking the arched gateway to the privy garden. Who was it? Shakespeare back again? No, the man was too large and broad. Had one of his patron's men secretly followed her from the hall, perhaps, and seen her speaking to Will? Had she been discovered in her disobedience to the Earl of Southampton?

'Who is there?' she whispered, suddenly afraid.

The man came slowly forward across the frosty grass, wearing the livery of the Queen's household. Was she to be summoned to the Queen's presence, perhaps? Then the faint moonshine fell on his face, illuminating a pair of familiar dark eyes and a beard, and her heart jerked in shocked amazement.

It was Master Goodluck.

Eight

'YOU WISH MY LADIES TO BE DISMISSED?'

'Yes, Your Majesty,' young Cecil agreed, waiting for her permission to rise, where Essex would not even have knelt in the first place.

'Oh, very well,' Elizabeth said wearily, and gestured her ladies to withdraw.

Sleepily the women curtseyed and departed the Privy Chamber, closing the door behind them. Elizabeth drew her furred mantle about herself, for the month was December and the vast log fire in the hearth could never quite shake off the cold at Nonsuch, for all that her father's grand palace was impressive to look upon.

For a moment she gazed upon Sir Robert Cecil, youngest son of Lord Burghley and his successor in terms of political ability. She felt no inclination to speak to the young man, who looked shorter and more deformed than ever on his knees. However distressing his looks though, there was no doubting either his loyalty or his wits. She did not know how the Privy Council would have managed if he had not tacitly taken on most of his elderly father's duties as secretary of state.

'Very well, you may get up now,' she told Cecil impatiently. 'How is your father?'

The young man rose to his feet with apparent difficulty. His face was sombre. 'Still in much pain, Your Majesty, and likely to be confined to his bed until the end of the month at least. My father sends his deepest apologies and begs to be excused a short while longer from his duties at court.'

'I suppose we can make do without Lord Burghley this Christmastide,' she agreed reluctantly, then caught a flash of something in Cecil's face. Irritation? Disapproval?

Her temper flared, and her voice rose. 'No doubt you think me cruel, sir, to keep your father in service when he has reached his allotted three score years and ten. But these are difficult times, and there is no man yet to replace him. Except you, perhaps. Though you will need to stop butting heads with my other courtiers if you wish to succeed.'

So Lord Burghley was suffering with gout again. While Elizabeth felt every sympathy over his unpleasant ailment, she cursed her old councillor for being absent from her side when everything was still topsy-turvy in the world. The Earl of Essex had been at loggerheads with Sir Robert Cecil ever since his ignominious failure and return from France, and now she had heard that Bess Throckmorton, who had begged leave to return to her home at Yuletide, had done so in order to be delivered of a son, having been secretly married to Sir Walter Raleigh for some time.

Cecil said nothing in return to this pointed remark, but merely waited with his gaze lowered diplomatically to the floor, his figure small and hunched over, oddly reminiscent of a bat in his long-sleeved black coat.

She did not sit for this interview, preferring to stand, for she was beginning to find it hard to get up again after sitting for too lengthy a time. But she did signal her newest privy councillor to pour her a glass of wine, the heat of the fire having made her head hurt. She took a few sips, wetting her dry mouth, then nodded him to speak.

'Well, what have you discovered?'

Robert Cecil drew a paper from his pouch and unfolded it. Quietly, he read aloud, 'His lordship the Earl of Essex has been in secret meetings with Henry Wriothesley, Earl of Southampton, also the Bacon brothers, Francis and Anthony, and sundry other noblemen and gentry of your court. There has been some talk of rebellion against Your Majesty, but no plans made as yet.'

Her lip curled. 'This is the same report you gave last time. Have you picked up the wrong paper, sir?'

Robert Cecil hesitated. His dark eyes flashed to hers, disturbingly like his father's steady gaze, then back to the paper in his hand. 'Southampton is to supply his lordship with followers, and of the Bacons, Anthony is to steer the earl in matters of intelligence.'

'Intelligence?'

'Now that the Earl of Essex has taken over Walsingham's work, he is in need of someone more . . .' Robert Cecil paused, and she read contempt in his suave expression. 'More gifted in the ways of codes and ciphers, shall we say? Bacon provides that expertise, in exchange, one must assume, for a promise of power to come.'

Elizabeth's eyes widened on his face. 'In the event of my death, you mean?'

'No, no.' The young Cecil looked shocked. 'I am sure his lordship does not plan so boldly, Your Majesty. I would suggest the earl merely hopes to share power with you in the years to come, presumably by making himself so useful to Your Majesty that you bring him closer to the ways of governance.'

'You mean, appoint Essex to the Privy Council?'

The young man's expression was grave. 'I do indeed. Your Majesty is most percipient.'

'I see.' She ignored his flattery. 'Well, I have not yet admitted him to the council, but that day may come. You may not have noticed this, Sir Robert, but I have few men of merit about me and must govern England with whatever tools I have to hand, however rusty or unfit for purpose. Now what other accusations do you have in that document? Anything to give me genuine cause for fear? To have the earl arrested for treason, perhaps?'

Robert Cecil looked almost disappointed as he shook his head. 'No, Your Majesty. That is all the information I have been able to gather.'

'Then why come to me in this dramatic way? I thought at least you had uncovered some plot against my throne, begging an audience so late at night.'

'With any other courtier, Your Majesty, such secret dealings and assemblies would be considered treasonous, and their perpetrators committed to the Tower.' He frowned, putting away the letter. 'Forgive my impertinence, Your Majesty, but after the Earl of Essex returned from Rouen, he argued violently with you in front of the court when reprimanded on his failure there. I even thought at one point that he would draw steel against you. Yet you took no action against him that day, and the matter was never mentioned again. Nor is that the only time Essex has abused you in public. Indeed, I find his many discourtesies towards Your Majesty vile and dishonourable.' He hesitated, seeming to catch her irritation, and bowed his head. 'But of course you must act as you see fit.'

'Thank you, Cecil,' she commented drily.

She did not dismiss him immediately, but thought for a moment. While the rest was known to her already, it was true that this news about Anthony Bacon was interesting. Anthony was a clever young man of dubious nature, or so rumour had it, as was his brother Francis. Wild tales had been told of orgies and indiscretions beyond those

193

ordinarily committed by young men of high birth. She had never pried too closely into such rumours, for they filled her with distaste, but if the Bacons and their circle managed to draw her handsome young Essex into such iniquities . . .

Elizabeth shuddered. 'Anything more?'

Robert Cecil hesitated. Seeing her gaze on his face, he looked down at his papers again and seemed to squirm, as though confronted with a difficult duty. Then he murmured, 'I have been asked to enquire again about the . . . erm . . . the question of your succession, Your Majesty.'

She stiffened. The impertinence of these young men. They couldn't wait for her to be carried out of the door and a new prince installed in her place. Power-mongering dogs.

'Asked by whom?'

'The . . .' Cecil did not like his duty. He cleared his throat. Shuffled his papers needlessly. Glanced sombrely at the small portrait of his father, Lord Burghley, which hung by the door. 'The other members of the Privy Council, Your Majesty.'

'Drew the short straw, did you?'

He waited. A small dog, a hunchbacked terrier, but a tenacious one. 'Have you had an opportunity to consider the question yet, Your Majesty?'

'I have considered it, yes. And I think it a great impertinence on the part of my own privy councillors to be asking me to decide who should warm my throne once I am dead.'

'If you had married, Your Majesty, and brought forth issue . . .' He took a precarious step forward into the most dangerous territory of all. Then saw her face and hastily retreated. 'But in the absence of an heir, the stability of the country is at risk. With no heir named, if by some terrible mischance or illness Your Majesty should suddenly . . .'

'Die?'

Robert Cecil cleared his throat again. Studiously avoided her eyes. 'England would be left in turmoil. The obvious choice must be King James of Scotland, with whom you share a common blood at least. But he must be *named*, and by you, the reigning monarch, while you still live. It is the protocol.'

'Better a Scot than a Catholic prince, is that the enlightened thinking of the Privy Council?'

He bowed, a slight flush in his cheeks. 'Forgive me, Your Majesty. To put these questions to you is not a duty I relish.'

'Enough! I am not dead yet, nor have I any idea to be in the next few years.'

She clapped her hands loudly, exercising her anger, and the sound echoed about the Privy Chamber, startling the young man so that he dropped some of his papers and had to bend to retrieve them.

She watched him in silence, waiting until he was ready. Then she waved the diminutive Robert Cecil towards the door. 'Very well, my pygmy, you may go.'

He gave her a look which spoke of some barely concealed hostility, and Elizabeth wondered if he disliked her nickname for him. Pygmy. But what was wrong with that? It was all in jest, after all, and she had always given her favourite councillors nicknames. Leicester had been her Gypsy. Walsingham her Ears. And young Cecil was short, he could hardly deny such a thing. So why cavil at having it acknowledged? She was the Queen. Did they not all address her as Majesty?

She looked at Cecil sourly as he bowed. 'Come back when you have something more to tell me than gossip. And ask my ladies to attend me again.'

'Your Majesty.'

Still bowing, her new councillor backed out of the Privy Chamber, and suddenly the room was crowded with women, rustling gently about her in their swaying, broad-skirted gowns of black or white silk, their hoods either jewelled or demure according to their station, removing the wine she held out and slowly extinguishing the lights about the chamber. The fire crackled in the hearth and she stared into its glowing heart, thinking of Essex. How different he was from Cecil. He was too young for her, she knew it, and yet . . .

A log dissolved in the fire with a crash, and she blinked. Time had passed while she had neither moved nor spoken, caught in a kind of dream. Elizabeth looked about herself, recalling the lateness of the hour. The chamber was but dimly lit now most of the candles were put out. The older women stood heavy-lidded and ready for bed themselves, the younger girls giggling when she staggered, missing her footing as she turned away from the heat of the fire. Perhaps they thought her drunk. Or too old to walk unattended.

Foolish children! What did they know of life?

She heard one of the girls whispering, and caught the name 'Essex' on the end of a laughing remark.

'What was that?' she demanded, suddenly furious. 'Which of you silly girls is gossiping about his lordship the Earl of Essex?'

No one moved or spoke.

She swore at one of the younger maids, the pink-cheeked and fair-haired Katherine Bridges, and the girl fell silent.

Elizabeth shook her head, trembling with unexpected rage. 'Mind your manners, girl. Or would you end up in the Tower like Mistress Throckmorton, whom I suppose I must now call Lady Raleigh?'

'Your Majesty,' Helena said soothingly, holding out her

arm for support, and Elizabeth turned at that familiar voice.

But even as her anger subsided into nagging irritation, she could not slow her mind, nor unthink the thoughts that pursued her into the dark reaches of the night. Had they been gossiping about her? About her and Essex? What did they know?

Nothing, she told herself vehemently. Because there was nothing to know or tell about her and Essex.

'Silence!' she exclaimed, sitting up in bed. They were whispering about her again, those wicked girls.

But her bedchamber was empty and in darkness, and only Lady Helena slept on the trestle bed beside her, snoring quietly.

The New Year's Day revels were finished, the masque at an end, the gold and silver fountains of wine stuttering into silence as the courtiers, still singing and laughing, retreated to their beds. Elizabeth allowed her closest attendants to draw her into the quiet hush of the Royal Bedchamber, too tired to speak. The women closed the door on the world and unpinned her vast ruff and her jewel-studded wig, combing out what little hair she had left beneath. Her sleeves were unlaced, then her heavy foreskirt and gown removed while she stood, her feet and calves aching. For it was nearly midnight and she had been standing – or dancing – most of that long day.

After her nightcap had been set in place, Elizabeth sat wearily on the edge of the bed while her stockings were unrolled and a scented emollient rubbed into her bare feet. She did love to dance. Indeed, she had surpassed herself tonight, leaping in a lively Volta to the applause of the whole court. Later, she had danced at a more stately pace with the charming and erudite Sir Christopher Blount while Lucy Morgan sang a traditional country lament from the gallery. Now, though, the balls of her feet throbbed with pain and she longed to stretch out on the bed, dismissing all her women so she could sleep in glorious solitude.

But first her night-time preparations must be concluded. How wearisome it was to sit through them, she thought, staring at the wall.

Lady Mary Herbert was reading aloud to them from what seemed to be a new manuscript of sonnets. Her soft voice steadied Elizabeth's nerves as she listened, seeking to unravel the clever conceits and arguments within the verse.

When she had finished, Lady Mary set the thick sheaf of papers aside and fetched her looking glass, so Elizabeth could check her reflection.

'Who is the poet?' she asked Mary curiously, taking the glass from her hand.

The young woman coloured delicately. 'I am, Your Majesty.'

'Those were *your* verses?'

'Forgive me if they offended you, Your Majesty.'

'Not at all, I enjoyed them.' Elizabeth smiled. 'As I enjoyed that French tragedy you translated so prettily. Your uncle Sir Philip would have been proud.' She sighed, remembering Pip's smile once as he presented her with a roll of his poems, bound with ribbons and flowers. 'He was a skilled poet, his works will never be forgotten.'

'Oh, my poetry is nothing to my uncle's,' Lady Mary insisted.

Her voice was a little breathless, as if she still held her uncle in awe, though poor Sir Philip Sidney was some six years dead now. Elizabeth looked at her assessingly. Mary curtseyed, perhaps sensing that she had not answered her queen as respectfully as she should, and hurried away to fetch the cleansing cloths.

Elizabeth glanced at herself in the looking glass, then abruptly wished she hadn't.

She allowed her ladies to smooth a tightening cream over her face and throat, then wipe it gently away with cloths steeped in some astringent solution. Yet although her skin felt softer to the touch afterwards, the glass in her hand told no different a story from before. The fragrance rising from such creams and potions was refreshing though, and masked the less pleasant odours about her.

She despised herself for the vanity which made her disguise her age, distracting from her body's decay with more and more elaborate gowns and ruffs, more jewels and paint on her face, more pomp to keep the roving eye away. But if she failed in that duty, if she allowed the court to see their queen wrinkled and ageing, she would never keep their love, nor hold their enemies at bay with just the mention of her name.

Yes, patch me up, Elizabeth thought wearily, raising her arms like a child as they slipped the white nightrail over her head and laced the bodice loosely. There would be more feasting tomorrow. More games and revels to be endured. Prepare me for another long day of forgery and dissembling, she thought.

There was a knock at the door to the Royal Bedchamber. All the ladies stopped their work, turning to stare at this breach of etiquette.

Lady Helena was holding out her white ermine-trimmed night robe, a frown in her eyes. 'The hour is very late, Your Majesty. What should I do?' Her gentlewoman seemed perplexed, as well she might, for it was now past midnight and few courtiers came to disturb Elizabeth at such an hour now that Leicester and Walsingham were both dead.

Those two men had been the great disturbers of her sleep. Elizabeth had to admit she half missed their visits, a welcome interruption to her relentless insomnia.

'My night wig,' she said, and waited impatiently while they set it on her head, placing her lace cap on top. 'Hurry, hurry. Now see who it is, Helena.'

It was Essex.

The young earl walked straight through her disapproving women – though 'swaggered' would be a better term for it, Elizabeth considered, watching him – and bowed before her.

'Your Majesty,' Essex addressed her, with no word of apology for this unwarranted intrusion, 'forgive me for missing the revels tonight. I am newly returned to court from my country estate, and would speak with you on a matter of great urgency.'

Elizabeth raised her eyebrows, looking him up and down. It was hard not to compare his arrogant approach to Robert Cecil's, who had knelt so awkwardly before her. Essex strode into every room like a young god, as handsome and athletic as Leicester had been in his youth.

'Indeed?' she remarked, and stood up from the bed, preferring not to let him see how tired she was.

Perhaps it might be possible to yoke Lord Essex and Robert Cecil together in her service. After all, Leicester and Burghley had worked well enough together, despite their differences. First, though, she would have to tame the unruly Essex, for he was wilder than Leicester at the height of his influence. Nor could she hope to bring him to heel with the same inducements of love and flattery that she had used with his stepfather.

Essex might continue to profess love for her, but she was convinced he felt none. He had sworn he loved her, then suddenly married Frances Walsingham behind her back, almost to spite Elizabeth for her rejection of his suit. Robbie was as selfish and greedy for attention as a child. It would be better if she felt nothing for him.

But oh, her foolish heart . . .

Elizabeth held out her bare hand, still perfumed from the cream her women had rubbed into her skin.

Essex came forward, kneeling to kiss it as she had known he would. He wore an immaculate ruff and a white silk jacket with a gold chain cast carelessly over his neck. Every inch an earl.

'Rise,' she told him graciously, and saw his dark eyes glance up at her frowningly, as though she had tricked him into showing deference. 'Now tell me, what is this urgent matter?'

No, she was no longer the red-haired siren she had been in her youth. Though to hear the poets' lavish descriptions of her charms, she thought drily, one would be forgiven for thinking she was still seventeen. But she had her feminine wiles, and the power to make men fear her. Essex would require a little of both if he was to serve her as Leicester had.

He glanced at her ladies-in-waiting.

She dismissed them reluctantly. 'Return in half an hour,' she told them, 'when I will retire for the night.'

It was not unusual for her to receive councillors privately, but Essex was not yet a member of the Privy Council and the hour was very late for her to be receiving him alone in her bedchamber. Surely, though, she had reached an age where she could be above suspicion of unchaste behaviour?

Even as she thought that, Elizabeth knew it was not true. In recent years she had encouraged the younger courtiers to see her as an ageless queen, almost a faery queen, as the fanciful poet Spenser had described her. She could not now complain if she was held to account as though still young and open to scandal.

'Your Majesty?' Essex began, glancing at her for permission to pour himself some wine.

She nodded, and he poured two goblets of red wine,

handing one to her with a careless gesture that reminded her so sharply of Leicester that her breath caught in her throat.

If only she could forget the past!

'I was concerned to hear that you had allowed Raleigh to return home to Devon after his disgrace,' he commented, sipping his wine. 'A man like that should remain in the Tower where he belongs. Seducing one of the innocent young maids under his care, and here at court!'

Her mouth twisted. 'Bess Throckmorton was not innocent, as her story of love and debauchery made clear. She only saved herself from complete disgrace by marrying Raleigh before their child could be born illegitimately. Not that I approve of such secret marriages, as you know to your cost,' she said sharply, 'but at least the wanton has not given birth to a child out of wedlock.'

'Lady Raleigh remains in the Tower still, I believe,' he murmured, not looking at her.

'Your point?'

'I know you dislike her particular sin, but she has been punished enough for it now, surely? I have no love for her husband, and would gladly have seen the man rot in the Tower's filthy confines until the end of his days, for all his service to your throne. But Bess is a sweet lady and has always been a friend to me.'

Essex raised his dark gaze to hers, and Elizabeth had the unsettling impression that her favourite was threatening her.

'The Tower in winter is no place for a woman. I would not wish to see Lady Raleigh succumb to illness, Your Majesty, or fall into despair at her continuing imprisonment.'

Elizabeth did not know how to respond. It would be the work of a moment to order the woman's release from the Tower. Yet she did not think she ought to bow to his will so easily. It would only encourage Essex to consider her weak and malleable.

Her calm surprised her. Why could she not be angry with Essex, as she would have been with any other man who spoke to her this way?

She waited a moment, staring down into her wine, then asked, 'Is this all you came to say?'

He hesitated. 'I have been over those documents of Walsingham's that I have been able to decipher, and spoken to some of his men. All are agreed that Walsingham believed your person to be in danger from someone close at court. As yet we have no name, nor any clue as to the traitor's identity, except that he is a secret Catholic. Which any fool could have surmised from the evidence.'

'So you are no further along the road than Walsingham was when he died? But with two years passed, you surely cannot believe the traitor still holds to his course?'

'It is not uncommon, I have been informed, for such agents to lie in concealment for years, never revealing themselves but waiting for a letter or agreed sign from their masters.' He paused significantly. 'A sign to proceed with their grisly task of assassination.'

'God's blood!' She drank deeply, almost draining the cup, then regretted it, the strong wine leaving her light-headed. 'How are we to discover him?'

'It has taken me much investigation, but a few months ago I finally managed to track down the man who first discovered this plot. He was one of Walsingham's most trusted agents, with great knowledge of these foreign spies and their loathsome work throughout Europe. Now that he is found, I have installed the man here in the palace, posing as a member of your own household, and instructed him to discover the identity of the secret traitor at the heart of your court. He reports directly to me, though none but you and I will know of his true identity.'

She was impressed, not having considered that Essex could achieve such a thing. Then she remembered what Robert Cecil had recently told her of Anthony Bacon's friendship with Essex, and wondered if he had been the one to find this missing agent and put such a cunning scheme together.

'His name?'

'Master Goodluck.'

A memory came to her. 'I know that name. He was Lucy Morgan's guardian when she was a child.'

'I did not know that.'

'He served Walsingham well on many occasions, and more than once thwarted a plot to have me killed.' She smiled warmly, holding out her hand to him. Even if Bacon had helped him to this goal, nonetheless the work had been conceived and planned by Essex. 'You have done well, Robbie. I shall sleep easier knowing there is a sturdy agent in my household, working to uncover this traitor.'

'I have done nothing but my duty to you, Your Majesty,' Essex said easily, stripping off his gloves to take her hand, but she could see he was pleased by her praise.

'Though I do not understand how any man, even a treacherous one, could live in a state of falsehood for years,' Elizabeth added in a low voice, not wishing her ladies to hear any of this secret exchange and become frightened, 'hiding his true intention from those around him, with the daily contemplation of a queen's murder staining his heart.'

She shuddered. A man's soul must be twisted by such evil until there was no hope of redemption.

'Those who serve Spain,' he observed, still holding her hand, 'do so with much zeal and passion, undergoing any sacrifice to strike at England and her queen.'

'Yet such a deed in his heart must be like a worm in an

204

apple,' she muttered, 'eating away at its wholesomeness from the inside. Surely such a man would reveal himself to us by his very nature?'

'If he exists and is at court, then our Master Goodluck will sniff him out,' he reassured her, and rubbed his thumb slowly back and forth across her palm. 'Do not distress yourself, madam. I will not allow this traitor to harm you.'

Essex was standing very close, she realized. She had been shocked and a little frightened by his passion last time they were alone together. Yet she had lain awake at nights remembering it since, and her body had begun to think its own thoughts about the Earl of Essex, thoughts she found it dangerous to examine too closely.

Shyly, she raised her gaze to his face: dark eyes, deep-set beneath thin arched brows, dark curly hair, an adventurer's abandon in the way he wore it too, brushing against his ruff.

She tried to shake off the illusion that this boy was Leicester and steeled herself to dismiss him.

'My ladies will return soon,' Elizabeth reminded him, yet lacked the strength to draw her hand from his. Was it a sin to wish for his youthful company a little longer? 'So if that is all, my lord . . .'

'Your Majesty,' he said huskily, and raised her hand to his lips. As he kissed her skin, his gaze burned into hers. 'You haunt my dreams and my waking hours. When will you grant this body some peace and permit me to love and worship you, as you should be loved and worshipped?'

'Never,' she managed, stumbling over her denial.

He ignored that and drew closer. 'I am no poet, so never think my words are false or honeyed. I love you with all my body and soul. That you are my queen I accept as only natural, for who else should reign here but one whose beauty and wit surpass that of every other woman in England? But that you resist my love is painful to me. I wish only to show you the depths of my heart.'

'You are a married man,' she reminded him. 'You must share your heart with your wife, Frances, not with me.'

She was no fool, she had heard many men praise her in just such an extravagant fashion in hope of advancement. But there was an honesty to the pain in his face, a sharpness to his voice that made her believe Essex truly suffered as he spoke.

'My wife has feet of clay,' he said bitterly, then lowered his head, kissing her palm. 'Forgive me, I should not speak ill of Walsingham's daughter. I am sworn to her before God. But she makes my life difficult. She does not understand why I must spend so much time at court, or go away fighting for England, or be alone in your company. She is a jealous wife, and fears to lose me to war as she lost her first husband.'

Elizabeth thought it more likely that Frances feared to lose him to his mistress the Queen, but she did not voice that. 'Perhaps you should have thought of such obstacles before you wed her behind my back, my lord.'

'Forgive me, Your Majesty. Frances caught my eye and my weak body thought only of begetting an heir.' Essex hung his head, and she was reminded of Leicester, weeping in her lap as he confessed his need for a son. 'A man must have a wife, and a young wife too, to ensure sons for himself and his name. But love can thrive beyond the marriage bed – as it thrives in this heart, for you.'

He placed her hand flat above his heart. Beneath the white silk she felt his broad muscular chest, the strong expanse of the ribcage, and beneath them, the quick rhythmic thud of his heart. His eyes watched her fiercely, his hand holding hers in place.

Elizabeth struggled to pull away, and he tore loose his ruff and the collar of his white jacket, and thrust her hand on to his chest. Touching his bare skin, she felt heat sweep over her, her cheeks suddenly burning, her body weak with physical desire.

'Elizabeth,' he murmured, and bent his head to hers.

They kissed like young lovers, her tongue in his mouth, inviting him to further outrages, his arm tight about her waist, one hand stroking sensuously down her back.

'My love,' he groaned against her mouth, and she let her head tilt back, encouraging his lips on her throat. 'You never married, which means you have no heir,' he muttered, kissing her skin fiercely, 'and that has put you in danger, my beautiful queen. For until the succession is agreed, you will never be free from those assassins who seek your life's blood. My fear for your safety is as strong as my love—'

Suddenly there was a quiet knock at the door, probably one of her ladies come to help her retire. Elizabeth only just sprang away from Essex in time to see it open, Lady Helena standing there with a candle in her hand, her face horrified.

'Forgive me,' her lady-in-waiting said hurriedly, but Elizabeth shook her head, coming back to her senses.

'No, come in, Helena. Our business here is concluded. His lordship was just leaving,' she said unsteadily, and watched in silence as Essex bowed and withdrew, his eyes dark with turmoil.

Until the succession is agreed, you will never be free from those assassins who seek your life's blood.

His kisses had served to distract her well. Oh yes, they had been a distraction. *Look over here at this shiny new love while I steal your throne, Your Majesty.* But now her head was clear, and she knew herself betrayed. Not openly, by young rebel lords as Cecil had suggested, but surrounded by those on her council who would force her into naming Mary Stuart's son James as her heir.

Mary Stuart's son!

207

She would rather any man sat on the throne of England than the Scottish whelp of her dead cousin, for all that the treacherous Queen died by order of her own hand.

Was that the real reason Essex had come to see her tonight? Not to make love to her, but to settle the question of the succession?

Part Three

Part Three

One

Greenwich Palace, January 1593

JANUARY CAME CRUELLY TO GREENWICH, FREEZING THE
Thames in dangerous patches of thin ice, a trap for the
unwary, and hanging glassy icicles from the courtyard
walls. Snow lay thick on the ground, making the many
outside steps and stone-flagged cloisters treacherous, and
not even the vast roaring fire that was kept burning
continuously in the Great Hall could seem to warm the
courtiers. Out of the Presence Chamber, cosy enough when
packed wall to wall with fur-wrapped gentry and nobles,
the only way to keep the limbs from stiffening and the
fingers from growing numb was to dance.

And to Lucy, dancing was like breathing.

So while others grumbled, and stubbed their frozen toes
on the hard stone flags, she took pleasure in being able to
move freely and hold her head up high. It was rare these
days that she was asked to dance before the court, since
younger girls had taken her place in the Queen's favour,
and she no longer remembered the more intricate steps
required of the entertainers. But she would be permitted to
dance with a courtier or two, along with the other ladies

211

of the court, and lose herself for a short space in the haunting lilt of music.

It had been nigh on two months since she discovered that Master Goodluck was in residence with the court. She had barely seen her guardian since that night he had surprised her in the palace garden, except about his duties, and while she could wish he had not overheard her shameful quarrel with Will, at least there was no longer any need to hide the doubts of her heart from him. Goodluck knew how it lay between her and Shakespeare, and she took some comfort from knowing she did not have to bear that grief alone.

'Beware Southampton,' Goodluck had told her that night, as he accompanied her back through the darkened palace to the ladies' chambers. 'He is part of a wild set of noblemen, youths interested only in power and pleasure.'

'But why does he pursue me with such hatred?'

'It may not be you he pursues, but Shakespeare.'

She had not understood that, and had told him so.

'Why this nobleman has threatened you is not important,' Goodluck remarked, kissing her gently on the forehead as they reached the door to the women's bedchamber. 'For now, try never to cross him nor let yourself be alone with him. These great men of wealth are cruel and vengeful towards those they consider their enemies, for whatever reason. The Earl of Southampton would think nothing of destroying you, as an entertainment for himself and his friends.'

'I know it,' she told him. 'I will be careful, and try never to put myself in his power.'

'I cannot help you beyond this advice,' Goodluck murmured, releasing her hands, 'though I dearly wish I could. I have been given a task which requires great secrecy, and I dare not risk my true identity being uncovered. Forgive me.'

She had not spoken to him since that night, but had been relieved to find herself largely ignored by the Earl of Southampton that winter, as though she was no longer of any importance to him.

With the whole court in attendance at that evening's lavish feast given in honour of the French ambassador, who appeared to have come seeking fresh help for their struggle against the Spanish, the Queen had insisted upon dancing. She loved nothing better than to show off her skill in the dance to visiting ambassadors, and indeed her athletic prowess, for she was as nimble and swift at the Gavotte and Volta as any woman half her age.

'Tonight everyone must dance!' the Queen had declared, holding out her hands, then waited impatiently for one of her nobles to lead her forward first, as was the tradition.

Now the hall rang to the clack-clack-clack of their heeled court shoes, the shuffles and thuds of their leaps, while the musicians played beneath the high windows, their faces raw with cold but filling the air with sweet sounds.

Lucy was dancing with Francis Bacon, whose fascinated smile had caught her eye from across the Great Hall, when someone tapped him on the shoulder.

'My turn, Francis,' a familiar voice drawled, and as Bacon stepped aside, bowing ironically, she looked into the face of Henry Wriothesley, the Earl of Southampton.

Her first horrified instinct was to refuse his hand in the dance. But such an insult would have drawn unwanted attention to her, and possibly gained her the Queen's displeasure. So she curtseyed, and slipped back into the swaying circle of dancers with this new unwanted partner, trying not to shrink when he put his arm about her waist.

'You are very tall, Mistress Morgan,' he commented.

'But not taller than the Queen.'

He glanced across at the Queen, comparing the two of them with a critical eye. 'You have the edge, I think.'

She looked away, and saw Cathy watching her from across the room. As befitted her position as servant to the Queen's ladies, Catherine's long fair hair had been hidden away beneath a demure hood. She ought not to be here, her duties sadly no longer permitting her to attend the feasts.

Lucy stared, bemused, and saw Cathy nod her head significantly, as though trying to pass on a message.

What could her friend want?

'Do you like to jump?' Henry Wriothesley asked, whispering in her ear. 'Or do you prefer to be lifted?'

She looked him in the eye. 'I like to jump, my lord.'

'I have heard that.'

She stiffened but said nothing. He wanted her to lose her temper, but she would not give him the satisfaction.

The music changed tempo, becoming faster, and she whirled before him in the steps of the dance, her broad skirts flying.

They were dancing a few steps from the Queen and her partner, the exquisitely dressed Earl of Essex, his doublet black and white, his slashed sleeves of gorgeous black velvet, pure white silk peeping through from beneath. A large pearl trembled in his ear as he bowed to the Queen.

The Queen leapt lightly up in the dance, laughing with pleasure, and Essex stepped forward to catch her. The many panels of her magnificent rainbow-skirted gown shimmered and swayed as she descended in his arms, her waist and chest still pleasingly small and narrow above their broad expanse.

'You are a bird of paradise, Your Majesty!' Robert Devereux flattered her, holding her with deliberate intimacy.

Watched by hundreds of envious eyes, the earl slid his

hands down her back in a display of ownership that Her Majesty did not seem disposed to object to. Her long white fingers gripped his shoulders as he placed her gently on her feet, as flushed as a young girl at her first dance, her eyes fixed on the earl's handsome face.

'And you are a swan, my lord,' she countered, though still smiling. 'A bird to be watched most carefully.'

Lucy leapt a few seconds later, not daring to jump higher or earlier than the Queen, and Henry Wriothesley caught her by the waist.

She looked down at him. Loathsome, dangerous man. But her expression gave nothing away.

His hands dropped to her hips, drawing her closer than she found comfortable. She felt Wriothesley's body against hers, the insistent press of his knee. His breath scorched her neck. Then he was forced to release her as she turned in the dance, her arms spread wide, her long white silk-lined sleeves hanging down.

As they came together again, he asked, 'Have you seen Master Shakespeare lately?'

Her glance was hostile. 'No, my lord. But I think you must know that already.'

'And has he written? Sent you any word at all?'

This time Lucy had to bite her tongue, keeping her tone light. He might be young, but he was influential at court as well as enormously wealthy, and therefore not a man to offend.

'No, my lord Southampton. I took your warning most seriously and have had no dealings with Master Shakespeare for many months.'

She leapt in the dance, and again he caught her. Only Henry Wriothesley did not let her go, pulling her even tighter into his body than before, his smile greedy and contemptuous.

'My lord, you must release me!'

'Must I indeed?' He laughed, and his hand squeezed one of her breasts quite openly, hurting her. She struggled, her eyes wide with shock, but he paid no heed, tugging at her white-beaded bodice as though to release her breasts in front of the whole court. 'Dancing is not for me, clearly. I seem to have forgotten the steps. But perhaps you can teach them to me.'

An icy voice from behind them drew Wriothesley up straight, his hands dropping to his sides.

'My lord, your clumsiness is not to be tolerated. You are holding up the dance.'

It was the Queen, who never seemed to miss any indiscretion among her courtiers, however small.

'Remove yourself at once, my lord, and pray do not dance at court again until you have the steps by heart.'

'Yes, Your Majesty,' Henry Wriothesley said stiffly, and backed towards the door, still bowing to the Queen.

At the Queen's cold nod of dismissal, Lucy curtseyed and slipped gratefully away into the crowd, heading towards the candlelit sideboard where the wine was being served. She wanted to get as far from the Earl of Southampton and his cruel hands as she could manage. Somehow she found an empty seat against the wall and sat there, trembling with rage at Wriothesley's treatment, barely dredging up a smile when one of the older courtiers stopped to ask if she was unwell. He called a servant and had wine brought, then moved on into the crowd, leaving her alone with her thoughts. She had given in to Henry Wriothesley's demands too easily before, that had been her error. He was still young, still learning the ways of the world. Her unquestioning submission had given the earl hope that he could treat her however he wished, speaking to her lewdly and without respect, even humiliating her before the Queen.

But how to correct her mistake without endangering her position at court?

Cathy found her, her look flustered. 'Thank the Lord, you are still here. I was beginning to think you had gone back to the ladies' chamber.'

'Cathy, what are you doing here?' Lucy stroked her friend's cheek, concerned by the tremble in her voice. 'You could get a whipping if you're here without permission.'

'That doesn't matter. I had to see you, Lucy. I couldn't wait until later.'

Catherine looked agitated, a strained look in her friend's face that Lucy did not like. A stray lock of fair hair had tumbled out from under her hood; she tucked it away with a shaking hand, biting her lip as she glanced about them at the thronging crowd of courtiers.

'What in God's name is it? You look awful, Cath.' She rose. 'Come, you must take my seat. Has something bad happened?'

Cathy shook her head. 'No, it's nothing, I'm just . . . a little unwell, that's all. Here, though,' she said, and drew a rolled slip of paper from her sleeve. 'This . . . This message came for you.'

Lucy took it, frowning. 'What is it? Who brought it?'

'A boy, I don't know his name.'

She began to unroll the paper, but Cathy put a hand on her arm. 'Not here, don't read it here,' she whispered urgently. 'Hide it, and come aside with me. I know a quiet place close at hand.'

Lucy pushed the message into the small leather pouch at her belt, then followed her out of the Great Hall, away from the state chambers and through a narrow maze of corridors. Soon they had left the noise of the revelry behind, the palace quieter here, only a few servants moving softly around, bearing empty trays back to the kitchens or replacing burned-out torches with fresh ones.

They passed along a cloistered walk, the uneven flag-stones slippery with ice; Lucy looked up at the night sky through the ornately carved archways and saw the moon rising in the heavens, mistily haloed.

It was bitterly cold.

'Where are you taking me?' she asked, her heart beating loudly.

It was unlike Catherine to be so secretive; nor had she ever seen her friend so frightened. Lucy peered over her shoulder in the darkened cloisters, thinking she heard foot-steps behind them, but saw only shadows and patches of moonlight on the icy stones.

'Cathy, I do not know this part of the palace. Where are we?'

'Have patience. We are nearly there.'

Just beyond the cloistered walk, Cathy reached a low wooden door in the stone wall and pushed it open, gestur-ing Lucy down the steps. The room below was small and dimly lit by a single candle, furnished simply with a table and a pile of straw, a stack of wooden crates to one side, as though the place was sometimes used for storage.

Lucy trod carefully down the steps, holding her skirts out of the straw, and looked up into the face of Henry Wriothesley.

Stunned, she nearly tripped, stumbling over the bottom step. 'You? My lord Southampton? What is this trickery?'

'Forgive me, Lucy,' Cathy said in a gasp, and now Lucy could see what she had missed in the darkness, her face flushed with shame. Cathy stood at the top of the steps, staring down at her. 'I . . . I didn't want to do this. His lordship made me bring you here. He gave me no choice, you must believe me.' She glanced at the earl, then hurried outside as though in sudden fright, dragging the door shut behind her and calling down, 'It . . . it's in her pouch!'

Lucy turned to face the Earl of Southampton. She did

not know if he intended her harm, though the pile of straw in the corner might serve as a mattress if he planned to rape her. She had faced such horrors from men before though, and felt no fear at what was to come, only disgust.

'Well, my lord? Your trap has worked and you have my attention. Though I fear you will have the Queen's attention soon, once she hears of this indignity.'

'I don't think so,' he said calmly, and nodded to her pouch. 'Take out the letter.'

She set her jaw at this command. Damn his eyes! He must have learned of the message – which came almost certainly from Will Shakespeare – and bribed Cathy to bring her and the message here. There could be no other explanation, though she would dearly love to know why Cathy had betrayed her.

Since there seemed little point in denying it, she undid her pouch, pulled out the message and held it out to him.

'Have you read it?' he demanded, not taking it from her.

'No.'

'Do you know who it is from?'

She shook her head.

'Read it then,' he insisted coldly, looking at it. 'Read it out loud, for I would know what this message contains. Though I believe we can both guess who it is from. Your lover, the poet Master Shakespeare.'

'He is not my lover!'

'Do not lie to me, whore!' Henry Wriothesley seemed to tremble with rage, his young face flushed with it. Then he collected himself and nodded again at the message. 'Your servant Catherine has been most helpful in this matter. Not trusting your word that you would never have any dealings with Shakespeare again, I set the slut to watch when you should receive any secret message, and bring both you and it straight to me in this place. She sent word to me at the feast tonight that such a message had just arrived, and then led you here, as arranged.' His smile made her blood chill. 'And if that letter is from Shakespeare, I shall convey you before Her Majesty the Queen this very night, and tell her of your whoring ways.'

'But you are Shakespeare's patron. Surely you cannot wish to see him in the Tower?'

'Master Shakespeare will not be punished as you will be,' he said softly. 'The Queen treasures his poetry and will be swayed by my defence of his good name. I shall argue that you seduced Master Shakespeare against his better judgement, and that you alone should bear the guilt of this transgression. He is a married man, and the Queen looks kindly on such men who are led astray. Though not so on her ladies, who face the whip and a prison cell for their sins. I could name half a dozen in the past few years who have shared that fate.'

She knew he was right, and raged against the unfairness of the Queen's judgement, who always forgave a lustful man more readily than a woman. Her fingers trembled on the message that would condemn her, wishing she could destroy it.

'Read!'

Well, why not? Might as well get it over with, she thought, and face the Queen's wrath. She could not stand there all night in her thin dancing shoes until her feet turned to ice.

Lucy stripped off her gloves, unrolled the message, and stared down at it in silence.

'Well?' he demanded impatiently.

She handed the paper to the earl, almost tempted to smile.

'What is this nonsense?' Southampton frowned as he turned the paper over in his hand, then examined its message again. 'These strange markings, what do they mean? This . . . This message is in code!' His eyes narrowed in accusation on her face. 'By God, it is worse than I thought. You are a spy!'

'Me? A spy?'

'Wait until the Queen hears of this. Do not think you will escape punishment because you are a woman. You will be burned alive for this treachery, Mistress Morgan, for that is the method of execution reserved for a woman who has betrayed her country. I believe it is a terrible and agonizing death.'

At that moment, the door above creaked open. She turned in relief to see the Earl of Essex at the top of the steps, a servant behind him with a flaming torch in his hand.

Essex looked briefly from her face to Southampton's, then called down, 'Come away, Mistress Morgan. I will see you safely back to your chamber.'

'No, wait, my lord, you must see this!' Henry Wriothesley swore, pushing past her up the steps to thrust the message under Essex's nose. 'You see this? I found it on her person. It is written in code! This is the traitor you have been seeking. Lucy Morgan is the one who has been spying on us for the Spanish.'

Essex took the paper, glanced down at it blankly, then handed it back to Lucy. 'This is yours, I believe.'

When his friend began to protest, Essex put a hand on his shoulder. 'Let it drop, Henry. Come to my rooms tomorrow, I shall explain some of what has passed here. But you must not speak of this to anyone. Do you understand?'

Wriothesley looked past him at Lucy, his face contorted with fury. But he seemed to grasp there could be no winning this argument, for he gave a short reluctant nod, and shrugged off Essex's hand.

'Very well,' he muttered. 'But say what you like, she is still a whore.'

Essex left her not far from the large chamber where she slept with the other women, his manner icily polite. She noticed he did not bow.

'Be warned to keep out of this game, Mistress Morgan, and tend the Queen only. That is your rightful place, whatever your guardian may believe.'

When he had gone, Lucy stood a moment in silence, her wits not quite steady, trying to understand what had happened. Then a bulky shadow detached itself from the others along the corridor and she turned to find Goodluck at her back.

He looked at her grimly without speaking, then laid a finger on his lips and drew her into a dark alcove.

'This is my fault,' he muttered, once he seemed convinced that none could hear them. 'I sent you that message and never considered that it would reach your enemy first. I simply wished to see you again, to ask how you are faring at court. But when I realized that your friend Catherine had betrayed you, I followed both of you to the storage room, then went to alert the Earl of Essex. Robert Devereux is an unpredictable master, and he is no Walsingham, more's the pity. But I trust him, for he holds the Queen's safety close to his heart.'

She remembered how Lord Essex had looked at her coldly before bidding her goodnight. 'He does not hold me in much regard, I think.'

'That his lordship does not,' Goodluck agreed wryly. 'But at least my lord Essex understood tonight why you – and my coded message – had to be rescued from young Southampton. My exposure could risk the Queen's life.'

So that was why he had come to court, working in the Queen's household like a common servant. He had not told her as much at their meeting, merely shaking his head at her questions with his customary air of mystery. But she had known him all her life, and ought to have realized. Why else would Goodluck have trimmed his famous beard so neatly, except in some vain attempt to disguise himself?

'There is another plot against Her Majesty's life?'

Goodluck nodded, then took her hands. He frowned, rubbing them between his. 'In God's name, you are so cold. Where are your gloves?'

'I'm not sure. I must have left them in . . . in that room with Southampton.'

'Then let me warm them for you.' He brought her fingers up to his chest, pushing them beneath the liveried jacket to keep warm. She could hear the beat of his heart, deep and steady.

She raised her eyes shyly to his. 'Thank you, Goodluck.'

'Do not thank me, for this is my fault. I should never have sent that message and risked your safety like this. In God's name though, how I itched to kill that arrogant young fool for daring to speak to you with so little courtesy, to lay his violent hands on you.' His eyes darkened with fury. 'And these are the noblemen who run our country. Braggarts and fools.'

'Forget him, Goodluck. There is no harm done. Southampton is a fool, yes, and a braggart. But he did not lay his hands on me.'

Not this time, she thought fiercely, remembering how the young earl had struck her across the face at their first meeting.

As though reading her mind, Goodluck stroked her face with the back of his hand where the earl's blow had caught her.

'You are my dearest love,' he muttered, watching her, 'and the only woman I truly care about. I could not bear it if anything were to happen to you.'

His hand was so warm against her cheek. She felt the shock of that touch run through her, her lips suddenly tingling as she gazed up at him. Goodluck was one of the few men she knew who was taller than her. She had never thought of it before, but if she were to stand on her toes, their mouths would be almost on the same level.

In her mind's eye, Lucy saw herself placing her hands on his shoulders and her mouth on his, and kissing him.

Desire coiled in her belly, sharp and pleasurable at the same time, an unfamiliar ache that was quite unlike her feelings for Will. Suddenly she could not breathe, but stood staring at him through the darkness, lips parted, eyes wide.

Kiss Goodluck?

She had never thought of her guardian in such terms before, and now could not quite believe her own naivety. For as she examined her turbulent feelings, it became clear that she loved Goodluck, not in filial affection for her guardian as she had thought all these years, but as a woman loves a man.

'Goodluck,' she whispered, then took a quick step back, shaking her head, scared to reveal her thoughts.

What if she were to kiss him and Goodluck pushed her away, shocked at her wantonness? She knew he was no cold-blooded celibate but a man who enjoyed a woman's company. To her knowledge though, Goodluck was not a frequenter of Southwark's many disreputable houses of Venus. He would certainly be shocked to know what she was thinking.

Her guardian had always treated her as a daughter, even his bear hugs fatherly, deliberately averting his eyes when she so much as showed an ankle.

'Lucy?' His voice was husky. 'What is it?'

'I . . .' She was lost for an answer.

'Come here.'

To her dismay, Goodluck enfolded her in his arms.

'Do not be afraid,' he murmured, frowning at her

expression, no doubt surprised by how she trembled. He stroked her back, his hand slow and reassuring, unaware of how his touch inflamed her desire to have him love her.

'The danger is past. It is not like you to lack courage.'

She studied him, thinking how much younger he looked with his beard trimmed.

He was right. It was not like her to lack courage.

'I love you,' she murmured in a sudden moment of daring, and raised herself on tiptoe to press her lips to his.

For a moment, Goodluck stood immobile, cold and stiff under her tentative kiss. She felt sure he would push her away. Then his arms tightened about her and he gave a muffled groan.

'Lucy,' he managed hoarsely.

He drew her closer, his mouth moving hard and compulsively against hers. The kiss deepened until she was breathless. Then Goodluck turned her in one swift movement so Lucy had her back to the wall, with him pressing urgently against her.

His hand crept up to her neck, holding her gently while his mouth explored hers. His kisses surprised her but were welcome. She was no innocent virgin, and could feel desire in the body which pushed so hard against her.

Goodluck wanted her too!

Boldly, she let her tongue stroke along his lips, and heard him groan again.

He drew back a little to look into her face. 'We should not do this. I am your guardian, dearest. It is not right.'

'You do not want me?'

'Of course I want you.' His voice hardened, a flick of self-loathing in his words. 'But I shall not take you. You are like a daughter to me, Lucy. It is not so many years since I was your guardian. It would be a betrayal of trust to give in to this desire and lie with you.'

She ran a slow hand down his body and felt him

respond, his eyes very dark as she stared into them. 'And if I tell you how much I want you too, Goodluck? Would it still be a betrayal?'

'It is too dangerous, Lucy. You are one of the Queen's ladies. You do not know what you are asking.'

She raised her eyebrows. 'I have not been the Queen's chaste maid since I was a child. I have been Shakespeare's secret lover these past years, as well you know, and been married and widowed in that time too. Oh, I may not be as *experienced* as you in the bedchamber,' she said deliberately, laughing at the flash in his eyes, 'but I have learned something of the nature of desire, and I desire you, Goodluck, whatever danger may come from it.'

Goodluck had listened with a strained expression as though he could not quite believe what he was hearing. She wondered if he thought her wanton, inviting herself so freely into his bed. But he did not reject her as she feared and half expected.

Instead, he cupped her face, his palm warm against her cheek. 'Well, then,' he told her huskily, 'I shall attempt not to disappoint you, my dearest. But not here, and not tonight. There are too many who might see us together and report you to the Queen.'

Nonetheless, he kissed her fiercely before releasing her, his lips scorching her mouth and throat. She clung to him, kissing him back, breathing him in, wishing they could be private that night, and every night. That they could lie together like man and wife for the rest of their lives. Her heart stuttered and raced as she imagined them in bed together, incredulous that she had never before realized the depth of her love for this man. Her love and her desire.

Goodluck rested his cheek against hers, breathing hard, and she knew he was fighting for control.

In that instant she could not conceive what she had ever seen in William Shakespeare. For Will was nothing to this man. He was a shadow compared to Goodluck's warmth, light, solidity, love.

'I am lodged at the top of the old west tower,' he murmured in her ear, his arm about her waist. 'Come to my chamber late on Sunday evening, my love, if you have not changed your mind by then. We shall be private there.'

Two

DAWN BROKE DARK AND BITTER COLD TO THE RINGING OF bells at Greenwich Palace. Soon the whole place was awake, courtiers being dressed for Mass by firelight in their tapestry-hung chambers, servants running to and fro in the narrow corridors, intent on their tasks. Outside, a wind from the north-east whistled through the icy court-yards and open spaces of the palace, bringing snow with it. Serving men in livery stamped their feet and blew on their cupped hands as they went about their duties, the women wrapped in shawls and thick woollen cloaks, only their red noses and chapped lips visible.

Goodluck heaved the empty barrel on to his shoulder, trudging up the cellar steps and along the towpath to a narrow jetty where two rivermen were loading their skiff.

'Is that the last?' one of the rivermen demanded, his leather cap tied under his chin to prevent the wind from whisking it away.

When Goodluck assented, the man threw the barrel aboard as though it weighed nothing. He turned to his raw-faced fellow on the bank, calling, 'That's us done, Master Penn. Cast her off!'

The river was partially frozen at that point, and the

heavily laden boat, sitting low in the water now, would not budge. To break free of the bank, the two men were forced to smash the ice with long sticks, showering themselves with flecks of slush. The thin ice gave way easily, and so they made their way across to the other bank, white with snow and swathed in early mists, shouting and smashing as they went.

Goodluck watched them for a moment, then returned to the small courtyard that housed the cellar steps and adjoined the kitchen. The icy path was treacherous, pitted with footprints, and he had to take care with his footing.

As he entered the courtyard, it began to snow again.

Goodluck shivered, clapping his gloved hands together for warmth. Despite the heavy snowfall, he was not permitted to wear a cloak over his livery. His boots were stout enough, but afforded little protection against the cold. Yet he had not heard any of those who laboured in the palaces complain about their treatment. Indeed they seemed proud to do it, and often spoke of the Queen with simple reverence, as though she were more saint than woman.

Apart from the rigours of the snow, Goodluck himself had found no hardship in the duties he was expected to perform while posing as a member of the palace staff. It was good work, decently paid, and there was honour in serving the Queen and her household.

One day I shall be too old to work, he reminded himself. Then what?

In his youth, when he had chosen the dubious trade of spy, foolishly welcoming death in the service of his country, he had not thought to last so long. But the honour of an early death had not been his. Now he looked ahead to his later years with some trepidation, for work was thin for an old spy, and those who lived too long found themselves on the streets, begging for alms with the other dregs and drifters. He could work in the theatres, it

229

was true, but when so many had remained closed for months after the riots and the scourge of the plague, it seemed a precarious trade for a man who needed daily bread and shelter to survive.

Now that he had been given a breathing space to reconsider, Goodluck knew he must put Lucy off with some lie when she came to him today. He loved her more than his own life, and once that would have seemed enough to him. For he was nothing. A shadow set to watch other shadows. What could he offer her except old age and poverty?

Goodluck stopped dead, seeing a cloaked figure ahead of him in the snowy courtyard.

He ducked out of sight behind a cart as the man turned, glancing over his shoulder, perhaps to check that he was not observed. He crouched and peered through the iced wheel spokes, then saw the man's face and drew a sharp breath.

It was Kit Marlowe, whom he had thought abroad.

Goodluck watched as Kit descended the short flight of steps into the palace kitchens, then followed hurriedly after. His heart had begun to thud, his senses suddenly alert.

What would young Kit Marlowe be doing at Greenwich Palace on a frozen Sunday, except visiting a fellow spy and conspirator while most decent folk were in church?

He had always had his doubts about this young man, instinctively distrusting him. Marlowe had lied to him on board ship from the Low Countries, certainly, and then had spoken to someone at one of the treacherous Stanley's houses on arrival in London. His lordship the Earl of Essex trusted him, but Essex was young too, and nowhere near as canny as Walsingham had been. It was easy for a man to play both sides in this game, but more difficult for any to be sure where his true allegiances lay.

Following Marlowe through the dim-lit maze of

corridors, Goodluck kept as close as he dared. He waited impatiently at each corner to avoid being seen, shivering in the bitter wind that whistled through the narrow stone-walled hallways. Perhaps Marlowe's contact at court would turn out to be the very man they sought, the traitor at the heart of the Queen's household?

Marlowe stopped before a low door and knocked three times quickly, then twice slowly.

The door was jerked open to reveal Essex himself, the fashionable earl at odds with such dingy surroundings, even clad in sober black and silver for Sunday. He did not appear surprised to see Kit Marlowe, but stood aside with an abrupt gesture, beckoning the young man inside.

Marlowe slipped past him, and the door closed.

The corridor was dark and empty. Goodluck edged nearer the door, listening hard for the sound of voices within. But all he could hear was a muffled exchange between the two men. They were speaking quietly, as though afraid of being over-heard. Then the earl suddenly exclaimed, 'No!' and Marlowe's voice dropped to a whisper.

The scraping of a chair indicated that the interview was at an end. Goodluck hurried into a shadowy doorway further along the hall and waited, his cap drawn down.

A moment later, the door opened and Marlowe emerged. Bowing briefly, the young man returned the way he had come, once more wrapped in his cloak, a huddled figure unlikely to excite comment among the hurrying palace servants.

Essex turned and came slowly towards Goodluck's hiding place, his head bent in thought, a hand resting on the jewelled hilt of his sword.

'My lord,' Goodluck muttered, and the earl's head came up, frowning.

He stared at Goodluck through the gloom, then a wry smile twisted his mouth. 'I should have known nothing would escape your attention, Master Goodluck.' He glanced over his shoulder but the corridor was still empty. 'You recognized my visitor?'

'Yes, my lord.'

'And now you are wondering at our business together?' Essex shrugged. 'I keep many irons in the fire. Some are hotter to the touch than others. Not that it concerns you, but to lay your mind at rest, I have spoken with young Marlowe about his presence in the Low Countries at the time of the Spanish Armada's launch, and his visit to Stanley's house. I am convinced by what he has told me that he plays the villain for our benefit, and at his late master Walsingham's express command.'

'He spies for both sides, then?'

'But is loyal to England, yes.' Essex was clearly impatient. 'I must attend the Queen for Sunday Mass. What of you, Goodluck? Marlowe tells me that our man may be a foreigner, not English as we originally suspected. But nothing is certain, and he fears this could be another false lead, thrown out by our conspirators themselves to send us off the track. So still we search.'

Essex hesitated, looking hard at him. 'Have you anything new for me? Are you any closer to discovering the identity of the traitor we seek?'

Goodluck had to admit that he was not. The earl swept on, leaving him alone in the corridor.

Contemplating the earl's disappearing back, his thoughts were bitter. But what use to complain that he was hunting for a thimble in the dark, when he had willingly accepted this task, knowing success to be unlikely?

He made his way back to the kitchens, for further tasks would await him there to be completed before the servants were called to Mass. There were several men he was watching within the Queen's household, but so far he had been unable to find evidence of any conspiracy or wrongdoing there. It seemed to him that this trail had indeed gone cold, as he had warned Essex before.

Yet Marlowe appeared to have brought the earl credible intelligence that some threat to Her Majesty was still afoot.

How was that possible? What leads had young Marlowe pursued that had been denied to Goodluck?

I am jealous, he thought ironically, and had to laugh. *Fool that I am.* Jealous of a young man for possessing more information than he had been able to glean. And yet they were both working for the Queen's safety. Or so Essex would have him believe. Perhaps the ambitious earl was more trusting of Marlowe than he should be, this hunt for a non-existent traitor merely a desperate bid to impress the Queen.

I must tread carefully, he told himself. *If things run foul, it will be my neck that swings, not his lordship's.*

Voices ahead, muttering together as though in some secret conversation, brought him up short. Suddenly alert, he flattened himself behind a stack of crates and peered round. The corridor was dark here, no torches nor openings to weather that might afford light. But he recognized one of the men's voices.

It was Marlowe, his back towards him, speaking softly to a hooded and cloaked figure whose face he could not see.

'Come, I must give them a date.'

The other man replied, his voice low and harried, accented. Possibly Spanish? 'Forgive me, but to give a date . . . It must be the work of a seized moment. She is too closely guarded.'

'The King grows impatient with your delays. He demands a date. This month? Next? He will not wait for ever, and then . . .'

The man sounded terrified. 'Yes, yes, I understand. But please . . . you must give us more time.'

'Your master has had years to prepare for this.'

'It is not an easy thing,' the man muttered. 'To take such a life . . .'

A serving man came puffing down the corridor under the weight of a tray of flagons, and both conspirators moved aside to let him pass, their faces hidden. The man glanced at both, his round face frowning, but continued on without comment. Goodluck drew closer into the wall, and was relieved when the serving man turned aside into another corridor leading up to the ground floor. It would not have done to be discovered down here, not when Marlowe knew him by sight.

The two men seemed to have been unsettled by this interruption; nothing more was said as they stood, listening to the man's receding footsteps.

'It will be done soon. That is all my master can promise.' The man turned and hurried away into the darkness.

If Marlowe knew the identity of the traitor, and was speaking to him or his servant here, why would he not have communicated this information to his master, Essex? The only explanation was that Kit Marlowe was not merely aping a double game between England and Spain, but was secretly in the service of King Philip.

Yet how to convince Essex of such treachery, when the young earl clearly favoured Marlowe above him and would hear no suspicion raised against him?

Marlowe pulled his hood down to cover his face and began to move away, then halted, glancing back over his shoulder as though some sixth sense had warned him that he was being observed.

Goodluck stood still, head lowered, hoping he would be hidden behind the stack of crates. A few uncomfortable seconds passed in silence, then he heard Marlowe walk on.

Had he been seen?

Goodluck had only meant to close his eyes for a short while, resting on his straw pallet after the day's labour, but when he woke, night had fallen and the room was dark.

A quiet knocking at his door had woken him. He rose and listened, frowning.

'Goodluck? Are you there?'

In a guilty rush he remembered his arrangement with Lucy, and was suddenly alert. He drew back the bolt and opened the door. She stood in the doorway, holding a small lantern, the flame sharply illuminating her face.

'Lucy, forgive me,' he managed, barely able to meet her gaze. 'I . . . I fell asleep. Come in.'

His blunt admission did not seem to ease the sudden awkwardness between them. Cloaked and hooded for disguise, Lucy looked as uncertain about this secret assignation as he was. Acutely aware of his own dishevelled appearance, Goodluck gestured her inside the room, then combed down his unkempt hair and fastened his loose-hanging shirt.

While he knelt to kindle a fire, Lucy stood in the middle of the candlelit chamber, keeping clear of the narrow window where she might have been seen from the court-yard below.

'I could not come any sooner. The Queen has not been well.'

'Yet still you came.'

She swung off her cloak, turning to face him as he straightened, her eyes lowered. Had she registered the surprise in his voice?

'As you see.'

'Did you check you were not followed?'

She bit her lip, then shook her head. 'Forgive me, I . . . I did not think.'

'No matter,' he reassured her, and managed a smile,

though in truth he was a little unsettled by her admission. To be discovered here, alone together, would not easily be explained, not even by their old relationship of guardian and child. For those days were long gone. 'I am sure we will be safe enough here from prying eyes.'

Goodluck knew his own fears about this meeting, but he had not expected Lucy herself to be shy. Not after her affair with Shakespeare. It pleased him, because it suggested feelings which matched his own. Or was that merely his own wish, preventing his ability to read Lucy as he would any other woman?

He saw her shivering, and frowned, cursing his own stupidity at not staying awake and kindling a fire earlier to warm the chamber.

'This place is too cold,' he muttered, glancing about the small, grim tower chamber where he slept. 'There is not even a chair for your comfort. I should not have asked you here at this hour.'

She came to him, rustling in her broad-skirted court gown, seed pearls along her white bodice. Her eyes met his in frankness. 'Do not say you regret it. I could not bear it if you were to send me away now. You do not know how much courage was required to climb those stairs.'

She smiled wryly, adding, 'And breath, for they are steep and many, and I am no longer young.'

He saw the fine lines about her eyes and mouth, and recognized the truth in that. He had been her guardian once, and had protected her like his own daughter. But Lucy was no longer a child. She had loved one man, and married another to hide her shame, then miscarried the ill-starred child in her belly. She knew her own mind now, and her appetites, and if she felt no strangeness in this, then why should he?

'You are younger than I am,' he pointed out.

Her smile faded. 'Goodluck, you are not old.' She put a

hand on his chest and stood, head on one side, as though listening to the beat of his heart. 'Besides, I love you.'

He drew her close, looking into her face. He had waited so long, so long . . .

And yet, if she was at all uncertain about this desire between them, he could wait a little longer. For ever, if need be. He would take nothing from Lucy that did not come willingly.

Goodluck stroked her cheek.

'And Shakespeare?'

She had not changed much since leaving her girlhood behind. Her cheek was still soft, her nature one of curiosity and goodness. Still, she was no fool, this woman he had raised. She could not only sing and dance to charm the coldest court, but could handle a knife, decode a secret message, and had even learned to smell out a villain, however cunningly he might conceal himself.

His traitorous old companion John Twist had taught her that lesson himself. Never trust anyone, however close to your heart.

Yet to love was to trust. Could Lucy do either, given her upbringing at the hands of a spy?

Could he?

'I love Will too,' she replied simply, rubbing her cheek against his hand. 'But not like I love you. When I was younger, I thought the world only turned one way. That if a woman loved a man, it was for ever and she could love no other. But I know the truth now.'

She looked stubborn, her chin jutting out, her eyes searching his in the candlelight as she struggled to explain her innermost thoughts. He let her speak, though she might have been describing his own feelings.

'There are many different kinds of love, and it is entirely possible to love more than one person at once, and even to fall out of love and into hate, then love the same person

237

again with all your heart, and not understand the reason why, but suffer the pain of this torment, and have no release except to tell them – and hope they feel the same.' Her voice broke suddenly. 'Which too often they do not.'

It was difficult to keep the anger out of his voice. 'Has Shakespeare hurt you again?'

'He no longer has the power to hurt me, Goodluck. But you do.'

'I would never hurt you.'

She smiled painfully. 'Not by design, perhaps.'

'Lucy,' he muttered.

Her gaze moved to his mouth, and he could not help himself. He took her by the shoulders and kissed her, his touch urgent. His hands stroked to her waist, then suddenly the chill air took flame, burning between them like the logs in the hearth.

She helped him with her gown, all intricate fastenings and frustrating silken layers he had not known with the women he had lain with before. Nor was her body like that of any other woman he had seen naked, being strong and black, her curves bold and womanly, almost statuesque. He wrenched at his own clothes, but she did not seem inclined to wait, so they collapsed together on to the straw pallet with him half clothed, his need for her obvious, her mouth on his. She knew what to do, as eager for this consummation as he was, her hands less shy than her smile as she moved him inside her.

He gasped, looking up at her naked and astride him. Her spirit shone out in the dark of the evening, her body glowing as she rose and fell as though dancing with him, her dark-tipped breasts flickering with firelight.

Beautiful, beautiful, beautiful.

'I love you,' he whispered, and she leaned forward, laughing, kissing his mouth.

'I love you too, Goodluck.'

He captured her hands in his, drawing them to his bared chest. Her skin was so warm. 'My Christian name is Faithful.'

'Faithful,' she repeated, then kissed him again, more lingeringly. 'I should have known. It suits you.'

'I cannot think why I hid it from you.'

Her smile was slow. 'Because I did not need to know you were Faithful until this moment.'

Her naked limbs rubbed against his, drawing a groan of exquisite pleasure from him. He could bear much more of this torment, he realized, and felt his control begin to slip.

Almost feverish in his haste, Goodluck drew her down to him. He kissed her bare shoulder, her throat, her delicious mouth, then turned her over on the straw pallet so that she lay beneath him.

He dragged off his shirt, suddenly burning hot in the chill of the wintry evening, then pressed her down into the rough mattress, muttering between her breasts, 'You truly want this, Lucy? You are certain? We must be careful. I do not wish to make a child.'

'I will not stop you.'

Lucy stroked down his back, her eyes huge and dark, her lips parted with passion, and it was all he could do not to achieve his end there and then.

'Then you should,' he muttered thickly, staring down at her naked body. 'God forbid I ever ruin you in the eyes of the court.'

Her presence in his bed felt like a dream. He had to remind himself that she was no longer a child, no longer his ward, his responsibility. Yet he could not control the desire driving him. To love her was a fantasy of such dizzying lustful power that it threatened to drive him out of his mind, his whole body shaking at the strangeness and yet familiarity of her warm skin against his.

Her kiss nearly undid him, her tongue dancing sweetly

with his. She whispered in his ear, 'Ruin me if you must, Faithful. But love me. Make me yours. I cannot wait any longer.'

'I have waited years . . .' Goodluck managed, then lost all hope of coherent speech as her hips rose to meet his, her strong legs wrapped about his back to urge him on.

'Lucy,' he groaned, and drove hard into her. 'My love, my love.'

Goodluck woke in the night to find her stroking him, her dark eyes watching him with passionate intent, and his desire rose urgently again to match hers. He had not withdrawn to prevent his seed from filling her the first time, and when he pushed her back into the warmth of the straw pallet, he knew he would not pull out this time either. There had been a recklessness and an air of inevitability to their first-ever lovemaking, and she had seemed to desire their union as much as he did. Now she wanted him again.

He groaned pleasurably as Lucy parted her thighs and drew him back inside her, their bodies moving with one purpose. All other thoughts were pushed aside before his desire for her, a need which kept him hard and eager, his stamina that of a young man again.

And yet he should use his head, for this night might bring dangerous consequences for them both. She was still young enough to conceive by him.

If there should be a child, he told himself firmly, he would marry her at once, and so prevent Lucy from falling into dishonour at court. Then he remembered Shakespeare, and how that young man had used her like this, night after night, with no thought of marriage, and his desire was suddenly tainted with bitterness and an old fury.

'Come away from court with me,' he urged her, slowing his thrusts. 'Before the month is out.'

'Leave court?' She sounded startled.

He stopped, supporting his weight on his hands. Looking down into her face, illuminated by the glowing embers in the hearth, he knew a terrible moment of fear. Fear that this flood of happiness would be fleeting, that the rituals of courtly life would soon intrude again, the dreariness of custom and habit, and they would be broken apart.

'It is the only way for us to be together. Come away secretly with me, and we shall be married in the country. I'll take you in disguise to my brother's farm in Oxfordshire. It is an isolated spot, and safe enough. No one will think to look for us there.'

'I cannot,' she whispered in the darkness, staring up at him. Her desire seemed to fall away sharply. 'The Queen—'

'You love me?' he interrupted her.

'Yes.'

'And you intend to be with me for the rest of your life?'

Lucy hesitated, her dark eyes wide with fear and uncertainty. His heart juddered with the sudden suspicion that she would reject him and go back to Shakespeare.

He did not know what he would do if Lucy were to put him aside after their lovemaking tonight. Find Shakespeare and run him through with his blade, and go readily to the gibbet for his murder. For there would be little purpose in staying alive once he had tasted this love, then been kicked aside for such a wastrel.

But to his relief she did not reject him.

'Yes,' she whispered at last. 'This change between us is strange, and yet not strange. It feels right to love you as a man, not simply my guardian. It is as though everything I have ever done has been leading to this. And I do love you, with all my heart. But for us to be married . . . No, it cannot be like this. Not without warning, without even Her Majesty's permission. We would be hunted down and punished. Let me wait for the right time to ask Her Majesty, not before.'

'I cannot lie with you, and not marry you,' he insisted doggedly, and hoped she would not mistake his sternness for tyranny. Everything else he would concede to her as his wife, but not this. Not her honour. 'I watched over you and advised you as a child, Lucy. Trust me to make this decision for you now.'

'Goodluck, I love you dearly, but I cannot let you make such a dangerous decision. I know the Queen, and you do not. She is a cruel and jealous mistress, and will not take kindly to any man stealing me away from court. I would not see you punished like others who have dared to love one of her ladies behind the Queen's back.'

'But—'

Lucy laid a finger on his lips. 'Hush, let me be your guide this time. I will marry you, I give you my word. But it must be done as I say, or we shall both suffer the consequences.'

'And if the Queen does not give her consent, and you find yourself with child, what then?'

Lucy stroked a slow wanton hand from his chest to his groin, leaving him throbbing with renewed desire, his need for her almost painful. 'Then we will run away from court as you suggest, and change our names, live as vagabonds, and hope they never find us. Tonight though, I do not wish to talk of the Queen, nor of spies, nor of running away.'

She smiled up at him, and he saw the same passion in her face. 'Tonight I just need you to love me.'

242

Three

STIFFLY, ELIZABETH TOOK UP THE REINS AGAIN AND TURNED her horse's head back to face the way they had come. It was February, and even encased in fleece-lined kid gloves her fingers were numb with cold.

'Let us ride back to Greenwich Palace,' she told her entourage, and saw the relief on their raw-nipped faces. Too long cooped up inside during the snows, they had followed her and Lord Burghley cheerfully enough through the palace gates and into the woodlands beyond, their bridles jingling, their horses' hooves sounding like gentle thunder along the ice-hardened paths. But as the air grew colder, even she had begun to doubt the wisdom of this excursion. Still, it was good to breathe fresh air again instead of the stewed fog of the smoky palace chambers.

Coming to a familiar clearing, Elizabeth had pulled up sharp and sat on her mount looking about at the woodland scene, remembering other wintry rides she had taken with Robert Dudley by her side. Robert had been her Master of the Horse for many years, his effortless horsemanship always a pleasure to watch. Essex held the post now, but he was no match on a horse for his step father. An excellent horseman but he lacked Leicester's vitality, the sense that he was one with the animal he rode.

Dearest Robert, she thought, and patted her horse's neck absentmindedly.

At her back, the impatient courtiers muttered among themselves and waited to see what she would do next, some walking their horses up and down to keep warm, the animals' breath steaming out in great clouds on the frosty air. And now she had turned her horse for home, the courtiers fell back in disarray to let her pass, their horses milling about in sudden confusion.

'Which of you advised me that the winter snows were thawing and it was safe to ride out again?' she demanded petulantly of nobody in particular. 'Whoever it was, the fool should be whipped. The snow may be melting, but it is too icy to ride, and the north wind is like a knife in my back.'

'Indeed, the spring is not yet upon us,' Lord Burghley commented, her secretary of state riding at her side in Essex's absence. She wished he would not make the effort to accompany her out on horseback, for his health had been ailing for some years now and it hurt to see his lordship so grey and drawn, sitting upright as ever but clearly in pain. 'Yet some greenery braves the cold to herald its coming, Your Majesty.'

She followed the direction of his pointing arm, and smiled to see a few doughty snowdrops piercing the scattered snow and ice along the woodland ride.

Elizabeth wished she had the same native courage as those flowers. But then her spring years were long over; all she had to look forward to was deepening winter, her body increasingly frail, even if she was not yet as elderly as Lord Burghley. The weather mirrored her own wretched state, each day since Advent dawning dark with an overcast sky and threat of further snow. Her people suffered too. This winter had been particularly hard, with tales reaching her ears of country folk found frozen to death in their own homes, or foolhardy commoners drowned by falling through ice on the Thames as they attempted to cross the ice-locked upper stretches of the river on foot. And the continuing fear of a Spanish invasion could not be shaken from them; like dogs with a bone, the people held firm to their hatred of King Philip and his Catholic hordes, and grumbled that she had not yet brought this long war to a successful end.

Some of her younger ladies, riding a short distance behind, broke the amiable quiet of the woodlands with a burst of immoderate laughter. Elizabeth slowed and glared over her shoulder. At her frown, they fell silent, most looking away with downcast eyes.

Ignorant young girls!

She looked for Helena among their number, meaning to reprimand her for allowing such misbehaviour, then belatedly recalled that the Swedish noblewoman had fallen sick and was being nursed in bed. The oldest of her ladies that day was Lucy Morgan, ducking her head as she rode beneath the ice-covered branches, her dark face glowing with apparent pleasure at this outing.

Elizabeth studied her suspiciously, for Lucy was not a natural horsewoman and was wont to look uncertain and fidgety on her mount. And there were still whispered rumours about her African lady-in-waiting. Rumours which Elizabeth tended to put down to ill will among the other women.

But this smiling look . . .

The path gradually opened up as they left the dark gloaming of the woods behind. Under a lighter sky, she urged her horse on and the others followed, the whole cavalcade beginning to ride more swiftly back towards the palace. Cows lowed sulkily from somewhere beyond white-encrusted hedgerows, and she caught the herder's

245

hoarse cries as he drove them back up the slope from milking. Closer now she could see the icy thread of the river through the trees, and smoke rising from a hamlet of ramshackle, snow-covered buildings along the road towards London.

Was Lucy Morgan once again playing between the sheets? There had been a poet who had pursued her once, then a short-lived marriage without permission, and a still-born child. Although a widow need not be watched as closely as a maid, nonetheless Elizabeth had a duty towards her attendants and she intended to uphold it. She could not allow her ladies-in-waiting to despoil their honour with every chance courtier who admired them. She had sent young Bess Throckmorton to the Tower for dallying with the roughly handsome Raleigh – that whole episode had left her sick and furious – so Lucy Morgan should expect a similar punishment if she had any secret love to conceal.

Elizabeth felt a profound distaste at the thought of any courtier lying with the dark-eyed, dark-skinned Lucy Morgan. And what of a child that might come from such a union?

It did not bear thinking about.

She shivered as the icy wind tore at her, and wished angrily that she was back in her Privy Chamber with a greedy fire in the hearth and a lacy woollen shawl to keep her back and shoulders warm. She was surrounded by fools and slatterns, obsequious charlatans who wrongly informed her that it was warm enough to ride out again, lustful women who could not keep their chastity much beyond their fifteenth year, and ambitious youths on every corner, jabbering at her for this and that, pestering her for honours she had no wish to bestow, and ruining her ladies while their keepers turned a blind eye to such whorings.

The palace gates were in sight, the liveried guards

standing stiffly to attention for her approach, their pikes upright.

Elizabeth steadied her mount and allowed Lord Burghley, riding sturdily some three hundred paces to her rear, to catch up with her.

'Any new word from my lord Essex?' she asked lightly, trying to sound as though she did not care, when in truth the earl's absence pained her more each day. 'Is he indeed unwell again, as he wrote to tell me yesterday, or is this another of his elaborate excuses not to come to court?'

Lord Burghley gave her a look which was not hard to read. He might not see through her as readily as Walsingham had always done, but he was no fool. 'I believe he has been taken sick, yes. Though not so unwell that you need fear for his safety, Your Majesty. Indeed, he was able to send me a note this morning, pertaining to various matters of state which we have been discussing in the council.'

Something in his tone made her take interest. 'Which matters are those? Our war with Spain?'

'Do you remember Don Antonio, Your Majesty?'

She nodded, bending forward to stroke her mount's black neck as the animal neighed restlessly, accustomed to a faster pace than this. As she recalled, the man was a Portuguese noble with some claim to the throne of Portugal, currently held by King Philip of Spain. Don Antonio had come to the English court a few years ago, begging asylum on the grounds that King Philip wished him dead, and she had granted it, even giving him some small property.

'I do indeed,' she agreed. 'You and the council advised me that he could prove a useful tool in our fight against Spain. But so far he has been nothing but an expense on our throne. If Don Antonio is demanding more money, he can go whistle for it in the streets. I do not care if the man is destitute, I shall not grant him a penny further until he can prove his worth to us.'

'He is not destitute, though near to it,' Burghley told her drily, 'but that is not why I mention him. The council has had intelligence of another Portuguese gentleman living within the walls of London, a rogue called Ferreira who was once in Don Antonio's pay. It seems he has turned his coat and now offers his services to Philip as a spy – and possibly a murderer.'

She frowned. 'And this has become common knowledge?'

'It seems he fled from his master once his treachery had been uncovered. Now he takes refuge in a Portuguese home in Holborn. But his secret is known only to a few, and we would like it to remain so. With the mood of the people so ugly these days, their hand turned against any foreigner whom they suspect of treason, we would risk Ferreira being killed on the streets if his guilt became more widely known.' He hesitated, glancing at her. 'Lord Essex feels this matter is worth investigating further. He would like a warrant to arrest Ferreira quietly, take him back to his master Don Antonio in Eton, and question him.'

'Why does Lord Essex wish to take this traitor all the way back to Don Antonio? If the man is already in London, surely Robert could question him more conveniently at Essex House?'

Burghley cleared his throat delicately. 'It appears my lord Essex has little command of the Portuguese tongue, and Ferreira is not exactly fluent in English. His lordship believes that Don Antonio will be able to provide a translator for this interview.'

She smiled grimly. 'So this move is not part of Robert's homespun campaign against the Spanish, a sop to placate Don Antonio who no doubt wishes to have this fellow thrashed and decked in chains?'

248

'I could not pass comment on Lord Essex's motives, Your Majesty. But I do believe we need to take this seriously. Ferreira may already have passed information to King Philip about our defences, even if he has no other information to give. Also, we need to discover whether he has acted alone, or if there is a nest of traitors involved in his plot to betray and possibly murder Don Antonio, whom – we should not forget – England has been supporting in his claim to the throne of Portugal.'

'A nest?'

Burghley hesitated. His face was troubled. 'I have not mentioned this to you before, Your Majesty. But there is a troubling connection between this man Ferreira and your royal personage.'

Their horses had walked side by side into the palace courtyard, and through the arched gateway into the inner court. She dismounted, aided by two gentlemen of the stables, just as the rest of the cavalcade filed through the gates, the clatter of the horses' hooves echoing noisily throughout the courtyard.

'How so?' she demanded coldly, preceding her secretary into the chilly maze of corridors that led to the Great Hall.

Courtiers fell to their knees as she passed, their heads respectfully bent, muttering, 'Your Majesty.'

She ignored them, worrying away at what Burghley had said. They passed through the busy Presence Chamber, crowded with courtiers hoping to put their petitions before her or present their young sons and daughters, but she did not stop until she was safely inside the Privy Chamber and had signalled the doors to be closed against the noise and bustle of the mob outside.

'I am almost afraid to disclose it, Your Majesty,' Burghley said quietly, going straight to the hearthside and pouring them both a cup of warm, spiced wine from the jewelled flagon waiting there.

She stripped off her gloves and took the cup from him, inhaling the fragrant warmth of the wine.

'Speak, old friend, and do not fear reprisals for being the bearer of bad tidings,' Elizabeth told him impatiently, and met his eyes with candour. 'I may be famed for my ill temper, and rightly so, but you are exempt from its worst ravages. Besides, after thirty-five years' service to my throne, surely there can be no need for such caution on your part?'

'Very well, Your Majesty. The house where this traitor Ferreira took refuge,' he murmured, 'is the home of Rodriguez Lopez, your personal physician, who is himself a Portuguese Jew – though he calls himself a Christian.'

Late that evening, fetched to the palace from his London home, Master Lopez was escorted into the Privy Chamber, flanked by four guardsmen with pikes as though she was at risk from this old man.

'You are dismissed,' Elizabeth told the guards, and they withdrew, bowing, though she noticed with some irritation that the men glanced at Lord Burghley and his son Robert Cecil for confirmation before backing away.

She remained standing to question her physician, as was her custom in the public chambers, for she disliked being considered weak. Catching Cecil's astute glance, she nodded briskly to Lopez, who had served as her doctor for many years and been more intimate with her than any other living man in England.

Master Lopez stared about the room in despair, as though fearing he had been condemned without trial. His sombre black robes declared his profession as physician, while a large silver cross hanging from his neck proclaimed him a Christian. His skin was dark, swarthy rather than olive, his eyes a deep nut-brown, and his features were markedly Jewish. She had never considered his personal history before, having once satisfied herself that he was a Christian. Now though she looked at her physician with fresh eyes, wondering if Burghley and Essex could be mistaken in their suspicions.

Surely they *must* be mistaken, though. Master Lopez had attended her for years without causing her or any other person in her household harm. Why would this Portuguese gentleman, having been well rewarded with wealth and respect, suddenly cast aside his many years of loyal service to the English crown to bow the knee to a Spanish king whose claim to Portugal's throne was tenuous and unpopular?

It made no sense whatsoever.

But no doubt Essex was hungry for success in his long fruitless hunt for a traitor in her household, she thought grimly. She recalled a short comedy presented before her the previous year, entitled *A Knack to Know a Knave*. She now wished fervently that she possessed such a knack. But lacking it, she must make do with asking questions instead.

'Come forward, Senhor Lopez,' she ordered him coolly. 'Do not look so afraid. You are not on trial here, nor accused of anything. I merely wish to address a few questions to you on the subject of your recent guest, Senhor Ferreira.'

Senhor Lopez came forward, cap in hand, and fell to his knees before her. 'Your Majesty, forgive me,' he began, his hands clasped together, his face upturned in the firelight. 'I am a foolish old man. I took Senhor Ferreira into my home because he was a fellow countryman who came to my door in the middle of the night, with a tale of having been turned out in the winter cold by his master over some misunderstanding. I had no knowledge that he was a traitor to the most excellent Don Antonio, nor to England, a country I have made my home these past thirty

251

years and would protect with my life. I swear there is nothing sinister behind my sheltering of this man, Your Majesty. My only sin was an excess of charity which I now bitterly regret.'

She listened in silence to this impassioned speech, then asked, 'I am told you are no Christian, as I was led to believe when you first joined my household, but in fact a Jew.'

'Not true! I swear by Almighty God that I am a good and devout Christian like yourself.' Her Portuguese physician crossed himself, then lifted the silver cross at his neck and touched it most reverently to his lips. 'I was born and brought up in Christianity by my enlightened parents, and am a true believer in Jesus Christ. I call on His most holy and precious blood to open the eyes of those who have wrongly accused me. May I die a thousand deaths in Hell if I have in any way wronged or deceived you, Your Majesty. I am your faithful servant, and no traitor.'

Elizabeth studied him thoughtfully. She did not believe he was a traitor. But as Burghley had suggested, the old man might have been led astray by promises of great rewards if he lent his support to the Spanish cause instead of his adopted country, England. And he did look like a Jew. Those who outwardly professed Christianity but practised their Jewish faith in secret were known as Marranos. Could he be one of those?

Lord Burghley stirred and came forward into the light, as though concerned that her questioning was not stringent enough. 'This is a Christian country, sir, and a Protestant one. If you are racked and found to be a Marrano and a traitor to your queen, you will die a traitor's death on the scaffold.' He waited, but the old man said nothing, staring up at his accuser in horror. 'Best to confess your crimes now and beg for leniency.'

'My lord, I have no crimes to confess,' Lopez answered

252

him, still on his knees. He turned his grey head back towards Elizabeth, and she saw terror in his face. 'Please, Your Majesty, spare my life. I have done nothing but take in a man from the cold of whose good character I felt assured. Indeed, I still cannot believe Senhor Ferreira to be a traitor to his master and his country. Why would he betray a nobleman who may yet, God willing, rightfully ascend the throne of Portugal?'

She nodded, and looked at Lord Burghley. 'I have heard enough, my lord, and am convinced this man has no guilt to answer. Let him return to his duties and his home unmolested.'

'But, Your Majesty, Senhor Lopez gave succour to a suspected traitor, a man who may well prove to be one of King Philip's assassins . . .' Robert Cecil stared at her, aghast, his voice only falling into silence when his father placed a cautious hand on his arm.

She heard the incredulity in the young man's voice, but would not relent. 'Closely question this Senhor Ferreira to discover the truth, as you would any other suspected traitor, and bring your findings before me. But I will brook no more false accusations against my physician. Is that understood?'

Lopez had begun to tremble, no doubt with relief that he was not about to be dragged away to prison and a traitor's death.

'I thank you, Your Majesty,' he managed hoarsely, settling his black velvet cap back on his head as he attempted to compose himself. 'I knew your mercy and compassion would save me. You are indeed the wisest prince in Europe, a most gracious and Christian queen.'

'You may leave us, Senhor,' she told him, her tone not altogether friendly, 'though in future, you would be better advised to bar your door against those of your countrymen who would trespass against your hospitality.'

'Yes, Your Majesty,' he whispered, and promptly withdrew, bowing so low his cap tumbled off and he had to snatch it up from the rushes. 'May the Lord bless and preserve you, Your Majesty.'

Robert Cecil hurried after him, taking his leave in a rushed manner, muttering, 'Forgive me, Your Majesty, but an order was sent out to arrest Senhor Lopez's son, who is at Winchester School. It must be rescinded at once.'

Left alone with her secretary in the Privy Chamber, Elizabeth raised her eyebrows at him. 'You were having his son arrested? A schoolboy?'

Burghley had the grace to look embarrassed. 'Lord Essex thought he might be better placed to extract a confession from Lopez if his son was also in custody.'

'I see,' she said drily.

'We have not acted out of malice or prejudice,' he pointed out mildly, 'but thought only to secure Your Majesty's person from a suspected assassin. Senhor Ferreira was unlikely ever to gain access to the court, even in disguise, so his threat was always more to Don Antonio. But if he had been able to influence your physician into some malignant action against you, a man so intimately placed in your household—'

She held up a hand, interrupting him. 'I understand your motives, my lord, and hold you in no less regard for your zeal in pursuing this matter. But equally it is clear that my lord Essex has not been successful in hunting down the traitor he believes to be lurking here at court, and that the unfortunate Senhor Lopez was to be his lamb to the slaughter, offered up to hide my lord's failure.'

'I am sure that was not his lordship's intention, Your Majesty, any more than it was mine. '

She became stern. 'Hear me, my lord. I shall not budge on this matter of Senhor Lopez, or not without the strongest, most irrefutable evidence against his loyalty. If you and Essex must seek a traitor at court, take care you search for him elsewhere, not among my most trusted and learned servants.'

Lord Burghley bowed. 'Yes, Your Majesty.'

'You will convey this instruction to Lord Essex straight away, if you please,' she told him, then called him back when he turned to leave. Her conscience was troubling her, for she knew Essex's temper was as sharp and easily roused as her own, and being still young, he lacked Leicester's charm and diplomacy in times of disagreement. After today's unsettling events, she did not have the strength to face another show of fireworks between them. 'Wait!'

'Your Majesty?'

'Be sure to tell his lordship that this failure has not prejudiced my belief in his loyalty and good service to the throne. Without his vigilance, this Senhor Ferreira might have continued his treacherous schemes undetected.' She considered for a moment. 'Ask Lord Essex to attend me promptly tomorrow morning, if he is able to rise from his sickbed, and we shall discuss his reward.'

Some premonition flickered in Burghley's face. He stiffened. 'You surely do not mean to admit his lordship to the Privy Council, Your Majesty?'

'Is it any of your concern, my lord?' she demanded icily.

Her secretary bowed, betraying a twinge of pain. Was he unwell again? 'Forgive me, Your Majesty. I did not mean to be impertinent. I will convey your message to his lordship tonight.'

'Send a servant with a note,' she told him, 'and get you to bed. It is late.'

He smiled wearily. 'Thank you, Your Majesty. Give you good night.'

'Good night, my old friend. And sleep well.'

Elizabeth signalled to the steward to allow her ladies to

approach, for she was overtired herself and ready for her bedchamber.

'We are safe enough from King Philip's assassins here, whatever Lord Essex might say. All the same, with this new worry, and the plague back in the city, it might be prudent to move the court out to Richmond for a few months.' She closed her eyes, already wishing herself among the peaceful open fields of Richmond, a good ride west of Greenwich. 'There should be better hunting there, anyway.'

Four

'SHAKESPEARE? WILLIAM SHAKESPEARE? WHAT IN THE NAME of all that's holy are you doing in a brothel in Southwark?'

Kit Marlowe stared down at the buxom girl in Will's lap, squirming pleasantly as he tried to study his cards around her fulsome figure.

'And a good evening to you too, Master Marlowe,' Will managed, then grinned, pleased that he had not slurred his words despite the large amount of ale he had consumed that day. 'What does it look like I'm doing?'

Kit's eyebrows shot up as he took in the unfastened doublet, the fresh pitcher of ale on the stained table, and the flushed faces of the good-natured fellows with whom Will was playing cards.

'I had heard that Master Shakespeare was a little wild these days, but this is beyond even what I had envisaged.' He paused, becoming serious for a moment. 'I am glad to see you in London though. I thought you had disappeared off to the country again.'

Will raised his brows at that unpleasant suggestion. 'Not I.'

Kit looked thoughtful. 'I have been reading that epic poem you sent me. *Venus and Adonis*. It is a rare piece of work, Will, far better than anything you have written for the stage. I tell you, reading it made me sick with jealousy. That poem will make your name.'

Will was surprised by this unexpected praise. He felt heat in his face, and did not know what to say. 'I thank you, Kit.'

'Your patron is the Earl of Southampton?'

'Yes, and a more generous patron I could not have hoped for.' Will caught an odd expression on Marlowe's face. 'What is it?'

'Only that powerful men make dangerous bedfellows.' Marlowe looked at the girl in Will's lap, and his friend had the impression that Kit was trying to distract him. 'Is this your catch of the night? Are you in such a rush to catch the pox? Because if so, I can suggest whores of even less repute than this pretty jug in your lap.'

'I'm here with Dick Burbage,' Will replied shortly, playing his hand to jeers from the other men. 'Damn, I'm out.'

'I'm not surprised, with cards that bad.' Kit frowned, glancing around the brothel's smoky room. 'Where is Dick?'

'Upstairs.'

'I see.' Kit smiled as Will extricated himself with difficulty from the whore's arms, amid her shrill protests. 'Are you not heading that way yourself, then?'

At that moment, Dick Burbage appeared in the low doorway, his clothing dishevelled. He spread his arms wide at the sight of them. 'Kit, my friend! What, are you here too? Come and join us, there's plenty of soft flesh in this house to go round, if you don't mind dipping your ladle in the same barrel as the rest of us.'

Burbage stumbled into the room, a fair-haired girl on his arm, her gown pulled down to expose large, pink-skinned breasts with prominent nipples, her face drowsy with too much ale.

'Will!' he exclaimed, dragging the girl forward so that she cried out and stumbled, almost falling into Will's arms. 'See, I found the girl I was telling you about. She's a trifle drunk, which mars all, but when her head clears, I swear she will show you a trick with her purse to surpass any performance you have ever seen, in bed or on stage.'

'I can't wait,' Will said drily.

'Well, sir, you must,' Burbage rejoined sharply, slapping him on the back. 'Consider our parts. I like to play the nobleman, you prefer to play the pauper. And as every fellow knows, the prince must be served before the pauper.'

Kit gave a bark of laughter at this exchange. He shook his head and moved away to speak to a foreign-looking man at the counter. There was a brief exchange, then the man handed him something and left the room.

Watching uneasily, Will could not see what it was the man had given him, but saw Kit push it hurriedly into the leather pouch on his belt.

Marlowe came back to the table, still laughing. 'Shall we retire upstairs then, and see this trick?' he asked, surprising Will, who had thought he had little love for women. 'I have a few shillings to throw in the kitty if you're short.'

'Short?' Burbage belched loudly at this implied insult, and shook his head in mock anger. 'No such thing, I promise you. And this little kitty will vouch for that later tonight. Why, she'll be walking stiff for a sennight after our sport. Won't you, my sweet Marjorie?'

'Margaret,' the girl corrected him sourly, no doubt sobering up at the prospect of three on one, but allowed Burbage to lead her back towards the stairs.

They passed an open door at the head of the stairs. Within the narrow smoky chamber Will could see men playing illegally at dice. Beyond their table, a girl lay nude and shameless on a straw pallet, so thin that her ribs showed through her skin. Her legs were still sprawled wide from where they had used her, her thumb in her mouth like a child, fast asleep despite the shouts and laughter around her.

'With the plague raging and the Rose shut down, what is there to do but lie with whores and play dice?' Burbage declared, staring lewdly in at the naked girl on the bed. 'Do the city fathers not understand that closing the theatres leads us poor players into sin, not out of it? Come, girl, where is this chamber? I am eager to be up and at it.'

The girl Margaret obediently showed them to a room further along the upper landing. It was cramped, just one bed, and stank like a fishhouse, but Will barely considered this as he kicked the door shut – this was no stage, and he would not be watched by strangers while he performed – and jerked the fair-haired girl towards him.

He kissed her mouth, which was not so sweet as he had hoped, then ran his hands over her full breasts. A driving need for debauchery had taken hold of him in recent months, his lust insatiable, as though each girl he used was another blow against Lucy's hold on his heart.

Lucy! Lucy! She was lost to him. He should not even think her name.

And yet he could not help but bring her to mind every morning when he woke and every night when he lay down to sleep. To remember her face was a pain beyond anything he had ever felt, a hammer-blow to his manhood. He told himself he hated her, and meant it, but the agony such reminders brought could mean only one thing: that he still loved her, and had been rejected.

The only way to drown out her incessant name in his head was to lie with other women, to indulge his lust for this sweet flesh until he was wholly emptied of it.

'Margaret,' he muttered savagely, and dragged her gown

260

down to her waist, rubbing his thumbs back and forth across her nipples until they grew large and stiff. 'Sweet Margaret.'

He remembered Lucy's voice in the darkness of the palace garden, spinning her wicked lies about his patron, telling him the Earl of Southampton had warned her not to see him again. And yet Henry Wriothesley, the earl himself, had given him a girl to enjoy at his grand palace; they had even shared the whore between them that night, and several times since, when Will had been invited to join Henry and his wealthy friends again as they drank and caroused through the long cold winter. So why would Henry warn Lucy off? It made no sense.

The only explanation must be that Lucy had fallen out of love with Will and sought an excuse to part from him that would not bring her blame.

Damn her, still haunting him!

'Hey, Shakespeare, not so greedy, if you please. Leave some for us,' Burbage told him laughingly. He lifted the girl's tousled fair hair and kissed her throat.

Margaret moaned and let her loosened gown fall obligingly past her hips to the floor. Burbage slapped one of her buttocks with a resounding crack; the girl gave a mewling protest but did not attempt to pull away, clearly used to such rough treatment.

'Come, shall we toss a coin to see who fucks her first? I call heads.'

But the girl was gazing across the room at Marlowe instead, brazen in her nakedness, licking her lips greedily as though drawn to his good looks.

Will muttered, 'I'll go tails,' though he was already erect and itching to sink himself inside her.

Oblivious to the girl's interest, Kit Marlowe had taken up a position at the window and was staring down into the dark street. He seemed uneasy, watching those passing below, not even glancing at the girl's nudity, and Will recalled some talk about Marlowe's preference being for young men. He had been friends once with the unfortunate Jack Parker, who had married Lucy and met his death at some brigand's hands.

Lucy, again. His mind had come full circle.

'Enough talk. Let's have at it,' he managed hoarsely, wishing it was Lucy before them, dark-skinned Lucy, her ripe breasts in his hands, her urgent whispers in his ear.

Marlowe had unfastened his pouch and withdrawn a small coin. This he tossed in the air, catching the coin as it descended and slapping it down on the back of his hand.

'Heads it is,' Kit declared, then grinned at Will's expression. 'Never mind, Master Shake-Your-Spear, you can go next. Indeed, I'll leave you two gentlemen to share the spoils between you. I've just remembered there's a man I'm to meet at the Angel tonight.'

'Wait, you're not staying?' Margaret demanded, suddenly coming to life, hands on hips, apparently vexed by this insulting refusal of her services.

'I cannot, my fair whore,' he replied, barely acknowledging her with a glance. 'Another time, perhaps.'

Her eyes spat venom at him. 'Such a fine gentleman too, walking in here like you own the place. I've seen you here before, and in better company than this, when there were three or four girls paid for, and other games besides. But I suppose I'm not good enough for you this time. Or perhaps I am not cut to your taste, being too womanly.' Lasciviously, she cupped her large breasts, her nipples so duskily pink it looked as though she had painted them with rouge, and offered them to Marlowe. 'I'm clean, you know. I wash every Sunday. Not like most of the whores in this filthy town.'

But Kit merely laughed at this naive speech, turning to leave. Margaret, infuriated by his response to her outburst, struck out at him, all sharp claws like a cat, hissing between her teeth. The player staggered backwards, taken by surprise, and fell across the narrow wooden-framed cot which passed for a bed. Kit grunted, jumping back to his feet at once, and fiercely slapped the girl's face before Will could intervene.

She yelped and clutched at her reddening cheek, staring up at him in hurt and accusation. 'Bastard!'

'You deserved that, you little wildcat.' Kit was breathless. He bowed briefly, tidying his clothes. 'Gentlemen, I wish you joy of this termagant. For myself, I have sweeter pleasures in mind tonight than those to be enjoyed at such a stinking nunnery as this one.'

Will bent, retrieving a glinting object that had rolled under the cot. 'This fell from your pouch, Kit.'

It was a diamond ring.

Burbage swore under his breath, then stared at Kit in narrow-eyed suspicion. 'Why, Master Marlowe, that's a pretty bauble, and fit for a nobleman's finger. Where in God's name did you get it? You could buy a share or two in Henslowe's company with a jewel like that.'

'Mind your own business, Burbage. Go back to your playhouse and leave me to mine.'

His face oddly pale, Kit snatched the ring from Will's open palm and thrust it back into the pouch on his belt, tightening the drawstring to keep it secure. He left the room without another word.

Burbage caught the petulant girl in his arms when she would have stormed after him. 'Quiet, wench, the fool's gone, do you hear me? And we need not miss him.'

Torn between curiosity at Kit's newfound wealth and his urgent lust for the girl, her breasts jiggling pleasantly as she struggled in Burbage's arms, Will gave in to his baser desire.

'Hold the girl still for me, Burbage,' he muttered, and

kissed her mouth again, this time pushing an exploratory hand between her thighs.

Burbage caught his lusty mood, grinning at him over her shoulder. He drew the whore towards the cot, already unlacing his hose. 'Come, Margaret, show my friend that trick you do with your rose purse, and there'll be an extra shilling in it for you.'

Wandering home alone, stumbling through the narrow streets with not even a lantern to light his way, Will found some solace in the moonless night. He felt empty and ashamed of his sport tonight at the brothel, his spirit poured out in lust for a girl who lay with any man who could produce her paltry fee of four shillings. The dark houses seemed to glower down at him like a row of judges. Not that earthly punishment was what he feared, for Anne knew nothing of his sins and no man in London would condemn him for whoring. But God's judgement on him as an adulterer and a fornicator was another matter.

How had it come to this? He had arrived in London as a fresh-faced youth, swearing he would not lie with whores but keep himself clean and faithful to his wife. Now he took a woman to his bed whenever he felt the itch, and thought nothing of such sticky pleasure, though he knew it for a sin.

'Anne sinned first,' he reminded himself unsteadily. His voice echoed off the walls as he cut through a dark alley-way to his lodgings. 'Like Eve.'

Reaching his lodgings, he found two servants outside the door, dressed in the livery of the Earl of Southampton and with a litter waiting that bore Southampton's distinctive coat of arms. The older man looked him up and down as he approached, his face expressionless. 'Master Shakespeare?'

When Will assented, surprised and still a little drunk,

the man handed him a note. He unrolled it and read the message inside.

Come at once, however late the hour. I must speak with you tonight. W.H.

He frowned over the initials, then understood. *Wriothesley, Henry.* It was from the Earl of Southampton himself.

'How long have you been waiting?' he asked.

'Two hours.'

'Is your master in London?'

'Aye, sir, and close at hand.' The man indicated the litter. 'If you would care to get in, we can be there soon enough.'

Will plucked at his dishevelled and stained clothing, in which he had been carousing most of the day. 'I would prefer to change, if you could wait a short space.'

But the man shook his head, his tone flat. 'I'm to convey you to him at once, sir.'

The journey was indeed a short one. The litter stopped outside a tall building only a few streets from Will's own lodgings, though a world away in terms of finery. He had passed it often enough when crossing the city, and admired the fine stucco and the beautifully leaded windows that overlooked the street, though he had no idea who lived there. Tonight the downstairs windows were dark, though light spilled generously from an upper room on to the street below, and two torches burned at the entrance, lighting the way.

The servants showed him inside, as courteous as if he had been a nobleman himself, and gestured him up a well-lit flight of stairs to the first floor.

He climbed the stairs, unnerved by the silence and grandeur of the place, and came to a half-open door at the top. Through it he could see a fire burning in a marble-topped fireplace, and a young man seated at a table, a wine flagon and two ornate silver cups before him, his head sunk in his hands.

Will pushed open the door. 'My lord?'

The young man stirred. It was indeed Henry Wriothesley, the Earl of Southampton. He jumped up, knocking the chair backwards. 'Will, you have come! I had begun to think you would fail me.' He seemed to be drunk, but no more than Will himself. 'Come in, come in – and close the door behind you. This place belongs to a friend. My own men are downstairs, but I cannot trust the other servants here. Can I offer you wine?'

'I thank you, yes.' Will watched, uncertain, as the earl poured wine for them both, holding out the silver cup with a smile. 'You wished to see me, my lord? An urgent matter . . .'

'Urgent? Yes.' Henry drank deeply from his own cup, then poured himself more wine. 'But here, you are not drinking.' He held out the flagon of wine and Will came forward, though his own cup was barely touched. They were standing close together. Henry smiled awkwardly, looking him up and down. 'Where have you been tonight? Out in the alehouses, by the look and smell of you. Or with a woman? And why should you not be? Even a married man must have some pleasure in these dark days.'

Will did not answer. He drank, then set his cup on the table. His hand trembled a little.

Sending for him late at night, meeting privately at the house of a friend, the place empty except for a few servants. What could this be but an assignation of the type Marlowe and his like secretly enjoyed?

Henry's arm came across his shoulder, friendly, undemanding. They were about the same height. Will was no nobleman, not even a wealthy theatre-owner like Burbage. Take away the poetry and he was nobody, a commoner living on his wits in a dangerous city where

266

commoners were dirt beneath the feet of the nobility. But in this at least he could be on equal terms with Henry Wriothesley. The thought was strangely seductive, and he found himself smiling back at the younger man, not moving away as he had intended.

Besides, part of him was curious to discover . . . .

'Will?'

He looked up from his contemplation of the floor and met Henry's dark steady gaze. 'My lord?'

'Your poem on Venus and Adonis . . . It touched me.' Closer now, his breath on Will's cheek. 'It is the best poem in English I have ever read. No, do not shake your head. It is worthy of such praise.'

'I thank you.'

'So, will you come into the country with me next month? Have you decided yet? It is to be a select party, only myself and a few friends. Afterwards we will all return to court, and drink the Queen's cellars dry instead. You will be most welcome to join us . . . if you can be spared from the theatre.'

'The city fathers closed the Rose this month, so I have no work to hand but writing. If the theatres are still closed in May . . .' He hesitated, the words coming stiffly to his tongue, barely knowing what he said, his eyes fixed on Henry's face. 'The plague, you know. I am surprised you risked coming to London, my lord, when the whole city is in fear.'

'I only stay tonight. Perhaps tomorrow too, if . . .'

Will searched the young man's face. His heart was beating so fast he felt almost sick with trepidation.

'If?'

'If you are kind to me, Shakespeare,' Henry whispered, and touched his cheek, just fingertips against his bearded jaw, tracing a butterfly's path to his mouth, so lightly Will thought at first he was mistaken. 'Will you be kind, dear heart?'

267

Will stared, and could not speak, repeating in his head the dizzying words, *dear heart, dear heart*.

Slowly, and with utmost caution, as though fearing a rebuff at any moment, Henry Wriothesley leaned forward and placed his lips over Will's own mouth.

He smelt wine on Henry's breath, felt the slight tickle of his boyish moustache, and stood wooden as a post, his whole being frozen in shock. He was being kissed by another man. The sensation was so strange, so beyond anything he had ever experienced, something violent leapt in his chest, and it was all Will could do not to knock the young man down and run from the room. Then, almost in the same moment, his groin reacted with fierce excitement, swelling in its confinement, and he heard himself groan.

Daringly, Henry pushed his tongue into his mouth, and all pretence of male friendship fell away.

Sweet Jesu . . .

Will had thought at first to suffer such unnatural attentions purely for the sake of advancement, or out of prurient curiosity, having read of sodomites in a few risky Latin passages forbidden to him at school. Instead he found himself drowning in this masculine embrace, every atom of his being shaking and falling to pieces as though he had been struck by lightning. He gripped the young earl by the shoulders, dragging him closer, his response so visceral, so unexpected, he could hardly breathe.

'Yes,' Will muttered hoarsely, and found he could no longer recall the name of that dark sweet wanton he had once loved so passionately, or the whores he had lain with since, or even the name of his fair-haired wife, waiting at home with his children. 'Yes, I will be kind.'

Five

Deptford, near London, May 1593

THE SKY WAS THICK WITH BLACK-HEADED GULLS, SCREAMING hoarsely to each other as they wheeled and circled the creek that ran down the middle of the mudflats. His cap sloping down over his face, Goodluck kicked his horse along the narrow country lane that led to Deptford and its scattering of buildings and storehouses for the shipyards.

It might seem like quiet countryside out here on the dusty road, but Goodluck could see the vast river snaking and glittering in the sunshine ahead of him, and knew he was not far from London itself. Deptford was a busy thoroughfare, a sheltered spot on the south bank of the river Thames where the old King's shipyards had been sited. Even though the threat of a Spanish invasion seemed to have passed, warships were still being built here, and as he approached the river, he could see smoke rising all along the dockyards and hear the place ring with the sound of hammering. Further into the town, he could tell from the clustered taverns and alehouses along the muddy banks that Deptford had long benefited from its river trade, and from the comings and goings of the shipbuilders.

It was about ten in the morning, and he had been shadowing Kit Marlowe since dawn.

The sun climbed steadily higher as he followed Marlowe past the church and on towards the river, the May heat intensifying the stench of exposed mud on the riverbanks, flies constantly darting about his horse's head or buzzing above the hedgerows.

At intervals, the man he was following would slow his horse, glancing over his shoulder. Goodluck too would halt, bending to brush mud from his mount's flanks, or pretending to consult the slant of the sun as it swung towards noon, one hand shielding his face. But he suspected that Marlowe knew only too well that he was being followed.

Reaching the row of taverns near the waterfront, Kit Marlowe finally slipped from his horse, secured the animal to a post, and ducked down a narrow alleyway.

Goodluck dismounted, tying up his own horse, and crept to the shadowy mouth of the alleyway.

Marlowe was standing in the shadows behind a row of houses built higher than the road to avoid the spring floods that were so frequent in this area. Head bent, he was fumbling with his riding gloves. Removing one, he tugged at a costly ring on his finger. A large golden ring that flashed as he slipped it into his belt purse. Then he dragged his glove back on and continued on his way.

Diamonds?

The back door to one of the houses stood open, a short flight of steps leading inside. Marlowe hesitated at the base of these steps, speaking to a man there, then entered the building.

Goodluck loosened the knife at his belt, then approached the house. It was no alehouse, but a rough sign at the back door signalled that ale could be bought there, and an old man was smoking a pipe on the step in the bright May sunshine.

'Good morning to you, master,' Goodluck said in a friendly manner, and touched his cap, adapting his voice to the softer accent of those who lived south of the river. 'The sun is hot today, is it not? I've heard there is good ale to be had in this house. I've been riding an hour long and could do with something to wet my throat.'

The old man looked him up and down with interest. 'From across the river, are you?'

Goodluck nodded. 'I'm looking for work on the docks.'

'Ah well, you've come to the right place. It's a busy port, Deptford, and there's always plenty of labour needed in the dockyards. Though you'll have to be strong.' The old man eyed him dubiously. 'It's work for a young man.'

'I'll manage,' Goodluck assured him easily. He glanced up the steps into the house. The corridor was dim, but he could hear voices within. Marlowe's, for certain. And another man's, deeper and more cautious. 'So the ale's good here. And it's not too crowded.'

'Aye, the ale's good enough. And Eleanor Bull only serves those she likes, so it's always a quiet house. Put on your best smile, and have a witty compliment ready for her. She likes a wit.' The old man tapped his pipe on the step, then pushed a small pinch of tobacco into the narrow bowl. 'Only don't be too forward. She's no whore, is Widow Bull.'

'Thanks, I'll bear that in mind.'

Goodluck went up the steps, unsure what he would find inside, or indeed whether he should enter the place at all. But the time for caution was past. Some five days earlier, he had received a letter from a contact in London which had worried him greatly. Marlowe had been arrested earlier in May, then mysteriously released without charge. Shortly afterwards, he had been seen in the company of

271

one Robert Pooley, one of Walsingham's inner spy ring and still known to some as a closet Catholic.

Because of this, it was muttered that Marlowe had been recruited by the Catholics. Either that, his friend suggested darkly, or Marlowe had renounced God altogether and become an atheist. In which case, he would soon die for his heresy.

Goodluck had read this letter with much misgiving, for the last time he had seen Pooley had been some seven years ago, at the arrest of that foolish young traitor Babington. It confirmed for him that Kit Marlowe was up to his neck in some conspiracy, though on whose side was still unclear. But he had never trusted Pooley, a duplicitous man who enjoyed playing both sides of every game, regardless of what it cost those who believed his smooth and consummate lies. It struck him that Kit Marlowe, clever as he was, could be an unwitting pawn in whatever game Pooley was playing. But pawn or outright villain, Marlowe might yet lead Goodluck to the secret traitor in the Queen's household.

He had taken the note to Lord Essex and been instructed not to pursue the matter any further.

'Forget Marlowe,' Essex had told him sharply. 'His activities are none of your concern.'

This in itself had made Goodluck suspicious, for while he trusted Lord Essex to guard the Queen against traitors, he did not consider the earl to be as cunning a man as his predecessor Walsingham, nor as able to steer a daring course through the devious machinations of his own spies.

So he had ignored his master's injunction to leave well alone. Although it had been difficult to explain his decision to Lucy, Goodluck had immediately quit the court at Richmond and tracked Marlowe down to the house of Sir Thomas Walsingham, cousin to Sir Francis, who was the playwright's patron. There he had waited under the trees just out of sight of the great house at Chislehurst, pacing and watching the lit windows where he could see Marlowe working by candlelight in an upper room. Early the next morning, just as dawn was beginning to lighten the dark country lanes, he had stirred awake at the sound of hoofbeats, and risen to see Marlowe riding away from the house.

Goodluck had grabbed his pack and clambered on to his horse, turning the animal's reluctant head to follow. Whatever Essex might insist, he knew that the young playwright was somehow linked to this traitor in the Queen's household, and that he must find out more.

And now he stood closer to the truth than ever. He negotiated a dark corridor in Widow Bull's house and came out into a cramped, smoky room where several men in good attire lounged at their ease, drinking and smoking as they played a game of dice. One of them, a man with a narrow, whiskered chin and small bright eyes like a weasel, was exclaiming over some poor roll of the dice, though he fell silent when he saw Goodluck, as though afraid he would report them for gambling. A thin-ribbed grey wolfhound was sprawled before the fire which lit the room. This mangy animal raised its head curiously as he paused on the threshold, then lay down again with a sigh, satisfied that he was no threat. The other men glanced up too, but seemed to lose interest when they saw his poor clothes and dusty boots.

Goodluck entered the room, and at once a sharp-eyed woman sprang out of the shadows to block his way. Her arms were folded across an expensive lacy bodice, broad skirts brushing the rushes, an apron tied about her waist. Her dark hair was streaked with grey, barely concealed by the fine widow's cap strapped under her chin.

'And who might you be?' she demanded, looking him up and down.

This must be the widow Bull, he thought, and was instantly on his guard, for his senses told him something was wrong here. This hostess was too genteel for such a house, and too much on edge.

Was this some kind of trap? And if so, for whom was it intended?

'A very good morning to you, mistress,' he replied, still using the local accent. He bowed his head, removing his cap as a mark of respect. 'My name is Master Goodcheer, and I was wondering if I could buy a cup of ale from you. I've heard there's not a finer drop of ale to be had in the whole of Deptford. Nor such a comely hostess.'

'This is a private house,' Mistress Bull told him, still barring his way. Her face was cold. 'Those who drink here do so by invitation only. There is an alehouse three doors along, the Golden Boar. Be on your way.'

'One cup,' Goodluck promised her, smiling. 'Have pity on a thirsty man, mistress.'

'Are you deaf, fellow? I have said you cannot drink here.' Her gaze dropped to his boots in disgust. 'Especially not in those dirty boots.'

'What, you cannot offer me even a small cup of ale? I have told you I can pay.' He looked at her steadily and, although he spoke quietly enough, allowed a suggestion of threat to enter his voice. 'Why, mistress, any man would think you had something to hide.'

Her gaze narrowed angrily on his face. She had just drawn breath, as though to call for assistance in removing him, when there was some commotion at the back door where Goodluck had just entered. Footsteps. Raised voices. One of them was familiar to him and he tensed, listening. Surely that was . . . ?

Mistress Bull had heard the newcomers too. She made an impatient noise under her breath and pushed past him.

'Sit down in the corner and wait,' she snapped over her

shoulder. 'I will be back with your ale, by and by. Then you must leave.'

Goodluck settled in the wooden corner seat, only too glad to be in the shadows, away from the firelight and the other men, whose curious glances had turned to the doorway now.

Replacing his cap on his head, Goodluck drew it hurriedly down to shade the upper part of his face, then turned up his jacket collar to shield the rest. He crossed one booted foot over his knee to conceal his body, then slumped in his seat like a drunkard, resting his cheek wearily on his hand. He was glad now that his beard had sprouted grey in places, for in this shadowy corner he might be mistaken for an old man, not worth a second glance.

The first man who entered looked about cautiously, then spotted the men playing dice and nodded in greeting to the weasel-like man. 'Ingram, how do you do?'

Robert Pooley, another of Walsingham's former agents. Not a man to be trusted, he was more a master of disguise than Goodluck himself, and with fewer scruples. It had once been said of Pooley that he would slit a whore's throat after using her rather than pay his shot. Certainly if he served any master, it was gold. Not England, nor the Queen, nor any of her nobles, unless they paid him for his loyalty.

The weasel-faced man at the table had stood up and shaken Pooley's hand, introducing him to the others so softly that Goodluck could hear nothing. But when a second man entered, younger than Pooley, a man with golden hair that curled to his shoulder like a girl's, this fellow shook hands with the man standing, then introduced himself to the seated dice players as 'Master Nicholas Skeres, at your service,' not bothering to lower his voice.

Goodluck showed no reaction to that name, but his heart had leapt. Nicholas Skeres. Named as one of the Babington conspirators, he had never been brought to trial. Now it was clear why not. Because he had been in Walsingham's pay all along.

And now Skeres was one of Essex's men, no doubt.

He felt a cold sweat break out on his palms and tried to remain calm. But it seemed to Goodluck that he had stumbled across a secret meeting in Mistress Bull's house. A meeting of spies to which he himself had not been invited. But to what purpose had it been called? Were all these men double agents in Spanish pay, or had Goodluck been excluded from his master's directives as no longer trustworthy?

Either way, it would almost certainly cost him his life if his identity was discovered.

Pooley looked in Goodluck's direction at that moment, his face sharp with suspicion. But suddenly Mistress Bull was there, chivvying the men from the room like children.

'I have set your table upstairs, Master Frizer,' she told the dice player briskly, 'with drinks and vittals as you requested.'

So the weasel-faced man was named Ingram Frizer – an unusual name, even for Kent. Goodluck thought he recognized the name, but could not place where he had heard it before. From another spy, perhaps?

Pooley asked the widow a question, *sotto voce*, and she shook her head. 'Don't fret now, Master Pooley, your friend is already up there, awaiting you. The room is very private, just as you desired, and no one will disturb you. There you may spend the whole day if you wish, or wander the gardens after lunch, for I keep a small garden and orchard here for the pleasure of my guests.'

Pooley paused in the doorway. He put a hand on her arm, his head bent, speaking to her again in his quiet voice.

Mistress Bull glanced across at Goodluck in surprise, then muttered something like 'Not staying long,' as she gestured him towards the stairs.

The three men – Robert Pooley, Nicholas Skeres and Ingram Frizer – ascended the stairs to where, Goodluck had to assume, Kit Marlowe was already waiting for them. He listened hard, but heard only scuffling feet and deep echoing voices as the men above greeted each other, then the whining scrape of a table being moved – away from the open window? – and after that, nothing but a faint rumble of voices as the men began to talk among themselves.

True to her word, the widow Bull brought him a small cup of ale a few minutes later, setting it before him so hard the ale sloshed out.

'Drink that and be on your way,' she told him, her voice hard as flint. 'And don't waste your breath asking for food. I'll have no filthy dockmen at my table.'

'I thank you, mistress,' he murmured ironically, and gave a grimace as he tasted the ale, which was so sour on his lips, he had to wonder what foul substance had been added to speed him on his way. 'A fine beverage, indeed.'

Mistress Bull looked him up and down in undisguised disgust, then swept away to take fresh orders from the dice players.

Glancing up at the uneven ceiling, Goodluck watched their comings and goings keenly, though he could see them only as mere shadows passing across gaps in the floor-boards. One man left the table, walked to the window – to check they were not being observed, or perhaps to give a signal? – then returned to his place. Another rose to fetch something from his bag, and the others fell silent as though waiting while it was spread across the table. A large document, perhaps, or a map. Sometimes he heard a word or two of their discussion, and an occasional burst of laughter. But always their voices would drop frustratingly to whispers afterwards.

'Essex', he caught several times, and once 'Spain'.

Suddenly there came the crash of a chair falling backwards, then an angry shout from Marlowe – the playwright's voice clear and unmistakable, trained as it was to carry to the back of a crowded theatre – exclaiming hotly, 'No, that's not true! Who dares call me a traitor?'

One of the others hushed him, and another said loudly, 'Don't be a fool, Marlowe. Sit down!'

The chair was righted, and the shadows stilled above his head.

After that, the men in the upper room fell to muttering, their voices inaudible to Goodluck over the crackling of the fire.

Mistress Bull came to remove his unfinished cup of ale after half an hour, and showed him the door when he asked for another, her expression as sour as her ale.

'Out, fellow,' she said shortly, pushing him down the steps. 'And do not come back unless you want a beating from one of my potmen.'

It was bright outside, the hour coming close to noon by the height of the sun. The old man who had been smoking on the steps before had vanished, the dusty lane now empty and sunlit. The greenish-brown spikes of salt rushes and marsh-grass grew among the tall grasses in the verge, suggesting that the place was prone to flooding from the nearby Thames. As Goodluck spat the sourness of the widow's ale out into the dust, a large green-backed toad crossed his path, hopping away into the shade of the undergrowth with an ironic croak.

Goodluck adjusted his cap, taking this opportunity to glance up without being too obvious about it. The window of the room above was open and unshuttered, but he could not hear any of the conversation within.

Robert Pooley was deep into every Catholic conspiracy, often playing a double part while ostensibly working for the Queen. But on whose side was he this time? Ingram Frizer he did not know, but the man had the cold look of a killer. And Nicholas Skeres was another of the earl's men, involved like Goodluck and Pooley in the uncovering of the Babington plot.

Their meeting had to be connected to this traitor in the Queen's household. Essex had suggested at first that it was Lopez, one of the Queen's doctors, but she had refused to believe it, and indeed Goodluck himself found the foreigner Lopez too convenient a hook on which to hang this conspiracy.

But if not Lopez, then who?

Marlowe must know the truth. He was at the heart of all this. He had spoken secretly of an attack on the Queen to that man in the kitchens – a man Goodluck had never seen about the palace since – and seemed to know more than anyone else of this latest plot. Yet the Earl of Essex had refused to hear of Kit Marlowe's guilt. Another Cambridge man, no doubt blinded by the playwright's charm and talent. Or else in alliance with him.

'No!' he exclaimed aloud, suddenly sickened by his own dreadful thoughts and suspicions.

It was unthinkable that a nobleman of Essex's rank and stature, so close to the Queen, could be secretly plotting her death while pretending to be her protector. And to what avail? Surely Essex stood to gain more by keeping Queen Elizabeth alive, if only while he was still in her royal favour. Unless he hoped she would name him as her heir.

Goodluck walked a little way down the lane until he came to where it petered out into dockyards and rough-hewn quays, a sudden breeze hitting him as he came out beyond the last buildings to find the vast greyish river rolling mightily past, dark at its heart, its skin shivering and flecked with rough white wherever the wind caught it. The other bank was too far away to be anything but a shimmering haze, with the dark specks of boats bobbing by the shore.

It seemed to Goodluck that he had spent most of his life working with Walsingham to avoid the Queen's assassination, lurching from one potential disaster to another and somehow averting them at the very last moment. Nothing had ever been terribly clear about this spying business, except that the Queen's safety was worth the lives of many good men. But now Walsingham was dead, and Goodluck himself was lost in a mist of lies and confusion, fumbling about in darkness while the truth danced just out of his reach. He was like a blindfolded man searching for the centre of a maze, all the while suspecting that it had none and yet unable to give up the hunt.

The wind blowing off the river was chilly, and he shivered. He had told Lucy he would leave spying and take her away from court, that he was ready for a new life in the country as a respectable married man. And it was true, he loved Lucy, and could no longer bear sleeping under hedges and waiting about in cold places to force another man to admit treachery. Yet if the Queen's death was the cost of his freedom, could he still live with his conscience after he had walked away from her service?

Frustrated by the vicious tangle of deceit with which he had to struggle, Goodluck walked back to his horse and led it to a freshwater creek, waiting until the animal had drunk its fill. Then he tied up his horse in the shade and wandered back along the lane. Within a few doors of the widow Bull's house, he sat down in the shade of an old ash tree gnarled and stunted by the salt winds. There was nothing more to do but wait for Marlowe to come out, then either follow him again or risk death by demanding straight out if he was planning the Queen's assassination.

No more after this. He would seek his release from service, take Lucy back to his brother's farm and marry her as he had promised. There had to be something honest in his life before he died. Else why had God brought him into this world in the first place?

It was late afternoon when he stirred for the third time, walking a little way down towards the river again to rouse his blood and keep his limbs from stiffening. He was just on his way back when he heard a woman screaming, and started to run. He leapt up the steps into the dimly lit house to find the widow Bull standing in his way, screaming and rocking, her hands over her face.

'Dead! Dead!'

The hairs crept on the back of his neck. Goodluck shouldered past her and ran to the stairs. There, stumbling down into darkness from the room above, his hands outstretched and stained with blood, was the weasel-faced man called Ingram Frizer.

'It was not my fault,' he kept repeating, his voice dull. 'He attacked me first. I had to defend myself, as God is my witness.'

Someone in the lower room had thrown open a shutter, letting in the dying rays of the sun. A large ring on Frizer's hand flashed red and gold. Diamonds? On the hand of a killer?

Ingram Frizer stared down at it, as though only just remembering its existence, then dragged the ring from his finger and stuffed it into the leather pouch at his belt.

'Who is dead?' Goodluck demanded from him, then ran urgently up the stairs, not waiting for a reply.

He stopped in the doorway and almost recoiled. Every instinct was shrieking at him to turn around and leave. To get as far away from this house of death as possible.

Marlowe lay sprawled backwards across the table, as though dragged there from behind. His once handsome face was a mass of blood. A dagger protruded from one eye socket, pushed in with such force that it had penetrated almost to the hilt. One arm dangled down from the table as though pointing to the letter that had been knocked to the floor, spattered now with blood.

He did not need to go any further to discover what he already knew. If Marlowe was not dead, he soon would be.

The two other men, who had been bending over the body in fierce discussion, straightened and looked round at him intently.

Goodluck descended the stairs two at a time, ignoring Frizer's shout from the lower room, stumbled from the house and ran back along the lane. Out of breath, his chest heaving, he dragged the horse's reins free and clambered into the saddle.

'Hie! Hie!' he gasped, and kicked the startled animal into a trot, then into a canter. Moments later he was fleeing Deptford at an ungainly gallop, men staring as he passed, clods of turf flying up in his dusty wake, his horse's head turned towards Richmond and the court.

Marlowe was dead. Horribly dead. And given the secret nature of their meeting, he had every reason to fear the Queen would be next.

It was dark before Goodluck reached Richmond, his horse exhausted and trembling as he slid from its sweat-slick back. The guards had only let him through the gate when he invoked the powerful name of Essex, a talisman against questions and delays. But now that he was here, Goodluck was suddenly unsure what to tell him, still trying to weigh up his master's allegiance to the Queen.

With Walsingham, it had been more clear-cut. A villain

had been a villain, even if sometimes it had been necessary for Goodluck to play that part himself, in the hope of bringing light to a dark situation.

With Essex though, he often suspected the earl knew more than he did about the plots they were constantly attempting to thwart. It was almost as though some of these villains were also in his employ. Which was not a thought he could ever voice, Goodluck thought grimly, unless he too wished for an early death.

Had Marlowe been reckless enough to suspect or question his master's loyalty?

Lord Essex, he was told, was dining late that evening with the Queen and the rest of the court. He stopped only to wash his face and brush the worst of the dirt from his clothes, then stumbled into the banqueting hall. His first thought was for Lucy, but she was not in the crowd of ladies milling about behind the Queen's table. Reluctantly, he put his beloved out of his head, and made his way up the hall towards the dais where Essex was dining at the right hand of the Queen.

Essex saw him at once, beckoning him over with a frown. He must have known Goodluck would never approach him so openly if it were not vital.

'Goodluck?' He wiped his lips with a napkin, then looked him up and down. 'What is it, man? Quietly now, what's the matter?'

Goodluck bent forward and whispered in his ear. 'Marlowe is dead, my lord. Murdered in Deptford this very afternoon, at the house of a widow named Eleanor Bull.'

'You were with him?'

'I was outside. I . . . I heard a commotion, then ran inside and saw . . .' He paused, not wishing to recount the rest of what he had seen. 'My lord, there were two agents of the crown present. Maybe three.'

'Names?'

'Nicholas Skeres, Robert Pooley, and one Ingram Frizer.'

Essex did not blink. He sat back instead, waving him away as though what he had said held no special significance. 'Very well, I see. Go now, change your clothes. Take some wine and get some sleep. I will send for you in the morning.'

'My lord,' Goodluck said urgently, 'I fear Master Marlowe may have discovered a plot against the Queen's life by these men and was silenced for his knowledge.'

A serving man was approaching the high dais, a vast platter of glazed fruits balanced most unsteadily before him.

Essex stared at Goodluck, his eyes cold. 'You have spoken out of turn, Master Goodluck. I regret Marlowe's death, but I can assure you that it was in no way connected to any plot against Her Majesty.'

Goodluck's belly tightened with fear. Lord Essex had known that Marlowe was dead, even before he had whispered the cold fact in his ear. He might even have ordered the playwright's execution himself. That could be the only explanation for his words, his calm dismissal of Marlowe's death. Today's meeting at the widow's quiet house in Deptford had been an assassination disguised as a secret rendezvous between spies. Though why had the killers not struck in the morning when Marlowe arrived? Why wait until the sun was almost ready to set before striking the vicious blow that would deprive the playwright of his life?

Because Marlowe held some information they had to extract first.

A confession, he wondered feverishly? Or perhaps the identity of the assassin hired by Philip of Spain?

The serving man was lowering the platter of glazed fruits before the Queen, wobbling slightly as he knelt at her side. 'Your Majesty,' he said hoarsely, 'my master sends you this with his compliments.'

'You must thank him for me,' the Queen replied graciously, then gave a sudden horrified gasp, for the man had pulled a long sharp blade from under the platter of fruits. Her pale fingers clutched Essex's sleeve as she recoiled in her seat. 'Robbie!'

'Die, you Protestant whore, in the name of King Philip of Spain and the Holy Roman Church!' the assassin yelled at the top of his voice. His hand drew back to stab her in the throat, his face twisted with triumphant rage.

The room seemed frozen, like a brightly coloured tableau at a pageant, as every courtier and servant turned to stare at the high dais. Then, with miraculous speed, before his knife had descended, three of the Queen's body-guards seized the assassin, sent the blade spinning from his hand and forced him to the floor. The man lay there grotesquely, arms twisted behind his back, face pressed into the greasy rushes of the banqueting hall, still yelling obscenities.

Above his head, the Queen's ladies screamed and stared and fluttered their painted fans, pressing close to see the would-be killer.

The Queen herself shrank back in her chair, staring first at the floored assassin and then at Lord Essex.

'You swore I would be safe, Robert,' she whispered accusingly, her face stiff and white as a mask. 'You promised me.'

Six

LUCY STOOD IN THE CENTRE OF THE GILT-CEILINGED LADIES' chamber, staring about in despair. The room lay in utter chaos, mostly made by the other women with whom she shared this chamber when Her Majesty was in residence at Richmond. Everyone had squeezed into the narrow room to change their gowns for tonight's dinner, given in honour of Sir John Puckering who had lately entertained the Queen at his house in nearby Kew, and then left the place in disarray. A bolt of white lace was veiling the mirror, petticoats and hoops lay abandoned on the floor where women had simply stepped out of them, velvet hoods and court slippers were strewn higgledy-piggledy across the numerous mattresses.

'Where did I put my pearl earrings?' she muttered to herself. The earrings Sir John had given her at New Year. She had looked everywhere and could not find them.

Lucy blew out her cheeks, suddenly fearful that she would miss the end of the banquet and be reprimanded for not starting the dances. The Queen had noticed she was not wearing them and sent her back to find them.

I shall be scolded so badly if I have lost Sir John's gift, she thought, and bent to rummage in a chest under the window. At last her hand fell on a small rose-coloured silk bag.

'Are they not in here?'

She loosened the drawstring and peered inside, then drew out the exquisite pearl earrings with a smile. Slowly, she fed the thin gold wire through the holes in her ear lobes. It was an uncomfortable sensation, and she was not yet accustomed to the weight of jewellery there. But Queen Elizabeth liked her ladies to keep up with the fashions, and the Lord knew she needed to remain in the Queen's good graces these days, for there was always some whisper against her at court.

Once again, she regretted that Cathy was not there to help her. But ever since her friend had so inexplicably betrayed her to the Earl of Southampton, Cathy had chosen to serve the other ladies of the court, and had never once spoken to her about that night. Lucy had passed her a few times in the corridors and in the ladies' chambers, but Cathy had always lowered her eyes and hurried away, her cheeks flushed.

Why had Cathy betrayed her?

It was a mystery, and one which still pained her. She had never treated Cathy as a servant but as a friend. Though perhaps such distinctions were not enough when their very different duties at court had kept them so often apart.

Lucy hurried alone through the corridors, her broad skirts brushing the stone walls, for Richmond Palace had been constructed long before this new rage for hooped skirts. She wondered where Goodluck was tonight. His last note had been terse, promising that he would return to court in a sennight, unless his business called him elsewhere.

Business. He meant spying, of course.

Her body tingled with excitement at the thought of how often they had made love since that first night in his chamber, skin against skin, taking risks which had terrified her with Shakespeare, yet which felt so natural and right with Goodluck.

As she reached the base of the west tower and turned to descend the winding staircase towards the banqueting hall, she gazed out across the Thames through the leaded windows as she always did, admiring the glitter and flash of torchlight on the current as it flowed past the west front of the palace.

A burst of deep male laughter from one of the rooms off the staircase caught her attention; she paused on the stair in surprise, glancing into the candlelit room.

Two men, standing close together, almost in each other's arms.

One was Henry Wriothesley, the Earl of Southampton, who hated her with such a passion.

Then her heart clenched in sudden dread as she recognized the second man. The voice first, once so beloved, then the dark head, the slim figure in a plain white shirt and leather jerkin, the traditional garb of a player.

William Shakespeare.

She stared, her heartbeat galloping, and cursed herself as a fool, thrown into confusion just by his presence. Yet what was he doing here at court? He must be here for some theatrical performance, though she had not heard that any company would be performing before the Queen tonight.

She lifted her heavy skirts to continue down the stairs, determined to leave her love for Shakespeare behind, and then it happened. Her gaze still locked on Shakespeare, she suddenly saw what she had missed before – the closeness of their bodies, the earl's arm draped so possessively about Will's shoulders, their hips pushed oddly together – and could not miss the moment when Henry Wriothesley leaned forward and touched his lips to Shakespeare's.

Not a kiss given in chaste friendship, but open-mouthed, kissing him fully, his hand clasping the player's dark head.

Lucy almost fell down the stairs, her hand flying out to the wall just in time to prevent her fall. She could not breathe, and thought herself under some kind of spell, for what she had seen was surely impossible. Not two men kissing each other, for she had discovered the existence of such unusual pleasures after her marriage to Jack Parker, but that he, her one-time lover Will Shakespeare, could find joy in the embrace of another man. And not any man but the Earl of Southampton, barely grown to manhood himself, and Lucy's most vicious enemy at court.

But that was why!

How blind she had been. How blind. No wonder the young earl had been so vile, warning her to stay away from Will. She almost ran the rest of the way to the banqueting hall, wishing she could undo that terrible glance, that moment of shock and amazement, that unravelling of everything she had ever known or thought about Will.

She was no longer a fool to his attentions, but all the same, her heart burned with shame at how she had been in thrall to such a man. She suddenly remembered her wedding night, the awkwardness of Jack's ribald jokes, and how Will had laughed at her for fearing rape at the hands of her new husband. Had Will and Jack been lovers too? Had they made love together at Will's lodgings while she was keeping house with Mistress Parker, then laughed at her simple trusting faith?

Her troubled thoughts were interrupted by the sound of angry shouts ahead, a clatter of benches knocked over. She stumbled into the high-ceilinged, torchlit banqueting hall. The place was in confusion, all the guests on their feet, the captain of the guards shouting orders to his men, ladies weeping into their hands, men staring and pressing forward to the dais.

What in God's name could have happened?

In the noise and confusion, she found herself facing Master Goodluck across the high-ceilinged room, his face the only clear one in the hall, while men crowded past her to the Queen's side.

Goodluck!

Master Goodluck saw her, and his eyes widened. But when Lucy would have approached him, he shook his head and motioned her to attend the Queen instead.

Her heart jerked in shock. For a few blinding seconds, in the chaos around them, Lucy had forgotten she must hide her love for him. At his gesture she had herself under control, her smile erased as she pushed through the crowd of courtiers to the high dais.

A man was being dragged away, his hands bound behind his back, guards on either side, his face red with hate and anger.

'I would to God I had murdered her!' the man spat at his captors, then shouted wildly, for all the court to hear, 'You are all sinners, to kneel and pledge allegiance to this whore. I go to my death with no sin on my conscience, for Elizabeth the bastard is a heretic and a usurper. I may have failed, but others will take my place!'

Lord Essex, dressed lavishly in cloth of gold, a diamond-studded gold star pinned to his chest, was standing over the Queen, who had sunk into her high-backed seat, her face white as plaster, her eyes wide and dark with fear. Behind her seat, her ladies crowded, jostling one another, trying to soothe their mistress with wine and comforting prayers.

'Your Majesty,' Essex was saying urgently, trying to support her, 'are you hurt? Did his knife cut you?'

'Let me be, don't fuss, I am unharmed,' the Queen

insisted in an angry mutter, pushing him away. She accepted a white lace handkerchief from Sir John and pressed it to her mouth, gasping, 'Though only by the grace of God, it would seem. Why in the name of all that's holy was this lunatic allowed into my presence?'

'That shall be discovered. For now, you must allow me to escort you to a place of greater safety, Your Majesty.' Lord Essex clicked his fingers at the captain of the guards. 'Your guards will accompany us to the Privy Chamber and secure the place. The villain may not have come alone.'

'Oh, very well. But I am vexed that I shall miss the dancing.' Queen Elizabeth sighed, then held out one pale jewelled hand, allowing his lordship to raise her from her seat. Lord Essex placed an arm about her waist. She did not protest but leaned against him, staring about the hall, her hand seeming to tremble on his chest. 'So that was my secret assassin. Not a terribly successful murderer, my lord, after all your fears that he would do for me. Who was he in the end? Does anyone know the villain's name? He was wearing my household livery. I thought you told me all my servants had been questioned to ensure their loyalty.'

Lord Essex looked furious. He was afraid too, his gaze seeking out Goodluck's above the crowd of startled courtiers. 'And so they have been. These things will be discovered in time, Your Majesty. But since we are still uncertain of the truth, let me take you back to the Privy Chamber under guard.'

Her voice was querulous, as though she suspected him of a coup. 'Take me back under guard? Your guards or mine? What, am I a prisoner in my own palace now?'

'They are your own royal bodyguards, Your Majesty,' he reassured her, 'and all hand-picked men. It is for your supreme safety that they will escort us, and no other reason.'

The captain of the guards had caught Lucy's eye, gesturing her to join the confused throng about the dais. She glanced about for Goodluck, but he had vanished. Gone ahead, no doubt, to check the Queen's state apartments were safe to receive the royal entourage. She knew what he would be thinking: that if an assassin could attack her so openly in the state rooms, an accomplice could easily have entered her royal chambers during the confusion and even now be awaiting the Queen's return.

Lucy fell into line, following the other shocked and whispering women along the corridors, though her mind was in chaos. First that disturbing glimpse of Shakespeare and the Earl of Southampton together, now an attack on the Queen in her own palace.

Goodluck was back earlier than expected. She had never seen his face so grim, and guessed instinctively it was not this unsuccessful attack on the Queen that had brought him back to court.

So what else had happened to put that frown in his eyes?

Even safely installed in the Privy Chamber, her bodyguards thronging at the door and her armed nobles about her, the Queen refused to sit but stood resolutely at the window, staring out at the darkness. Lord Essex spoke to her urgently, his voice kept low so only the Queen could hear. She waved him away after a moment, then turned to face the room as the doors were shut and barred against the rest of the court.

Lucy watched in silence, concerned by what she saw; the Queen was trembling, her face pinched with worry and fatigue. Anger too, and small wonder. Who could she rely on to protect her but these men?

Cautiously, not wishing to draw attention to him, Lucy's

gaze moved round to where Goodluck stood, his back against the door. His eyes sought her out, not reassuring but their gaze steady enough, then he looked away. He knew something. But like the old campaigner he was, he was not going to speak unless there was no help for it. Truth, as he had often told her, was a dangerous thing when spoken out loud.

'How could this have happened?' Queen Elizabeth was demanding, glaring at each of her nobles in turn. 'Where is Lord Burghley?'

His strangely hunched son, Robert Cecil, stepped forward in his customary black robes. He bowed before her, his look apologetic. 'My father was not well enough to leave his chamber tonight. But I can answer for him, Your Majesty.'

'I might have died out there. The villain had a knife. Did you see it? Mere inches from my throat.'

'I did indeed, Your Majesty.' Cecil turned his accusing gaze on Lord Essex; Lucy shivered to see the malice in the young councillor's face. 'Monitoring plots and threats of assassination is your province, my lord Essex, is it not? I take it you were unaware of this man's existence in Her Majesty's service, right under your nose?' He paused, as though for effect. 'Wait though, I seem to recall being told of some plot involving a servant of the Queen. But perhaps you considered those who work in the kitchens too lowly to be a threat to Her Majesty?'

'Last year we spoke at great length to all who serve Her Majesty,' Essex spat out angrily, 'and dismissed all those we could not trust. But these serving men come and go each year, and more are employed whenever the Queen moves residence. Besides, my men tell me this villain who attacked the Queen was not known to them. An outsider, they said. He must have bribed someone to let him into the palace—'

'Bribed someone? But if all here are so loyal to the Queen, who would be open to a bribe?'

Queen Elizabeth clapped her hands, bringing both men to attention. 'Enough! I cannot think!' She paced the room, barely seeming to notice the weight of her elaborate gilt-edged ruff, her jewelled slippers peeping out from under the heavy golden skirts of her gown. 'My lord Essex, I know you have worked hard to secure my palaces against would-be assassins. Yet it is also true, as Cecil suggests, that any blame for this event must fall on your shoulders. You said one of your own men was stationed here in my household, watching the other servants for signs of treachery. Is he still here? Did he miss this attacker?'

Essex pointed to Goodluck standing against the door, and the nobles parted so the Queen could see him more clearly.

'That is the man, Your Majesty, and Master Goodluck is his name. He left the palace some days ago, against my clear instructions, following the trail of a fellow spy instead of watching for conspirators here. He returned just in time to see this Catholic traitor make an attack on your royal person.'

Queen Elizabeth clicked her fingers at Goodluck, who came forward at once and fell to his knees before her.

'You, sir, Master Goodluck,' she said coldly, 'you will be so good as to explain yourself. I have been attacked by a traitor within my own household, the very crime you were set to watch for, and now it seems you were not even on hand to prevent this villainy.' The Queen stared at his bent head. 'Speak, sirrah, what do you have to say for yourself?'

Lucy watched in silence, struggling to keep her emotions hidden, though her nails were cutting into her palms.

'Forgive me, Your Majesty,' Goodluck said plainly, looking up at his queen. 'Lord Essex speaks the truth. I have indeed failed Your Majesty on this count. Though if I may be permitted to speak in my defence, some months ago I recounted my suspicions to his lordship about a serving man in your household, whom I had never seen but heard, and was told not to pursue the matter any further.'

He hesitated, glancing warily at the door to the Privy Chamber as it swung open. But it was only the Earl of Southampton being admitted, no cap on his head, the youth's hair in disarray, his fair face flushed. Lucy saw his untidy appearance and shivered, for she could guess what it meant; that he and Shakespeare had been sporting with each other when the earl was informed of the attack on Her Majesty.

'As for not being on hand in recent days, that also is true,' Goodluck continued, his face sombre. 'But I have been following the trail of a suspected traitor, who met his death today in most dreadful circumstances. I absented myself from court in an effort to discover more about his activities, and for no other reason. This I will gladly swear on my life.'

'Which should be forfeit anyway,' Essex muttered savagely.

'This traitor's name?'

Goodluck looked cautiously at Essex, who shook his head. 'You must excuse my disobedience, Your Majesty, but his name may only be disclosed in secret, not before this company. The question of his treachery is not yet certain.'

The Queen turned from him and paced back and forth, fanning herself, her face still white and pinched with strain.

'My lord,' she asked Essex without looking in his direction, 'is it true that your attention was drawn to this serving man by Master Goodluck, and that you did nothing to discover his identity?'

Essex had folded his arms across his chest, a look of sullen rage on his face. 'The matter is more complicated than you can grasp, Your Majesty.'

'Being a mere woman, and therefore a simple-minded fool?' she threw icily over her shoulder at him.

'I believed this other man to be pursuing the traitor on my behalf.' Essex sounded bitter. 'I had paid him handsomely enough for his loyalty, after all, and thought him a true Englishman.'

'And all the while he was working for Spain behind your back?'

But Lord Essex refused to be drawn. 'That remains to be seen, Your Majesty. Either way, the man was a danger and had to be removed.'

Queen Elizabeth stopped pacing and stared at him. Her lips opened, then closed again abruptly, as though she had remembered that they were not alone.

'Very well,' she began tartly, 'since I cannot find it in myself to condemn him for having done his best to uncover this traitor's identity, I shall demand no punishment for Master Goodluck.'

At these words, Lucy felt herself sag in relief. Still on his knees, Goodluck glanced at her briefly, a slight frown in his eyes. Carefully, she looked away, schooling herself not to react so openly again.

'But you, my lord Essex, will leave court immediately and dwell on your mistakes at Essex House until I give you leave to return.'

Essex stared at the Queen in disbelief. 'You are punishing me for his failure?'

'I entrusted you with one task, my lord, which was to discover all secret movements against my throne and person. Tonight I was nearly murdered in my own palace, in front of the whole court.' She shook her head, not bothering to hide her anger. The other nobles shrank as she gazed round at them, her tone accusing. 'I hold you to blame for this, my lords. Think how the heads of Europe will laugh when they hear how vulnerable my court is to such attacks. As for King Philip, he will be sending assassins over by the bushel-load when he hears of this, for if one lone man can almost accomplish my slaughter, it stands to reason that several at once would be more successful. After all, a monk killed poor Henry of France in the same way, a lone fanatic with a knife. Why should they cavil at murdering a queen in the same cowardly manner?'

The Queen gestured Goodluck to stand. 'Get you gone, Master Goodluck, and in future you will take your findings to Sir Robert Cecil there.' She indicated Cecil, deliberately snubbing Essex by favouring his rival. 'Is that clear?'

Goodluck said nothing, but bowed his head. Lucy saw the hard flush in Essex's cheeks, and thought she had never seen him look so humbled and ashamed.

The Earl of Southampton started forward with a cry. 'Your Majesty, do not put this shame on Lord Essex. He does not deserve such a burden. Nor does this creature,' and he pointed forcefully at Master Goodluck, 'deserve your mercy. For he has not failed through Lord Essex's fault, but through his own hardened lust for one of your own ladies, whom he has bedded on many occasions, here in this very palace.'

Lucy could hardly breathe. She stared from him to Goodluck, and then, terribly, turned her head to face the Queen.

The Queen had frozen where she stood. 'If this is a lie, my lord Southampton—'

'It is the truth, I swear it.'

'And which of my ladies has Master Goodluck been bedding? Or do you lack the courage to name her openly?'

'I lack no courage, Your Majesty, and will name her in front of the whole court, if need be.'

To her horror, Henry Wriothesley swivelled on his heel, ignoring Goodluck's instinctive movement to protect her, then looked directly at Lucy. The earl seemed almost to be smiling, his eyes narrowed in malice, the jerk of his head contemptuous.

'The woman he has been panting after is none other than that black slut, Lucy Morgan. Her serving maid, Catherine Belton, will swear to it, for she has several times followed Mistress Morgan on my instructions and seen her enter the spy's room . . . not to emerge again until dawn.'

Rigid with outrage, the Queen beckoned Lucy forward, and watched with stony eyes as she knelt before her. 'Speak, is this true? Have you lain wantonly with this man?' Then she held up a hand. 'Wait, is this some poor jest on the earl's part, or else some error? Goodluck is your guardian, is he not?'

'He was, Your Majesty,' Lucy agreed, trembling.

'And now?'

She could lie to save them from punishment and imprisonment. She could claim they had spent the night together chastely, as guardian and ward reunited. She could tell them that Cathy was lying, that her old friend wished her harm, though she did not know why.

Lucy looked at Goodluck. He returned her gaze for a long moment, then nodded. It was time, he seemed to be urging her. Let the dice roll.

'Now he is my lover, Your Majesty.'

As soon as the tide was favourable the next morning, they were escorted to the Tower on separate barges. Goodluck had been bound hand and foot in case he attempted to escape. Yet his look had been proud as he was pushed aboard, her last glimpse of him standing between the guards' raised pikes, not cowed by his punishment at the Queen's hands but fierce with longing as he gazed back at her.

'It will not be for ever, Lucy,' he had called to her over the water as the barge danced on the spring tide. 'Keep patience, my love.'

One of the guards struck him, harshly bidding him, 'Be silent!', but Goodluck did not fall. He straightened stiffly after the blow and looked ahead to their destination, the grey ribbon of the Thames leading them to London, just as though he were sailing for the New World and their liberty, not under guard to the Tower.

Lucy herself was taken aboard her prison-bound barge with gentler hands, though some of the guards eyed her sideways. She had forgotten how discomfiting such lewd stares could be from a stranger, it had been so many years since she had returned to court and the protection afforded by its rules of etiquette, where a courtier might look but not touch, and a servant must keep his head bowed when a lady passed. Behind closed doors, sinful outrages might take place, and often did, but never publicly. So to find herself suddenly at the mercy of these common men, the youngest cupping his crotch in a suggestive way when she glanced in his direction, was not an easy thing to face.

Her hands mercifully unbound, she gripped the rail all the way down the river. It was a long and chilly journey, for the sun was behind clouds that morning and the river breeze was cold, snatching at her hood and cloak. Her fingers were soon numb, but it seemed pointless to dwell on such a trifle. After her arrest for unchaste behaviour, a serving woman had been sent scurrying away with the order to 'Pack a bag for Mistress Morgan,' and to fetch her travelling clothes. It seemed her gloves had been forgotten in the woman's haste.

She did not wish to consider Cathy's terrible betrayal,

299

nor how Goodluck had looked at her with such fortitude when the Queen pronounced their fate: 'To the Tower with both of them, and let Master Goodluck be flogged until he is bloodied!' All she could think of was how to obtain Goodluck's release.

Even if she herself must agree to live and die within the Tower's confines, Goodluck must be freed. She owed him that for all the times he had helped her when he was her guardian. Lucy smiled, remembering his words of comfort. 'It will not be for ever.' Brave to the end. She could face any torment if Goodluck was at liberty, living out his days peacefully on his brother's farm.

By the time the barge drew alongside the high, forbidding walls of the Tower, bobbing uneasily at the watergate while the men secured it with ropes, she felt sick and frightened. But she refused to show it.

Taken ashore, suddenly dizzy after the constant movement of the boat, she stumbled and fell in the damp, breezy space before the steps. The stones hurt her hands and knees. When she looked down at them, both palms were bleeding.

The young guard beside her grinned, dragging Lucy back to her feet. 'You're to enjoy a show before they take you to your cell. Your lover is to get his shirt and then his skin stripped off his back.' He pretended to shiver, glancing up at the clouds. 'A sharp day for it, but the whip will soon warm him up.'

Sure enough, as she entered the Tower confines and began to ascend the steep slope to where the guard had said she would be housed, she looked ahead with trepidation and saw a low wooden platform on the green. Standing on it with his legs set wide apart, bare-chested and bare-headed, his hands bound to a wooden post, was Goodluck. Behind him stood a man with a sturdy leather whip, his face impassive as he waited for the signal to begin.

Goodluck saw her in the assembled crowd before the platform. He made no comment this time, but his eyes tried to reassure her.

'I've seen women faint and strong men weep like girls under that whip,' the guard remarked, looking at her sideways. 'It's no disgrace. They say the pain is more than flesh and blood can bear once the skin is cut.'

She gripped her hands together, acutely aware now of how foolish and reckless they had been, loving each other in breach of the Queen's command. Some of the others in the crowd had turned now, staring openly at her, and she forced herself to watch without flinching. This flogging would be hard enough for Goodluck to bear; she would not disgrace him further by crying out. To watch her lover being flogged was part of her punishment, and it was only thanks to the Queen's great mercy that she too had not been sentenced to a flogging. Though she would gladly have changed places with Goodluck now, given the agony he was about to endure as his reward for lying with her out of wedlock.

Silence fell. One of the gentlemen on the platform lifted his hand in a signal. The man with the whip raised his fearful burden, then brought it down hard between Goodluck's shoulders, and she saw him jerk in response.

After that first stroke, Goodluck's face set hard. He stared directly ahead at nothing, as though determined not to break. But his stoicism could not last, and after twelve strokes he gave a muffled cry, and closed his eyes. His back was already a mass of ugly red stripes.

A few strokes later, his knees sagged, and one of the guards stepped forward to dash a bucket of water into his face. He revived at once, gasping and spluttering, and the flogging began again. This time Goodluck cried out in pain after each stroke. Lucy wanted to hide her face in her hands, but she made herself keep watching, though she could hardly bear to see him suffer so cruel a punishment. By the time it was over, he was clinging to the post like a dying man to a raft, his back bloodied from the terrible welter of shallow cuts.

Goodluck was cut loose and fell to his knees, groaning and bowing his forehead to the wooden platform.

The guard steered her away from the green, handing her into the care of a well-dressed gentleman who examined the papers that had come with her from Richmond, then asked her a few questions. He spoke in a friendly enough way, assuring her that she would not be molested while in his charge, but Lucy could not bring herself to reply, merely staring at him blankly.

A stern-looking woman in a coarse black gown appeared at his side. Her new jailor, she guessed. This woman led the way up a winding stair in one of the towers and into a small, low-ceilinged room which smelt as though bats had nested there. It held one rough-looking stool, one table and a straw pallet for a bed. But it was not a horrid dark little room, as she had feared, and from one narrow side window Lucy could even look down to the boats on the greyish-green river.

'My name is Mistress Hall, and these will be your quarters here,' the woman declared coldly, 'until Her Majesty sends further orders.'

Quietly, Lucy asked if she was allowed ink, quill and paper. The woman agreed that she was, albeit with obvious reluctance, and swept away to procure some.

As soon as the writing materials had arrived and she was alone in her prison cell, Lucy sat down at the uneven table and began to draft the most difficult letter of her life.

To his noble lordship, she began, *the Earl of Essex . . .*

Seven

WILL OPENED HIS EYES AND STARED UP AT THE FINE embroidered silk hangings of the bed in which he was lying. The curtains had been drawn against the coming dawn while it was still dark, but he could tell it was morning now. And a fine June morning, by the sound of it. Outside the high windows of the earl's London residence he could hear the watermen at their work below, calling for trade and shouting to each other as they ferried goods and passengers across the broad grey flood of the Thames. Servants were moving about in the old palace in the same way; he could hear voices in the antechamber, kept low for fear of disturbing their master, and the rumble of cartwheels in one of the back courtyards as a delivery arrived. Everyone was awake, it seemed, except his lordship himself.

Rolling over, Will stared into the young man's face. Sleeping, Henry Wriothesley resembled one of the solemn-faced cherubs from the pages of Will's grandmother's old Catholic Bible. A somewhat dissolute cherub, to judge by the amount of wine they had consumed the night before, and the delicious sins they had committed together before the fire. Yet charmingly innocent, almost childlike, in his sleep.

303

Kit Marlowe came into his head unbidden. He was sleeping now. He would sleep until Doomsday. What a waste of a great talent. He had not quite believed it when he heard of the playwright's death. Or murder, rather. Some brawl in Deptford that had brought about his end.

He reached out, tentatively brushing the curly hair back from his lover's forehead.

'My lord?'

The earl stirred, then opened his eyes. For a moment they stared at each other and the world stopped moving, the globe still and silent as it waited for one of them to speak.

'Will.'

Henry smiled drowsily, and the world moved on. The cries of the watermen came again under their window, and now Will could hear the lapping of the tide against the wooden spars below.

'So I did not dream last night's pleasure. And this time you did not melt away with the dark but stayed to keep me company.' Henry pinched Will's shoulder. 'Solid.'

'Where would I have gone?'

'You had all of London to wander. A hundred worlds to describe in your plays. Yet you chose to sleep beside me, docile as a lamb.' Will made a bleating noise, and Henry laughed. 'I sometimes forget you are a countryman.'

'I am your servant.'

'Hardly.' Henry trailed a hand down Will's bare chest to his groin. Their eyes met, and heat flared between them. 'I served *you* last night. Did you like it?'

Will found he could not speak, but nodded dumbly, staring as he remembered Henry's mouth working skilfully between his thighs, his lips and tongue more knowing than any woman's. He had held on for as long as he could, then spent into the earl's mouth, the intense pleasure almost painful. They had dozed together for a while in the warmth of the firelight before kissing and caressing each other again, and then Will had performed the same act for his lordship.

Thinking back on what they done last night, first on the floor and then, later, in this very bed, Will could not conceive of anything more marvellous – or forbidden – between two men.

Henry leaned forward to kiss him. 'I am glad you are not still angry with me,' he murmured against his mouth, 'for failing to save that woman and her lover from the Tower. I knew you could not hate me for ever. Besides, they are where they belong.'

Will closed his eyes at the reminder. When he had first heard of Lucy's arrest, and the earl's part in it, he had not been able to believe that Henry would be so vindictive. He had even lost his temper and struck the earl, an act which could have served as his death sentence if Henry had chosen to enforce the law. But instead the earl had forgiven him, kissing him and explaining how Lucy had betrayed both his trust and the Queen's by lying frequently and wantonly with Master Goodluck, and how the best place for her was a prison cell.

At first, Will had not believed such lascivious behaviour of Lucy. Not his Lucy. Not even though she had spurned him, and lied on more than one occasion, claiming that the earl had warned her not to see him again. Such a wilful lie! And he was sure that Master Goodluck must have seduced her. For Lucy had sworn to him many times that she was not in love with her guardian. How else could he have slept with her except by cunning or force?

He had always distrusted Master Goodluck. The man was a spy, for certain, and a slippery fellow. He might have worked in the playhouses when he was younger, and even acted once or twice before the Queen according to what Lucy had told him, but he was no theatrical. Theatricals were like brothers. They did not seduce each other's women nor lead them into such danger that they were dragged away to the Tower.

'Lucy . . .' He had not meant to say her name, and looked at Henry in sudden trepidation. 'Forgive me, my lord, I swore not to mention her name again. But it grieves me to think what she must be suffering in that place. You know our history, what little I have told you of it. I wronged Mistress Morgan greatly in the past with false accusations, and . . . and by getting her with child when I was not free to marry.' He hesitated. 'Is there nothing you can do to help her, my lord?'

Henry said nothing for a moment. Then he spoke quietly. 'You must forget her, Will. This desire to save your one-time mistress does you much credit, given how falsely she has played you in the past. But she's a shilling whore, and beneath your notice.'

Will struggled not to argue. They might have lain together as lovers, but he was under no illusions. This young man was his better, and if he could not learn to rein in his tongue, he would soon be made sorry for it. He disliked the disparity between them, but accepted it as inevitable. It would be dangerous to press for greater power when what he did have was merely lent to him while they were in bed together.

'Come, think of what awaits you,' Henry murmured, and drew him into his arms. 'You are already renowned in the playhouse, and more deservedly than that godless fool Marlowe ever was. The groundlings stamp their feet and call for you after the play. But if you wish for true glory, to have your name raised among the great poets, you must leave Lucy Morgan to her fate and allow my influence at court to advance you.'

'I still cannot believe Kit is dead.'

Henry sighed, and kissed him on the lips. His hand

slipped beneath the silken covers again, arousing him with ease. 'Are we to talk the morning away, Master Shakespeare? I am summoned back to court today, and you must attend the playhouse. Since we must rise soon, let us spend our time more pleasurably than in speech.'

'I have risen already,' Will told him, only half smiling at his jest as Henry pressed him back against the pillows. 'My love.'

The sun was high in the sky when Will finally left the Earl of Southampton's great house on the Thames. Not quite daring to use the main entrance, which was guarded by liveried servants day and night, he slipped out of the back door near the kitchen quarters. Several women were washing linen in steaming tubs outside the door, sleeves rolled up and skirts tucked into their belts, their bared arms redraw to the elbow. One of the youngest lifted her coiffed head and stared as Will hurried across the courtyard and turned right into the narrow stinking mews that ran behind the residence.

Although it was bright, there was a chill wind blowing off the river. Will pulled down his cap, shrugged deeper into the fine woollen cloak he had borrowed from Henry, and was just nearing the end of the mews when three figures emerged to block his way. Three men of the street, dressed in filthy rags, their faces swarthy, staring at him.

He slowed his pace, suddenly wary.

'You Shakespeare?' one of them asked. He was thickly built, with filth-blackened hands and a scarred face that spoke of many fights. His voice was gruff, as though he was disguising it. 'Master William Shakespeare?'

Will shook his head, though he knew there was little point in denying his identity when the man so clearly knew it. He stopped, looking about for some means of escape. One of the men slipped past him with a sly wink and stood at his back with folded arms, as though blocking any retreat to the old palace.

'You look like Shakespeare.' The one who had spoken spat on the ground, then looked at him in a measuring way. 'That dagger at your belt. Come now, lay it down. We're not here to kill you. But we will if you fight back.'

Will fingered the dagger, his eyes on the man, considering what his chances would be if he drew it. He had some training with the weapon, but only for stage-fighting. If he had his sword . . . But he did not have it. And he was alone here, one man against three.

'You're a married man, I hear,' the ruffian commented, no doubt guessing at his thoughts. 'With three little children.'

Will stared, his blood chilling. What was this?

'I'm a married man myself. I know how it is. If you want to see your wife and children again, you'll throw down that dagger and take your beating like a man.'

So he was to be beaten, was he? On whose orders, he wondered, and thought wildly of revenge.

The man was still staring at him, waiting for an answer. Could he call out for help and be heard by those women in the courtyard? Yet even as he wondered that, he knew it was futile. He was too far from the gate now, and even if someone heard, they would not come in time to save him.

Slowly, Will drew his dagger. The thick-set ruffian tensed, crouching as though to defend himself. He heard a rasp of metal and knew the man at his back had drawn a weapon too. The odds were against him living to see the end of such a fight. He thought of Anne, then suddenly of young Hamnet. Fear struck him and he threw down the dagger. It fell to the dirt with a dull thud.

'Ah, I knew you'd see sense, Master Shakespeare,' the ruffian told him, then nodded sharply to the man behind Will. 'Hold him there. We'll do what's necessary.'

Before he had a chance to strike a blow, Will's arms were seized and dragged painfully behind his back. Kicking out, he tried to shuffle nearer to the wall, to shake the man off, but it was too late. The heaviest of the three men, who had neither moved nor spoken, came rushing forward and struck him hard in the belly with his staff.

Will doubled over, his breath knocked out of him, then felt himself being jerked upright again by the man behind him.

'Keep on yer feet!' came his curt order.

The ruffian punched him in the face. Fist collided with bone. Will's head was forced back by the strength of the blow. He found himself staring up at the sky, too dazed to think what was happening. A black-headed gull wheeled above the mews, crying hoarsely. A second appeared, then a third and a fourth, the hungry birds gathering overhead, perhaps in hope of a dead body to feed on. Another blow, this time to his nose, and he heard a distinct snap.

He cried out, then sagged in the man's arms. Momentarily he lost all strength in his legs. Blood was dripping down his face in a warm trickle. He could even taste it in his mouth now.

'We've a message to deliver, Master Shakespeare.' Another punch landed in his face, splitting his lip. The pain seemed to wake him from the nightmare; he yelped like a wounded dog and once more struggled to get away. But his hands were still held tightly behind him, the man's grip unyielding as iron. 'A message from his lordship the Earl of Essex.'

The Earl of Essex?

The man with the staff came forward again, grinning like a madman. He slammed the staff mercilessly into Will's lower legs, then into his belly again, which still ached from his earlier blow. The pain was excruciating and he choked on his cry, terrified and furious at the same time. They had claimed they would not kill him if he dropped the dagger, but perhaps they meant to anyway.

'Stay away from Henry,' the ruffian snarled, then smashed his fist sideways into his face again. 'Stay away from him or you'll meet this fist again, you whoreson rogue. Only next time you'll be joining Marlowe in hell. You understand me?'

The man behind him suddenly released Will's arms. He collapsed and fell face down in the dirt, gasping, his breath bubbling in his throat. He was going to choke to death on his own blood, and it was all his own fault. He should have known that first night with Southampton that it would not end well.

One of them bent and turned him over so roughly, he tore his shirt. A boot was aimed at his side, then came stamping on his crotch, an agony he thought would never end. He jerked, trying in vain to roll away, and groaned out his pain through a mouthful of blood.

Barely able to form words, he whispered, 'No more, I beg you,' but his plea was lost in the raucous cries of the gulls overhead.

'You understand me?' the man repeated harshly, stooping over him as though to strike again.

'Yes . . . yes.'

In case the man had not heard him, Will summoned the effort to nod his head.

'Your word on it, master.'

'My . . . my word,' he repeated vaguely, then closed his eyes against a too-bright sky, the men blurring to shadows as he drifted in and out of this nightmare.

Stay away from Henry.

The message was clear. He had looked too high and this was his fall. The Earl of Essex had seen the love Henry bore him, or else someone had seen fit to tell him, and his lordship had acted to separate them before the whispers grew too loud at court. Blood pooled in his mouth, perhaps from a broken tooth, and he twisted his head sideways, spitting out the foul liquid so he could breathe.

He tried to sit up and could not manage it. So he lay still instead, groaning, and attempted to gauge if any of his bones were broken. It was hard to be sure, his body was such a mass of pain.

The men left him there in his blood, moving away in silence. No one else passed in the narrow mews, overlooked by the rough wattle walls of a barn belonging to Southampton's estate. He stared at the cross-hatched patterns made by the wooden frames, waiting for his strength to return.

At last he felt able to turn over on to hands and knees. He groped for his unused dagger in the dirt, stuck it back in his belt then staggered to his feet, leaning against the wall as he made for the street ahead.

However bad his hurts, he could not go back to seek refuge with Henry. The Earl of Essex had made his anger clear, and Will did not have a death wish. But there was always his lodging place. He could rest there for a few hours at least, if he could make it that far. Though how long he would be safe there was less certain. Those men had known his name, and no doubt knew where he lodged too. They could easily return to finish him off if the earl chose not to trust his word.

Will scrabbled in his purse. A handful of shillings. He could pay a carter to carry him home if he could not walk that far. But as soon as he could, he must get out of London.

As he stood on the corner, looking up and down for a passing cart, his memory snagged on that final threat, *you'll be joining Marlowe in hell*. Had Kit been caught *in flagrante delicto* with some noble lord? The thought

311

chilled him. Kit had been a thousand times greater than him as a playwright. Yet now he was snuffed out, nothing but a name left behind, a tale to frighten fools away from their lovers. How easily a life could be lost if a man strayed from his proper place . . .

By the time he reached home, his limbs were already stiffening like a dead man's, the blood dried on his face and hands. He thanked the carter who had borne him home from the riverside in the back of his wagon, jolting him agonizingly every step of the way, and handed over his meagre fee of four shillings.

The man grunted, studying his bloodied face with apparent interest, then spat on the ground. 'Salt water first, master, then try a weak solution of vinegar. That should ease the bruising.'

Will smiled his thanks, and split his lip again as a reward. With the taste of fresh blood in his mouth, he limped painfully back to his lodgings. He had meant to take a larger place this year. But somehow all his money had gone on wine and wantons, fine apparel for his court visits, and such little gifts for Henry as he had been able to afford. With the theatres so often closed against the spread of the plague, it had been hard to earn enough to keep himself in bread and beer, and since he had chosen not to tour with the company earlier that year, the only money he had received had been from his patron. Which he had spent most unwisely, not thinking ahead to the day when it would dry up.

But all that was finished now, he thought wearily. Lord Essex would soon persuade Henry to drop his patronage, and then he would be without even that fee.

Before he could reach the door, it was flung open.

Will staggered back in sudden fear, throwing up a hand

to shield his face. They had got there before him. They had been waiting to finish him.

'No, do not strike!' he cried hoarsely. 'I will never see him again. I will do whatever you say, I swear it. Only spare my life!'

There was a silence. He lowered his arm and stared, shocked and numb with disbelief. It was not the men who had attacked him who stood on his doorstep.

It was his wife.

He gaped like an idiot. 'Anne?'

She looked him over, her face aghast. 'Where have you been, Will? I asked your landlord to let me in, and have been waiting for you here these past two days. I went to the Rose yesterday and found the playhouse still closed. A neighbour told me you might be at court. But now you are here, and your face . . .'

Still stunned by his wife's presence on his doorstep, Will put a hand to his mouth and dabbed at the fresh blood trickling down his chin. 'I . . . I was attacked.'

Anne stared at him, uncomprehending.

'You should not have left Stratford, Anne. This is not your place.' He pushed past her into his lodgings. How in God's name was she here in London? 'What was my father thinking to have let you come here? And where are the children? Surely you did not travel alone?'

Anne followed him inside, speaking hurriedly, her voice unnaturally high. 'The children are safe at home in Stratford with your mother. I came with Cousin Richard.'

He hesitated, swaying as he gazed stupidly about the room. His wife had been making herself at home since arriving in London. The hearth was still cold with yesterday's ashes, and a candle was burning, an extravagance he only indulged when he needed to write after dusk had fallen. He pinched it out, the air wreathed with thin twisting smoke.

'Close the door,' he told her shortly, and swung off his soiled cloak, depositing it over a chair, 'unless you want the whole world to hear our business. And do not burn candles while there is daylight, it is too costly. Throw open a shutter, let the sunlight in.'

Anne obeyed, then stood with her back to the door, watching him in silence. He lurched about the small room as though she were not there, gathering up belongings and shoving them into a bag. His legs were trembling, and when he stumbled over his old walking boots, he fell to his knees and had to stagger up again, his whole body racked with pain.

She must think him drunk, he realized, catching a look of contempt on her face. Better drunk, though, than afraid. He was ashamed of his fear. It made him less than a man. Yet he seemed unable to control it.

'What are you doing?' she asked, staring at the bag.

'I have to leave London for a few months. I'll come back in the autumn. There's no work in the city anyway, not with the theatres still closed. I've a new play I'm working on. It's good, it'll fetch in the crowds. We'll travel back to Stratford together and I'll finish it there.' Talking quickly seemed to ease his uncertainty. He frowned though, the haze slowly lifting from his thoughts now that he was home and, for the time being at least, safe from Essex's men. 'Where is Cousin Richard?'

'He had business across the river. He plans to return on Monday in the afternoon.'

Monday was too late, he thought, frowning.

She seemed to read his mind. 'If I am no longer here when Cousin Richard knocks, he is to travel home to Warwickshire without me.'

The bag would hold no more. He struggled to fasten it, then gave up, staring down blankly at the bulging sides, the clothes spilling out. This is how terror feels, he realized.

He sat, turning to look at her properly. She was pale, her blue eyes wide in an apprehensive face, a soot smudge on her white cap. Mistress Anne Shakespeare. She looked every inch the good country wife, and yet here she was, in the midst of the ugly city. Her first time in London, a thousand times noisier and more frightening than the little market town of Stratford, and her husband had not been at home to welcome her.

'Why did you come, Anne?'

'To see you,' she said simply.

'I'm sorry I was not here when you arrived.'

'I did not mind waiting,' she said in a colourless fashion, and he knew she was lying.

Two days she had waited for him, living alone in his dusty, untidy lodgings while he was sporting with the Earl of Southampton. He shuddered at the thought of what gossip she might have gleaned from his neighbours. Nothing good, that was for sure.

He set his teeth, trying not to sound angry. 'Anything could have happened to you, alone here at night. You should have made Cousin Richard wait with you. Or you could have stayed in Stratford and waited for my return as you have always done.' He saw some flicker in her expression. 'Has it been so long since my last visit?'

'Nigh on a year,' she told him, then shook her head angrily when he stared at her in surprise. 'You have not come to see your children since last summer, and then you only stayed a night. The summer before you came for a sennight. Do we mean so little to you that you have missed the months passing since last you were in Stratford, kissing your daughter Susanna and holding little Judith and Hamnet?'

'Anne,' he began in self-defence, but got no further.

Her voice accused him, sharp as a knife. 'Your children miss you. I cannot for ever answer Hamnet with a lie when

315

he asks why you do not visit. I tell him his father is working hard for us in London, working every hour God sends, so he can earn money . . .'

Her voice broke and she turned away, hiding from him. Perhaps she could no longer bear to look upon his battered face.

'It is no lie,' he insisted. 'I do work hard. And I send home money for your housekeeping.'

'When?'

'What do you mean?'

'When did you last send us money?' Anne choked out, and looked back at him. Her cheeks were wet. 'When, Will?'

Surprised by her question, he counted silently backwards in his head. It must be almost a year since he had last consigned a purse for her to a courier, he realized, and was shocked by the discovery.

'I can't recall exactly when,' he said guiltily. 'Though I'm sorry it's been so long. The city fathers closed the theatres because of the plague, so I haven't earned enough to pay my rent and send money home too. Am I to be blamed because this city is riddled with disease?'

'Yet you have managed to buy yourself a fine suit of clothes,' his wife remarked, gazing pointedly at his torn shirt and bloodstained doublet, 'and ruin them in a street brawl.'

He opened his mouth to deny that it was a brawl, then closed it again. How could he reveal the truth?

'It is expected,' he muttered. 'I am called to court sometimes. I cannot attend the Queen and her nobles in my workaday clothes.'

Anne said nothing, but took a few steps towards him, angrily twisting the folds of her skirt between her fingers. She glanced behind him at the low table before the fire, where a pool of spilt wine had stained the wood.

316

'I cleared that table of empty cups and trenchers when I arrived,' she told him coldly, 'for the place stank of wine. You had left cheese and bread on the hearth, and the mice had been at it. There was a flagon of beer too, standing uncovered on the windowsill. It must have been there some days, for it had more than a dozen flies and cockroaches dead in it.'

'I have been away, though I am not a good housekeeper even when I am at home. If I had known you planned to visit me, I would have set the place to rights.'

'Where were you last night? And the night before?'

He hesitated a space before replying. 'I dislike your tone, Anne. You are my wife, not my keeper.'

She shouted, 'What is her name?'

He stared, shocked by her sudden rage, and could not speak. His heart began to race. What secrets did she know? Nothing of him and Southampton, it would seem. But a little perhaps of his long affair with Lucy Morgan. Or his more recent taste in whores. The local women gossiping . . .

Or had some bawd come round from the brothel, looking to collect on a debt? He owed money at one of the houses of Venus across the river. Not much, but enough perhaps to prompt a visit.

'I swore to myself when I found the place empty that I would not ask your whereabouts,' Anne continued angrily. 'I promised myself that I would not shout at you, nor make demands you could not meet. That I would be a good wife. But then Cousin Richard went about his business and the hours passed. It grew dark outside. I felt so alone here, I sat by the fire and cried. There were men shouting and wandering the streets half the night. Drunkards, thieves, rapists. And I did not know where you were, Will.'

Awkwardly, he took her in his arms, blaming himself for

the fear she must have suffered. It felt strange to feel her soft body against his. His wife. A woman. He had grown accustomed to the hardness of a man, a mouth as hungry and demanding as his own.

He bent his head to kiss her, though his lip burned and throbbed where it had been split by that man's fist.

'It is my fault,' he told her. 'Don't cry.'

'I didn't mean to.'

'This wrong I have dealt you is soon remedied. Tomorrow I will take you back to Stratford, and stay with you until summer's end at least.' He managed a smile when he saw the hope in her face. 'Is that what you want? To have me home again?'

Anne nodded, drying her tears. 'Oh Will,' she said faintly. 'Yes, it is what I want. Forgive me for what I said, the way I spoke to you. But even in Stratford we have heard strange rumours. Unkind whispers about you and . . . and your friends.'

He froze, staring at her, a sickness like bile rising in his throat. *Even in Stratford we have heard strange rumours.* He had thought her innocent of his recent sins. But perhaps his long-suffering wife had merely chosen to ignore the rumours.

God, he was tired. So tired of London, tired of constantly lying, tired of everything. And his body hurt now with a vicious throbbing pain, like he had been kicked repeatedly by a horse. He needed to sleep soon, to close his eyes before he collapsed or vomited.

'All envious falsehoods, of course,' she continued, not quite meeting his eyes. 'We did not believe them. But even if they were not . . . What a man does when he is not at home should not concern his wife. Besides, I am hardly unblemished myself.' Gently, she touched his bruised cheek, and he held still under the caress. 'It was wrong of me to speak of this, William. I shall not mention it again.'

'The past is forgotten. Did we not agree that? There is no one else in my heart,' Will tried to reassure his wife, perhaps too hurriedly. He felt wretched. He despised himself even as he lied, the falsehood so smoothly delivered he was sure she must suspect. 'No one but you, Anne.'

Part Four

Part Four

One

Essex House, London, October 1593

SOMEWHERE OUT IN THE DARKNESS, DEEP AND GRAVE, church bells announced the hour. Eleven o'clock. Goodluck turned away from the window and stared at the half-open door through which he could occasionally hear whispers and see shadows passing to and fro in the great house. Impatience twisted within him again, fretting, and he tried to damp it down, telling himself that this summons meant nothing. There had been no indication in his master's letter to give him cause for hope. Yet still he hoped, grimly and stubbornly.

His feet hurt from long standing. Goodluck sat at last, but could not settle in the uncomfortable high-backed chair which was the only furniture the room afforded to visitors.

He had been waiting in the small antechamber to Essex's study for over two hours. How much longer before he was admitted to the earl's presence?

The door to the study opened. Essex stood there, dressed sombrely in black, a single diamond pinned to his doublet, a gold-hilted dagger at his belt.

'Come,' the earl said briefly. He stood aside to let Goodluck enter, then closed the door again. 'I have a task for you.'

The room was warm, a good fire burning in the grate, and all the windows were shuttered against the chill October wind. Bookcases filled with leather-bound volumes lined the walls, and a portrait of the Queen hung facing the ornately carved desk, strewn with documents and open books. The place reminded Goodluck of Walsingham's old corner study in Seething Lane – and of happier days, both for himself and for England.

'My lord?'

Essex handed him a rolled-up letter. 'My men took this from a man who came into the country at Sandwich yesterday. A Portuguese commoner. The name on his papers is Gomez d'Avila. The man appears to have little English. Do you know this language? Or the hand?'

Unrolling the letter, Goodluck glanced down at it and frowned. 'I do not know the hand, but this is written in Portuguese, my lord.'

'Can you translate it?'

'Given time, yes.'

'I need it within the hour.'

Goodluck was surprised. 'So urgently?' His senses prickled. There was more to this than a suspect letter.

'We have found a translator to aid in d'Avila's interview, but he is also Portuguese. I cannot entirely trust that we will get the full account. I would have you listen from a secret vantage point, and afterwards tell me if you believe anything was missed out by the translator.'

'Yes, my lord.'

Essex sat down behind his desk. He looked heavy-lidded, his face drawn, as though he had not slept much in recent days. 'So now to you. What news do you have for me? You have been out of the Tower since June, yet I have had few enough reports of your progress.'

'I have been watching Don Antonio as you requested, in the guise of a servant,' Goodluck told him, and shrugged. 'I have seen nothing but a Portuguese nobleman going about his daily business. Foreign letters sometimes arrive, secretly or via couriers, and I take pains to find and read them where possible. But there is never anything suspicious or written in any code that I can discern.' He paused. 'His son, Don Manuel, is another case, however.'

The earl's gaze narrowed on his face. 'You suspect Don Manuel to be a traitor?'

'He has received a few visitors at night lately. Foreigners, possibly Spaniards. I have not been able to overhear their conversations. But I did find a note once, signed by him and then torn up, the pieces discarded when he was called away suddenly. I was able to reconstruct part of the note before he returned, and there was some mention of a bribe. And initials which could have been a reference to King Philip.'

'If his father were to die, Don Manuel would presumably inherit his mantle as next in line to the throne of Portugal.'

'Yes, my lord.' Goodluck frowned. 'But it may be that Don Manuel is prepared to forgo that honour if King Philip offers a lucrative enough inducement to relinquish that right for ever to the Spanish.'

'Or perhaps the King hopes to recruit Don Manuel to his feud against Queen Elizabeth.' Essex leaned back in his chair with a grim expression. 'He would make an excellent rallying point for traitors and dissidents in this country, for the Queen refuses to believe ill of his father.'

'Rightly so, I believe.'

'The Queen does not understand the danger in which she stands. She allows these secret enemies into the country, then hampers my efforts to have them watched.'

Essex glanced at him, his face suddenly shuttered, as though realizing the disloyal nature of what he had just said. 'You will not repeat what is said here to any man, you understand? And after tonight, you will return to your post and watch Don Manuel more closely. I want to know everyone he speaks to, and what is said. And keep copies of any letters you intercept. I did not have you released from the Tower to waste my time with half a story.'

Boldly, Goodluck replied, 'I shall continue to serve you with all loyalty, my lord. But you told me on my release that Mistress Morgan would also be freed if I performed my duties to your satisfaction.'

Essex said nothing, though his eyes betrayed a flicker of impatience.

Goodluck continued, refusing to be silenced, 'I am concerned for Lucy's health now that the cold weather is here, for I have heard she has not been well in recent weeks. Nor have I been permitted to visit her, even though it was my own reckless behaviour that brought her to such a cruel fate.' He hesitated. 'I will always be deeply grateful for your mercy towards me, my lord. But you have the Queen's ear. Is there no way you can also arrange for Lucy's release?'

'It was not mercy, Master Goodluck, as I am sure you have guessed. I needed your services. But the Queen has no such need of Lucy's services. And she is still angry about her wantonness in lying with you while unmarried.'

'That was my fault. I persuaded her.'

The earl smiled drily. 'And I have no doubt she was willing to be persuaded.'

'My lord—'

'Listen, it was not my mercy which brought about your release. It was a trade agreed between myself and your lovely Mistress Morgan. Your release in return for some information which interested me greatly.'

Goodluck stared. 'Information?'

'Its nature need not concern either of us now. The situation was resolved. Yet although the Queen agreed to your release on my request, as a man who could still be useful in this war against Spain, she would not hear of allowing Lucy Morgan to go free.'

Essex looked at him with some degree of pity, then added, 'I have informed the Queen that Mistress Morgan's health is suffering in the chill confines of the Tower, and have arranged for one of her former servants to wait upon her there, so she is not alone in her sickness. But I fear Her Majesty will not countenance your lady's release. She is too angry over Lucy's betrayal of her trust.'

There was silence in the warm book-lined study. The fire crackled cheerily in the grate. Goodluck stared at it dumbly. So Lucy had traded information with Lord Essex to obtain his release. He had no idea what she had known that could be of such value to Essex that he would go against the Queen's orders and release him after he had served only ten days in the Tower. Though they had been the longest days of his life, he reminded himself, spent staring at the sky through a narrow iron grating in his cell and wondering where Lucy was being held, if she was safe.

At least she had been spared the pain and humiliation of a flogging. He had borne that punishment gladly for her. It was only flesh and blood, after all. The human spirit was not destroyed by such physical trials, though it could be crushed by the withholding of love, light and liberty for too long a period of time.

Her Majesty will not countenance your lady's release.

His lust and impatience to enjoy her body before they could be properly wed had brought his beloved to a small, dank cell in the Tower of London. And Lucy would almost certainly die there if he could not find a way to have her released.

'However,' the earl continued speculatively, 'perhaps if you could prove your worth to the Queen . . . If you were to perform some great service to her throne, Her Majesty might find it within herself to forgive your transgression and consent to Mistress Morgan's release – and to your marriage.'

Goodluck scrutinized the Portuguese letter again. His attention was arrested by a phrase that seemed oddly convoluted. He frowned, reading on, the florid hand yielding up its secrets with difficulty. Something about the gift of a costly ring from the King's own hand, sent as a gesture of good will, and had it been received yet by the proper person?

A gold and diamond ring.

'Perform some service to her throne?' he repeated, rolling up the letter again.

His lordship meant some *further* service, surely?

'You mentioned an interview with this man d'Avila that you wished me to hear, my lord?'

He removed his cloak and draped it over his arm. His heart was beating fast, for some parts at least of the puzzle that had nagged at him ever since Marlowe's murder were beginning to fall into place.

'Then I will need ink and paper if I am to translate the letter he was bearing.'

In a threadbare suit and patched hose, Gomez d'Avila looked like a man at the end of his resources. His face was turned away from Goodluck's vantage point for most of the interview, but he could see the coarse dark louse-ridden hair that d'Avila scratched at nervously while he spoke, and the scrawny neck painted with designs that Goodluck had seen before on the bodies of Arabs.

'I swear to you, my good lord, I am merely a courier,' he was telling Essex, via the translator, a man whose impatience and tendency to leave out half of what Gomez said marked him out as unreliable. 'I was asked to bring this letter to England, a letter which contains nothing but negotiations of commerce between two gentlemen, and to wait for a reply. That is all I know. I swear this on my life. On my mother's life. Read the letter, I beg of you, my lord. It is an innocent letter.'

He waved his hands as though performing a spell to make his guilt disappear. 'Innocent.'

His hoarse whining tones were oddly familiar. Goodluck put his eye more closely to the spyhole, studying the man intently.

Of course!

In Nieuwpoort, Goodluck had known him as Juan. A quiet man, Juan had served in some minor capacity on Stanley's staff, speaking nothing but fluent Spanish in public. Indeed, Goodluck had never suspected that he might in truth be Portuguese.

'And to whom were you bearing this letter?'

'I . . . I cannot recall at the moment, my lord. All these questions . . . It has gone out of my head.'

'I need a name.'

'It will come back to me. But I swear, no one important. An English merchant looking to buy some jewels. Some pearls, that is all. You will see from the letter.'

'His abode?'

A helpless shrug. 'Somewhere in London.'

'You recall neither this man's name nor his place of residence, yet you were to have delivered a letter to him?'

Gomez nodded, as if this was a perfectly credible story. 'Forgive me. My memory is not so good. I will tell you both when I remember them, my lord.'

'Who gave you the letter to bring to England?'

'Ah, *si, si*!' The man nodded sagely when the translator had finished relaying this question to him. 'I have forgotten his name also. But he was a very wealthy man in Flanders. A merchant. He gave me the letter on the docks.'

Essex made a brief note on the paper in front of him. 'What was your original purpose in sailing to Sandwich?'

'To visit England, my lord.'

'For what reason?'

Gomez spread his hands wide. His translator worked pithily, picking out the gist of his explanation from among Gomez's excessive and unlikely compliments. 'I came because I desired to see your great and beautiful land for myself.' He nodded at Essex's incredulous look. 'But how can you doubt it, my lord? Portugal is a dry land. Where I come from, the soil is parched and nothing grows there. England enjoys the rain all year round. So many green fields. All the little white sheep. What other reason could there be?'

'Master Gomez, England is at war with Spain, and therefore with Portugal, which is currently under the rule of the Spanish King,' Essex pointed out drily. 'What in God's name made you think a voyage to the land of your enemy, just to see its natural beauty, was a good idea?'

'Now that I have been arrested,' Gomez conceded glumly, 'I can see my mistake.'

Essex looked at him for a long moment in silence. 'So you did not in fact run this errand on behalf of His Majesty King Philip of Spain?'

This was too close to an insult for d'Avila. He stood up, knocking his chair over and swearing a violent oath in Portuguese, as though outraged to have been accused of such a crime. 'I have answered your questions most faithfully, my lord, and the hour is late. Why must you continue to hold me against my will?'

'If you are innocent, you have nothing to fear.' Essex also rose to his feet. 'Meanwhile, you are required to spend a little more time with us at Her Majesty's pleasure, while we verify your documents and the contents of the letter found in your possession.'

The interview having been brought to a close, Essex bade his guards keep watch over Gomez d'Avila, and stepped outside to speak with Goodluck.

They walked a little way down the corridor, their voices lowered.

'Any thoughts, Master Goodluck? The fellow is lying, certainly. But for whom is that letter intended, and who wrote it?' Essex glanced at the sheet in Goodluck's hand. His eyes grew keen. 'You have already translated it? Good work. What does it tell us?'

'On the surface, exactly what Senhor Gomez told you. It appears to be an inconsequential letter in Portuguese, addressed to "Your Worship". It promises information on the price of a gold and diamond ring, and some pearls, that had previously been mentioned in discussions between the two men, and then enquires about the reader's requirements for "musk and amber", which the writer of the letter is now ready to buy.'

Essex looked disappointed. 'Nothing more?'

'It is the wording that must be attended to, my lord, not the words themselves.' Goodluck smiled, and read aloud from his translation: ' "But before I resolve myself on this matter, I wish to be advised of the price of the musk and amber you are selling. If it please you to be my partner in this business, we shall make good profit." '

'Musk and amber?'

Goodluck mused a moment. 'Pearls are precious jewels.'

'And one of the Queen's chosen symbols.'

'And musk and amber might be found in a doctor's medicine chest.'

'Senhor Lopez?'

'My instinct leads me in that direction, yes. But you could not arrest the doctor on such scanty evidence. The thread in this letter is tenuous at best. As it was intended to be, to confuse any who might read this without possessing the key to these code words.'

'I am constantly in the dark over this business of Lopez. And the Queen protects him. She favours him, despite our warnings.' His jaw clenched. 'I wish to God I could wrest this simpering doctor from her side and consign him to the Tower. Lopez would soon bleat when faced with the rack.'

Goodluck thought of Lucy, imprisoned in the Tower through no fault of her own. It was hard to stay silent.

He studied the letter again. If he could find a Spanish plot among all this, a coherent plot with a gallows at the end of it, he might yet be able to obtain Lucy's release.

The gold and diamond ring.

He had seen such a ring before, first on Marlowe's finger at Deptford and then on the hand of his murderer. Though Ingram Frizer was not to be charged with the playwright's murder, he had heard. No, for the man had killed Marlowe, it was claimed, in self-defence.

Self-defence!

He dwelt on the memory of that costly ring. A bribe from King Philip himself?

Lopez would soon bleat when faced with the rack.

'Give me a few hours,' he told Essex, 'then have this man Gomez conveyed to the Tower.'

'Your plan?'

'I shall install myself in a cell there, and be submitted to the rack by one of your torturers. When Gomez is brought in, he will recognize me at once, for I knew him briefly in Nieuwpoort. I will be introduced to him as a fellow Spanish spy and traitor, and this will help him to trust me.' He paused. 'Once we are left alone together, I will get his story from him.'

'It could take days to gain his trust.'

332

'Let us hope not. I will ride back to Essex House with the information as soon as I have it.'

'God speed then, sir!' Essex clapped him on the back. 'I shall write a note for the captain of the guards at the Tower. But you are a brave man to set foot inside the Tower again.'

The Tower might be a grim place, Goodluck thought, yet it is where Lucy lays her head each night. And where Lucy is, there I should be also.

Despite his wish to be near Lucy again, Goodluck had to admit to some trepidation as the barge neared the dark walled mound of the Tower. Only a few months ago he had been a prisoner here, and his beloved was still kept in this place against her will. The river was misty, the eerie sound of lapping water bouncing off stone. He stared up at the forbidding towers beyond the wall, saw a light burning steadily in one of the high window slits and wondered if it was Lucy's cell. A shout went up inside as the barge came slowly in to moor alongside the damp, mossed steps that led up to the gate. A few moments passed while they waited, the barge bobbing uneasily back and forth, tugging at its ropes on a strong outgoing tide. Then a man came out in the livery of the Tower, carrying a lantern, and made his way down to the riverside.

'No one is allowed to enter after dark without permission. Who are you? What is your business here?'

Goodluck jumped ashore and handed over the note he had brought from Lord Essex. The man read the note with a dour expression, then lifted his lantern, shining it full in Goodluck's face.

'Follow me,' the man said shortly, and climbed back up the steps. 'Though I do not know what the Constable of the Tower will say to this. Master Goodluck, is it?'

'That's right.'

'You've been here before.' It was a statement, not a question.

'I have.'

'Ah.' The man looked back at him, his face unreadable in the long shadows of the watergate wall. 'I daresay you'd know your own way then. But no one is permitted to walk unaccompanied here.'

He was led through the ancient gate and inside the Tower confines, then up the sloping track and past the green where he had been flogged before a watching crowd that had included Lucy herself. Now the place was empty, though a wooden platform still stood below the grey towers, as though awaiting its next victim.

Coming to a low door in one of the dark buildings that had loomed up through the mist, the man knocked and after a moment's wait was admitted by an unseen guard. He turned and gestured Goodluck silently to follow him up the winding stair.

The stairway was narrow, lit only by the swaying light of the lantern. Goodluck knew he was not there as a prisoner this time. Yet this simple message had not been communicated to his heart, which beat sickeningly fast as he climbed the stone steps.

At the first turn of the stair, the man pushed open a studded door and pointed down a corridor that led into darkness.

'This should serve your purpose. Though there is only one interrogator working tonight,' he muttered. 'Master Topcliffe.'

Master Topcliffe!

Goodluck halted, suddenly too unsteady to go on. At the mention of that dreaded name his knees had begun to buckle, his innards turning to water.

'I . . .' he began shakily, then saw the malicious gleam in his guide's eyes and knew he was being mocked. How

334

could he hope to be a man for Lucy when he could not even be a man for his own sake? 'The name of the interrogator makes no odds to me. I am a servant of the Queen, as is he. Lead on, fellow.'

Two

IT WAS VERY LATE WHEN FOOTSTEPS CAME SHUFFLING UP THE steps to her cell at the Tower, and someone began to unlock the heavy wooden door. Lucy turned without interest from the narrow window, through which she had been watching the bright flecks of torchlight reflected on the water, and the dark shape of a barge struggling slowly across the river currents as though intending to dock at the watergate. She did not bother to adjust her simple coif, for the place was dim enough at night to conceal any faults of face or attire. She had extinguished her candle stump some hours ago, and now the cell was lit only by a small fire burning in the grate, though its fuel would soon be exhausted and she knew there would be no more wood until tomorrow.

She ought to have been asleep, but she found her nights of captivity at the Tower more difficult than the days, and often put off retiring to bed as long as possible.

Carefully, Lucy sat to receive her jailor. She draped her lace shawl low across her shoulders so that its folds obscured her body, as was her custom with visitors these days.

Except the woman who entered was not Mistress Hall. Lucy stared, and felt slightly sick. She did not know what to say.

It was Cathy.

Her sombrely dressed jailor pushed past her former friend, who had halted on the threshold, staring back at her.

'Not abed yet, Mistress Morgan?' her jailer demanded, and glanced at the fire. 'You will burn through your fuel allowance before time.'

There was a disapproving look on her face. More disapproving than was usual, Lucy noted, for Mistress Hall had the kind of turned-up nose and curling lip that always seemed to be sneering.

Lucy said nothing, staring past her at Cathy.

Mistress Hall motioned Cathy into the room, then turned to Lucy. 'We have received orders from his lordship the Earl of Essex that you are to be provided with your own serving woman, to which end he has sent this woman, whose name is Mistress Belton, to wait on you and share your cell.'

Lucy's throat constricted with anger and despair. Surely she had fallen asleep and this was a nightmare? Why would Lord Essex send a serving woman to tend her, and not just any maid, but the woman who had betrayed her to the Queen?

'I shall arrange for a straw pallet to be brought up tonight for your bed,' Mistress Hall was telling Cathy, her manner cold and unwelcoming. 'The chest you brought will be sent up in the morning, when the Constable has checked its contents. If you wish for anything that cannot wait until my daily visit, you may knock upon the door to be released. There is a guard on the stair who will attend you.'

'Thank you, Mistress Hall,' Cathy murmured.

'Goodnight,' Mistress Hall told them both sharply, then slammed the door shut, locking it behind her.

They continued to stare at each other in silence for a moment, no sound in the room but the crackle of the miserable little fire, then Cathy took a few tentative steps forward.

Her face crumpled as she looked about the room, taking in the dusty floor with its stale rushes, the narrow window looking down to the river, the small grate with its wretched flames that barely kept the chill October draughts at bay.

'Oh sweet Jesu,' Cathy whispered, tears in her eyes, and fell to her knees before Lucy. 'What have I done to you? My good friend, my dearest, truest Lucy.'

Lucy put out a hand to her friend. Then she drew it back slightly, on the edge of tears herself. There was only one question to ask. 'Why did you betray me?'

She too was whispering, for she half suspected Mistress Hall to be listening at the door, and this was not a conversation she wished to share with her jailor.

'What wrong had I ever done you?' she demanded. 'Tell me, Cathy, for I have searched my heart these past months, with nowhere to go but this room and the yard below, and have found no cause for your betrayal.' She heard her voice quiver and was angry with herself for not being more controlled, but she could not seem to contain her turbulent emotions. 'Was I too distant, perhaps? Did I neglect our friendship once I had been advanced at court? For I can think of no other reason that you should hate me so much.'

Cathy shook her head, weeping quietly. 'You did me no wrong. It was not you who drove me to betray you, but his lordship, the Earl of Southampton. One of his spies told him that I have a son back home in Norfolk, and his lordship told me he would . . . He threatened to send men to

338

my father's farm and have James killed. He said it could be done this easily,' she snapped her fingers brutally, her mouth trembling, 'and made to look like an accident.'

'Henry Wriothesley threatened to kill your son?'

'If I did not help him.' Cathy looked at her directly. 'He made me follow you and note to whom you spoke, and when, and whether you met with any man privately. But I swear, I had not understood what he planned to do with the information.'

'But you knew he wished me ill.'

'Yes,' Cathy agreed reluctantly.

'Why did you not come to me with these threats? I might have been able to help you.'

'Against the Earl of Southampton, a young man of fortune and nobility, favoured by the Queen herself?' Cathy's eyes were desperate. 'We are only women. These noblemen hold the true power at court. And if his lordship had discovered my betrayal, my son would have died for it. I saw it in his eyes. He would have had James killed and thought nothing of it. I promise you, I had no choice.'

'Rather my life than your son's,' Lucy murmured, thinking aloud, then nodded. 'I cannot hold you to account for that.'

'I knew the earl disliked you, I cannot deny it, though not how much. To condemn you to this . . .' Her friend shuddered, glancing about the bare cell. 'And because of that, I do not ask you to forgive me. For what I have done is unforgivable. But perhaps in time, knowing how much I love my son and that I acted only to protect his life, you may bring yourself to forget a little. Just a very little.' Cathy hesitated. 'Enough to trust me to be your servant again.'

Lucy folded her arms across her belly, unsure what her answer should be. Cathy had been her friend for many years – ever since they had been court entertainers together as girls, indeed – and she had not thought it possible that anything could come between them. But her betrayal had led to Lucy's ruin and, worse, to Goodluck's disgrace. He at least was free of this place, and so she was content with the four dreary walls of her prison, knowing he had escaped the same fate.

Yet could she now, given what she had been brought to, forget Cathy's betrayal and accept her presence here?

'Come.' She held out her hands to Cathy, her mind made up. 'I have wept too many nights, wondering how I wronged you. I do not wish to spend another night in tears now that I know the truth. Let us embrace each other as friends, not as servant and mistress. For we can be friends again in this grim chamber, a place where the court does not intrude, where we are equals before God.'

Stumbling to her feet, Cathy embraced her at once. They clung together, kissing each other affectionately, and soon Lucy found herself weeping despite her wish. It was the first time she had felt loving arms about her since the spring, when she had been arrested and brought to this dreadful place.

'What is it?' Cathy asked, seeing her tears. 'Are you hurt?'

'No, I . . . I miss Goodluck, that is all.'

'I heard Master Goodluck had been released, though I did not understand why. Was it to serve Lord Essex?'

Lucy nodded, unable to speak her mind, to explain why she was so distressed by Goodluck's absence. It was not safe, not even with Cathy. Though now that she had a woman attending her, rather than seeing to her needs herself, it could not be very long before her secret was discovered.

Her friend stepped back, releasing her. She stared at Lucy in silence for a long moment, her face perplexed. Then her hand flew to her mouth. She glanced at the door

340

as though suddenly afraid, then leaned forward, whispering hoarsely in Lucy's ear, 'You are with child, aren't you?'

There, it was out. At long last, her secret was out.

Lucy sighed with a kind of terrified relief, then pulled aside the lacy shawl to reveal her too-tight bodice and the hard ball of her stomach below, pressing up under her ribs. She had loosened the stitches in her day gown herself, and widened the side panels by taking material from the under-skirt, but it would be impossible to hide her state much longer. Any day now, Mistress Hall would stop making sharp comments on Lucy's greedy habits, and notice that only her breasts and belly had enlarged over the summer, not the rest of her.

'How far gone are you?' Cathy asked, her face almost ghost-like with fear. No doubt she was imagining how the Queen would react to this news. For one of her ladies-in-waiting to lie with a man while unmarried was sin enough. But to conceive a child out of wedlock . . .

'Seven months, by my count.'

'And no one suspects?'

'No one has come near enough to suspect, except for Mistress Hall, who accompanies me outside sometimes. And she merely thinks I have grown fat and sloth-like through over-indulgence,' Lucy whispered, then lovingly stroked her swollen belly, 'though it cannot be long before even she sees the truth.'

'Does Master Goodluck know? He is the father, is he not?'

'He is the father, yes. But I have not told him this. How could I? He might make some desperate attempt to be with me, or else to have me released, and I do not wish him to endanger himself.' Lucy smiled, thinking of her absent lover. 'He is such a good man, Cathy. The best man I have ever known.'

'Lucy, I cannot imagine how you have suffered, alone in this place and concealing such a secret, even from the child's father.'

'It has not been so very hard as I feared,' Lucy mused. 'I have always enjoyed solitude, and although I dislike the unvarying confinement of this little room, I have grown to prefer my isolation to the perils of court life. Here at least I am safe from plots and counter-plots, from the many subtle intrigues that seemed to dog my steps at the Queen's side. And so long as Goodluck is at liberty, I shall be at peace with myself. Though I admit that it has not always been easy, concealing my condition from those who guard me here.'

The early days had been the worst, arriving at the Tower with the faintest nagging suspicion that she might be with child. Bouts of nausea had followed in those first weeks away from court, her sickness hard to conceal from her jailor. She had lied, saying she was unhappy and could not face her food because of the injustice of being imprisoned.

In a way, it had been true. Early that summer, she had indeed been pining for Goodluck; as the days and weeks passed, she had grown resigned to her fate. The mere fact of his freedom gave her pleasure, and although her heart ached that she had been forced to betray Shakespeare in order to obtain Goodluck's release, she could not be wholly angry with herself for telling what she knew. Lord Essex would not have wished to risk a scandal at court over his friend Southampton's nature, so he could not have openly attacked Shakespeare. To her mind, the affair would have been quelled with more subtlety than that, perhaps with a warning or a threat. Nor had she heard anything of trouble for Will in the occasional gossip brought to her by the Tower servants, the shy girls who brought the food and laid the fire for her. The theatres had been reopened after the summer plague, and one of the girls had been taken by her uncle to a new play by William Shakespeare at the Cross Keys Inn.

It seemed that Will had not unduly suffered for her letter to Essex, and Goodluck was free. What was there to regret?

Later in the summer, grown too large and clumsy to make her way easily down the narrow winding stair to the yard below, she had claimed ill-health and refused to walk outside each day at the allotted hour. Mistress Hall had argued bitterly over this refusal, swearing that river air was beneficial to the health of all prisoners in the Tower. But her jailor had given up when the first winds of autumn came, and allowed Lucy to remain inside without protest. Now that she had a companion, though, she would doubtless be expected to walk outside again. And her swollen belly would be more visible in the cold light of an October morning.

Cathy took her hands, kneeling by her side. 'My dear friend, my mistress, will you listen to me for once and hear sense?'

'Speak and I will listen,' Lucy told her softly, though she was still thinking of the child within her.

Goodluck's child. Their child. She could not help remembering the poor dead babe they had brought stillborn from her womb after her fall at the Parkers' house. A boy, and so perfectly formed, yet tiny. Too tiny to live in this harsh world. Every day she put a hand on her belly, whispering to the unseen child within her, and prayed to God that this one might live, son or daughter, to grow up strong and meet its father.

'It will not be possible to conceal your condition much longer,' Cathy began gently, 'and you do not want the Queen to hear of it from the Constable of the Tower, as a secret brought to light by that awful woman Hall. Trust me, that would do you greater harm than if you made the admission now and of your own free will. Let me fetch you paper and ink, and you can write to the Queen tonight.'

'The Queen?'

'No, hear me out. You promised that you would. If you confess your sin, throwing yourself on her royal mercy, the Queen may soften and permit you to marry Master Goodluck before the babe is born.'

Lucy considered her friend's suggestion for a moment. 'But when my condition is known, Master Goodluck may be punished again for . . . for this miracle,' she whispered, touching her belly.

'Maybe so. But better to risk further punishment now than face it later, when it is too late and the babe is born out of wedlock.' Cathy made a face. 'Remember, I was in the same position when I was carrying James. We had to marry with a child in my womb, and his mother never let me forget the shame of it. But how much better to face that humiliation now, than for your child to be born into it. Do what I suggest,' she urged Lucy, kissing her hands. 'Write to the Queen and admit your shame. Take this last risk and see what it brings you.'

To marry Goodluck, to be his wife at last. It was a temptation. But there were greater things at stake here besides her own happiness and the future of their child.

'I will write to the Queen and beg for clemency,' she agreed slowly, 'but not yet. Give me a few more days in which to consider what to say.'

She smiled at her companion. It was strange to be so comfortable in her presence again. Yet despite the betrayal between them, it felt almost as though Cathy had never been away. They were still firm friends, regardless of the horrors of the past year. Now at last she had someone to confide in, and would no longer need to pace the room at night, her heart almost bursting with all the secrets it had to keep.

'Besides,' she added, 'in the last note I received from

Goodluck, he indicated to me that he was working in disguise, watching a man for Lord Essex. If his mission is interrupted too soon, it may endanger the Queen's life.'

Three

A MAN WAS BEING DRAGGED AWAY AS GOODLUCK WAS BROUGHT
into the Tower cell where Topcliffe enacted his interroga-
tions. He averted his eyes from the barely conscious
victim, stripped to raw flesh and unable to walk, all the
fingernails ripped off his right hand and both his knees
crushed in some mangling device, leaving a bloodied mess
of lacerated skin behind. He understood the necessity for
torture when the information to be garnered was of vital
importance to the state. When it was merely a matter of
determining a man's faith, however, the agonies inflicted
were too barbarous to be Christian.

The cell was large, holding a rack and an iron cage as
well as other implements of torture he recognized: long-
handled irons thrust into the red-hot heart of a brazier, a
high bar on the wall where a man could hang for hours
until his arms were wrenched loose from their sockets, a
leather whip, a small bundle of birch twigs for tormenting
the feet, pincers to remove finger- and toenails, and a
variety of smaller tools laid out on a rough board, their use
thankfully unknown to Goodluck.

Topcliffe perused the letter from Lord Essex, then
dismissed the guard who had brought him. Alone in

the cell, the two men looked at each other in silence.

Slowly, Topcliffe walked around Goodluck, sizing him up as though considering how he would fit on the wall chains or the rack. His eyes gleamed with malice. 'I remember you, Master Goodluck. I remember all the men who have been brought before me. As I recall, you were strong. But not strong enough to resist the hot irons.'

'I am not here to be tortured this time,' Goodluck reminded him. 'Only to persuade a Portuguese spy to trust me. He will follow soon. We may not have much time.'

'If we are to convince this man you are in the pay of the Spanish, it will not be enough to chain you up and crack a whip in your direction. You must be made to bleed a little.'

Goodluck could see the sense in that, though his skin crept at the look on Topcliffe's face. 'A very little, perhaps,' he agreed.

He glanced at the implements laid out on the side tables, many still bloodied from their last victim. He felt sick at the thought of being subjected to any of them, but could see that his chances of success depended on making this look real.

'What do you suggest?'

Topcliffe fingered the whip, glancing at Goodluck speculatively. 'There is this.'

'I thank you, no. Something that will do less harm, yet still bloody me enough to suggest a night of torture at your hands.'

The Queen's interrogator hesitated over the smaller implements, then selected one, a narrow coil of metal lined with tiny sharp teeth and topped with a stout wooden handle. This fearsome-looking tool he shoved into the glowing brazier.

'Strip off your shirt,' he instructed Goodluck. Once he was bare-chested, Topcliffe secured him to the damp cell wall, fastening metal cuffs about his wrists. 'Now you are my prisoner.'

Topcliffe removed the toothed coil from the red-hot brazier, then approached Goodluck. Close enough that Goodluck could smell his foul breath, Topcliffe rolled the coil slowly down his chest and belly, searing his skin, pressing so deep that the metal teeth tore into his flesh with every cruel rotation.

When the coil reached his lower belly, digging into the tender flesh there, Goodluck uttered a cry and jerked instinctively against his restraints, though he had promised himself not to show any weakness.

Topcliffe smiled, removing the metal coil from his flesh. 'My own invention. You admire it? If you were in truth a suspected traitor, the metal teeth would be heated in the fire until they were red-hot. Then you would be stripped completely, so that I could continue lower, tearing into your groin and thighs. That is when most men break down, begging to make their confession instead.'

'I can readily believe it,' Goodluck managed from between gritted teeth.

Laying the implement aside, Topcliffe ran an exploratory hand over Goodluck's chest and belly. He probed the deepest holes with his fingers, as though taking pleasure in his suffering. Which no doubt he was.

'I do this for your own good, for you have not been tortured enough for a suspected spy.' Having cruelly plumbed his wounds, the interrogator rubbed bloodied fingers back and forth across Goodluck's face. 'There, that looks better.'

Topcliffe turned away, and began to write something in a volume that lay open on one of the tables. A note of his torturings, no doubt. Goodluck closed his eyes and tried to ignore the pain across his chest and belly. The injuries were neither deep nor life-threatening. The dozens of holes stung as they bled, however, and he could only hope there would be no infection.

Soon there was the sound of footsteps in the corridor. Topcliffe laid down his quill.

'It seems your friend has arrived. Shall we make this look more convincing?' He plucked up a short bundle of twigs from the assortment of whips and scourges on the table, then added mildly, 'Perhaps a few cries and oaths to promote the illusion?'

The birch twigs were applied brutally and repeatedly to his bare chest. This was no illusion, Goodluck thought grimly. He cried out with genuine pain, and dragged on the rattling chains that bound him to the wall. Topcliffe continued to birch him as the cell door was flung open, each stroke hard enough to break his skin, a look of malicious amusement on the interrogator's face.

'Enough, enough!' Goodluck called out hoarsely in Spanish, and meant it. 'In the name of our sweet Saviour, I swear that I have told you all I know.'

Two guards stood in the doorway, with Gomez between them, his wrists and ankles chained together, then linked to a rope about his waist. The Portuguese spy looked terrified as his small darting eyes took in the cell with its horrific implements of torture, then its unfortunate prisoner, his chest bare and bloodied, who had cried out in Spanish as he entered. Finally his gaze turned to the interrogator, clad in a leather apron stained with the blood of many victims.

'Save thy miserable servant, O Lord Jesus!' Gomez muttered, and clumsily attempted to cross himself, though his hands were chained together.

Topcliffe threw down the birch twigs and turned away, as though no longer interested in Goodluck.

On his way out, he spoke briefly to the guards in the doorway. 'A new prisoner for me to interrogate? Take him to a cell until I have time to deal with him. It is late, I have finished for the night. And you may put this other Catholic wretch in with him. The spy has said little, but the rack should loosen his tongue tomorrow.'

To his shame, Goodluck felt his knees buckle beneath him when the guard unchained him from the wall.

'For show,' Topcliffe had said, but Goodluck knew the Queen's interrogator would happily have continued with that flogging until half the skin was flayed from his body. At least his bloodied appearance and unfeigned cries of pain seemed to have had the desired effect on Gomez d'Avila.

The man said nothing further, but there was an air of terror to his silence which told Goodluck his performance had been credible. Still, it would take rather more than a few bloodied cuts to wring a confession out of this close-mouthed spy.

Left alone with Gomez, he wasted no time but groaned, clasping his head in his hands. 'What a fool I was,' Goodluck muttered in Spanish, rocking back and forth as though he had lost his wits, 'to think I could succeed in tricking the English court. They are demons!'

Gomez watched in silence for a while. The chains binding his hands had been removed on entering the cell, but his ankles were still fastened together, hobbling him. The Portuguese spy had therefore settled himself on the damp floor of the cell, his back against the wall, his knees drawn up. Although he was clearly in fear of his life, Goodluck could tell that he was wary and would not easily be deceived.

When Gomez finally spoke, it was with a note of deep suspicion in his voice. 'Señor,' he replied carefully in Spanish, 'I think perhaps I know you. Were you at

Nieuwpoort in the Low Countries with the English knight Stanley and his men?'

Raising his head in mock surprise, Goodluck stared back at him. 'Yes, friend, I was indeed,' he said, trusting Gomez would not recall he had been posing as a Dutchman. 'What, were you there too?'

The man hesitated, still frowning, then nodded.

'And now you have come to these ungodly shores, the English have arrested you, just as they did me?'

Again, Gomez nodded, but said nothing.

'Do you see what they have done to me?' Goodluck indicated his bloodied chest. 'I was charged by Stanley to bring a secret message from him to a gentleman in England, for the señor knew I spoke a little of his filthy tongue. But I was arrested at Sandwich and charged with conspiring with the Queen's enemies, and then they tortured me. Nor is my ordeal over. Tomorrow I shall be returned to their man Topcliffe, who will all but squeeze the life out of me with his torturing ways before I am taken to be executed.'

His companion stayed silent, but there was sympathy in his face. Goodluck spoke of more trivial matters after that. The poor food he had been served, more like pig slops than pottage, the cruelty of the English guards, and the stench of human ordure about the place. Eventually Gomez began to relax, even passing a few comments himself.

'So what is your sin, señor?' Goodluck asked casually. 'Or is it merely the taint of foreign blood that makes you a criminal? For I recall from my days in Nieuwpoort that you are not Spanish, but Portuguese. These English would hang a man for not speaking their tongue!'

Gomez muttered, 'I was to have carried a letter from Flanders to a man here, but I was arrested at the docks. There is nothing else to tell.'

351

'May the holy Virgin spare you from their interrogator Topcliffe, then. For I have been tortured and scourged, and if I say nothing upon the rack, Topcliffe says I shall be pressed inside a box loaded with spikes. When the lid of this box is shut upon me, the spikes will pierce my skin all over my body. And if it does not pierce my heart and pop my eyeballs out, I shall be dragged behind a cart to their Tyburn Hill, and there strung aloft. But even then my suffering will not be at an end, for I shall be cut down while still alive, then quartered by the executioner, my heart dragged still beating out of my chest, and my severed head stuck on a pike for all men to jeer at.'

Gomez listened to this horrific description of what lay ahead of him. 'It was a fearsome chamber,' he agreed, and there was sweat on his forehead now. 'That evil man . . .'

'Topcliffe,' Goodluck supplied helpfully. He spat on the floor in a venomous manner. 'He is the Protestant Queen's chief interrogator. They say Topcliffe hates us Catholics so much, he takes the greatest pleasure in his work and makes us suffer more than other men. Some even say . . .' He hesitated, then shook his head. 'No, I cannot speak of it. It is too horrible.'

'W-what?' Gomez stammered. 'Tell me what this horror is, for the love of God.'

'They say he inflicts unnatural practices on Catholics,' he whispered, looking up and meeting Gomez's horrified gaze with mock shame. 'Male or female, it makes no odds to him. So far he has not touched me in that way. I swear to you, if he does that tomorrow, I will beg the fiend for death rather than commit a sin against God.'

The man was terrified in earnest now. 'And you say that if we betray our masters . . . he will not . . .'

'So they claim.' Goodluck shrugged. 'But I have nothing

more to tell, so my case is hopeless. You should save yourself the worst, though. There is no shame in begging for mercy. But come, let us pray together.'

His companion nodded slowly, and raised a hand to cross himself, trembling. 'Christ have pity on my soul.'

Goodluck hushed him as a guard passed close by their door, his face suddenly apprehensive. Then he bent his head. 'Dear Lord in heaven, if I had known I was going to my death when I bore that letter to Senhor Lopez, I swear that—'

'Senhor Lopez?' his companion repeated, startled into betraying himself by the mention of this name. 'But that is the very man . . . That is to say, I was to bear a message to Lopez too.'

'Your letter?'

'No, I was to speak the message to him.' The spy shook his head, putting a finger to his lips. 'It was safer that way.'

'Discharge your message before you die. Speak it to me, and I will take it to my grave. Otherwise you will never rest in peace!'

'I cannot!'

They were whispering urgently now. Goodluck gripped his shoulder hard. 'Be a man, Gomez. Do not allow these English to frighten you. Discharge your message before you are tortured, and I swear, your heart will be lighter for it.'

'The message . . . The message was from Tinoco.' Gomez was now sweating profusely. He ran a hand over his forehead, his eyes unfocused. 'If by any chance you survive this terrible place, and I die, will you deliver this message to Senhor Lopez for me?'

'Yes.' Goodluck crossed himself again and spat on the ground between them. 'I swear it.'

'I . . . I was to tell Lopez that it is all arranged. That Tinoco has been ordered by our master to bring fifty thousand crowns secretly into England, to be handed over to Lopez as a reward when the deed is done.'

'The deed?'

Gomez gave him a significant look. 'The *deed*. You know.'

Some leap of faith had to be made if he was not to reveal himself. 'You mean the murder of the Queen?'

The spy nodded, lowering his voice. 'Lopez has been reluctant to fulfil his mission, as you must know. But now he has accepted the King's bribe, all shall be well.'

'A bribe?'

'A very fine ring, cunningly wrought of gold and diamonds, taken from King Philip's own finger. What man would refuse such a lavish gift, especially if followed by fifty thousand crowns when the Queen is dead?'

'Friend, I shall carry your message to the noble Lopez if I survive. But this plan will never succeed. Even if the doctor is willing to be bribed, how are fifty thousand crowns to be brought into the country without the English finding it as soon as Tinoco lands?'

'Tinoco is to write to the Queen from Brussels, offering her Spanish secrets which he is willing to sell, and thus be granted safe passage into Dover. It is a perfect plan. The English Queen is a fool surrounded by fools. She is always greedy for secrets, and will readily grant Tinoco what he desires. Once he has arrived at court, Lopez will poison the Queen, and when the church bells toll to announce her death, Tinoco will hand over the fifty thousand crowns' reward as arranged.'

He smiled at Goodluck, unaware that he had just betrayed himself and his fellow plotters. 'And thus the mighty Queen of England will meet her death, not from a vast Spanish army of invasion but at the hands of a few stout Portuguese.'

'A work of genius indeed,' Goodluck murmured

appreciatively, then stood and limped to the cell door. He hammered on it with his fist. 'Open this door, in the name of the Queen!'

Four

'*MAGNIFIQUE!*' THE FRENCH AMBASSADOR EXCLAIMED, clapping his hands as he watched Elizabeth leap into the air for a fifth time, to be caught round the waist by Lord Essex and lowered gently to the floor. 'Your Majesty, I have never seen La Volta performed with such skill and daring. Your Majesty enjoys the grace and strength of a young girl, I swear it!'

The music came to an end, and Elizabeth finished triumphantly before the ambassador, her forehead damp with a fine sheen of perspiration. Her legs ached cruelly and she was short of breath, but she was determined to show no indication of infirmity in front of her courtiers. Besides, she hated to miss her regular dancing practice. It was one of the few pleasures left to her these days.

'I thank you, monsieur,' she told him, and graciously held out her hand so the ambassador could kiss it. 'This is your first visit to Whitehall, is it not? How do you find the palace?'

'Like its beautiful owner, Whitehall is *magnifique*, quite *magnifique*!' The ambassador flashed his oily smile at her again, bowing. 'If a trifle cold in the evenings.'

'London is always cold this late in the year, but a little dancing will soon warm you up.'

On the advice of her doctors, she had kept to her bed for the past sennight over some trifling sickness, but had returned to her duties that morning with unusual vigour.

'There will be more dancing after the banquet tonight, and you will dance the Saltarella with me. That should test your mettle, for I am told we dance it faster here than in France these days.'

He bowed very low. 'I am all gratitude for your generous attentions, Your Majesty.'

A dry cough behind her made Elizabeth turn.

She gave a little frown at the sight of Robert Cecil in the doorway to her dancing chamber, his narrow face disapproving. She knew Cecil had not wanted her to rise that morning but to remain in bed, cosseted and wrapped up like a sick hound at the fireside. But the chill November sunlight had beckoned to her as soon as the shutters were drawn back, and she had demanded her court gown and ruff instead of her day robe, determined to walk out among her courtiers again.

It was not for her privy councillors to insist that she was too unwell to face the court.

'Cecil?' She held out a hand, seeing the rolled-up document he was carrying. 'More bad news, by the look of your long face?'

Burghley's sombre son glanced past her at the musicians, maids and ladies gossiping comfortably among themselves under the tall sunlit windows, and the ambassador at her shoulder, his inquisitive face eager for some tittle-tattle to send back to the French court.

'There is some business that has been left to one side during your sickness and now demands your attention. But it is of a delicate nature.' Cecil hesitated. 'If we could converse in private, Your Majesty?'

Elizabeth sighed. Tiresome youth. Always trying to spoil her good humour, and rather too often succeeding. If only he was more like his father, moderate even in his dislikes.

'You here again, Cecil?'

Robbie had come up behind her while Cecil was talking, and now placed his hand outrageously on her hip. Just as if she were his wife. Or his mistress.

The thought made her light-headed.

'What, are we finished for the morning already?' Robbie sounded annoyed.

'Some business of state I must attend to,' she told him soothingly. 'You should take an interest, Robbie. You are a member of the Privy Council now.'

'I have not forgotten your generosity in that quarter. But there is still La Gavotte to practise, Your Majesty,' he murmured in her ear. 'The kissing dance.'

She smiled, then hid her smile behind her fan when Cecil turned his cool gaze in her direction.

'Shall we retire into the next chamber, Your Majesty?' he suggested. 'Or dismiss the dancers?'

'Let the musicians keep playing. I will return to dance when this business is concluded. You are a cloud darkening my sunny morning, Cecil, but if there is some business that will not wait . . .' She clicked her fingers. 'My lord Essex, you will accompany me. And two of my ladies.'

Cecil bowed as she swept towards the door. But she caught his look of acute dislike thrown at the nobleman following in her wake.

So the two boys still squabbled over her royal favour, did they? The thought both amused and irritated her. As long as they could learn to pull together in time of war, as Leicester and Burghley had finally done, all would be well.

And yet England was at war, and still they fought.

The white-haired Lord Burghley was waiting in the next chamber, leaning on his cane rather than occupying the only chair in the place, his black velvet cap on the table. 'Your Majesty,' the elder statesman said as she entered, bowing with difficulty, and she waved him to sit down.

'Your son has ruined my hour of dancing, Lord Burghley,' she told him curtly. 'What do you say to that?'

'It is a matter of great urgency,' he replied, surprising her with his stern tone.

What was this? Not more conspiracies?

So it was not simply a matter of signing a document and returning to her dancing practice, she thought, and regretted giving away the only seat. She admitted to a little fatigue, and some stiffness in her legs after those high leaps in La Volta. But she did not consider herself old enough to require such props as a cane or seat. For now, her own two feet would sustain her.

Elizabeth stood, tapping her foot impatiently as the door was closed behind them and her ladies sank to the floor near the fireplace, one taking up a book and reading quietly to the other. Helena, looking more tired than ever these days, and Lady Mary, whose gift for poetry could delight even the dour Cecil on occasion, it was said.

'Speak,' she urged Cecil, and held out her hand again for the document he was clasping so tightly. 'Come, let me have this bad news. I am eager to return to my dancing practice.'

Essex had come to her side. Now he stood with his arms folded, like a man about to be accused of a crime.

'What is it?' she demanded.

With a grim expression, Cecil handed over the paper. She unrolled it and glanced down at the contents. A warrant for the arrest and detention of a Portuguese Jew. Her temper rose when she saw the familiar name on the warrant.

Rodriguez Lopez.

'God's blood, are you all mad? My doctor? Is this your poisoning plot again, Robbie?'

'Your Majesty—' Essex began, but she refused to let him finish.

'I told you not to pursue that nonsensical charge, my lord. I will not have an innocent man accused of treason.' Elizabeth raised a hand, silencing his protest. 'No, I will not be gainsaid. For a man accused of treason is always tortured, and it is my belief that most men will confess to any crime, however dreadful the punishment, if it will save them even a moment's torment on the rack.'

'Where your safety is at stake, Your Majesty,' Lord Burghley said gravely, 'there can be no mercy shown, no infirmity of purpose.'

'You believe in this plot now, my lord? I thought you and Cecil were against it. When Lord Essex came to me again on this matter earlier in the autumn, you advised me to dismiss it from my mind. Now you too think my doctor guilty of plotting to poison me?'

'I did indeed advise Your Majesty not to lend too much credence to Lord Essex over this particular conspiracy. But in recent weeks I have been brought to a new understanding of the problem, and there is some evidence now to support his claim.'

'Evidence?' She glanced at Robbie searchingly. Was he behind this change in Burghley's position? 'Out with it.'

'I set a man to watch Lopez at his home,' Essex told her, though she could see he was not happy that she had doubted his word, and in front of Cecil too, 'and to follow whenever Lopez travelled about the country, which the doctor does with surprising frequency. This fellow sent me back reports on Lopez's dealings and meetings with others, and even conversations where he was privy to them. Some of the men with whom he has met in recent days, other Portuguese exiles with links to Spain, are also suspected of conspiring against your throne.'

360

'That is not evidence but hearsay,' she muttered, still loath to hand her doctor over to these men.

'There is a ring,' Essex countered swiftly. 'A gold and diamond ring, taken from the finger of King Philip himself, by all accounts, and sent as a bribe to Lopez. My man has seen Lopez wearing this ring at his house in Holborn, where no doubt he thought himself safe, that none would report him for it.'

'A bribe?' Her voice faltered.

She did not wish to think such evil of Dr Lopez. Was there no one at court she could trust?

Elizabeth walked to the leaded window and stared out, unseeing. 'How can you be sure this ring came from King Philip?'

'We have letters to prove it,' Lord Burghley told her. He threw a bundle on to the table, tied with a red ribbon. She looked round at them, but did not move. 'I took the liberty of having all such correspondence copied out, so you might study it at your leisure and draw your own conclusions. The most damning evidence is a letter which arrived only last week, from a Portuguese gentleman of the name of Tinoco. He is working as a diplomat in Brussels, and wrote begging us for safe passage to England so he might share state secrets with Your Majesty, secrets which he swears you will find vital to the health of your kingdom.'

'And will I not?'

Essex replied for him, coming urgently to her side. 'Your Majesty, a Portuguese spy we apprehended and tortured in October gave us this man's name. He said a Senhor Tinoco from Brussels would write and beg safe passage for this very purpose. And that when he arrived, bearing no fewer than fifty thousand crowns from the King of Spain hidden secretly among his luggage, this would be the signal for Lopez to poison Your Majesty, accepting the crowns as his reward.'

361

She drew in her breath and held it. 'And this letter from Tinoco has arrived, you say?'

'And been replied to,' Burghley agreed.

'You have granted him safe passage?'

'Indeed we have, Your Majesty,' Cecil told her, and limped forward to stand at her other side, his gaze locking with Robbie's. 'As soon as Senhor Tinoco lands at Dover, he will be arrested and searched. If these fifty thousand crowns are in his possession, will you give us leave to arrest Dr Lopez and question him on the matter of this ring, and the bribe sent by the Spanish King?'

Elizabeth wished she was still dancing. She could forget her cares while the music played. Here was no respite.

Wearily, she sifted through what they had said, but could formulate no argument to set against their cold and brutal 'evidence'. Even Lord Burghley, a councillor of eminent good sense and judgement, seemed determined that her servant should be arrested. Was it possible that a gentleman as close to her as Lopez, a respected doctor with frequent access to the royal bedchamber and to her person, could be in league with her greatest enemy?

Part of her suspected that Essex, in his struggle for power, would stop at nothing to best his rival Cecil. This latest plot might prove to be merely a wild attempt to make himself seem as powerful a spymaster as Walsingham had been.

But the gold and diamond ring from Philip himself . . . The letter written by this spy, Tinoco . . .

These seemed hard to refute, if they could be proved. Then she recalled how Lopez had feared for his life when interviewed about this business, as though he had some guilt to hide.

'Robbie,' she said, without turning to look at him, 'your man who has been watching Lopez . . . Is he Master

Goodluck, Lucy's seducer whom I had committed to the Tower?'

'Yes, Your Majesty.'

'When you asked permission to have him released so he could spy for you, I thought it was on some great state business. Not for this frippery.'

Robbie touched her and she stiffened. It was a daring gesture in front of the other two councillors, his fingers brushing her arm just below her shoulder. But she did not shake him off. Instead, she revelled in the warmth of his hand on the red velvet sleeve, and wished they could be alone together.

'The safeguarding of your life is no trivial matter. Besides, Goodluck was the best man for the task. If Walsingham had been alive, he would have made the same decision.'

At her other side, Cecil coughed drily. 'For once I must concur with his lordship. You should consider your safety as paramount, Your Majesty, and not allow your natural passions as a female to interfere with this business. Dr Lopez could feed you any poison he wished, disguised as some healing tonic or potion, and none of us would be any the wiser until you were found dead in your bed. If we could question him before this Tinoco arrives . . .'

'I will not have my servant arrested before I am sure of his guilt,' Elizabeth insisted shrilly, then forced herself to be calm again.

She must maintain control. Otherwise they would wrest it from her and claim her unfit to rule. Such things had happened to princes before, those who could not control themselves and their people.

Gazing out of the window, Elizabeth watched in silence as the sun hid behind a cloud and the November day grew suddenly dark. The bright morning and its promise of joy had gone. These late autumn days were so short. In only a few hours, dusk would begin to fall again. Then a river mist would creep in across the palace roofs, masking these whitewashed façades below and striking a chill into her bones.

Soon she would send one of her ladies for a warm shawl to set about her shoulders. Once night had fallen, her courtiers would drag themselves away to play cards or enjoy whores where they thought she would not hear of their sin. Then she herself would retire to the comfort of a book and a roaring fire in her Privy Chamber.

It was a horrible thought, but Robbie was right. She had grown old and fragile. It was only the presence of these men about her throne that prevented villains and traitors from taking her life away from her, reducing her to nothing.

And yet she could not admit how vulnerable she had become. Stare hard at one hand and ignore what the other is doing.

'The trap has been baited,' she remarked to the grey sky. 'Now let us wait and see.'

Later that evening, when the business of the day had been concluded and her ladies sat quietly about the Privy Chamber at Whitehall, setting neat stitches into their embroidery frames or whispering among themselves in the firelight, Lord Burghley returned. As soon as Elizabeth saw his face, she dismissed Mary and Helena, who had been smoothing an emollient into her white hands, dried her fingers on a square of muslin and beckoned her chief councillor to approach.

'My lord, what's the matter? Are you unwell?'

'No, Your Majesty, though I'm afraid I do come bearing news which may distress you. Not wishing to add to your burden earlier, I decided to wait until a later hour to bring this to your attention.' Lord Burghley hesitated; she saw a letter in his hand. 'Indeed, I received this some days ago from the Constable of the Tower. It was addressed to Your Majesty, but the constable is a sensible man and suggested I should read it first, then decide how best to deal with its contents.'

She stiffened. 'It comes from the Tower?'

'From Mistress Morgan.'

'I do not wish to read her words. Tell me what this letter contains.'

'Mistress Morgan writes that she is with child, and that the father is Lord Essex's man, Master Goodluck.'

'God's blood!'

'I know Your Majesty's views on this, but Mistress Morgan has been in the Tower since spring, and her health has suffered of late.' He hesitated. 'I would suggest that Master Goodluck be summoned and permitted to wed her with all haste, which I believe from Lord Essex has been his intention all along. Otherwise the child will be born a bastard, and the mother's reputation ruined beyond repair.'

'Lucy ruined herself when she played the whore in my service.' Elizabeth's fists clenched. 'If she did not wish to bring a bastard into the world, she ought to have kept herself chaste. My answer is no, my lord. Is that understood?'

'Yes, Your Majesty.'

Lord Burghley waited a moment, as though hoping she might relent and change her mind. Then he withdrew, leaving Elizabeth to stare at each of the unmarried ladies in the room, wondering which of them were chaste and which wanton.

Her lips tightened, her hands clasped fiercely in her lap. There they sat, innocent enough, heads bent over their stitchwork or their books, giving no outer indication of their inner thoughts. Lucy too had sat like that, pure on the surface, while inside must have been seething all manner of heated and wanton yearnings.

There was no way to tell, she thought feverishly, just as there was no way to tell which of her servants were true and which were traitors. All that could be done was to watch them carefully until they revealed themselves with a word, or a look, or a letter.

Towards the end of November, Elizabeth woke one frosty morning to aches, sweats and a fever. Her doctors were summoned, and among them came Master Lopez, modestly dressed in a black velvet gown and cap, his head bent.

There was some fuss as he tried to approach the bed. Word had got round, no doubt, that the physician was under suspicion. She stirred angrily, turning her head on her pillow. 'Enough there! I wish Master Lopez to attend me.'

She knew only too well how it felt to be innocent, yet held under suspicion of treason. To have done no wrong, yet face the terrifying prospect of a cruel and unjust death.

Yet it would not hurt to be cautious.

Lopez soothed and attended her with his customary solicitude, fluttering about the bed like a black moth. 'Your Majesty,' he murmured, bowing low before placing a hand on her temple. 'Your ladies tell me you have the ague. The danger of such a condition deteriorating should be heeded. We must endeavour to cool your body.'

'Is that so?'

Elizabeth pulled herself up on her pillows and stared at his hands. No gold and diamond ring. No ring at all, in fact. His thin fingers were bare, like twigs in winter.

Sir Robert Cecil appeared, sidling in behind Lopez as though he had been set to watch him.

Cecil said nothing, but stood beside her bed, just out of sight behind the rich green and gold hangings that kept out the draughts in the winter months. She presumed he was there to watch that Lopez did not force some poison down her throat under the guise of a medicament.

But her Portuguese doctor merely suggested the application of cool cloths steeped in hyssop, which sounded pleasant, then outraged her by diagnosing an infection of the jaw and advocating the removal of several more teeth.

'I have a fever,' she told him flatly. 'Not toothache.'

'So your teeth do not hurt you at all, Your Majesty?'

'No,' she lied.

'This swelling under the jawbone,' Lopez remarked, daring to prod her where it hurt. 'It does not pain you?'

'There is discomfort. Nothing more.'

'The swelling is caused by a rotten tooth. And the rot is gradually spreading to its neighbours.' Her chief physician seemed oblivious to her grimaces, continuing blithely, 'The best course of action would be to remove the bad tooth without delay. The swelling in your jaw would then subside, and the fever with it. If left untreated, your fever may climb even higher and the infection spread to your ears and throat. I have seen it happen before, and death is not infrequent.'

She stared. Was the man a fool to suggest such horrors, when he must know the suspicion of treachery hung about his head?

'Shall I call for a surgeon to come with a bowl and his instruments, Your Majesty? There is a preparation which will ease the pain of its removal considerably.'

'No,' she roared, and knocked him away.

Her ladies had already fled the chamber, all except patient Helena and two or three of the younger girls, who were staring with horrified fascination from behind the ornate screen. The others knew better than to remain on hand when the subject of toothache came up.

Lopez knew how averse she was to the idea of losing another tooth. Yet like all physicians he did not worry unduly about distressing his patient. Indeed he was already opening his medicine chest and rummaging inside for something to ease her dread. Some sharp-tasting solution of poppy, she thought, or perhaps a poison to help her to sleep until the last trumpet.

'I understand your distress, Your Majesty. But the pain of removal is only momentary, and fever can be very dangerous for a woman of your age,' Lopez was saying, inspecting a phial of some cloudy fluid.

A woman of my age?

Did he possess no sense of self-preservation? Elizabeth wondered, clasping a hand to her throbbing jaw. Or was Lopez genuinely unaware of the accusations Lord Essex had laid upon him in recent weeks?

Certainly Lopez would never get her tooth. Or not without the bitterest of struggles.

At that moment, the jolting agony of her tooth reasserted itself, radiating throughout her head and down her spine. It felt as though a pike had been thrust through her jaw. Her pity for the doctor evaporated in a painful rush. 'God's blood!'

Elizabeth glared round the bed hangings at young Sir Robert Cecil in a meaningful way.

Lopez shook the phial, then turned towards the bed, his smile almost sinister. 'Three drops of this cordial in your wine, Your Majesty, and you will soon feel sleepy. Then the troublesome tooth can be extracted.'

'Cecil?' she demanded shrilly.

Her councillor took Lopez by the arm and led him away. 'Sir, you had better come away with me. Her Majesty does not wish you to attend her any further today.'

'But the tooth—'

'I believe Lord Burghley and Lord Essex have some questions for you.' Cecil summoned the guards from the door to the Privy Chamber. 'One of you men, carry the doctor's chest of medicaments. That will need to be examined too.'

Her other physicians gathered around the bed to probe and question her, some wearing self-righteous smiles at Lopez's removal.

Too worn down by pain to resist, Elizabeth eventually allowed one of them to drug her, though she would not agree to a removal of the rotten tooth. She had few teeth left and needed them. Whenever she was persuaded to have one removed, she suffered for months afterwards, unable to chew properly and constantly in pain. At least while the bad tooth remained in place, the pain might be acute but it would come and go, allowing her whole weeks without discomfort.

Sleep would be a blessing, she considered, easing her body into it with reluctance. Their faces gradually dimmed, their voices draining away into the darkness.

Torchlight woke her in the late evening. Elizabeth stared blearily about the royal chamber, her view hampered by half-drawn green hangings fringed with gold.

What dreary bed curtains, she thought, studying them through half-closed eyes. I must get someone to replace them. But she knew at once that it would never happen. Or not in her lifetime.

Whitehall was an old palace, and this was an old bed, to suit its old occupant. Besides, the coffers would not take another palatial renovation. Not while this war with Spain dragged on and on. If only she had kept her cousin Mary alive. That bodged beheading was what had brought on this business. Mary's head rolling.

She started. 'Who's there?'

A man stepped into view. Torchlight behind him. Handsome, his cloak furred, a jewelled sword by his side. Her heart sang with relief and pleasure.

'Ah, Robin,' she said in relief, and held out her hands to him. 'Come to visit me at last? Those dogs wanted to butcher me, to tear out this rotten tooth. But I stood up to them. What do physicians know? Only what will pay their fee or keep them from the hangman.'

He came to the bedside and took her hands, looking down at her strangely.

'What is it, my dearest Robert? You may speak your mind, we are alone here.'

'Who am I?' he whispered.

She smiled, playing along. 'Leicester,' she said confidently, then saw the frown in his eyes and reconsidered. Stammering, she managed, 'My lord Essex. I thought . . .'

Not Robert Dudley. Robert Devereux, his stepson. Stupid, stupid, stupid. Her own darling Robin had been dead these past five years.

'I have been asleep for hours,' she said hurriedly. 'They gave me a sleeping draught. For my toothache, you know. What . . . What news do you bring, my lord?'

She dropped his hands and sat up, tidying her own bedclothes like a servant. Where was Helena? Who was meant to be watching her this evening?

She babbled on, nodding, responding to his news, hoping to distract Essex from her error. She did not want him to think his queen in her dotage. A trick of the light, that was all it had been. The wall torch behind his head, throwing him into relief. Her sleepiness. A natural mistake, in fact.

'Cecil had the doctor taken away,' she commented, snatching at a true memory. 'Has he been questioned again? I regret my temper now. If Master Lopez is innocent, and I do still believe him to be . . .' Her voice died away at his expression. 'What is it? You have spoken with Cecil? Discovered something?'

Essex shook his head, a sombre look in his face. 'We

have questioned your doctor at length. Lopez continues to deny his guilt.'

'Then what troubles you?'

'Senhor Tinoco was arrested yesterday evening, Your Majesty, on his arrival at Dover. He was questioned and his possessions searched. It is as we feared. In the false bottom of one of Tinoco's travelling chests we found fifty thousand crowns, and a letter in Spanish code which we have not yet been able to decipher.'

Fifty thousand crowns. The bribe King Philip was supposed to be sending to Lopez in return for her death.

'This proves nothing,' she said uneasily. 'Except Tinoco's guilt. We have no evidence that Lopez would have taken the bribe.'

'Your Majesty!'

'Lopez has always been a good servant to me.'

'And I have not?'

'Your loyalty is not in question here, Robbie.'

'Yet you doubt me. You toss aside my hard-won proof that Lopez wishes and intends your death, as though you have no faith in me. Or more in him, perhaps. A foreigner in the pay of our enemy, and you rate his word above mine. Would you have doubted Leicester's word?' His voice grew bitter. 'Shall I go out of the room and come back in the guise of my stepfather, so I may be believed when I say Senhor Lopez means you great harm?'

She did not know where to look. 'Robbie, that is hardly fair. I was drowsy, I was still half asleep.'

'Lopez should be taken to the Tower and made to confess his guilt on the rack. Topcliffe will soon have the truth out of him. Will you ratify that decision or must we take it without you?'

Elizabeth stared up at him, shocked by such an outlandish suggestion. Was this a *coup d'état*?

'Torture one of my servants without my permission? You forget yourself, my lord Essex.'

'Better to forget myself than be forgotten by a woman twice my age, who sleeps the day away in a drugged state while those who plot her death wander the country freely.'

She considered whether to call her guards and have him thrown into the Tower.

But he had not finished.

'Elizabeth,' he continued, ignoring her anger at this familiar address, 'I beg you to see sense. Lord Burghley told me of your conversation with him about Mistress Morgan. You continue to keep a faithful servant locked up in the Tower, a lady who is with child and in failing health, for no greater crime than that she was foolish enough to love without your permission. Yet you will not allow us to arrest your doctor, a traitor who is clearly in league with the Spanish and even now may be plotting your death.'

Her mouth thinned. Assault on every side. So be it. She knit her fingers tight together and glared at him.

'Lucy Morgan has trespassed against our authority.'

'The man who led us to Tinoco and the fifty thousand crowns is Master Goodluck, who will marry Lucy Morgan if he can obtain your permission.'

'You ask too much!'

'The Queen whom I revered as a youth, the beautiful Gloriana, she would not have needed this debate. She would have committed Lopez to the Tower in a heartbeat, and rewarded her spymaster and his men for saving her life from another Spanish plot.'

Whom I revered as a youth. But now despised, it would seem. *The beautiful Gloriana.* That stung.

No, he was not Leicester. His stepfather would have come about this business an entirely different way. The other Robert would have flattered and cajoled her. He would have been courteous, then passionate, and left her smiling in the end, believing it was her own idea. He would not have bludgeoned her with insults, then made these paltry demands for recognition of his skill.

But Robert Dudley was long gone. He was a bag of bones and dust under a memorial. This handsome young cockerel, and his arrogant fellows, were all she had left to protect her throne.

Her head throbbed as she regarded him through narrowed eyes. She needed to give a little on this matter, to retain the young earl as an ally. Things were still too fragile for the English court to be split by an argument. And Essex would make a dangerous enemy.

Her knitted fingers flexed, then wound together again, ravelling up her emotions until they were a hard little ball pressed between her palms. This she clasped to her chest, hating herself for her weakness.

'Do it then,' Elizabeth conceded bitterly. 'Throw Lopez to your interrogators, release Lucy Morgan from the Tower, even wed her to your lascivious spy if you must. I am prepared to grant permission for all this. But I am not convinced of the doctor's guilt and shall never sign a death warrant for Master Lopez without proper evidence that he has conspired against me. *That* I can promise you.'

Five

WILL WOKE IN A CHILLY ROOM TO THE FAMILIAR SOUND OF small clattering hooves accompanied by incessant, bell-tongued bleating.

For a moment he lay in a bemused stupor, wondering why on earth he could hear sheep below his window. Then his mind groped sleepily towards the explanation: he was back in Stratford, and what he could hear were the good farmers of Warwickshire driving their sheep to market along the street outside. Then the memories returned that he had been trying to suppress: arriving in Stratford with Anne late at night, his father throwing open the door to stare at his bruised and battered face. Then the faltering explanation Will had given his mother, that he had been 'set upon by vagabonds', and the look on their faces.

His parents had not believed him. They knew what he was and what he had done.

From Anne's looks and sparing comments on the journey back from London, it was clear that rumours of his wild behaviour had reached even the little market town of Stratford-upon-Avon.

Nonetheless his parents had welcomed him back home and drawn him inside to the fire, black sheep that he was.

'I did not wish Anne to visit you in London,' his father had said quietly, taking him aside before bedtime. 'But your wife would not be gainsaid, and your cousin Richard swore he would take good care of her on the journey. Besides, I was hopeful she would be able to persuade you to return with her. It has been too long since you last visited, Will, and the children have missed you. Particularly the boy.' He hesitated a moment before adding, 'Young Hamnet needs his father.'

Was John Shakespeare unsure of himself? It would be the first time. But it was a hard thing for a father to say to his son about his own offspring, Will supposed.

As the two men had stood silently beside the fire, the sound of women's voices had come from above, one singing a lullaby, the other whispering reassurances as she tucked a child into bed. Feet had creaked across the floorboards by the light of a candle, its thin glow reaching down through gaps into the room below.

Now, beside him in bed, Anne stretched and yawned. Briefly he felt her stockinged foot touch his leg, then flinch away.

They were awkward together, like newly-weds who were still not sure what would please or offend. He thought of how she had edged backwards into their bed last night, her thick nightrail and stockings necessary against the bitter cold of an icy night in Warwickshire, then had blown out the candle without speaking or looking at him.

The message had been clear: don't touch me.

He had lain next to her unmoving body the night before, and felt on the brink of something new in their marriage. Some astonishing revelation about Anne's character. His brain had still been wearily untangling the problem when he fell asleep, leaving it unsolved. Perhaps it would never be solved. His wife had changed and matured over the years he had been away from Stratford, but he had only glimpsed that change in snatches, during those fleeting days and weeks when he had felt able to return home and be with her.

Now the changes were complete, it seemed. Anne was no longer the woman he had married. She was a stranger to him. And his position as her husband was somewhat tarnished by these whispers of orgies in London. Neither of them had come innocently to bed last night.

Something new could be forged between them though, if both wished for it hard enough. There was always a chance they could start afresh, strangers to the other, lying in the same bed and with nothing to lose now that the early love between them had gone.

'Are you awake?' Anne whispered, and he dismissed the temptation to lie.

'Yes.'

Boldly, her hand found his hip. Then his groin. So she was not indifferent to him, then. Despite the pain of his bruising, he felt desire flicker and return.

'Will . . .'

He turned at the sound of his name, and took his wife in his arms. He kissed her throat, her pale breasts, but never her mouth. The intimacy of her lips against his would have been too much. His heart could not love her again, even if his body could.

Not that he expected to take genuine pleasure from the act. He knew too much of that other secret life with the Earl of Southampton to be satisfied with just this ordinary woman, this conventional marriage. Perhaps he would never again experience such intense joy now that he had been forced out of Wriothesley's bed.

His physical needs were still alive, however. And she was his wife.

But it seemed she too had changed in her carnal

376

appetites since they had last performed this dance together. Anne lay sprawled beneath him, her thighs splayed greedily, a stranger in his bed, pulling her own nightrail up to demonstrate her readiness.

'Yes,' she exclaimed, panting hard, then whispered lewd suggestions in his ear, begging him to touch her, to push his fingers inside her. When he finally mounted her, her eager hands reached for his buttocks, clawing him, pressing him closer.

He cried out with surprised pleasure at the climax, and heard her sigh beneath him, her hips lifting.

Anne lay warm and sleepy for a space afterwards, her limbs tangled heavily with his, her woollen stockings scratching his legs. She seemed content at last, like a purring cat on a sunny windowsill. Then she stirred, gently pushing him away.

The sun was rising. He had performed his duty as a husband. Now that delicate business was over, the day could begin.

'I must tend the children,' she told him, and he released her.

Wandering out into the street after breakfast, he found Hamnet kicking a football with some of the other Stratford boys. The morning was dry but frosty, and once or twice he saw his son slip on the icy puddles in the street. The boy did not cry out though, Will noted, but rose again immediately and continued with his game.

Susanna was seated on the wall, braiding Judith's hair. Her younger sister squirmed as her hair was pulled tight, and Susanna chided her.

'You must look your best, Judith. See, Father has come to visit us. You don't want him to see you crying like a baby, do you?'

Judith, still not quite nine years of age, glanced at Will,

taking in his bruised and swollen face, and shook her head. Her little mouth hardened and she raised her chin, as though determined not to cry in front of him. She still gave a cry when her sister began to thread a narrow green ribbon through her hair, but Will felt it was uttered more in fury than in pain. Judith had a touch of her mother's stubborn nature, he thought wryly, though her older sister still possessed the quiet shyness of her early years.

He smiled at Susanna, and she stared, also taken aback by his battered face.

Her gaze dropped, as though his elder daughter did not wish to seem too friendly with this man who looked like a vagabond. The girl's thin arched brows were slanted in a frown, and suddenly he was reminded of Anne, that air of disapproval that seemed to haunt every room whenever he had done something to annoy her.

Even my children are strangers to me, he thought, and felt his temper prickle under his skin like a fever. Had Anne spoken about him in such a way that Susanna was growing up in fear of her own father? Even Judith, whom he barely knew, had seemed tentative and unsure when he addressed her. And Hamnet . . .

But things were less clear-cut with Hamnet and Judith, who could easily turn out to be another man's children. The illegitimate offspring of his father's apprentice, perhaps. In all fairness, how could he open his heart in love to the twins, when at any moment his faithless wife might announce they were not his blood?

Hamnet had seen him now.

The boy came running, mud from the road on his tunic, his cap tumbling off, breath steaming on the wintry air.

'Father! Father!' he piped, and threw his arms about Will's thighs and stomach, embracing him so fiercely that Will staggered backwards, surprised but laughing at the young boy's enthusiasm. 'You have come home at last!

Susanna said you were too busy to come this year, but I knew that you would! Will you stay for Christmastide and New Year, sir?'

'Alas, I cannot,' Will told him, and ruffled the lad's hair. 'The theatres have opened again now the plague has eased. I must return to London soon, or risk losing my place in the company.'

Hamnet's face fell. The boy nodded stoutly though, accepting his father's reason as just. He picked up his fallen cap, dusting it down and replacing it on his head.

'What happened to your face?' Hamnet enquired, staring up at his ugly bruising.

'I was set upon by thieves,' he lied. 'I put up a good fight, but they stole my purse. London is a dangerous place.'

Hamnet's eyes had widened. He seemed quite impressed. 'We are playing at football. Grandfather says it is a dangerous game and I should not play. Will you join us?'

On the point of refusal, Will hesitated. Then he grinned. 'Why not? The day is so cold, I could do with a little sport to warm my blood.'

'Thank you, sir.'

He grabbed Will's hand and dragged him down the street to where a crowd of boys were kicking a tattered pigsbladder about the place. The pigsbladder had once been carefully covered in leather, but its shape was now uneven and lopsided.

'Look, my father has come to play. Stop, stop! We will begin again, only you must give him first kick.' Securing the ball, Hamnet placed it in front of Will and nodded earnestly. 'Our goal is at the end of Henley Street, sir.'

'Did your grandfather make this ball?' he asked Hamnet.

'Yes, sir, he did.'

'Aha. I thought I recognized the stitchwork.'

Will kicked the football down the street as hard as he could, and watched with a grin as the other young lads dashed towards it, some trying to urge it further, others attempting to drive it back to the other end of the street.

'Come on!' Hamnet urged him, running off in pursuit.

Will needed no more persuasion but took to his heels at once, following the lad down Henley Street at a swift pace; faster than he had run since he was a young boy himself, he realized. Hamnet was quick too, agile and slender, darting between the older boys time and again to retrieve the ball.

Will watched him with pride. He wondered what kind of man Hamnet would make when he was grown. The boy's mind was keen, his father had told him so several times, and he learned his lessons well and obediently at school. Perhaps he should take the lad down to London once he was old enough to be apprenticed, and teach him the theatrical trade.

He could train Hamnet himself, let the lad follow him about the theatre, pick up a few tricks here and there, maybe learn to speak a few lines. Boys were always needed to play the women's parts, and if he was a quick study . . .

'Father! To us, to us . . .!'

The ball came to him several more times, passing back and forth in a crowd of heaving bodies between the goal-ends, and Will was soon out of breath, gasping as he limped down Henley Street after the boy.

My son, he thought proudly as Hamnet slammed his foot into the leather ball, raising it a good few feet into the air.

His son?

Hamnet turned on his heel at that moment as though to see where his father was, shielding his eyes against the cold bright glare of the morning. Will saw himself in the boy's

380

delicate, shining face, and suddenly knew that he was indeed Hamnet and Judith's father. Judith might take after her mother, but Hamnet was surely his. That high forehead, those dark eyes . . .

He owed his wife an apology, he realized with a start.

'Did you see that?' Hamnet called excitedly.

'Yes, quite a kick!' He grinned, then raised his hand in a wave when the boy would have come trotting back to him. 'No, go on. Don't wait for me, I'll follow.'

It was a noisy family luncheon that first day home, not only his wife and children gathered for the meal but his younger brothers and sisters too, squeezed in around the table in the narrow kitchen. They sat squabbling and teasing each other with jests, accepting Will's presence there with easy good humour. The servants hurried around them as the stew bubbled in the pot, fetching knives and trenchers from the cupboard. They leaned in to place them on the freshly wiped table, its clean linen runner an indication that a special guest had come to lunch.

Glancing about at their eager faces, hands reaching for food as soon as it was placed on the table, spiced cabbage and pulses, flatbreads of rye hot and scorched from the oven, Will was reminded of his childhood. The square wooden trenchers they were using were still the same from when he was a child, his own cracked and warped, its much-rubbed greasy salt hole holding a generous pinch of salt. There was a good fire burning under the pot, his mother directing the servants what to serve and to whom. The dogs ran in and out, sniffing after the bones and scraps. The noise was incredible, and he was used to the din of a busy theatre.

His father came in, wiping icy boots and throwing off his cloak. He stood looking at them all, stripping off his leather gloves. 'What's all this commotion?'

A whispering silence fell among the younger children, then Hamnet stood and helped him pull off his boots, leaving the wet leather to steam before the fire.

'Here, Grandfather,' he said, and handed him a cloth for his hands. 'It's rabbit today.'

John Shakespeare exchanged a smiling glance with his wife. 'Excellent, my favourite.'

'Can we go fishing after luncheon, Grandfather?'

'It is a little cold for fishing, boy. Snow's on the way, by the feel of it, and once the water is frozen, there'll be precious few fish to be had. Now don't look like that, lad. Oh well, I suppose an hour or two by the river this afternoon could do no harm.' John Shakespeare smiled at the pleasure on his grandson's face, then hesitated, looking over his head at Will. 'But have you asked your father, Hamnet? He might prefer to take you himself. What do you say, Will?'

'Father?' Hamnet turned to him, and suddenly Will, who had been thinking *Rather you than me in this sharp weather*, found himself smiling and nodding his assent.

'Very well. But I will have to borrow a rod.'

'Oh, you can have Grandfather's best rod, he won't mind,' Hamnet offered excitedly, without asking John Shakespeare what he thought of this plan. 'I can show you where bait is to be found too, in case you have forgotten. We never come back without a good catch, do we, Grandfather?'

It seemed the boy had a way of getting what he wanted, Will thought wryly. He remembered himself as an eleven-year-old lad, pleading with his father to take him on the long journey from Stratford to Kenilworth, just so he could see the Queen and her court. Perhaps such charms and snares were in the blood.

'I will accompany you part of the way, then,' Anne said

calmly, passing him the platter of ryebreads. 'There is something I would like you to see.'

He was surprised. 'In town?'

Will was more surprised when his wife took his arm while they were walking, suddenly forceful, and steered him into the town square.

'This is not the quickest way to the river,' Hamnet protested, but fell silent at his mother's glance.

'One of those,' Anne whispered in his ear, indicating the row of town houses opposite. 'Or a place very like it. That is what I want.'

Will stared across at the fine houses, several storeys high, expensively timbered and fronted with broad casements.

He turned to Anne, aghast. 'I cannot afford such a house. You are dreaming.'

'No,' she assured him firmly, with the air of a woman who had already made up her mind and would not be budged. 'These past ten years, I have been putting a little by every time you have sent me money. And you have told me yourself how popular your plays are becoming. Everyone in Stratford knows your name. The other wives envy me for being married to such a man, whose plays are performed before the Queen, and even the shopkeepers are allowing us to have food delivered again, not asking for the money first as they did when your father was in such trouble.'

Her tone grew bitter. She stared at him accusingly, not caring that they were drawing curious glances from passers-by. 'Yet still we live with your parents, cooped up in that house on Henley Street like a penniless young couple. When the children were babes, I could manage. But now they are grown, there is little room left for all of us. We need a new home, Will. And if you do not provide it soon, I will not be able to hold my head up in this town. The younger women are already laughing at me behind my back, whispering that I have a miser for a husband.'

He opened his mouth to deny her, then closed it again. He thought of Southampton in his palatial residence by the Thames, and of the glittering court itself, the great halls and chambers echoing with music and laughter. These wonders Anne would never see. It was her place to be here in Stratford, dutifully tending his children as they grew, just as it was Will's place to be in London, his ready quill lining the pockets of Burbage and the other sharers. When he had found her waiting in his lodgings in London, the shock of seeing Anne there, in *his place*, had been profound. She had not belonged there, any more than he belonged in this little Warwickshire town. And he knew it was an experience he never wished to repeat.

She must wait here in Stratford until the theatre was finished with him. If it ever would be. It was her sacrifice to their marriage. And he owed her something for that sacrifice. One of these houses.

'Very well,' he agreed, keeping his voice low so that the boy, waiting so impatiently behind them, his arms full of fishing rods, would not overhear. 'But you must understand that you can never come to London again if I do this.'

She licked her lips. A nervous habit. He remembered it from their days of courtship, how it had tormented him with desire to see that little pink tongue running along her lips. Now it was merely a gesture that indicated indecision. He watched and felt nothing. There was a kind of freedom in that, he realized. A hard-won liberty he could rejoice in, even in the depths of this prison that he had built so eagerly for himself as a youth.

Anne looked at the houses, seeming to weigh them up against her loneliness and jealousy. Then she agreed.

'Never again,' she whispered.

Hamnet, distracted by a display of bows and arrows in the window of a shop, glanced at them over his shoulder as though checking his father was still there.

Will smiled, and bent to kiss her on the cheek. 'I owe you an apology, by the way,' he murmured in her ear. 'Now my eyes are cleared of anger, I see that Hamnet is my son. I was wrong to accuse you of that.'

There was relief in her face. Silently, she nodded to acknowledge what he had said. No doubt she was still angry that he had doubted her in the first place.

'All the same,' he warned her, 'we cannot take one of these fine houses yet. Not for another few years.'

Anne looked at him sharply, but did not argue. She was a pragmatic woman at heart, he thought, and willing to wait for what she wanted.

He left his wife in the market square, perhaps calculating how long it would take them to amass enough money to buy one of those expensive houses, and continued to the river with Hamnet. The sky had darkened with a threat of snow, just as his father had said it would. If they did not hurry, snow would begin to fall before they had time to catch a fish.

Will took a rod from Hamnet to lighten the boy's load, and the two of them marched briskly along in companionable silence.

The air was sharper in Warwickshire than he was used to. He drew his cloak about him, wondering what the weather was like in London, and if his lordship the Earl of Southampton knew yet that he had left town. It felt strange to be so far from the noisy bustle of the London streets. Already Will missed the lazy pace of days when the playhouses were closed: lying abed with Wriothesley until noon, then meeting his friends in the taverns, arguing passionately about plays and actors, and ogling the wenches who brought them ale, then staggering home again in the early hours.

On the way out of town, heading into open countryside, they passed a cart pulled on to the grass verge at the side of the frosty track. Recognizing the man unloading sacks into a barn, Will halted.

'It's Master Dun,' he murmured to Hamnet. The boy looked worried, perhaps thinking they would be delayed by this encounter. Will would have continued, but already the man had heaved his sack into the back of the cart and was straightening. It was too late to avoid him without causing offence.

'Christopher!'

His friend turned, smiling when he saw who it was. 'Will!' He wiped his dirty palms on his tunic, nodded cheerfully to Hamnet, then shook Will's hand. He raised his eyebrows, gazing at Will's bruised face. 'Fell down the stairs?'

'Vagabonds.'

'I see.' His voice was dry. His gaze lighted on the fishing rods. 'Off fishing? I'd join you, but I must get home before it snows.'

'Perhaps next time,' Will said.

Courteous words, that was all. For he had remembered his friend's pretty wife. Round with child last time he had seen her, and her eyes more inviting than they should be for a married woman. A danger to be avoided in a small Warwickshire town.

But Christopher was still smiling. 'Sally,' he called into the barn. 'Come out here. Look who it is.'

Sally came out, staring and holding a small child by the hand, a boy clad in a coarse brown smock. Her belly was rounded again already. They were wasting no time, Will thought drily, then tried not to imagine himself in bed with pretty Sally Dun. If he was her husband, he doubted whether he would be able to resist filling her again either.

'Master Shakespeare,' she murmured, and curtseyed, rising to look at him with a shy smile. 'I didn't know you had returned from London.'

'I only came home last night.'

'Oh, but your face . . . !'

Her husband touched her arm. 'Master Shakespeare was set upon by vagabonds.' He glanced at Will, and this time his mockery was plain. 'A large band of them, I presume?'

'Three only,' he admitted. 'But they got my dagger off me, and after that I had no chance.'

Sally shook her head. 'How dreadful!'

'That's London for you.'

She looked at him secretively from under her lashes. 'Well, I still wish I could visit London. Christopher said he would take me there one day, to see the great bridge spanning the river Thames and all the traitors' heads stuck up on pikes.' She caught her husband's warning glance, and pouted. 'But little Ned would miss me sorely, even if I left him with my mother. And I shall have another child come the spring, so I suppose I must stay at home.'

'It is a long journey,' Will told her uncomfortably.

She smiled. A delicate twitch of her lips. 'Yet I heard your wife, Anne, travelled all the way to the city last week to visit you.'

And to fetch you back, were her unspoken words.

Will was suddenly angry, despite the young wife's loveliness and the bloom in her cheeks. Was this one of the women who had been mocking Anne behind her back?

'Yes, and then I brought her home again.' Pointedly, he touched his battered cheek. 'The city is no fit place for a decent woman.'

There was an awkward silence.

An icy wind whistled past his ears, chilly on the back of his neck where his cap was not pulled down far enough. Snow was on its way, or something even colder. Less forgiving.

He glanced at young Hamnet, then back at his friend. 'Forgive me, Christopher, but we must get on. The afternoons draw in so early these days, and I do not wish to lose the light.'

They walked on together, again in silence, following the course of the river. The Avon flowed sluggishly past under a darkening sky.

Will found the glassy pool on the bend where he used to fish as a boy, and waited there while his young son slipped like a shadow along the river bank, hunting for worms to bait their rods. Once he had done the same for his own father. Now it was his turn to stand and wait, staring at the river as it rolled inexorably past.

The widening current of the Avon ran greyish-green past the bend, under trees stripped bare by winter. Yet where the water steadied itself against the edge of the pool, it seemed lighter, reflecting stark fingers against a back-cloth of cloud. And a man, though his face was unclear.

While they waited for the fish to bite, Will showed Hamnet how to whistle through a blade of grass, making a sound like a wild duck crying overhead.

'That's it,' he said encouragingly, listening to his son's strangled efforts. 'Though not so hard. Don't force the breath. It should come natural.'

It started to snow. Hamnet smiled, gazing upwards as tiny flecks of white swirled down and coated his little cap and shoulders. Then he stuck out his tongue, as all small boys do, and laughed when an icy snowflake landed there, melting swiftly.

'You will not be able to return to London if the snow becomes too deep for cartwheels to pass,' Hamnet said after a while, then sat down beside Will on the bank.

'Unless I ride back,' Will commented lightly.

His son looked at him for a long moment, all his childish joy at the snow abruptly forgotten. 'Are you going to ride back, sir?'

How cruel he was. The boy was crestfallen. His dark eyes stared as if in anticipation of a blow. He just wanted to hear that his father would not ride, that he would stay until Christmas, until New Year, until spring . . .

Or maybe for ever.

'I have to return to London soon,' he told the boy gently. 'You know that I must, Hamnet, that I am needed in the theatre. That is where I earn my keep. And must continue to do so, more so than ever now, since your mother has set her heart on a fine new home.'

Hamnet nodded, then dragged up the rough collar of his jacket against the wintry air. His hand crept into Will's and bunched there, as though trying to warm itself. He squeezed the boy's fingers. They were cold as stone.

'Your hand is frozen. Where are your gloves?'

'I forgot them,' Hamnet admitted sheepishly.

Will sighed, then drew off his own sheepskin gloves and slipped them over his son's hands. 'Here, put these on.'

His gloves were ridiculously huge on the boy, like cows' udders dangling from each hand, but at least Hamnet would not suffer the danger of frostbite. He himself could always blow hard on his fingers and clap his hands all the way home, to keep the blood moving so it would not freeze to ice in his veins.

'Father, will you take me to London one day? To see the big round theatre where your plays are performed?'

His voice was a thin piping against the wind, almost drowned by its chill whistle. The snow was falling more heavily about them now, beginning to whiten the grassy banks of the river. The boy looked down at the gloves Will had given him, studying the stitchwork, as though afraid to meet his eyes.

'I know you will not take Mother, because she is a woman. But will you take me? Not now, but when I am older? Please, sir?'

'When you are older,' he said, 'I will take you to London with me and show you the world. That I promise you.'

Hamnet's face lit up with incredulous pleasure, as though the boy had not expected that answer, would never have expected it.

Will smiled down at his son. A promise. Such a simple thing to bring such joy.

'Now, young Master Shakespeare, how about those fish?'

Six

'IT'S SNOWING!' CATHY EXCLAIMED.

Lucy came to stand at her shoulder, pressing her own cold face into the narrow angle where the window looked down to the river Thames. On the path below, between the high stone wall and the tower that blocked the afternoon light, was a faint dusting of snow. As they watched, flakes began to come more thickly, whirling past the window and whitening the path down to the river.

Shivering, Lucy wandered back to her chair and sat down. The sun would go down soon and there was a brisk wind off the river, whistling through the crack under the door and about the window frame. It was November now. Already her small cell was icy at night. Would she be kept there all winter, she wondered?

Perhaps she would stay here for ever, a prisoner of the grim Tower. Or until the old Queen died and she could sue for pardon from the new monarch.

It was not a comforting thought, and she put it aside.

She drew on her gloves again and clapped her hands together, trying to keep warm. Cathy had brought a book of sonnets with her, and Lucy had discarded her gloves in order to turn the pages. But it was too late for such pleasures now. The daylight was failing. Within an hour it would be too dark to read except by candlelight, and she did not want to waste her candle allowance unnecessarily.

'Snow makes everything look so pure,' Cathy murmured.

'And cold,' Lucy added, pragmatically.

'You have no poetry in you,' Cathy complained, frowning.

'Sometimes it is better that way. Poetry can be beautiful, I will not deny it. But too much poetry can blind you to the harsh truths of this life. Such as being too cold to think, let alone read a poem.'

'Perhaps we should build up the fire before it gets dark.' Lucy glanced dubiously at the low fire, barely giving out any heat, then at their meagre store of logs on the hearth. 'Mistress Hall will be furious if we ask for more wood.'

Irritable now, Cathy picked up the book of sonnets she had brought and flicked through it. 'Let us burn poetry to keep warm then. I could read a poem, and then if it is no good, we will tear out the page and burn it. How about this old one by Thomas Wyatt?' She glanced over the first few lines of the poem, then giggled. 'This will make you laugh. Listen to how it begins . . .

'They flee from me that sometime did me seek,
With naked foot stalking within my chamber:
Once have I seen them gentle, tame, and meek,
That now are wild, and do not once remember,
That sometime they have put themselves in danger
To take bread at my hand; and now they range
Busily seeking in continual change . . .'

'Hush, put it away,' Lucy warned her hurriedly, for she could hear heavy footsteps on the winding stair. 'Someone is coming. Besides, that is quite the wrong poet to have chosen, for did not Master Wyatt almost lose his head in this dreadful place? And indeed his son lost his after a revolt against Queen Mary.'

Cathy looked aghast. 'You are right. I had forgotten.' She threw the book down. 'Horrid thing.'

The door was being unlocked, the key being turned, the outside bolt drawn back.

Lucy heard Mistress Hall outside, talking to someone urgently. She sounded almost angry.

A man replied, his voice low and somehow familiar, and the hairs prickled a sudden warning on the back of her neck.

She sat forward in her chair, breathing quickly now, a protective hand resting on her rounded belly. What was it now? She had so few visitors these days, any change to her routine had become a cause for alarm. Every now and then, when the wind was still, she would hear the distant cries of the crowd as someone was whipped or hanged out on Tower Hill, and her blood would run cold. Perhaps one day they would come for her, she thought wildly. Once the babe was born, of course, for no woman in her condition could be hanged. Though the Queen could not hate her that much, surely? Not over a simple case of wanton behaviour. Yet still her mind ran on, unable to rest, fearing the worst of the Queen's anger.

The door was thrown open at last. Master Goodluck stood there on the threshold, cloaked and capped, his beard more silvered than ever, but his eyes bright and intent on her face.

'Lucy, my love.' He opened his arms and she stood up, gasping, then stumbled towards him. He caught her before she fell. 'Your ordeal is over. We are to be married.'

She stared. What had he said to her?

'Married?'

'Here in the Tower chapel. It is true, I swear on my life.' He put a hand to the hard swell of her belly, his touch

393

oddly gentle for such a large man. 'I do not wish to hurry you, my love. But the priest and witnesses are waiting for us below in the chapel of St Peter, and the place is very cold indeed. I will help you down the stairway, you need not fear that you will slip.'

She saw Cathy staring too and wondered vaguely if this was a trick. But why would Goodluck trick her? She could not think. Everything was topsy-turvy.

He put a finger under her chin, raising her bewildered face to his. 'Look at me, Lucy. We shall be married this very day. Then I am taking you home with me to Oxfordshire.'

'But Her Majesty—'

'Calm yourself,' he told her, and pulled off one of her gloves to kiss her hand. His beard tickled her cold knuckles. 'It was the Queen herself who signed the papers for your release.'

Inexplicably, Lucy began to cry.

'Hold me,' she whispered, and paid no attention to Mistress Hall's cluck of disapproval when he finally took her in his arms. 'I am so tired. Please hold me.'

She lay against his chest, limp and exhausted by the months she had spent in that place, mostly alone, mostly in fear for her life, and hardly ever knowing where Goodluck was, whether he was alive or not, whether he still loved her. Now he was there, and she could scarcely believe it.

Two guards entered and spoke to Mistress Hall. Two more people to witness her tears. She buried her face deeper in his chest and listened to his heart.

'I thought you would not come. That this was the end for me.'

'Forgive me,' he said deeply, then hesitated. She knew he could not speak freely before the others. 'I had things to do. You know my calling.'

'I know, I did not doubt *you*. I doubted myself.'

'I believed in you, Lucy. I knew you would be strong. Indeed, it was only that knowledge which allowed me to go about my business.'

He shook his cloak back to hide her from the others, the thick material flecked with wet from the snow, and drew her aside to the tiny alcove space where she slept.

It was not much in the way of privacy, but at least she was shielded from their curious gazes by his broad back.

'You are frozen!'

She heard the anger in his voice. Goodluck looked about at the ugly bare walls of the cell, the narrow window which let in the draught, then at the modest glow of the fire, almost burned out now.

'This place is barbaric. No woman in your condition should be kept a prisoner here. Come, I know you are not strong, but you must allow me to help you down the stairs to the chapel, and then on to Oxfordshire as fast as we can.' He took her bare hand and began to rub it between his own, warming her skin. 'It is a wonder you are not dead from the cold in this godforsaken place, you and the babe too!'

'Are you angry with me, Goodluck?'

'Angry with you?' It was his turn to stare, uncomprehending. 'Over what?'

Deliberately, she drew his hand back to her hard belly, and laid it there, pressing down. At that moment, the babe within kicked. She saw his gaze widen in shock, then fly to her face, startled by the presence of another being between them.

'The child,' she whispered. 'Are you angry that I kept it a secret all these months? That I did not tell even you, though you are the father?'

Goodluck closed his eyes. Slowly, he shook his head. When he opened them again, there was a hint of laughter in his face. 'My dearest love, I know I am the father. There was never any thought in my head otherwise. Though I admit, when I first learned that you were with child, I was angry with you for not telling me as soon as you knew yourself.'

He stroked her swollen belly, and the child kicked again, provoking one of his broad smiles. The room was suddenly warmer. She basked in his presence, his smile. She had never thought to see that smile again, nor be held in his arms like this, nor listen to his deep voice that always struck at the chord of her heart.

'But then I thought of how you are, Lucy. Of how you have always been. I thought of your pride and stubbornness. And I understood.'

'You forgive me?'

He kissed her, and she felt a sudden, fierce desire beat beneath her skin with a wildness that was almost uncontainable.

'There is nothing to forgive,' he murmured against her mouth, then drew back to gaze at her sombrely. 'How could there be something to forgive? You were alone here, Lucy, and made your choices as you thought best. I would have done the same in your position.'

'You are a man. You could never be in my position. But I should have told you. Only I could not trust that you wouldn't . . . I thought it might lead to more grief.'

'Let us have no more grief,' he said flatly. 'Surely we have taken our fill of grief. It is time for fate to release us so we can live out our days in peace.'

'Amen.'

He thought for a moment. He held her hands, his head bent. 'When I heard you were with child, Lucy, I was overjoyed. All my life I have considered myself unworthy to be a father. Then, when you and I first lay together, I began to think . . . I dared to hope that we might have a child together.'

'You wanted a child?'

'A child from our love. And son or daughter, it will be loved.'

She smiled, drawing strength from his words. 'Yes, it will be loved.'

'Come then, now that we have agreed that, and let us be married before God and the witnesses below.' His smile was weary, but it was self-mocking. He had been released from captivity, but he too had been alone. He had wandered in the darkness and doubted her love. 'Unless you do not wish to be my wife. You have had ample time to think, up here in your cold tower room. Perhaps you have grown to enjoy solitude. Perhaps I am no longer the man for you.'

'Don't,' she managed, choking. 'Please don't.'

Goodluck let his cloak drop away. The glow of the firelight intruded, and the stares of the others, watching. They were no longer alone.

'Forgive me,' he murmured. 'But I had to be sure. Now that I am, are you ready to be married, my love?'

'My things . . .'

'Cathy will pack them for you while we descend to the chapel.'

She glanced at her friend, and Cathy nodded her consent. She was smiling now, but Lucy could see she had been crying.

Cathy too had suffered from the life they led at court. She had been forced to lie and betray, though it was not in her nature to be so cruel. She was not even free to be with her son, James, who was growing up in Norfolk. She had not seen the boy for years.

Lucy put a hand to her belly. She would not be separated from this child, even if it meant her disgrace. Even if it meant her death.

'Then I am ready.'

Outside, snow had fallen white across the grass and pathways that threaded the confines of the Tower walls. The wind from the river was still blowing sharply, like a knife under her skirts as she raised them, stepping carefully through the snow. Though only late afternoon, it was already darkening to dusk, the November sky heavy with more snow.

Goodluck led her across to the chapel of St Peter ad Vincula, where they knelt on the cold flagstones to speak their vows. The chapel was long and narrow, a row of fluted columns supporting the roof. The remnants of daylight poured through high windows. God's light, falling upon their shoulders. She spoke quietly, affirming her faith, her hand in Goodluck's. His voice echoed hers. In the shadowy side aisle, she caught an occasional glimpse of priests moving about their business, lighting glimmering banks of candles against the winter's dark.

They were not alone for their strange wedding. Cathy came to kneel behind her during the final prayers, and kissed her affectionately on the cheek when Lucy rose from her knees, now Mistress Goodluck.

'I shall miss you,' she told Lucy, and this time did not bother to conceal her tears.

'Come and live with us in Oxfordshire,' Lucy insisted. She knew that loneliness in her friend's eyes. She had tasted it too often herself, waking in the night to cry alone and silently. There was no remedy for that pain, but love and good company could hold the shadows at bay for a little while at least. 'No one will force you to stay at court, not any more. Walsingham appointed you and he is long dead. Ask formal leave to depart, then bring James and come to us. Not as a servant, but as my friend and companion. You will be made welcome there.'

They embraced for a long moment outside the chapel, the snow falling around them.

Cathy asked, 'Are you sure?' but she was smiling.

'Goodluck will give you the directions.' She kissed her oldest friend, then let her go. 'I will not rest happy until I see you and James in Oxfordshire, Cathy. Do not fail me.'

'I shall not,' she promised.

An odd shuffling figure at the back, hiding behind one of the Tower guards during the ceremony itself, turned out to have been Jensen, the barge woman. She pressed a clay pipe into Goodluck's hand after the service, took off her cap to Lucy, then disappeared into the whitish dark, shambling back towards the river.

Wearily, Lucy accepted the nods and winks of some of the Tower servants and guards. Men who would have taken her to the block if a death warrant had arrived. They had meant her no harm. It was only duty.

The snow continued to fall, gently whitening the cruel grey towers around the walled enclosure. Lucy began to shiver, her teeth chattering. Someone put a cloak about her shoulders. She gripped its folds tightly, wondering if they would even manage the long journey into Oxfordshire, for if there was another day of snow the roads might become unpassable. Mistress Hall had been looking after her gloves while Lucy said her vows, but had vanished.

Summoned at last from her supper, her jailor handed her gloves back with a thin smile.

'I wish you well, mistress,' was all she said before sweeping out, stiff-backed and broad-skirted, towards her quarters.

Soon Master Goodluck was the only one she had not spoken to. It was late and she was cold. The sky was almost black, no stars burning yet. Lucy turned to look at him. Her husband.

There was joy in her heart. But such weariness too, she could barely stand now that it was all over. Her body felt heavy and overwhelmed with exhaustion, as though she could have lain down in the snow and slept in its frozen stillness for the rest of eternity.

Goodluck kissed her on the forehead, as if she were a child again. 'You look tired,' he said simply, and took her hand. 'Not long now. One more task, and then I can take you home.'

'One more task?'

'The Queen is at Whitehall. She has sent for us, and we must obey her summons before we can leave London.' He nodded towards the river. 'Jensen is waiting to take us on her barge. But we must hurry, for the tide will soon be against us.'

As they approached Whitehall by river, with all the long windows of that great palace illuminated by torches, Lucy began to feel less brave. She had told herself it was necessary to face the Queen again, to beg forgiveness for her acts of wantonness, and to thank Elizabeth for releasing them both from the Tower. But now that the moment was at hand, Lucy could almost wish herself back in her cell again.

'Have courage, my love,' Goodluck told her. 'You must have faced worse than this over the years.'

'True,' Lucy agreed.

Yet still she shivered in Goodluck's arms and could not seem to take comfort from his whispered encouragement. The day was like a strange dream that was shifting slowly into nightmare. She had not thought to return to court ever again. Yet here were the jetty and the water steps, the choppy water making her sick, and there was the intimidating expanse of the Palace of Whitehall, unseen pennants flapping on the towers high above the river.

Goodluck helped her ashore first, then stopped to exchange some muttered words with Jensen. Lucy looked ahead, her hard belly aching. She rubbed it absentmindedly.

Liveried servants were waiting for them in the palace gateway, flaming torches keeping the dark at bay.

She had not thought to see Goodluck again either, let alone become his wife. Yet here he was by her side, and she bore his name now. They had spoken their vows before God and their child would be born in wedlock. Born legitimate, wanted by both its father and mother.

Whatever Queen Elizabeth intended to do or say to them, she could not change her mind and take away their marriage. It was done now.

The steward led them through the long torchlit corridors Lucy had trodden once as a lady-in-waiting. It seemed so long ago now, as though another Lucy Morgan had served the Queen, a younger woman she no longer knew, a woman who lived in fear. She saw faces in doorways and through arches, watching them curiously as they passed. Most she recognized. Others were new.

The court was like that, she thought, meeting their eyes in silence. Constantly renewing itself. Throwing up new courtiers to dance attendance on the Queen, still sweet and young, come fresh to the whispering and the intrigues. The old ones were washed away in the dark stretches of the night, dismissed or imprisoned, anywhere their lost reputations would not cause a stench.

The old Lucy had feared everyone. Suspected everyone. But the long silences of her Tower cell had brought her to a new understanding of the court. Now she knew the only person to fear in this place was the Queen. For although Her Majesty had signed her release papers and agreed to her marriage to Goodluck, that did not mean she had finished with Lucy. All it meant was that someone had been persuasive. But who?

She asked Goodluck this question, and he looked at her grimly. 'Lord Essex.'

Essex had been her champion?

They arrived at an antechamber and an uninterested secretary, intent on his paperwork, instructed them to wait. A servant came to offer red wine. Lucy refused, but Goodluck accepted a cup with thanks. The wine was from the southern regions of France and darkly fragrant. It made Lucy feel queasy, sensitive to such smells in her condition. They stood slightly apart, waiting to be admitted into the Queen's presence. Someone opened a door elsewhere, and a sharp wind blew through the room, rustling the secretary's papers and filling out the tapestries which hung about the walls.

Goodluck looked at her over the rim of his wine cup. 'What was the information you offered Lord Essex?'

She stared at him, thrown off guard by the sudden question.

'In exchange for my freedom?' he continued, watching her closely. 'Do not bother to lie, Lucy. I know you too well to be taken in.'

She hesitated. 'I cannot tell you,' she said in the end.

'Why not?' His gaze narrowed on her face, and she had the suspicion that Goodluck was angry. But at least his anger did not seem to be directed at her. Not that it ever had been. 'Was it about William Shakespeare?'

Did he know everything?

'Yes,' Lucy admitted, and felt her shoulders drop with the relief of not having to conceal it any longer.

'You betrayed him to save me from imprisonment?'

'Information was the only thing I had of any worth. And even then I was not sure it would be enough. But it was.'

The flicker of something unfathomable passed across his face. Then he nodded. 'Thank you, Lucy. I know how much it must have cost you.'

She put a hand on the windowsill. Her sickness increased. It was not just the strong scent of the wine. She was sweating even in these wintry palace draughts. The room was spinning, the secretary's face alight with avid curiosity as he looked up from his documents. No doubt the young man hoped she would faint and give him something to gossip about later. What a stroke of luck if the Queen's disgraced lady-in-waiting, the Ethiopian whore they called Lucy Morgan, should come to the palace large with the child of her sin, and pass out on the floor of his antechamber.

'Did . . . Did Will suffer for it?' Her guilt was almost unbearable. 'I swear I did not want that. I just wanted to obtain your release from the Tower.'

Goodluck put down his cup and took her hand. 'Breathe,' he told her, and stroked her palm. 'You will only make yourself unwell like this. I do not know if Shakespeare suffered by your information. But I will always be grateful to you for volunteering it so bravely to Lord Essex, for your letter bought not only my freedom but our marriage. And when I finally get you home to Oxfordshire, and our child is born away from this city, safely and in good health, then it will have bought my happiness too.'

Someone had come to the door while they were talking. Lucy looked round, her heart beating rapidly. It was Lady Helena.

'Her Majesty will see you now.'

Goodluck removed his cap. He smoothed down his bushy hair and beard, tidied his clothes. Then glanced at Lucy, suddenly uncertain. She gave him an unsmiling nod.

Courage, my love.

Though it was late, the Queen had not yet been prepared for bed. She was still in her magnificent court gown, the broad skirts a shining swathe of cloth of gold, her sleeves russet velvet seeded with pearls. Had there been a banquet tonight for some visiting foreign dignitary, earmarked to be dazzled by England's wealth and grandeur?

No doubt Her Majesty had been kept busy with state business after supper, Lucy thought. Hence the weary secretary outside, picking through the stack of papers she had signed. If Elizabeth had taken after her father Henry, those papers might have been composed of death warrants, seizure of lands, confiscation of goods. And their own death warrants would have been among the documents. Thankfully, it was more likely to be petty matters: import and export, land division, and release of yet more funds for expeditions, secret campaigns and seafaring offensives against Spain.

Her ulcerated leg must have been paining her, for Queen Elizabeth had chosen to be seated to receive them. She sat upright, gripping the arms of her high-backed chair as though in pain. Her face was whitened with paint, her ruff a perfect halo slipped down about her neck. All her ladies appeared to have been dismissed for this interview, except for faithful Helena, who stood a few steps behind the Queen's seat, not meeting Lucy's eyes.

The Queen turned her head, surveying them both in silence as they came into the chamber and fell to their knees before her. Something like resentment flickered in her eyes at the sight of Lucy's heavily rounded body.

Despite the lustrous cloth of gold, and those chaste seed pearls that matched the colour of her skin, Elizabeth looked old.

Lucy gazed back at her with sudden pity, an emotion she had not felt for the Queen since she had been a young girl, newly brought into her service.

But it seemed the Queen felt little pity for her.

'Even you,' she muttered, her lips twitching with disgust as she examined Lucy's belly. 'Mistress Morgan, who was once so proud to remain a virgin by my side. Now everyone can see the mark of lasciviousness upon you.' Helena leaned forward and whispered something in her ear. The Queen sighed and nodded. 'But you are Mistress Goodluck now. I had forgotten you were to be married to your seducer. And this is he. Stand up, Master Goodluck, so I may look upon you properly.'

Goodluck stood, bowing his head in deference. 'Forgive me, Your Majesty.'

'That remains to be seen,' she said drily.

'Yes, Your Majesty.'

'Lord Essex has sent me . . .' The Queen glanced at Helena, who handed her a paper. She unrolled it laboriously and read for a moment, frowning. 'Yes, your family were disgraced under my royal sister. Is that not so? Your father executed for heresy, your lands confiscated and given to . . . Catholics.' She sighed, reading on, then handed the roll back to Helena. 'Master Goodluck, I am told by his lordship the Earl of Essex that, despite your lecherous nights with my lady-in-waiting, you have done good service to our throne. He informs me that by your bravery and skilled understanding, certain other men's sins and intrigues have been brought to light that might have endangered our life. What do you have to say to that, sir?'

'I have done nothing but my duty to Your Majesty and to England,' he said clearly, 'and would do so again tomorrow.'

'A good reply,' she said approvingly.

Of course it was a good reply, Lucy thought proudly, watching them together. Goodluck was a man in a court of boys and fools, and now her husband.

Elizabeth extended one of her hands, still thin and pale, jewelled. Goodluck knelt before her and bent his head, kissing it.

'I am Your Majesty's servant,' he said deeply, and Lucy heard complete obedience in his voice.

'You are a younger son, I understand.'

Goodluck hesitated, then nodded cautiously. 'I am indeed, Your Majesty. My brother, Julius Goodluck, is the head of our family.'

'At Lord Essex's suggestion,' Elizabeth announced, not looking at Lucy but at her husband, 'your original estate will be returned to your family. However, your lands have been granted to you alone, Master Goodluck, and not to your older brother. If he has any grievance with this, he may approach the Privy Council for compensation.'

Goodluck was staring up at her, still on his knees. For a moment he could not speak. Then he managed a hoarse 'I thank you, Your Majesty.'

'Save your thanks for Lord Essex,' the Queen countered sharply, 'at whose suggestion all this has been arranged. May you endeavour to deserve these honours, Master Goodluck, and live out the rest of your days in allegiance to this throne.'

It seemed their business was concluded. Queen Elizabeth looked past him at Lucy. Her eyes became suddenly misty. She drew an unsteady breath, and her fingers tapped on the arms of her chair in a long-familiar gesture.

The Queen raised her hand in the air. 'A blessing on your union,' she said, 'and on your child.' Then she dismissed them with an abrupt gesture. 'That is enough. Out, out!'

Taking Lucy's hand, Goodluck led her to the door, still bowing to the Queen. Outside the door, ignoring the secretary's angry stare, he kissed her as passionately as though they had only that moment been married.

'My lands restored,' he said in her ear, 'you my wife and carrying my child. What have I done to deserve such joy?'

Lucy smiled. 'Take me home, Goodluck.'

Epilogue

Greenway Manor, Oxfordshire, January 1594

WEARILY, GOODLUCK LAID DOWN THE LETTER HE HAD received from a man he knew at court – he had learned not to call them spies, for that word distressed his sister-in-law – and looked out of the window. So Lopez had been arrested at last, and committed to the Tower. Poor foolish man, thinking he could keep King Philip happy without ever doing his bidding, yet still escape detection. His possession of the diamond ring sent from Spain would be enough on its own to convict him, but Essex was apparently leaving nothing to chance. He wanted Lopez tortured until he confessed. The Queen was having none of it, of course. She did not believe the charges against her old Portuguese doctor either. But Essex would win in the end. Queen Elizabeth would eventually concede that a confession of some sort was required, and then Topcliffe would be called to work his dreadful trade.

The busy world of London and the court seemed so far away here. It had been snowing again in the night, and even the old barn had been obscured, a white shape where a row of tiny indented pawprints showed the cat had been climbing after robins. Twice Goodluck and the servants had been out in the night with the dogs, chasing off a fox who kept coming for their hens. Snow had gleamed like daylight across the valley, muffling their footsteps across the yard, the icy wind freezing his nethers under a too-short nightshirt.

Then just as he was settling back to sleep, Lucy had woken him again, complaining of pains.

'The child is coming,' she had whispered. 'Rouse Cathy. She will know what to do.'

He had shrugged back into his coat, still damp with snow, and woken Cathy. She had run down to the kitchen for hot water, her son James staring up from his bed with wide eyes.

'What is happening, Master Goodluck?'

'Nothing to make you fret. Go back to sleep, boy.'

He had woken the servants, then gone back to find Lucy kneeling beside the bed, not praying but moaning and gripping the coverlet in her fists as the pains strengthened.

'Have young John Sky ride for the midwife,' she whispered, sucking in her breath as another spasm rippled across her belly, 'and send Thomas over to your brother's farm. Agnes wishes to be here for the birth.'

It had been hard, leaving his wife in Cathy's care while she was in such pain. But he was a man, and men were not wanted at a birth. So Goodluck had called for some ham and ale for breakfast, then spent a few solitary hours pacing restlessly before a smoking fire in his study, waiting for the other women to arrive.

The midwife was bustled straight up to their bed-chamber, the door closing sharply, but not before he had heard his wife's moaning cry. His hands clenched into fists, he had stood silent in the hall below, listening in case her cries worsened – or stopped altogether.

Then his brother and sister-in-law arrived. Agnes kissed

him and went straight upstairs, her arms full of linen for the new baby, a gift. Behind her ran his young niece Eloise, carrying copper pans and other implements, as though they had been preparing for this event ever since he had come home to Oxfordshire, accompanied by a wife big with child.

His brother Julius, leaning heavily on a cane, laughed at his expression. 'Come, Little Brother. Let us go into your study and wait where it is warm. We can do nothing in this business. It's best that we leave this to the women.'

'But Lucy is in such terrible pain. She may need me.'

'Birth pains are always bad, but they are soon forgotten once the babe is born and is seen to be healthy. Women have amazingly adaptable memories. You will see.' Julius limped painstakingly into the study and eased himself into a seat beside the fire. 'What is this you have been reading, Faithful? Some news from London? Forgive me if it is a private letter, but you left it lying here on the seat.'

Goodluck could not seem to gather his thoughts. He forced himself to sit on the high-backed settle opposite his brother, though his impulse was to run upstairs and demand to see his wife, to know how she was faring.

'Yes, it is news of Senhor Lopez,' he muttered. 'The court doctor I was telling you about.'

'The Portuguese Poisoner?'

Goodluck smiled, allowing himself to be distracted for a moment. 'I suspect Lopez had no intention to poison his mistress. He should have brought the letters he received, and the bribes, straight to the Privy Council. Instead, he acted out of fear. No doubt he thought he would not be believed if he went to the council, not being English. Yet he did not wish to offend the Spanish King either, for Philip has a long hand that stretches even to the English court.'

'Good God.'

409

'Indeed.' Goodluck took the letter from Julius's hand and rolled it up. He would read it again later. 'Lopez tried to be clever, to play a double game, as spies are known to do when necessary. So he replied to the King's letters as far as he could without committing himself to any action, appearing to be on the side of the Portuguese rebels while doing nothing for them.'

'But what did they stand to gain, these Portuguese rebels?'

'Who knows? Certainly I do not. Perhaps they were offered lands in Portugal if they helped Philip dispose of Queen Elizabeth, and power as minor officials there. I imagine there was some promise of a place at Philip's court for Dr Lopez if he succeeded.'

'I am glad he did not.'

'Oh, he would never have tried it.' Goodluck shook his head. 'I spent some time observing Lopez, keeping an eye on him for Lord Essex, and the man may be a fool, and perhaps even a coward, but he is no murderer. His nerve failed him when he should have taken these bribes to the Queen in the first place. And for this failure of nerve, Senhor Lopez will die a traitor's death on the gallows tree, his neck wrung and his innards dragged out for all the world to see.'

'Yet if he refuses to confess, and if they have so little evidence against him as you claim, then surely his guilt cannot be proved.'

'Trust me, Julius. Once a man is in prison, and the torturer on hand, it is only a matter of time before he confesses to whatever nonsense they put before him, from having sex with a sow to conspiring to poison the Queen of England herself.'

'Is it so bad, the torture?'

His brother had such a marvellous gift for under-statement. 'The torture chamber is a worse place than you could possibly imagine, Brother. Few men do not break down when faced with the physical and mental torments that Master Topcliffe can supply. Only the very bravest and most principled have ever withstood his . . . persuasions.'

'But if a man is innocent . . .'

'Innocence is an irrelevance in the Tower of London. That is the first lesson you learn there.'

Goodluck recalled how he had wept like a child under Topcliffe's skilful ministrations. He shuddered, reminded of Lucy's moans and cries as her time finally came upon her. Birth was like torture, he thought. And he could not help his wife while she suffered. He could only sit and wait, as he had done with Lucy's mother so many years ago, her rounded body writhing in the agonies of childbirth.

The night of Lucy's birth would never leave him. Wandering home through filthy backstreets after a performance at the Cross Keys Inn, Goodluck had come across an African woman terrified out of her wits. She was fleeing from a man, no doubt her master, and her back still bore the marks of his whip.

Goodluck had concealed her in a doorway while the man passed, then taken the woman home with him, though he could clearly see she was heavy with child.

Later, he had paid for a simple burial when she died in childbirth, and taken her baby, crying and wrapped in swaddling, to be brought up by his sister Marian. He had not even known the dead woman's name, for although she had tried to tell her story in faltering Spanish – how she and her husband had been stolen by slavers from their village in Africa, where her husband had been the leader of his tribe, a prince among his people – she had never told him her name, nor that of her husband. All he knew was that her husband had died on the voyage to

Europe, and that she had run away from her new master on arrival in England, not wanting her child to be born into slavery.

As the child's self-appointed guardian, Goodluck had instructed his sister to baptize the infant with the English name of Lucy Morgan, despite her black skin and African origins, and had paid for her upbringing.

Now Lucy was his wife, and about to bring forth their own baby. He only prayed to God she would survive this birth, not die as her mother had done.

'Besides,' he struggled on, hearing voices from above, the sound of the servants running up and down the stairs, 'Senhor Lopez has grown old. He will be more accustomed to the luxury of a feather mattress than the cold hard floor of his cell in the Tower. First he will be threatened with the arrest and torture of his son, and perhaps his wife too, if Lord Essex is heartless enough to suggest it. If the doctor still refuses to confess to the crimes they put before him, his body will be stretched and broken on the rack, his flesh burned away with hot irons, his fingernails torn out—'

'God's death, enough!' Julius waved a horrified hand at him. 'I believe you, Little Brother. Pray spare me the details.'

Being a spy meant noticing the details, Goodluck thought wryly. But he fell silent. Topcliffe's cell was not a place he wished to think about here in Oxfordshire, with the snow lying on the ground and a robin redbreast perched on the tree stump outside his window.

'The manor is looking rather better than it was last month,' Julius commented. 'When will it be finished, do you think?'

'Not before the summer, alas. But the repairs are going more quickly than I had expected. We have four rooms habitable now, and the kitchens are in good shape.' Goodluck glanced at him. 'You do not regret accepting the

Queen's decision to restore the estate to me, rather than you?'

'You are welcome to it, Faithful.' His brother indicated his bad leg, for he was still crippled since the fall from his horse. 'I can barely walk half a mile without exhaustion, and have no thought of living in such a large manor. My little farmhouse is enough for me. Besides, I wish you joy of the vast costs and endless hammering that it will take to set this ancient barn to rights.'

Suddenly young Sky was at the door. 'Master Goodluck, sir?'

The boy had stayed on to serve him when he moved back into the manor, and very useful he had been too, suggesting the best – and least costly – local craftsmen to make repairs to the property so that they could at least inhabit a few of the rooms. Now he seemed one of the family rather than another servant.

'Yes, Sky, what is it?'

'You are wanted upstairs, sir.'

Goodluck thanked him, and took the stairs two at a time. The door to their bedchamber was open, and from within he could hear the quiet sounds of women talking.

No sound from Lucy. No crying babe either.

His heart clenched in sudden fear, Goodluck pushed open the door and trod heavily to the bedside.

'My love?'

Lucy was lying still against the pillows, her black springy head of hair fanned out. For a terrible moment he thought she was dead. Then she opened her eyes and looked up at him, weary but smiling.

'You have a son,' she whispered.

'A son?'

Agnes came to his side, bearing a small bundle wrapped tightly in white cloth. Cathy stood behind her, folding up squares of muslin, a broad smile on her face.

For a moment, Goodluck's chest tightened and he could not breathe. The child was perfect. Dark skin, dark thatch of hair, dark eyes staring up at him as though the child knew who he was.

'He is miraculous,' Goodluck managed, suddenly finding tears in his eyes. Not wishing the other women in the room to see them, he leaned down and kissed Lucy on the forehead. 'I am proud of you, my love. You are the best wife any man could have.'

'What shall we call him?'

Goodluck hesitated. 'Christopher,' he said in the end, and stroked the baby's cheek. 'After a brave man who died in the service of his queen.'

Christopher Marlowe.

Whatever mistakes Kit had made that led to his death, Goodluck did not believe him disloyal to his country. Kit Marlowe had been betrayed and murdered by his friends, the other spies working for Essex who had been at Deptford that day. Perhaps on Essex's own orders, so as to prevent some dangerous information reaching the Queen. Perhaps the earl was planning to seize the throne for himself one day, and Marlowe had been unfortunate enough to discover some incriminating evidence that had necessitated his death.

He recalled the strange conversation he had overheard between Marlowe and a servant in the palace corridors. Had he been the same man who later tried to stab the Queen? A man hired to kill her in truth, or hired to fail so that Essex could lend credence to his position as spymaster.

Reluctantly, he gave up the puzzle. It was impossible for him to get at the full truth. Some things were simply unknowable.

Goodluck admired the curl of his son's lashes, and how immaculately his small mouth yawned.

Although Lucy did not seem to object to the name Christopher, she studied him thoughtfully as he played with the babe. 'I hope you do not intend to make a spy of our son when he grows up.'

He grinned. 'Come, my love, where's the harm in teaching little Christopher a few tricks of the trade? I taught you some things you found useful, did I not?'

'It's over though, isn't it? All that business?' Lucy would not let it go. 'You won't go back to spying?'

'Not for five thousand crowns,' Goodluck promised her.

Author's Note

Queen Elizabeth, the Spanish Armada, and the Lopez Plot

In the summer of 1588, England was braced for imminent invasion by the hated Spanish. The Battle of Gravelines, a port in the Spanish-held Netherlands – near where we find my fictional spy Master Goodluck working under cover at the opening of this book – had seen many Spanish vessels destroyed or routed, but more were expected any day. Troops were stationed at Tilbury in Essex, at a makeshift camp overlooking the River Thames, a stretch the Spanish fleet were expected to navigate in their push for the all-important port of London. To strengthen her people's resolve at this desperate time, Elizabeth made the unusual – and highly dangerous – decision to walk among her troops with only a light guard of honour. She famously gave these troops a stirring speech, which in the end was not needed, for the bulk of the Spanish fleet was broken up by storms and its remainder routed. But her words served to mark her out in history as a strong and determined leader: 'I know I have the body of a weak and feeble woman; but I have the heart and stomach of a king – and of a King of England too, and think foul scorn that Parma or Spain, or any prince of Europe, should dare to invade the borders of my realm.'

Not all Elizabeth's subjects were pleased to have a strong Protestant Queen on the throne, however. The Catholic plots she had faced throughout her reign rose to the height of religious zeal during this threat of the Armada, and that previously loyal and trusted subjects were among the plotters must have infuriated Elizabeth. One of these was Sir William Stanley, a closet Catholic whose long and faithful service to the Queen in Ireland was forgotten when he abruptly turned traitor and handed the English-held port of Deventer over to the Spanish in 1587. His goal? To oust the Protestant Queen from the throne and install a Catholic monarch there instead. Stanley's fanatical hatred of Elizabeth in the years following the failure of the Armada led even the Spanish to hold him in contempt. But it seems likely that Sir William Stanley would have continued to engineer plots against the Queen's life from his exile abroad, such as the Portuguese plot in this book. Nor were such efforts always in vain. Henry III of France was assassinated by a fanatical Catholic monk in 1589 – though not as early in the year as I have described here.

During his colourful life, Robert Dudley, Earl of Leicester, had always been at the Queen's side to protect her from such fanatics, having enjoyed the position of court favourite from early in her reign. There is no doubt in my mind that Elizabeth and Robert were in love. But as the years passed, their love had become as much about friendship and mutual understanding as physical passion. When Robert died unexpectedly of fever, only a short time after the rout of the Spanish Armada, Elizabeth was heart-broken. Accounts suggest that she locked herself in her chamber for days, her grief so violent that in the end Lord

Burghley ordered the door to be broken down. After Elizabeth herself died, Robert's final note to her before his death was found in a casket beside her bed, marked 'His last letter' in her own handwriting. It is perhaps no surprise then that his stepson Robert Devereux, whose looks were oddly similar to Leicester's, was soon court favourite in his place, and rapidly became one of the most influential noblemen in England.

The Portuguese plot against Queen Elizabeth during the post-Armada years was tortuous in its complexity: the version I present here has been simplified, the conspiracy scaled down. It is possible that the plot was at least partially inflated by the Earl of Essex, determined to prove himself a worthy successor to Walsingham, but the number of players involved makes it unlikely that none of it was true. Accounts vary, but the gold and diamond ring seems to have come into play slightly later than I mention it, via a young Portuguese spy named Tinoco, who had been working in Brussels in the pay of the Spanish at the time of his visit to England. Following information received by Essex's sources, Tinoco was arrested on arrival at Dover and questioned at Essex House.

Perhaps in return for clemency, the Portuguese spy claimed that a ring from the hand of King Philip of Spain himself had been sent to Lopez, possibly as a bribe or incentive to poison the Queen. When questioned, Lopez admitted to possessing the ring: this admission alone appears to have sealed his fate, even though it is by no means certain that he would in fact have murdered his mistress of many years. After all, as one of the Queen's senior physicians, he would have had ample opportunity to poison her, yet never did so. Curiously, Lopez claimed that the ring had been legitimately intended for Elizabeth as a gift from Philip some years before, that the late Sir Francis Walsingham had known of its existence – and that

Elizabeth herself had refused to accept his gift and told Lopez to keep the ring for himself. Personally, I believe Lopez was a scapegoat for Essex's hatred of the Spanish, and was sacrificed to his driving ambition.

It must have worked, too, for following the shocking discovery of this 'Lopez plot', Essex's influence at court grew more powerful than ever.

Shakespeare, Southampton, and Lucy Morgan

We have no definitive record of Shakespeare's sexuality. We know that William Shakespeare of Stratford-upon-Avon was married to Anne Hathaway, had three children by her, and infamously left his 'second-best' bed to her in his will – an insult or a sentimental gesture? But that is about all we know as regards his love life. If we include his body of work as a resource, his love sonnets do seem to suggest sexual intimacy with men as well as women, though whether this was reflected in Shakespeare's personal life is open to conjecture. But in my story, Shakespeare falls in love with both his 'Dark Lady' of the sonnets – here, Lucy Morgan – and his wealthy patron, the Earl of Southampton, who by all accounts was a handsome young man just out of university.

Lucy Morgan, as I discussed in my notes for the previous two books in this trilogy, *The Queen's Secret* and *His Dark Lady*, is a semi-fictional character. That is, she exists as a repeated name on official records of the time, as a paid lady in Queen Elizabeth's service, and also possibly as Black Luce of Clerkenwell, who was imprisoned at one stage for being a 'bawd', or woman of loose morals. But her depiction as Shakespeare's 'Dark Lady' is mere conjecture on my part, and we have no hard evidence for who or what she was, beyond a name on a few official rolls. However, her later imprisonment in the Tower of London for lack of chastity is entirely in keeping with the Queen's hardline policy towards her ladies-in-waiting. When one of her favourites, the sailor and adventurer Sir Walter Raleigh, was found to have secretly married Bess Throckmorton, a young maid of honour, Elizabeth ordered both to be imprisoned in the Tower of London in the summer of 1592. Required for state duties, Raleigh was soon released. But poor Bess, whose baby son died during her imprisonment, was left to languish in the Tower long into that harsh winter.

In connection with Shakespeare's work with James Burbage at the Rose, I have taken various liberties with dates here to fit the structure of my story. *Venus and Adonis*, his epic poem, was published in 1593, four years later than I have it here. However, as a work of great length and complexity, based on a passage from Ovid's famous *Metamorphoses*, it is likely to have been a work in progress for several years prior to publication. Both *Venus and Adonis* and *The Rape of Lucrece*, which followed it, were epic poems dedicated to the Earl of Southampton, who was evidently his patron by the time the second poem appeared at least. As for Shakespeare's reception by his theatrical peers, Robert Greene actually criticized Shakespeare three years later than this scene, in 1592:

for there is an upstart Crow, beautified with our feathers, that with his Tygers hart wrapt in a Players hyde, supposes he is as well able to bombast out a blanke verse as the best of you: and being an absolute Johannes fac totum, is in his owne conceit the onely Shake-scene in a countrey.

The chances of an embryo-playwright, freshly arrived from the country, provoking that amount of ire from an established writer is unlikely, all of which points to Shakespeare having been in London some time before this outburst. It should be noted, however, that, to my knowledge, we have no official record of the companies playing at the Rose in 1589. So it is merely speculation that Shakespeare might have worked there around this time, and indeed some authorities would suggest he was still at home in Stratford during these early years. Since our knowledge of Shakespeare's life is scanty at best, it seems acceptable to make such leaps of interpretation in a work of fiction.

Shakespeare's son Hamnet, the twin of Judith, died in the summer of 1596 at the age of eleven, possibly while Shakespeare was on tour with his company. There is no record of what caused the boy's death, but it may have been the plague. Although he left behind no record of any personal grief for his only son, we have testimony of his feelings in the plays, notably *King John*, written around this time, where a mother is driven to distraction by the memory of her dead son, imagining him talking to her and filling out his 'vacant garments' as though still alive. In *Her Last Assassin*, I stop just short of Hamnet's death, leaving my fictional Shakespeare perpetually suspended at a time when his son was still alive and all things were possible.

Christopher Marlowe: playwright and spy

Christopher Marlowe was probably the most noted Elizabethan playwright of his generation after Shakespeare, who was born in the same year. It is likely, from what little we know of his life and movements just before his death, that he worked as a spy for the English. But he may also have been a 'double agent', trading information with the Spanish in return for money or favours. The truth of his loyalties may never be known, nor the circumstances behind his sudden death, but I feel it unlikely that he would have betrayed his country. For a start, his patron was cousin to Sir Francis Walsingham, the

Queen's spymaster and probably the man who first recruited him to spy for England. And though Marlowe was arrested for blasphemy and heresy – possibly on a charge of atheism – just prior to his death, he was questioned by the Privy Council, which seems extreme, and no record was kept of those proceedings. That Marlowe was in fact giving them a secret report, following his recent activities abroad, is more likely.

Shortly after this Privy Council summoning, however, Christopher Marlowe – or Kit as he was known in theatrical circles – was murdered. He was stabbed to death on 30 May 1593, in a quarrel that apparently blew up out of nowhere in a private house in Deptford, where he was drinking with a number of underworld acquaintances in an upper room. His self-confessed killer, Ingram Frizer, a well-known 'fixer' and confidence trickster, was later pardoned on the grounds of self-defence. My account of Marlowe's murder is loosely based on the legal testimony given by those witnesses present, most of whom appear to have had connections to espionage, a situation highly suggestive of a pre-arranged 'hit'. Precisely why this talented young playwright was murdered is an Elizabethan puzzle that many have tried to solve since. But whatever information Christopher Marlowe held that was so important, he took it with him to his grave.

Select Bibliography

Among these books, I am particularly indebted to Lytton Strachey's entertaining old volume on *Elizabeth and Essex*, from which I took much of my inspiration for the uncovering of the 'Lopez Plot'.

Ackroyd, Peter, *Shakespeare*, Vintage, 2005

Borman, Tracy, *Elizabeth's Women: The Hidden Story of the Virgin Queen*, Jonathan Cape, 2009

Cook, Judith, *Roaring Boys: Playwrights and Players in Elizabethan and Jacobean England*, Sutton Publishing, 2004

Cooper, John, *The Queen's Agent: Francis Walsingham at the Court of Elizabeth I*, Faber, 2011

Clark, John and Ross, Cathy (eds), London: *The Illustrated History*, Penguin, 2011

Glasheen, Joan, *The Secret People of the Palaces: The Royal Household from the Plantagenets to Queen Victoria*, BT Batsford, 1998

Gristwood, Sarah, *Elizabeth and Leicester*, Bantam Press, 2007

Haynes, Alan, *Sex in Elizabethan England*, The History Press, 2010

Hutchinson, Robert, *Elizabeth's Spy Master*, Orion, 2007

Knutson, Roslyn Lander, *Playing Companies and Commerce in Shakespeare's Time*, Cambridge University Press, 2001

Sim, Alison, *Pleasures & Pastimes in Tudor England*, The History Press, 2009

Southworth, John, *Shakespeare the Player*, Sutton Publishing, 2000

Strachey, Lytton, *Elizabeth and Essex*, Chatto & Windus, 1928

Trow, M. J., and Trow, Taliesin, *Who Killed Kit Marlow? A Contract to Murder in Elizabethan England*, The History Press, 2001

Now is the Month of Maying was written by Thomas Morley, 1557/8–1602. A popular composer of Tudor secular music, this is one of his better-known pieces, still performed today.

Acknowledgements

My grateful thanks must go first to my agent Luigi Bonomi, as always, and his wife Alison, who are beside me every step of the way. The writing of historical fiction can be a laborious process, undertaken alone or in the hushed surroundings of academic libraries, and the pleasure of an occasional working lunch with one's agent cannot be overstated.

My thanks are also due to the marvellous and professional team at Transworld, especially my editor Emma Buckley, whose thoughtful insights and patience have made this a far better book, and to Lynsey Dalladay for being such a brilliant publicist.

Nearer to home, I am eternally grateful to my husband Steve, to whom this novel is dedicated, for having made endless cups of tea and ferried children about while I sat struggling with Elizabethan plotters. I was only very haphazardly a writer when he married me, so he did not sign up for being Mr Lamb. Yet there he still is, happy to take on the often problematic mantle of novelist's spouse. Equally, my long-suffering children have learned to tiptoe about in the evenings and fetch snacks to keep me at my desk: my thanks to Kate, Becki, Dylan, Morris and Indigo for being indispensable members of the team.

Thanks, finally, to all those librarians, writers and researchers who have helped along the way, and to my friends and readers online, whose daily encouragement continues to nudge me towards exciting new writing projects.

The Queen's Secret

Warwickshire, 1575.

Pomp, fanfare and a wealth of lavish festivities await Elizabeth I at Kenilworth Castle. Organized by the Earl of Leicester, he knows this celebration is his last chance to persuade the Queen to marry him. But, a fickle man, he is unable to resist the seductive wiles of Lettice Knollys.

Enraged by the couple's growing intimacy, Elizabeth employs a young black singer and court entertainer to keep a watch on them. Brought up by a spy, Lucy's observational skills are sharper than anyone at the castle realizes, and she soon uncovers far more than she bargained for: Someone at Kenilworth is plotting to kill the queen.

Can the knowledge Lucy is gaining prevent the death of the monarch? Or has it put Lucy in mortal danger instead?

His Dark Lady

London, 1583.

William Shakespeare has declared Lucy Morgan the inspiration
for his work. But what is he hiding from his muse?

Meanwhile, Lucy has her own secrets to conceal. Tempted
by love, the lady-in-waiting also bore witness to the one
marriage forbidden by the queen.

England is in peril. Queen Elizabeth's health is deteriorating,
her throne under siege. She needs a trusted circle of advisors
. . . but who can she turn to when those closest have proved
disloyal?

And just how secure is Lucy's fate, now she has learned the
dangerous art of keeping secrets?